Copyright © 2017 by Laura E. Obolensky
Print ISBN: 978-1-48359-085-1
eBook ISBN: 978-1-48359-086-8
All rights reserved

COVER DESIGN BY BRUCE STEINKE

In Loving Memory of A. and G. HUN

TINA'S WAR

A NOVEL BY
LAURA OBOLENSKY

PROLOGUE

She sits in the train compartment watching the drop of perspiration slowly taking shape on the forehead of the old man across the aisle. He must be close to eighty. A frail little face with skin so sheer the nexus of blood vessels asleep under it give it a cyanic translucence. Xavier's skin is like that too, right above the temples where it stretches tautly over the baby's bones. But on Xavier's temples you can actually delineate each vein, three of them, as if someone had drawn them on purpose under the skin with a blue ballpoint pen. Clear. She often traces them with her finger when he sleeps against her breast. It doesn't wake him. He keeps on napping, his pink lips gaping over the ripe, luscious fruit of his tongue. On the old man's face it's different. You can't see the veins: the topography is blurred like on those photographs sent back by the American astronauts on which the earth looks like a ball of blue cotton candy.

The drop of perspiration, now a swollen tear, proceeds to dribble down his nose, slowly, a little off center. His lower jaw has dropped faster than his head: it's hanging limp over the knot of his skinny tie. Then he startles, blinks his eyes: the drop poised on the very tip of his nose has tickled him to wakefulness. He crushes it with the gnarled knuckle. She shifts her eyes, encounters the window. She doesn't want to embarrass him but she can feel him looking at her as she tallies the electric poles flying past the grimy panes.

It's drizzling and everything is cat gray outside: one of those late May rains steaming all over the countryside. They will reach Château-Thierry soon now and then it's only twenty more minutes to Dormans. She is a little sad but it's a sadness like that of love, mellow. The morning's thoughts are on the back-burner for a time ready to be tackled again when she snaps out of the mood.

Click-a-tee-clack, click-a-tee-clack: the wheels under the carpeted floor are devouring the kilometers of rail tracks. She doesn't like trains, planes: travelling. Alain chides her about this idiosyncrasy every time they travel together. He is a born adventurer, Alain. The year before they were married right after he proposed upon completing his internship at the Paris Children's Hospital, he bought a used land-rover, loaded it with camping gear, three pairs of jeans and ten T-shirts and took off: "Will you marry me? Goodbye!" She drove with him as far as Nice, then flew back to Paris and waited for him. It took him six months to see the world but when he returned he was eager for marriage, spoke a smattering of ten languages and had accumulated enough stories to last their conversational lifetime. She has tried to explain it to him, her dread of trains but he doesn't understand.

It starts from the moment she dusts the suitcases out of their Parisian hibernation and keeps growing until by the time they reach the railway station, the airport or load the Peugeot, the anguish is so overwhelming that it borders on panic and she wants madly to run back to their apartment, lock the door behind her and sit in the cretonne armchair by their bedroom window. Irrational: he is right. Actually if she tries to analyze the anguish -- and she has – she comes up with a reason which is entirely plausible from her psychological standpoint. It's the act of departure, of leaving, which is the root of the neurosis, of closing up the lovely apartment where they are so very happy, Alain, Xavier and she, and fearing something will happen along the journey to prevent either one or all of them from returning to it. Leaving is like shedding her past, discarding her identity and the history which is part of herself and for a while, until she gets to wherever she is going, being a non-person adrift on the raft of a present which has suddenly broken anchor.

"Château-Thierry! Château-Thierry!"

The voice blaring out of the loudspeaker jolts her back to reality. The old man gathers his brown overnight bag, his newspaper and the silver pommel of his cane. She tucks her feet under the seat sliding her knees sideways because he is standing in front of her, wobbling. But he makes it to the door, tips his hat to her and whispers a polite "Good-day". She smiles back at him but wonders why she did not return his friendly good-bye when the train starts again. But it's too late: his silhouette has already drifted past the rain-streaked window.

Dormans next. She opens the alligator handbag tossed next to her on the maroon plush of the seat and extracts from it the wire she has read many times. Like all wires it's what it doesn't say which weighs on her mind as she reads it again:

Madame Tatiana d'Evry

51 Rue du Bac

Paris 6eme

"Regret inform you Marcel Germain passed away this morning STOP Funeral to be held May 28 STOP please attend if you can STOP Guy Marchand."

It couldn't have come at a worst time Alain had complained when the boy had delivered it two days earlier. There was the dinner party planned for the same day, the decorators scheduled to begin work on his study that very morning and above all, the fact that she had promised him – promised him! – she would attend the Sixteenth International Pediatrics Congress on the twenty-ninth because he was one of the featured speakers. They argued over breakfast, not much, just enough for her to convince him that her decision when she had finally reached it was one she had arrived at after taking into account his disappointment. Silenced by kindness he had said he understood and kissed her before leaving for the hospital. She had called off the dinner guests and the decorators and written a sweet note to tell him how good his speech read and how proud she was of him. Later her mother had come: she had told her the guest room was ready and where Xavier's things were and what he should be fed tonight and tomorrow. Her mother had said everything would be fine because she wasn't new to motherhood, "Remember?" They had kissed good-bye and she had taken a taxi to the Gare de L'Est to catch the two-thirty train to Dormans.

Now the train is slowing down: she can see clearly the beach across the Marne river and the fields stretching beyond it to her left and on her right the still familiar main street halving the town and its double row of modest houses sandwiched at almost equal intervals by an array of shops, most of them new. Also the bridge rebuilt over the Marne river. She was right to come: she owes it to Tina.

Then she sees them standing in the drizzle, cloaked in the persistent sadness of the May rain and their own grief. They spot her behind the grimy window before the train comes to a halt and an ever so pale ray of sunshine seems to show over their gray faces. God how old they look! Antoinette is biting her lower lip as though on the verge of tears and Gilbert tries to hide his emotion behind a stiff smile.

Indeed she is right to have come to Dormans for Marcel Germain's funeral. Already she can feel it surging inside of her, this slow eruption of dormant emotions that have lurked for those many years simmering and rumbling they are, ready to surface into the present, to glitter and glimmer again as they did once for her and for Tina. As Antoinette embraces her, weeping now, she wonders why she has never told Alain about them. A slip of too-long buried memory. But now she will tell him as soon as she gets back to Paris after the funeral. Then perhaps he won't mind so much her having broken her promise and it might help him understand this thing she has about trains.

CHAPTER I

"What happened to the Boche, Nanette?"

"What Boche, child?"

"The one last week."

"I told you a hundred times, Tina: he left. Ain't no use your asking me over and over 'cause I'll just have to answer the same thing over and over. You are like a bee about my ears: buzz, buzz, buzz! Eat your bread instead and mind your home work!"

Nanette was laboring over the porcelain sink at the far end of the kitchen, peeling wrinkled rutabagas and anemic turnips for tonight's soup while I sat perched on a wooden stool and two green encyclopedias faced with a week-long problem, a slice of stale bread and a square of ersatz chocolate I didn't feel like eating.

The month was April, the year was nineteen-forty-four. I was nine years eight months and twelve days old hurrying toward my tenth birthday with great anticipation for reasons as varied as they were my own. I had recently read in one of the omnipresent encyclopedias that "Wolfgang Amadeus Mozart, as the tender age of nine, had performed before the Imperial Court of Vienna," and nurtured dreams of performing a similar feat upon reaching this seemingly prophetical age. Besides, Nanette, Bébert and Guigui kept drumming into my head that when I reached my tenth birthday I would be made privy to some of the secrets which, due to this maddening contretemps of a few months, they so far persisted in keeping from me. And if the Americans managed to make it to France round about that time, I would even be allowed my first glass of Champagne to celebrate both their long-anticipated landing upon French shores and my birthday. In short that spring, I was in the untenable position of desperately hankering for my birthday while paradoxically faced with the prospect of having to defer its celebration to accommodate the Americans if they didn't make it to Dormans by August 4. Fortunately, I never considered that they might make it earlier thereby avoiding another dilemma whose burden might have been too much considering the other inextricable problems confronting me that particular April, of which the question of what had happened to the Boche was the most pressing.

"Well girl, what are you gawking at now? You still ain't touched your bread and it's almost time for supper. And your homework?"

"It's Thursday tomorrow, no school!"

"It wouldn't hurt to start on it now!"

"But I don't have to –"

"You don't want to girl, I wasn't born yesterday you know!"

Nanette always had the last word with me, but then she had the last word with everyone her husband, Bébert, her mother-in-law Mémé who lived with us, with Bébert's uncle, Uncle Marcel and his wife Louise who lived across the avenue from us, with Guigui her son and, of course, with me, her charge. Even with the omniscient Doctor Martin who owned the big house next to the Town Hall on the Place de la Marne and whose waiting room was full of diplomas, all written in Latin, attesting, I was convinced, to his supernatural intelligence. Yet even with Dr. Martin she managed to have the last word although she went about upstaging him in a subtler manner using a litany of less blunt but just as effective "but-don't-you-think-Doctor-Martin" that invariably brought the good doctor to an exhausted surrender. Bébert sometimes in a sudden itch of rebellion would try to put her down but although his sporadic last-stands filled me with admiration I also knew that they were doomed to failure. Nanette could outlast any of us: she won her arguments by attrition because none of us were obstinate enough to out talk her. But being argumentative was Nanettes's only flaw and the sum of her qualities was such that we all put up with her contentiousness more willy than nilly. Bébert when he was in the mood to laugh about it even went so far as to remark that it was a pity she couldn't unleash it on the Boches because she was a Maginot line all by herself and much more defensible than the real one had proven back in thirty-nine.

"What's the matter with you today child? Cat's got your tongue? Wonder what happened to Mémé."

"Where'd she go?

"Up the fields to cut grass for the rabbits. We were all out."

"Where?"

"You know where, Tina! Behind the saw-mill on the road to Chavenay."

"Think I'll go after her." I said an idea suddenly popping into my mind. I was determined to find out what had happened to the Boche and if anybody was likely to enlighten me, Mémé was it.

I jumped down from my perch atop the encyclopedias, snatched the ersatz chocolate from the plate, ran out of the kitchen into the hallway and grabbed my red coat and yellow muffler from their assigned place on the mirrored coat-hanger behind the front door. I was already in the street when Nanette called out to me:

"Tina! Tina!" She had run after me, caught the hem of my fleeing coat.

"What?"

"Come back here, child. Inside, quick. Put your satchel away, and the plate: in the sink. And put on your shoes: You can't run half-way through Dormans in your slippers. Tsk! Tsk! Did you hear the quarter off siren of the saw-mill yet? And give me that chocolate, too late for it now, almost time for soup."

"No"

"What do you mean, no?"

"I didn't hear the siren," I yelled back. I would probably bump into Mémé at the corner of the street and that sure wouldn't give me enough time to find out about the Boche. You had to work on Mémé before she came through, lull her into thinking your questions weren't all that important.

"Tina! Tina!"

What did she want now? I swooped around. Nanette was leaning out of the kitchen window, waving her left arm frantically.

"Stop by the Co-op and see whether Guigui is finished for the day. It's dinner time, tell Pottin I want him home now" she bellowed half-way down the block.

Then she spotted Soldat Mueller coming out of the café across the street with three German privates and her head disappeared back inside the kitchen, I heard her close the window behind her as I stood petrified, smiling back at Soldat Mueller who was waving "Hello" to me the way he always did every time I passed the Town

Hall which he pretended to guard. He had even tried to talk to me once, Soldat Mueller, a couple of months back as I had passed him on my way to school. But I knew better. Bébert had warned me that all sorts of things happened to Frenchmen who fraternized with the enemy they disappeared one day and no one ever knew what had happened to them. Besides, the Germans, they did things to little girls that the devil himself wouldn't think of. I found his warning hard to believe as far as Soldat Mueller was concerned because he really seemed harmless, but still, I preferred to play it safe and the extent of my fraternization with him was limited to a stiff grimace which was meant to a s a smile but seldom came out as one.

The muscles of my cheeks ached when I turned my back on Soldat Mueller and his companions. I walked gingerly to the corner of the street, sensing their eyes on my back, gathering echoes of their guttural laughter. As I turned into the alley leading to the Faubourg de Chavenay, the siren releasing the workers of the saw-mill for the day shot above my fear and the Germans' laughter and I ran toward Mémé whose black and grey paisley smock had suddenly appeared at the sunny end of the high-walled and weed-grown alley.

"What's with you child!" Mémé asked as my face rammed into her skirts.

"Soldat Mueller!" I panted out my words muffled in the folds of her ankle-long skirt and the layers of the petticoat under it. Mémé's skirts were thick and soft like and eiderdown: a refuge where I cried, laughed and loved.

"Come now, baby, he won't hurt you. It's that son of mine putting all these tales into your head, frightening you like, child. They won't be here for long, the Boches, you mark Mémé's word." She continued petting my cheek.

"They won't?"

"No, dear. We got them out in eighteen and we'll get them out this time, and sooner than they think. You be a good girl and stop fretting your little head about Soldat Mueller 'cause I got my sickle and it's much more dangerous than him."

She pushed me away from her, laid the sickle safely atop the pungent wild grass and clover stacked in the basket swaying from her left arm and took my small hand in hers. My head almost reached her shoulders. I was as small for my age as she was for hers, her frailty being hereditary and mine circumstantial. According to the town folk of Mémé's generation and those beyond who were still alive to tell you about the Germains of Dormans, all the Germain women had been short like a winter day and lean like Good Friday. But notwithstanding their physical frailty, the local gossip also had it that every one of them from Mémé on to her mother and grandmother and down to her aunt and sister, God rest their souls, had ruled their households like little corporals and managed their husbands and sons like drill sergeants. Even now, long after Pépé had been killed at Verdun, after all her widowed years which one might assume would have eroded the potency of the Germain genes in her, she still enjoyed a definite ascendency over her son and Bébert, at forty-four would not have dreamed of contradicting his mother although he might make a fair try at contradicting his wife. So, even though Mémé's frailty was deceiving and I knew better than to take her size at face value, the realization that I would soon overtop her endeared her to me more than the rest of the family.

Between Soldat Mueller, Mémé's skirts and my height almost equal to hers and the ever present question of what had happened to the Boche, Nanette's summons for me to fetch Guigui had slipped my mind. As I filed into the kitchen behind Mémé, Nanette scolded me.

"Where's Guigui?" she bellowed no sooner had she spotted me, holding her knife threateningly over the strips of rancid lard she had been dicing.

"I am going now, " I said trying to sound casual.

"Oh you are, are you? You know Pottin closes at six. It's six twenty now, how are you going to get in?"

"By the backyard, through Rigaux's warehouse!"

"And how do you know about Rigaux's warehouse?"

"Bébert showed it to me."

"Bébert is a fool. Rigaux is a collaborator, everyone in Dormans knows that. What would happen if he found you loitering about his place, Rigaux?"

"He wouldn't 'cause I'd hide!"

"All the same, I don't want you hanging round there especially now that the Boches are almost done for. A lot of accounts are going to be settled and Rigaux is sure to be one of them. Well, what are you standing here for, go fetch Guigui but not through Rigaux's place: knock on Pottin's front door, he's bound to be there still."

I watched her as she went back to dicing her lard. I thought about what she had just told me about Rigaux and some of my courage was sorely tested. What if Pottin was in his back-room and didn't hear me? I would have to go through Rigaux's warehouse anyway, sneak my way through his place to the Co-op's backyard, and old Pottin's dog would bark the alarm long before I made it. Rigaux would catch me and the whole German army would follow in his trail to do things to me that the devil himself wouldn't dream of. I made a tacit appeal to Mémé, but she pretended not to notice me and busied herself with her upper false teeth which had dropped out of their sockets once more.

Like a condemned man marching to the scaffold, I turned my head back on their complicit indifference and stared at the handle of the kitchen door suddenly in line with my mouth as if it were Damocles sword ready to drop and halve my brain. That's when I heard the muffled giggles and snickers: the giggles were Guigui's the snickers Bébert's. Both originated I soon detected from the lumber-room under the staircase at the end of the hallway, where we kept pinafores and blue overalls, brooms and mops, firewood, snow boots, umbrellas, Marseilles' soap and bleach, Mémé's old ankle-boots studded with black buttons, Bébert's discarded pajamas turned dust mops, and where a few spiders and an occasional cockroach cohabitated in a stack of old, long-yellowed newspapers preserved by Nanette for plugging drafts in winter, lighting the stove, stuffing the tips of Bébert's old shoes so Guigui might "finish" them, or for lining the rabbit's cage when straw became scarce.

The giggles grew louder as I opened wide the kitchen door. When Guigui catapulted himself out of the lumber-room into the darkened hallway, taunting me with a string of "Got you, got you, chicken!" I punched him in the ribs once and hard. By now Mémé and Nanette were at the kitchen door joining in the chorus of laughter. Mortified, I silently hoped Mémé's dentures would burst out of their socket once and for all. But they didn't. They shook and quivered, and played a bar of castanets but hung on.

"Hey! Hey! Fooled you this time, Tina, didn't we?" Bébert said catching his wheezing breath.

I didn't dignify his taunt with an answer, but I was grateful when he told Guigui to stop roughing me up, and I sneaked behind him down the hallway back into the kitchen, holding on the his shapeless bottle-green sweater as if it were my salvation.

"Let go of my apron strings girl, "Bébert said as we reached the stove because not only was I holding on to Nanette's masterpiece of knitting, I had started tugging at it quite frantically. Bébert swooped around. As he did so he sighted Guigui who had been pulling my pony tail throughout our procession.

"What do they teach you at catechism, son?" he berated his son upon whom my eyes settled smugly. "About to make his first communion next month, spending his time with the curates and all those sacristans, washing their faces in the church's stoop several times a day, " he ranted taking the panoply of pots and pans as witnesses. "What does he teach you Father Rocas? To torment girls half your age? A bunch of hypocrites, that's what they are, and so are you, boy. But I'll have none of that mendacity in my house, no Monsieur Guigui, not in my house! Keep that for catechism, Father Rocas and his harem of bigoted womenfolk!'

"That's blasphemy, Bébert!" Mémé objected crossing herself, "you'll sure go to hell!" her dentures were shivering with anger.

"Alright Mother. I've spoken my piece. Say a couple of Ave Marias for my soul tonight to straighten me out with your boss!'

"Bébert!"

"Alright, alright, Goddam it! Where's my dinner Nanette?"

"Gilbert!" Mémé called out resorting to her son's Christian name in her indignation.

"Sorry, Mother, I won't swear again."

"I should hope not, I want to see you up there."

"Where?"

"In God's heaven where your father is, God bless him."

Bébert didn't answer. He believed neither in heaven nor in hell, although he was convinced there was a purgatory: his life had been nothing but one since the Boches had occupied Dormans. He didn't believe in priests, bishops, saints or the Pope and especially not in the virginity of Mary because he had been a gay blade in his prime and knew that babies weren't conceived in heaven. There was nothing holy about that notorious conception, he would tell everyone when the occasion arose and Mémé was not around, except Joseph's gullibility. Bébert was neither an iconoclast nor an atheist, he was a registered communist, or had been before the Germans had decreed that communism was anathema to the new order of National Socialism. He was a rabid patriot through an accident of history and a communist through a need for idealism: one had to find utopia where one could in these days. Bébert was too old for heroism and too practical for fanaticism. But because of the German occupation he was unable to determine which was more important: patriotism, communism, anti-clericalism or pro-Americanism for he was indeed fiercely pro-American. Just as politics makes for strange bedfellows, so does history, and in Bébert's philosophical bed their cohabited many ideologies not altogether reconcilable but which had landed there to see him through the long ordeal of France's occupation and helped him to survive the seemingly endless night of the war. I was proud of him for being what he was as I sat nights next to him at the dinner table. I respected him for standing up to Nanette once in a great while, for working as a carpenter in the German barracks of the Château every time they summoned him because I knew how much he hated those assignments. I loved him for knowing tenderness instinctively, for being able to be angry for the right reasons and wise for what everyone in those days considered the wrong ones;

for being not merely a survivor but a selfless provider to us all; for sensing precisely when I was on the verge of tears and drying them up with a story often told but which he – no one but he – could make sound so new every time.

The ingestion of the soup every evening had a ritualistic quality that had struck me as almost religious when I had first entered the Marchand family three years earlier. Its pattern was immutable.

The altar upon which we officiated silently was the long scarred kitchen table. It stood permanently pushed against the seldom used dining room wall, thus leaving only three sides for five of us. Mémé headed one side of the table while Bébert was her vis-à-vis on the other; in between them sat Guigui on Mémé's right, Nanette next to her son and then I between Nanette and Bébert. I always suspected Nanette had selected this vantage point between Guigui and myself to act as a buffer between us. At any rate, each evening at precisely seven o'clock we would sit at our assigned places and unfold our napkins. Mémé's was folded in a triangle, Nanette's in a square; Bébert's had for years been girdled by the silver ring that had been given him by his godfather upon his baptism, Guigui was never folded at all, and mine was usually covered with tell-tale signs of previous meals. Because of a perennial shortage of soap, we kept them for a week and they consequently served us for twenty-one meals so that it was essential that they be readily identifiable as to which belonged to whom.

Thus we all sat at the table in a row like garlic strung up for winter, all of us that is except Bébert who ladled the soup. I never understood why he undertook this chore since Nanette did everything else around the house and therefore might have considered this an encroachment upon her prerogatives. He always served his mother first. As soon as the steaming plate of soup was placed in front of her and Bébert's back was turned, she would mumble grace with a verbal dexterity that was as impressive as it was unintelligible. "Thank me, not God! He isn't down at the Château working for those bloody Boches!" he had exploded at her once a couple of months back when she hadn't been fast or surreptitious enough about her graces. Although she was a devout Catholic the war had put her devoutness to a strain: she knew in her heart that God didn't have anything to do with providing the food she ate and that only Bébert was responsible for that miracle. But cornered as she was between faith in God and gratitude toward her son, she did her best to preserve her future place in heaven while safeguarding her interests here on earth.

Once we had all been served and Bébert had settled himself behind his own plate, we ate the soup. But even then, it was not until he himself had attacked his steaming plate: none of us would have dared upstage him. Then there reigned a slurping symphony over the dinner table: no one said a word although sometimes livening up the ritual there was a tacit race between Guigui and me as to which one of us would finish first. Otherwise the only sounds one could hear were the rhythmical clang of spoons against china, Mémé trying not to swallow her dentures with her soup, Nanette's occasional sniffles – she had a chronic sniffle although nothing was wrong with her respiratory system - or Bébert blowing like Vulcan on each spoonful because the soup was too hot. In retrospect it might have been that this silence of ours was more pragmatic than pious since it is easier to speak with a mouthful of solid than a mouthful of liquid. But for whatever reasons, the Marchands ate their soup in utter silence and so did I.

I beat Guigui to the finish that night, wiped my mouth dry, heaved my anticipated sigh of contentment thereby summoning all eyes in my direction. The pace of the spoons against china grew more rapid and Bébert finished second. To my chagrin Guigui had not noticed my feat: I found him staring blankly at Mémé's right ear when I bent around Nanette to give him the winner's leer. After a shrug I started playing with my knife and grinned innocently at Bébert when I caught him frowning at me. In no time Nanette was up.

"Well, did you talk to Chalembert, Bébert?" she opened up as if the question had been debated long enough and was now despairing of an answer.

Guigui and I immediately perked up our ears. The question of Bébert talking to Chalembert had been on the family's agenda for the best part of a month. But so far Bébert had done nothing about it despite Nanette's initial pleas and then her vociferous ultimatums.

Chalembert was a farmer who lived in Coudouart on the road to Epernay. He was as ugly as a rhinoceros and as ill-disposed. He was also a misanthrope and a reputed miser who scared me far more than Soldat Mueller when I happened to catch sight of him in Dormans. Before the war his domain had extended over some ninety hectares of choice land where he cultivated grapes for sale to the Mercier Champagne factory in Epernay as well as corn, potatoes, beets and various other profitable crops. Since the war however, most of his land had either been requisitioned by the Germans, bombed to craters, or following historical precedents, scorched to the ground by agents of the resistance. Not one to be deterred by such misfortunes, he had turned to stock and on what little acreage remained after occupation and retaliation he bred a variety of pigs, calves, nanny goats, cows and horses most of which he sold at cut-rate prices to the German Commissariat and the rest at exorbitant prices to his compatriots. Unlike Rigaux who collaborated for ideological reasons, Chalembert was a businessman first and a patriot second. His ideology was restricted to the state of plumpness of his mattress where, according to the town gossip, he kept a substantial cache of gold.

Chalembert had outlived all of his relatives thus proving once again the legitimacy of the old adage that wickedness preserves. His wife had died in childbirth many years before, and the son born from this dead woman's womb had died shortly after of a combination of paternal neglect, chronic melancholia and meningitis. Until recently, Chalembert's only surviving kin had been a younger brother, paraplegic since birth, whom Chalembert had taken in his care out of necessity when the war had closed down the state sanatorium where he had spent the better part of his life. No one in Coudouart, Dormans or Epernay had ever seen him, but Rosalie the retarded girl who kept house for Chalembert (and was also his bed-warmer, if one were to believe the venomous local tongues) used to call him a poor soul upon whom God had never spread his mercy and who would be better off dead than alive to serve as whipping-boy to her boss. When news of the brother's passing reached the hillocks of Dormans no one missed him but the consensus was that at last God had smiled upon him by putting him out of his misery.

It was his brother's death which had brought Chalembert one day to visit Bébert's workshop. Being the only carpenter in town, Bébert was an indispensable member of the community. Among other things, he built cradles for the newborns, beds for the newlyweds, and coffins for the dead. And so Chalembert had called upon him to build the cheapest coffin possible to bury his deceased paraplegic brother in. Lumber being a scarce commodity in those days, the bill had proven quite substantial and Chalembert having squandered no money on his brother while he was alive saw no reason to do so now that he was dead. The bill had remained unsettled for six weeks and the unpaid-for coffin a bone of contention long after it and the brother had been interred in the good earth of Champagne.

At first Bébert, who was not a mean man himself and who had a chronic distaste for haggling over money, had more or less given up on the coffin and Chalembert. He temporized his abdication by pointing out to Nanette that, in the eyes of God, he would come out better than Chalembert and that a good deed done is a blessing received: "It's a down payment on heaven, Mother, isn't it? It's thanks to me that poor soul was buried like a God-fearing man!" But Nanette would have none of it, she wanted her heaven down here and her money now. Besides, Guigui's first communion was coming up in May and as yet she had nothing for the family feast that was to be the crowning glory of this memorable day. Since Chalembert didn't want to pay in cash, he would have to pay in kind: she wanted a pig in payment for the coffin. The idea had become such an obsession in her mind that she already had the poor animal quartered and cooked, smoked and put in brine as ham, lard, chitterlings, pork roast, suet, sausages and paté. When Nanette had first suggested this compromise, Bébert had objected: even to Bébert, the anticlerical, there was something heathen about swapping a pig for a coffin. But over the weeks the idea had gained traction and with Nanette's knack for bringing to the taste-buds the savor of all those delicacies one could extract from a hog, Bébert had reconsidered his objections and yielded some of his expedient piety. Soon enough, Nanette had convinced him that a pig for a coffin was a trade which even God himself might condone in those ungodly times.

Since Chalembert came down to Dormans every Wednesday to black-market his stock, Nanette for the last five days had intensified her siege. As for the rest of us, having stood as silent witnesses to this struggle of wills and wits for the best part of five weeks, we were eager for the fight to come to an end preferably with Nanette the winner.

"Yes, I talked to Chalembert!" Bébert relented at last, watching the impact of his words upon our faces.

"Well?" Nanette said expectantly.

"Well, what?" Bébert shot back, all innocence.

"What did he say?"

"He said a hog was too much."

"He did, did he? And did you tell him his poor brother's soul was worth at least a hundred pigs like I told you to tell him?"

"I did."

"And what did he say?"

"He said his brother wasn't worth a chicken, that he'd never been able to earn a sou in his life and that he saw no reason why he should be out a hog on his account!"

Nanette was fuming now as she dished the turnips and lard: her lower lip was quivering and her nostrils swelled in anger. I knew she was about to explode and watched fascinated. But suddenly, and for a reason I started to perceive, on my right Bébert broke in a low chuckle.

"That Chalembert should be shot or bled like a rabbit! A devil, that's what he is! No consideration for anyone, he has, none at all, even for his deceased brother. He'll rot in hell, won't he Mémé, and I'll dance on his grave. I hope the resistance do him in, might even talk to a couple of them, I know who they are, don't worry. Yes, that's exactly what I will do, and then we'll see what's what!"

She grumbled and rambled in her frustration, threatened reprisals, cursed Chalembert, and forked her turnips with a vengeance. But I knew the pig was ours when Bébert poked my elbow.

"You'll do no such thing, woman," he said at last "cause I got you your bloody pig. You just never let me finish, do you, just ranting and raving, that's all you know if you don't get your way. Well, I am smarter than you. I told Chalembert I'd patch up his barn in my spare time, and between the coffin and the barn, he seemed to think a pig was a fair price so he's bringing it over to us next Wednesday, and you'd better start thinking where you'll keep the darn animal till it's ready for slaughter."

Upon these words, pandemonium broke over the table led by Nanette who, reaching over me, plucked a resounding kiss on her husband's cheek. Bébert who was not a demonstrative man and who had been caught by surprise, took it with bad grace, mostly because in her unleashed enthusiasm Nanette had provoked a table-quake of major proportions and, even worse, forgotten to wipe her lips clean of grease before branding his cheek. Still, while he grunted and mumbled his disapprobation, the rest of us made merry: Guigui because he was anxious that his first communion should be a success and the pig would contribute its share to that end; Mémé because at the doorstep to Heaven gluttony was about the only sin she could indulge in without fear of divine retribution; Nanette because the rarity of the acquisition would make her the envy of the local housewives next market day, and I because like all children I was a chameleon and joy was the color of the moment.

"How many kilos?" Nanette queried with sudden mistrust.

"What kilos?"

"The pig, Bébert, the pig! He's so crafty Chalembert he's liable to give you an old carcass with two feet already in the grave and more bones than meat under its hide!"

Bébert shot her a frozen stare through his steel-framed glasses.

"It'll be big enough…Anyway, I'm sure you'll tell Chalembert if it isn't."

"Damn right I will. Sorry Mémé. I'll even go to the Coudouart and pick one out myself if Chalembert tries to put one over on me!"

And I knew she would too. So I sat back and savored my stewed apple. For want of further good news we finished dessert faster than usual and the siren of the saw-mill rang curfew as Mémé finished sucking her last spoonful. We fell back into the familiar routine: Bébert went outside to close the shutters of the kitchen and dining-room while Guigui went upstairs to draw those of our bedrooms. Mémé took out her mending while I helped Nanette clear the table.

After supper in Dormans the April 1944, we did what we had done in March 1944, what millions of families did throughout France and would, I was sure then, do for the rest of eternity. Curfew, like summer rain or winter snow, had become a natural condition about which everyone complained but for which no one had yet found a remedy. After eight in Dormans, in April 1944, we huddled in one room, the five of us – always the kitchen because it was still warm from the cast-iron stove which had cooked our evening meal – and clustered like moths under the forlorn electric bulb. Sometimes because of a bombardment that had hit the nearby power station or on orders of the German Kommandatur, power would be cut off and the bulb was then replaced by a tall and fat ivory candle whose sallow flame danced upon our faces and cast long shadows in every nook of the kitchen. I loved candle nights better than bulb nights: they made the evening mysterious and eerie and each one of the Marchands a little less familiar. Indeed, candle nights in that year of 1944 were my favorites. So I had hoped through my stewed apple that the pig night might be a candle night: between the joy over Chalembert's capitulation, the unlikelihood of Bébert being able to read his newspaper or Mémé darning his socks in the stingy light, like a Trojan horse infiltrating the Greek compound, I would break their companionable silence with a volley of questions which might at last provide me with the answer as to what had happened to the Boche. Alas, when Bébert returned from closing the shutters and switched on the light, the bulb lit up casting its lunar glow over our faces.

Guigui who for the past three weeks had been having a one sided affair with Monsieur Dumas' "Three Musketeers," suggested a game of dominos. He had finished the book the previous night and although his infatuation with Milady had been a sore point between the two of us I felt sorry for him. He was at the age when a boy approves of fictional vixens far more than ingénues, and whereas I had an undaunted love for Cosette of Monsieur Hugo's Les Misérables I also knew that Guigui could not admit to the same inclination. At the self-conscious age of twelve, mourning the execution of the beautiful but spiteful Milady added a reassuring dimension to his budding manhood and made him soul-mates with D'Artagnan and Aramis whom she had also deceived. He associated with heroes while I associated with victims: he was trying to be a man while I remained hopelessly a woman.

But I could tell our hearts were not in the game because neither one of us tried to cheat. I thought about the Boche while Guigui thought about Milady's severed head being tossed in the river Lys. The pig was forgotten. The only noises to be heard in the woolen silence came from Nanette as she scrubbed – and banged – her pots and pans, rinsed our plates and glasses under the running tap. I started looking forward to bed.

But then Bébert suddenly broke into our silence.

"By the way, has a Sergeant Schroeder been here?"

"What Sergeant Schroeder?" Nanette asked untying her faded blue apron.

"I met Uncle Marcel on my way back to Dumont's place this afternoon and he told me the Germans were going around Dormans asking all kinds of questions about one of their soldiers - - - " he broke off abruptly when he caught sight of me, shot a glance at Nanette. I sensed it was meant to convey to her some news of importance which couldn't be discussed in front of us.

"I haven't seen anyone all day except Soldat Mueller, but he didn't ask any questions. Did he ask you Tina?" Nanette replied impervious to Bébert's signal.

"No!"

"He wouldn't," Bébert said with finality.

"What's this about?" Nanette persisted

"Apparently that guy Schroeder has been asking questions. He was even at Pottin's place asking about the missing soldier. They think he went over the wall, but they aren't sure and that's bad if you know what I mean."

It became apparent that Nanette finally did because she dropped the subject and shot a knowing glance at her husband in the tacit understanding he had been trying to get from her. They would talk no more about the incident, at least not until they were in the privacy of their bedroom.

"What if they ask ME questions," I jumped in thinking ahead of them.

Nanette shot a glance at Bébert. He stared back at her. I had a good point and I knew it.

"Come to think of it they might do just that, the krauts. They know us adults won't talk. I wouldn't put past them to try to get their answers from the young ones…" Bébert opined folding his newspaper.

"So what? What can they tell them: they don't know anything," Nanette replied forcefully as if she were trying to give us a message. "Do you Guigui?"

But Guigui had already stopped listening and was once again staring at Mémé's right ear seeing beyond it, I guessed, the tender lobe of another ear stained with blood.

"Guigui!" Nanette bellowed.

"What?" Guigui jumped.

"When will you ever listen?" Nanette scolded him, "About the Boche! If they ask you any questions, you don't know anything, right?"

"About what?"

"About where he's gone to."

"Should I?"

"See what I mean!" she voiced looking smugly at Bébert. "He'll drive them crazy the Germans and it will serve them right."

Guigui's daydreaming which usually launched Nanette into monologues of frustration was paradoxically turning out to be an asset. Even Bébert nodded his head in assent having a simpleton for a son had its rewards. I watched them with contempt and felt like throwing the box of dominoes at Guigui's dumb face. I promised myself never to speak to him again and to be very nice to Soldat Mueller the next time I saw him. Resentment was turning me into a collaborator.

"Well, I might tell them what I know!" I broke in desperation.

"You'll do what?"

Nanette strode the length of the kitchen to the window beneath which I sat on the floor. Towering over me she gave me a frigid stare. The gust of her fury as she had charged through the kitchen had blown on Mémé waking her from her nap. She blinked her cataract-bleached blue eyes and smiled her usual tentative smile the one which automatically broke around her ill-fitting dentures whenever we caught her dozing in the middle of a family gathering.

"You'll do what?" Nanette boomed standing over me like Colossus her arms crossed over the breadth of her generous bosom.

I fidgeted, looked at Bébert who stared back at me without sympathy, at Guigui who had forgotten Milady, and at Mémé who was trying to piece together what she had missed of the confrontation.

"I'll. . . . . I'll have to tell them about the Boche. Won't I Nanette?" I stammered at last.

"What Boche?"

"The one last week, the one I've been asking you all about. Remember, The Gaux? Easter?"

I was regaining some of my self-assurance. Fast. It was now or never my finding out about what had happened to the Boche.

Nanette exchanged one of those knowing grown-up looks with Bébert which only served to arouse my curiosity even more. She was all smiles when she looked at me again but her unexpected change of heart did not fool me, not one bit.

"Well now, Tina?" she voiced more conciliatory, "You've been fretting about him long enough. Must've scared you, drunk as he was. But I told you a hundred times if I told you once, he left! Bébert saw him leave too, didn't you Bébert? He's probably back in Germany by now, seeing his kinfolk and getting drunk all over again. Isn't that so, Bébert?"

"It sure is!"

"So don't you be scared any more, Tina," Nanette continued patting my cheek. "Good riddance, it is! He'll never show his face round these parts again. A disgrace, that's what it was. Him drunk as he was and telling you all those ugly things. But he won't be back again. So if the Germans ask you about him, you never saw him. It's better that way, child. We don't want to get in trouble over a drunk kraut, do we? Besides, as Bébert says, the devil only knows what they would do to us the Germans if they knew about him."

She stopped gazed into my blinking eyes.

"Right, Tina?"

"I guess so…"

"And you won't tell them about the Boche?"

"I won't" I capitulated.

"There's a good girl."

But that she should sound so relieved only increased my suspicion: I was more determined than ever to get to the bottom of the whole affair and promised myself to spend the best part of Thursday cajoling Mémé into a confession. After all, wasn't it Mémé herself who had told me one catches more flies with honey?

* * *

CHAPTER II

Our house in Dormans was situated on the town's main artery, the Avenue de la Marne. Actually the Avenue de la Marne was nothing but a slice of the national highway that left Paris some one hundred and fifty kilometers before Dormans and resumed its course towards Nancy, Metz and Saarbrucken as soon as it passed the Dormans sign-post on the other side of town. But to the people of Dormans, the Avenue de la Marne was what Avenue Foch is to Parisians or Park Avenue to New Yorkers: the mere mention that one lived there gave one a definite standing over one's interlocutor.

The Avenue de la Marne was also the functional heart of the town and the villages scattered about its countryside. I often thought in those days that I could live my entire life just moving up and down its length like the Marchands had done for generations without having or wanting to reach beyond its boundaries for the necessities, chores or even the joys of life. I went to school and Sunday mass on the Avenue de la Marne, borrowed wonderful books from the public library located in its Town Hall. Bébert worked and banked there, Nanette shopped, argued and gossiped along its strip. You could be sired, born and schooled, married and divorced on the Avenue de la Marne; you could practice a trade or adultery there, become a saint in its Gothic church or an alcoholic in its friendly cafes; you could find a doctor for your ailments or a vet for those of your livestock, have your wedding photographed for legitimacy or your will drawn up for posterity on the Avenue de la Marne. Indeed, the only thing you couldn't do on the Avenue de la Marne was to be buried there because in Dormans people kept their grief to themselves. Once dead, the sons and daughters of Dormans were laid to rest in the cemetery on the road to the Château, an oasis of serenity delineated by a belt of indolent cypresses which wavered uniformly against the leaden sky whenever a summer storm lashed out at their conical tops.

The Marchands' house on the Avenue de la Marne consisted of three stories, two-rooms wide, sandwiched between the café where Soldat Mueller and his friends drank their morning beers and after-dinner schnapps on its right, and the house of the widowed Madame Tardieux on its left. The late Monsieur Tardieux had worked for the state-run railway system all of his life and then died peacefully of a heart attack two months after his retirement a year before I came to Dormans. Nanette always insisted that the poor man had died of a "concert" rather than the heart attack diagnosed by Dr. Martin, the latter being a divine punishment meted out to people who burnt the candle at both ends which certainly was not true of the Monsieur Tardieux.

At any rate, Madame Tardieux was our immediate neighbor. Having been blessed by neither children nor friends, she possessed a big fat rusty colored cat up which she lavished all the love and care which the passing of her husband had left unquenched. Albert, the cat was her confidant, her lover and her son all wrapped into one furry ball of feline opportunism. His stomach's capacity and culinary discrimination never ceased to amaze me.

I liked Madame Tardieux even though her solicitude tended to be excessive. She was built like an Amazon and had the strength of a stevedore. When she spoke her voice, which was a rich contralto, seemed to come from beyond the mere confines of her body, a sound born in the deepest and hollowest cavern whose belated resounding echoes when they finally made it to the surface thundered about one's bewildered ears. Bébert used to say that Madame Tardieux had a built-in bull-horn inside her capacious chest and I believed him. Notwithstanding her impressive stature I felt sorry for her because, although she never complained about it, I sensed that the passing of Monsieur Tardieux had left a big hole in her life which even the snooty Albert, no matter how obnoxious he might be, had not succeeded in filling entirely. I made it a point of visiting her every Thursday and Sunday afternoons for a half hour at most, and although our conversations were more in the nature of monologues, hers or mine depending upon our respective moods, she seemed to enjoy my presence and always managed to save enough ersatz butter and milk out of her weekly ration to concoct a sweet of some kind which she invariably watched me eat with the same unselfish pleasure she took in watching fat Albert wolf down one of her own dinners. She would talk while I ate, sometimes about her youth, often about Albert, but mostly about her late husband. She always spoke of him with an adoration that baffled me. Somehow it did not seem plausible that the bald-headed and stern-faced station master glaring at me from his picture frame above the parlor's mantel piece should have been able to command such worship as Madame Tardieux devoted to him. But this bafflement itself became the source of endless questions on my part, questions that made Madame Tardieux think I deeply regretted not having known her late husband and so convinced her that I felt cheated by the loss that she would summon forth a whole array of dusty memories to restore him to life for my benefit. Thus, between her devotion to and my curiosity about her defunct husband, we soon established as pleasant a relationship as our age difference would allow.

Madame Tardieux' house was a replica of ours except that what was left in ours was right in hers. This architectural quirk had disoriented me upon my first visiting her but by April of 1944 I had mastered the topographies of both houses to the point where I could have found my way in either one blindfolded. However what was comfortable size house for the five of us was a barn for Madame Tardieux. So the Germans whose occupation force was ever in need of lodgings had requisitioned her second floor to put up their very own Oberleutnant Redlich while Madame Tardieux and Albert retained occupancy of the ground floor.

Oberleutnant Redlich had created quite a stir when he had first appeared in our midst. Nanette who was suspicious of any one not born in Dormans be they French, Senegalese or Chinese, promptly decreed that he had been planted there by the Gestapo to eavesdrop on our prosaic dinner conversations and ascertain that Madame Tardieux and Albert were all that they seemed to be. After all, the Germans were bound to know that Monsieur Tardieux had worked for the French railroads and there were so many of their supply trains being blown up these days that they might well suspect his widow of being in the cahoots with the résistance. Bébert who was an incurable realist scoffed at his wife's notions: Madame Tardieux was far too loud to be involved in any sort of clandestine activities. She couldn't even whisper without people hearing her as far away as the Place du Luxembourg. Besides, she was for the Vichy government and thought of Marechal Pétain with almost the same reverence as she did her late husband.

It soon became apparent to the lot of us, except for Nanette, that Oberleutnant Redlich was as wary of being billeted in Madame Tardieux's house as we were of having him live so close to us and that a polite compromise on the part of all concerned was all anyone could hope to reach from this forced proximity. We developed a kind of apologetic attitude toward him which he reciprocated by appearing embarrassed whenever we ran into him. Notwithstanding this mutual malaise Madame Tardieux claimed he was a very considerate lodger as Germans went, always managing to pay her a rent although he didn't have to, seeing to it that his rooms were kept neat and clean, and being extremely polite whenever they met in the kitchen mornings. Besides he spoke fluent French, Oberleutnant Redlich, without a trace of Teutonic accent. His father had been a military attaché to the German Embassy in Paris between 1930 and 1935 and he had gone to college on the Boulevard Voltaire. He knew Paris like his native Munchen, and the works of Stendhal as thoroughly as those of Kierkegaard. Of course, these admissions on his part were above our heads, but the fact that he was willing to make them made him a little less of an occupier and somewhat more than a polite admirer of our endangered French culture. The war prevented us from liking him but we were conscious that given different circumstances than those of the times, we might, him and us, have shared a true mutual respect.

Our house in Dormans consisted of a first floor where we ate, fought, worked, played and entertained; a second floor where Bébert and Nanette, Mémé and I slept and where all of us washed our bodies and relieved our respective bladders and a third floor which was really an attic but spacious enough despite its mansard roof to accommodate Guigui, several families of dormice and a brood of sparrows not to mention a few skylarks and daddy-long-legs whose tenancy was strictly seasonal. The attic was the most frightening part of the house because it was alive with noises, especially at night, which I could no more explain than I could listen to them without reaching a paroxysm of dread.

Nanette had assigned me to one of the two attic bedrooms when I had first arrived in Dormans. She had showed it to me by the crisp daylight of a January morning and I had been enchanted by the winter white sunlight pouring in from its only window, the pink and red giant-flowers wall paper, the high mahogany bed buried under a foot of red eiderdown, the austere crucifix entwined with the branch of dried boxwood that had been blessed by Father Joseph, the same Father Joseph who had officiated at her first communion. I had spent two hours in my room in the attic that first day toying with the pear-switch dangling at the end of its electric wire at the head of the bed, thinking I was rid of all the maternal lights-out commands, lounging on this huge raft of a country mattress or diving into the carmine silk of its eiderdown.

However, it turned out that notwithstanding my diurnal delight I did not sleep a wink that first night of January 1942 in the attic of the Marchands' house. I was seven years old and a Parisian at heart. I was used to people living right and left and up and down of me, to the noisy silence of a small street of Paris' Ninth Arrondissement, to the cataract of Monsieur Michoux's toilet upstairs or the marital wrangling of the Duprés downstairs; my ears were attuned to the early morning clangor of garbage trucks, the song of the street sweeper, or the occasional monologue of the drunkard on his way home or hell. I had never experienced the noises of a country attic. The night's utter darkness gave the sounds breaking about it a demonic quality from the roof beams at work under the assault of a winter snow fall to the scurrying of the frozen dormice or the rhythmic snoring of a ten-year old boy sleeping in the room next to mine. I tried to hide under the blankets and eiderdown only to fear that when I hid a hundred demons surrounded my bedside. I switched on the light only to discover Christ nailed as a giant corpse to His crucifix about to drain me of my Parisian blood in vampire fashion. The gigantic flowers of the wall-paper became a jungle of man-eating tropical flora waiting to swallow me whole. In short that first night in the attic of the Marchand's house that January 1942 turned out to be a trip into a frightening world far removed from that of Nanette, Bébert and Mémé who slept below it. I stuck it out for three nights, pretending I liked the room until Nanette caught me sleeping on my soup and Mademoiselle Rouleau found me napping over my dictation at school. The family was apprised of my ordeal and Bébert who had a talent for making a child's fear sound entirely reasonable, decreed that my being assigned to the attic had been a mistake; that there was a small alcove in Mémé's bedroom next to theirs on the second floor which, provided he did some work on it, could turn out to be a very cozy nest for a bird like me.

Thus I slept in Mémé's room. However Bébert, out of respect for his mother and in an attempt at making my occupancy of her quarters as inconspicuous as her advanced age required, had fenced me in. A little niche to the immediate right of her bedroom door as one entered it was my habitat. The niche was just profound enough to accommodate me and my fantasies, Pépé's old army cot and his field chest in which I hoarded my treasures. Despite the absence of a door between Mémé and me, the demarcation line so ingenuously created by Bébert's two waist-high sidewalls joined by an arch opening on my sanctuary enabled us to cohabitate while at the same time protecting our respective autonomies; she could soak her dentures every night in the glass of water she kept on her night table, and I could bite my nails in the privacy of my alcove without either one of us having to fear the other might observe such intimate proceedings. We experienced none of the embarrassment of communal living while simultaneously enjoying a discreet intimacy. This situation encouraged me to consider Mémé as my only ally in times of hostilities with Nanette, or, more frequently, use her as an unwitting informer whenever the rest of the family turned a deaf ear to one of my probing questions.

I was hopeful when we went to bed the night of the pig that Mémé might be maneuvered into revealing the ultimate fate of the Boche. Unfortunately, when I got through my teeth-brushing and face-scrubbing chores, I found her abed in the dark, having resumed her napping interlude over Bébert's socks for what appeared to be the long haul that would see her through morning. Still, I crept to her bedside, just to make sure. A moonbeam sifting through the clover-leaf design of the wooden shutters shown on her face. Her toothless mouth when I peered at it gaped and her somewhat stale breath whistled its way out of the narrow gorge of her throat. Mémé was asleep. So I tip-toed my way back to my alcove. There was still tomorrow I thought and if she knew anything, Mémé , I would yet get it out of her. The problem was, did she know anything – more that is than what I knew myself?

The Boche! We all knew about him because all of us had been together when we had come upon him. Lying on my cot, biting the nail of my right thumb (thumbs being my favorite worry beads), forced to postpone my strategy and kept awake by frustration, I evoked as I had done countless times during the past week the night of the Boche.

Only a week ago! In retrospect it seemed that the Boche, Easter and The Gaux were already part of the distant past. Because it was still so fresh, my memory of those two days remained as potent as when I had lived them. Yet, I had so belabored the incident in my frantic search for clues that my general impression of it already had the remote quality of a recollection that has gone through the sifting process of time. Soon, I sensed, the emotions I had felt then would be out of my introspective reach and although I would be able to put a label on them, like fear, anguish or disgust, they would never again throb inside my throat or pulse beneath the skin of my wrists with the same intensity or for the same reason they had that Easter week-end.

My first emotion Saturday morning of Easter week-end had been one of excitement. We were going to The Gaux, Nanette had sounded reveille at six and by six-thirty the five of us were ready and accounted for around the kitchen table. While we ate a quick breakfast, laughed in anticipation, searched the patch of blue sky showing through the curtained window above the serrated roofline of the houses across the street and generally opined that the weather would be with us, Nanette assigned chores and explained logistics.

The Gaux was the Marchands' country retreat. I had been made to understand that what it lacked in comfort and other amenities was made up by the beauty of the scenery surrounding it. It was six kilometers outside of Dormans. Thus far enough from town in those days of rudimentary conveyances to turn the trip into a hiking expedition while still close enough to satisfy Nanette's xenophobia. The house had been in her family for three generations, and for almost seventy years it had been the tradition to open it for the season Easter week-end regardless of whether Easter happened to fall in March or April, under sleet or sunshine. Even under the German occupation, a time during which a lot of old traditions were being discarded out of fear or necessity, the Marchands had not missed one single Easter trek to The Gaux.

And so it was again in this year of 1944 that we stood at attention in the vestibule, ready for Nanette's final inspection.

"Now you understand Bébert? Guigui and me will go on ahead with the bicycle We'll take the cart in tow. Did you tie it to the rear fender? It's all uphill after Matthieu's farm so I'll need him in case the cart breaks loose. Don't want to lose it: got all my pots and pans in there, and your tools so you can mend the broken chairs Adélaide gave me: two years they've been up there, might as well mend them so we can use them come summer! Now let me see: I've got the youngsters' sleeping bags in there, your long-johns, soap and bleach, Mémé's sewing and pills, iodine…Sweet Jesus: yesterday I had it all straight in my mind, now I'm not so sure. Did you children pack your things? In the wheelbarrow? Better be right 'cause when we get up to The Gaux it'll be too late!" She caught her breath, reached for the front door handle, swiveled back: "Remember to lock everything now. Got a list all made up on the kitchen counter child, so you see to it that Bébert checks everything on it. And Bébert you take good care of Mémé, it's a long hike and I want her to rest every half hour. Got some chicory in the thermos, child and a bit of saccharine in your coat pocket…"

"Please, Nanette," Bébert cut in. "We'll be here come Monday if you run on so."

"Alright! But if I don't think around this family nothing gets done! Still, 'guess we won't miss anything. Don't forget the wheelbarrow, Bébert," she went on half-way through the front door. "'Got all our food in there, and the linen and my seeds, Mémé, don't forget.

The Lord knows we must do some planting while we are up there else we'll all be eating rabbit's eggs come winter."

At last she shoved Guigui ahead of her out the front door, turned once more to look at the three of us as though it were for the last time, came back to kiss our six cheeks and left. I had never felt so loved in my life.

Our trek to The Gaux turned out to be quite an expedition but I savored every moment of it. The morning was young, seven-thirty and early April with neither a cloud nor a soul in sight. The sky was a chalky white like a giant canvas waiting to be painted with the brush of my expectations. The brisk air streamed through my parted lips like cool lemonade drunk through a straw.

Thus we paraded through Dormans: first the wheelbarrow, Bébert behind it, then myself and Mémé behind me. On past Dr. Martin's big house and Professor Lucas' home, and left into the weed-grown alley right into the Faubourg de Chavenay and Madame Grimiaux' lopsided row houses, the one she rented and the one she lived in with her widowed son. On and on, past the Elementary School, through the large grounds of the saw-mill with its neat and pungent stack of fresh lumber and its two watch dogs, the one which barked at nothing and everything and the one who did not. Occasionally I could detect the flutter of a lace curtain behind a window pane, a lone inquisitive eye retreating under the probing of my own, and I could almost hear the whispers echoing from kitchen to parlor: "Here go the Marchands! Off to The Gaux for sure. The wife and son probably gone ahead. Nice Easter weather they'll have up there." I embraced Mémé, Bébert and our wheelbarrow in a proprietary glance. I owned them and the world, the day and my almost ten years, and marched through the streets of Dormans like Joan of Arc leading Charles VII to his coronation through the streets of Reims.

Once past the last warehouse of the saw-mill, we left Dormans behind. A pot-holed and gravelly path assaulted the steep hill. It was bordered on its left by the high wall topped by shards of broken glass which girded the grounds of the German-occupied Château, and on its right by a patchwork of desiccated fields and freshly ploughed ones. A small brook ran on the right side of the path its unseen water gurgling under a brush of dried blackberry bushes and budding nettles. Bébert pushed the wheelbarrow up the uneven path while Mémé had started huffing stoically through the climb. I walked now ahead of them, scanning the horizon and sniffing the spring, stopping occasionally to make sure they followed in my blazing trail. Pebbles rolled under our feet and ahead of me, slightly to the right, a still convalescent sun shone without warmth behind a line of trees still scarred by winter.

At ten sharp we reached The Gaux. Fists balled on her hips, Nanette stood waiting for us by the rusting wrought-iron gate fencing the garden. Guigui was nowhere in sight. Her welcome was as effusive as her farewell had been teary three hours earlier.

"There you are! How are you Mémé, not too tired? I've set up the long-chair out in the sun so you can rest your bones before lunch."

"I'm not tired, daughter," Mémé objected. "Got to give you a hand.'

And Nanette:

"I won't hear of it. Bet your rheumatisms are acting up again the way you hold your hips."

"Got to put my hands somewhere, don't I, son?"

"Tssk! Tssk! Off you go now. Bébert and me will take care of everything."

Nanette's order was final and although I could tell from Mémé's pinched lips that it was not to her liking, I knew she would comply. There was between those two a bit of the aboriginal rivalry between daughter and mother-in-law and although Nanette never tried to impose her will on Mémé in a confrontational manner, she used a feigned benevolence much to the same ends and accomplished through it what she could not through intransigence. No one was fooled by it, especially not Mémé . It was just one of those pas-de-deux one performs to maintain social harmony. So Mémé ambled along and I followed her thinking she might appreciate my solidarity.

The Marchands had been downright honest when they had warned me that The Gaux was not much by way of a summer residence. Surveying it again reminded me of a drawing I had made years before at the behest of a kindergarten teacher who had the knack of coming up with what I deemed stupid assignments. "My Dream House" as I drew it was a big square plot with a small rectangular house in its upper half stabbed by two smaller squares for windows and a wobbly rectangle for a door. An alley shot straight as an arrow from the door to the end of the garden. On either side of the alley I had planted rows of what might have been petunias with my red pencil and symmetrical cross lines of vegetables with my green pencil. Such had been my "Dream House" at five years of age: The Gaux was its embodiment. The house itself contained only two large rooms on each side of a small corridor, each with a window fronting the garden, and a windowless (and airless) cubicle at the far end of the hallway which ran between them. The cubicle served the dual functions of kitchen and washroom with its antique cast-iron stove, the broken mirror hanging on the wall above a small metal table topped by a blue enamel washbowl and its matching water jug. Three slightly cracked chamber pots were stacked almost out of sight but not out of reach behind a row of brooms, mops, scrubbing brushes and a rusty toolbox.

It was chilly inside the house. Emanating from the thick walls was a musty smell of unused fruit cellars and winter dampness blended with the acrid scent of long doused chimney fires. I peeked inside the two rooms. The furnishings were eclectic but uniformly sturdy, cast-offs of forgotten lives and old without a claim to antiquity. Nanette had opened the windows wide and together with the cleansing whiff of spring, a yellow butterfly fluttered its way inside the house. Far away and unseen, skylarks and swallows were chirping.

That Saturday at the Gaux was an enchantment: each hour was tinged with the pastel glow of serenity. The sun dutifully drifted across the April sky, the birds bustled about in search of nesting supplies, butterflies hunted for still scarce pollen. A toad leapt between my feet when I caught it dozing on the grassy bank of the small pond near the gate. We ate lunch outside, wrapped in frayed sweaters and sunning our noses. I wolfed down the boiled rutabagas of the occupation while looking forward to the capon Nanette had promised us for Easter Sunday. Over lunch Nanette planned her sowing and despaired of the state of winter disrepair of the grounds; Bébert mused about the likelihood of finding game in the fields that afternoon; Mémé ate with solemn care, and Guigui teased to confusion a convention of ants with the tip of his shoe. We ate left-over stewed apples for dessert.

After lunch Bébert loaded his old hunting rifle and promising to bring us back a couple of fat hares, embarked on an afternoon safari through the hills of Champagne. Nanette disappeared inside the house to give it a muscular cleaning while Mémé retreated to the long-chair by the cistern with her perennial darning. After some deliberation Guigui opted for a worm-gathering trip: the fishing season was about to open and a supply of bait might just convince Uncle Marcel into letting him on his boat. I idled away a half hour inspecting the rear of the house. There was an old abandoned well there whose black and stagnant waters exuded a putrid smell when I tossed a couple of pebbles into its untested depth. I listened but the pebbles seemingly never reached the bottom of its abyss if indeed the well had one. I ambled toward the stone wall which separated the rear of The Gaux from the grounds of the Château. It was not so high that with a push from Guigui I could not have reached its summit, but the broken glass spiking it precluded such an attempt. I couldn't even find a crack between the uneven stones of the wall to steal a peek at what laid beyond it. Apart from the wall and the well behind the house, there were the usual garden tools leaning against the back wall: rakes, spades, scythes along with discarded pots and pails, stacks of moldy logs. Anyway, it had turned chilly in the shade so I walked back to the front of the house and Mémé whose gaping mouth as she dozed under the cool sunlight attracted two flies which I swished away with a flicker of my hand.

The sun was smack at the heart of the sky as I left the garden; Bébert and Guigui were already long out of sight. I went through the gate and turned left on the dirt path hugging the small brook on my right. I walked a long time, my eyes tracing the weed-choked ditch, my ears attuned to the gurgling rush of its unseen water until the trail came to an abrupt end. The water pursued its upward course through a tangled growth of impossible brambles. Higher ahead of me beyond it, gnarled and leafless oaks huddled over shadowy mysteries which kindled in me a sense of utter loneliness and a vague feeling of dread. I could still see The Gaux below me but Mémé was now a black speck on the grayish background of the untilled soil, and the house looked far too small to contain even Nanette. I felt small and forsaken inside the infinity of the countryside. The shrill call of a blue jay shooting out of the clustered trees sent me scurrying as fast as I could down the path, back to The Gaux.

That evening at supper I told them I had walked far and long in search of the source but that, obviously, Bébert had been wrong and the brook had its beginning far beyond my ambulatory capabilities. Guigui sensing an easy victory wagered that, come the next day, he would succeed where I had failed and the matter was laid to rest leaving me torn between my earlier cowardice and resentment at Guigui.

Easter Sunday was as uneventful as Saturday had been. That is in the morning. The same sun continued to hang high in the sky. Guigui tended to his harvest of wiggly worms while Nanette planted neat but invisible rows of seeds she promised us would turn into potatoes, cabbages, string beans, tomatoes lettuce and strawberries come June or July. Bébert repaired Adélaide's chairs and Mémé busied herself in the kitchen while I set the table in the garden. Despite its advanced age the capon tasted scrumptious and its partaking made us all sated and mellow. To conclude our feast, Nanette, Bébert and Mémé indulged in a glass of apple-brandy and Guigui and I were allowed to savor a brandy-dipped lump of rare sugar, both being exceptional treats.

I remember as though it was yesterday that I was slowly sliding down Mémé's bony lap, sucking on my lump of sugar, when the thunder roll of distant heavy vehicles on the move broke our silence. I remember also that Bébert shot up from his chair and that Guigui started running toward the gate only to be stopped midway by Nanette's admonition to return to the fold. The sun above turned cold and the swallows vanished in a swift brown swarm.

"Planes?" Nanette asked Bébert.

He searched the sky, an unseen muscle twitching under the skin of his neck.

"A German convoy. Guigui sit down! Don't any of you move. Nothing to be afraid of," he went on tentatively. "Maneuvers probably. We are just enjoying our Easter Sunday, sitting in our own garden: nothing wrong with that."

And yet I felt guilty for no reason, but then most Frenchmen felt an irrational collective guilt under the German occupation. I was also scared as I stiffened on Mémé's lap and my arm slid from around her neck. She squeezed my waist and held me down. Tight.

Soon the thunder was upon us. At first a jeep loaded with four German soldiers moving up the dirt path beyond the rusty iron fence. There were shouts and calls and undertone of urgency permeating the men's voices. The driver spotted the five of us sitting at studied random under the April sun. His foot crushed the brake pedal and he turned to the officer who sat next to him, mouthing a few words. The officer got out, rounded the jeep and standing by the gate, beckoned to Bébert. Nanette made a move but her husband motioned her down. I watched a vein in Bébert's neck throb as he walked to the fence: we all did. He did not open the gate to the German officer: instead he spoke across it. The man talked and Bébert shook his head. The German persisted and still Bébert waved his head in negation. At last the man barked on last question and Bébert fished in his pant pockets. Papers! I felt like fleeing but sat paralyzed, searching Nanette's' stone face for reassurance.

Meanwhile, the two soldiers who had been riding in the back of the jeep had jumped out of the vehicle and now shouldered the officer who was obviously senior to them. They exchanged more words at the gate while the three men pored over Bébert's papers. Then the officer stepped closer to the fence: his eyes surveyed the garden, from the pond to the cistern at the right of the house, from Nanette's rows of seeding to Mémé's discarded long-chair and sewing, then back to us again. They attempted to read our innocent faces, the table with the scraps of our Easter feast. I heard a bird warble and a fly started to scale my neck as the man's steely eyes focused on me. I sat transfixed under his stare. And then he did the most unexpected thing: he broke into a smile, waved his hand in my direction.

"Wave back, Tina!" Nanette prompted me in a whisper. And I did all nerves on edge. He said something to the others and they all laughed: even Bébert. His papers were returned. There were good-byes exchanged and Nanette heaved a silent sigh of relief across the table. The cloud of anxiety broke over the garden and Guigui finished his aborted dash to the gate. He stood next to his father, waved at the Germans with him. The lump of sugar had melted in the palm of my hand: mixed with the apple brandy the concoction had glued the walls of my small fingers together.

"They are looking for one of theirs," Bébert reported as he made his way back. "Told them we haven't seen anyone round these parts since yesterday morning. God forbid they catch him!"

Behind him a truck loaded with fully armed soldiers machine guns at the ready, followed the lead jeep, and then a second jeep closed the small convoy. Guigui came back just as Bébert was pouring himself another round of apple bandy.

Guigui did not go on his source-finding expedition that afternoon and Bébert contented himself with the two partridges and the skinny hare he had killed the day before. We huddled close together the rest of the afternoon. The Gaux was a haven and our togetherness the safest harbor.

It was much later that night that we heard the Boche. Ten o'clock or perhaps a little after. A full moon poured its skimmed milk over the countryside, casting long shadows over each hollow and The Gaux itself. Guigui and I were sitting on the door-step gazing at the night sky while Bébert ambled through the garden smoking a rare cigarette. I remember I was crossed at Guigui's ability to name out of the stellar maze shapes and forms which to me remained hopelessly inextricable. I had just told him he was making it up, the Big Bear and the Little Bear, when suddenly we heard a deafening clangor coming from behind the house. Metallic: like someone crashing into a stack of tin pails. I searched for Bébert who was at the garden gate lost in thoughts. And then immediately it seemed, Nanette sprung out of the kitchen behind us: a stiff index across her lips motioned us to silence. And as we held our collective breath, our ears riveted to the silence, the noise broke again. Angry this time, pails being kicked by and angry foot each thrust accompanied by an outpouring of guttural curses.

"Bébert! Bébert!" Nanette yelled at last breaking our paralysis. I jumped up as did Guigui. "Bébert!"

He came running down the central path toward the house: I had never seen him run that fast. He flew past us, trampling Nanette's seedlings and then I don't know how or why but we were all running behind him, even Mémé come out of nowhere who puffed behind me.

Then I saw him. He stood opposite us thirty meters away maybe, almost at the far end of the house. He was a huge man with a massive frame, weaving a bit but clearly as startled as we were. He cut a husky black silhouette against the background of moon-speckled ferns and bushes. A half-empty bottle dangled from his left hand and in his right one a gun pointed at us caught a glimmer of light. Bébert started toward him. The man stumbled back flapping the air with the bottle as though looking for a prop. Still weaving he retreated further back soon emerging in the open space between the end of the house and the walls of the Château where the moon now poured its wheyey glow on his face: a human animal with alcohol-crazed eyes, haunted from deep within. He was completely bald and his square skull glistened from sweat as though with fear. He wore no coat or jacket. His shirt muddied and torn in places was open on a hairy muscular chest. I couldn't take my eyes off of him. None of us could. And then, as my eyes moved down the length of his body, I noticed his trousers hung undone about his lower hips. His genitals rested flaccid over the coarse material of his trousers like the innards of a slaughtered calf I had once seen on the butcher's stall. Slowly, the evening supper started working its acid way back from my stomach to my throat. I gasped for air.

He must have noticed my eyes staring at him because suddenly as I stood watching that thing at the hollow of him from his island of light his hand moved to the front of his trousers and started fondling the flaccid mass. "Lutscher Klein Madchen, Suss lutscher, klein Madchen, kom hier." Like a nursery rhyme. "Klein Mad-chen, Klein Mad-chen." His eyes had grown glassy, and always, still, he kept chanting his monotonous singsong: "Klein Mad-chen, Klein Mad-chen," faster and faster to the rhythm of his fingers. I screamed and screamed at that point. I couldn't stop though my throat was being torn to painful shreds. And then my ear was on fire and the screams choked inside my throat. Nanette had slapped me.

"Take them away, Mémé, take them away!" she ordered.

Guigui grabbed my hand, tried to pull me away. Then the fire again stinging my cheek, Mémé this time. Half way between nightmare and reality. But I could move now.

"Schwein, Franzosisch Schwein!"

And:

"I've got him, Nanette, got him! Quick, the scythe, a shovel anything, quick. Can't hold him much longer. He's like a mad bull, Nanette, quick!"

And then:

"Pick up his gun! He's breaking loose, Nanette! Kick him, kick him, yeas, right there!"

And she:

"Here, Here, you filthy Boche! Take that!"

Then a moan and a thud. Nothing. Silence. Mémé had closed the door behind us. And I was gasping for air. The brandy she was forcing between my clenched teeth dribbled down my chin and Guigui's knees were shaking as he stood by the iron stove, his face the dirty white of a turnip. Mémé was in turn wiping my chin, shaking me by the shoulders, burying my face into her skirt.

"It's alright, my Tina, just a dirty drunk Boche! Bébert'll truss him good like a sausage and throw him in the fields yonder. His kinfolk will find him soon enough: throw him in the brig they will." She patted my cheek, kissed my forehead, my cheeks. "Drink some of that brandy too, son! Your teeth are rattling like old bones," she called to Guigui over my head.

The chamber pots neatly stacked behind Mémé's skirt caught my attention: suddenly I had an uncontrollable urge to use one of them.

I did not see either Bébert or Nanette until the early dawn of the next day when we closed the house to return to Dormans. I rode down in Bébert's now empty wheelbarrow but took no joy from the ride. Despite their presence little was said: somehow I sensed theirs was a silence which one could not break. I just began to hope we would soon reach Dormans and our house, for it to be Tuesday and oblivion, for that queasiness which felt so much like guilt to go away.

It started pouring with April rain as we reached the saw-mill and for some unexplained reason, I wanted to cry.

* * * * * * * *

CHAPTER III

By May First, Labor Day, I had relegated the question of the Boche to the back of my mind mostly because Mémé's pretended ignorance left me stumped. Besides Dormans was swept by a tidal wave of rumors about an impending allied landing: Leclerc had liberated Sfax, De Gaulle had been to Algiers, Mayor Chancel was standing up to "them", "they" were running scared, and no one had seen or heard from Rigaux, the collaborator, for over a week. A virus of hope had swept the town and I had caught its symptoms. De Gaulle was Santa Claus and the Americans the good guys: with them would come in abundance all those things the Marchands had missed most, like butter and sugar, tobacco for Bébert, meat and real bread, soap to lather in and red wool to knit me a brand new dress. The first bars of Beethoven's Fifth were as popular as Edith Piaf's latest hit and Petain and Lavalle back in Vichy were talking to a growing nation of deaf ears, Nanette argued much less, Bébert smiled in defiance whenever he came back from a day's compulsory work at the Château, and Guigui dreamt of joining the resistance with Pottin's son Jean-Claude when school was over. At school Mademoiselle Rouleau was surreptitiously teaching us the verses of the Marseillaise and a few English words of welcome that made us giggle. In short we were all expectant and on the brink of the coming freedom, and even though Freedom was to me quite as esoteric a concept as Catholicism, heroism or patriotism, I knew that whatever it was was good.

Closer to me was another happiness, one with which I could identify. Our very own Lisette was in love and although love's mysteries still escaped me, I recognized its stigmata: Lisette carried them around like the signs of a benign allergy and her eyes were aglow with its fever. Our old Lisette, despite her thirty-four years, her thick glasses and double chin, had overnight turned into a belated beauty. She blushed whenever his name was mentioned and sometimes, I could tell, was near tears when Nanette dared to whisper something about a problematic wedding night. Yes, Lisette was in love and I loved her for it. It was as if I expected that I might somehow become tinged with the same mellowness just standing in the shadow of her. Like the frog I had seen sunning itself at The Gaux, I wanted to bask in Lisette's sun, in the warmth of her love for Raymond Langiers and dissolve under it into a puddle of sweet bliss.

Lisette was Bébert's niece: uncle Marcel and aunt Louise's only child. She had been considered an old maid for eight years ever since she had turned twenty-five because in Dormans girls wed early or not at all. Somehow Lisette had missed the connubial boat. She had thus joined that lusterless brood of spinsters one meets in any small town who socialize together, knit black socks for the church's poor and dark green scarves for the orphanage; who tend to their elders with abnegation and pray for their soul while craving for someone to come and fill the enduring void at the small of their belly, who collect recipes they will never use and dream of a life they will never have; who blush at off-color jokes but are bolder than most in their secret fantasies. But who also are more tolerant of other women's children because they are doomed to be denied their own motherhood.

Lisette was all of that and more. I had a special fondness for her much like that I had toward Mémé perhaps because spinsters and widows have much in common. I had spent many Sunday afternoons with her since coming to Dormans: we strung beads together, she taught me crochet while we talked in whispers about love. She was an avid reader of mellifluous novels and knew which movie star had taken up with what singer even before they in turn learned of it through the Mirror of Paris which she purchased from the bookstore of the Place du Luxembourg every Saturday morning. I found her a wealth of knowledge and the fact that she worked at the town Hall as the official Registrar in my mind contributed no small part to her stature. No one was born, married or deceased without notifying her first, except in the latter case when the bereaved survivors would see to the chore. Perhaps because of her official role she spoke in a slightly affected manner, and even when explaining a new recipe, she would often sound like Mayor Chancel when he addressed the townsfolk on special occasions. The history of Dormans going back to the Middle Ages was enshrined in her office at the Town Hall which was appropriately somber and musty.

I often went to visit her at her office when I was off from school Thursdays. I would watch from behind the lace curtain of our kitchen window until the awful Cerberus Soldat Mueller left his post to go have his high beer and would then bolt across the street and up the steps of the Town Hall before his return. There were many Germans inside the Town Hall but they seldom stopped me: "I am going to see my cousin Lisette!" I would proclaim loudly throughout my dash down the marble corridor. Still, once I had shut the door of Lisette's office, I would plop my body on the nearest bench and invariably comment that I had been "scared to death." Whereupon Lisette would rise from her cluttered desk behind the chest-high counter separating us and inquire in her most official voice: "Yes, Mademoiselle Tina? What will it be today: births, deaths, or marriages?" Then, depending on my mood, she would hand me over the wooden countertop one of the mammoth registers that otherwise gathered dust on the floor-to-ceiling shelves which covered the walls of her office.

I had taken a fancy to the death registries of late. It was not that I had developed a morbid taste but over my many weeks of research in Lisette's office I had soon determined that one was born either one of two ways, male or female, and that one invariably married someone of the opposite sex. Death, in short, was were my interest could best be cultivated because of the variety of ways in which it could occur. Murders were my favorite but they were few and far between. Childbirth deaths were my second favorite because I could fantasize umpteen situations each more heart-wrenching than the next which in sheer pathos rivaled anything found in Lisette's tear-jerker novels. Besides which, in the death registries, there were the trite but educational variety of causes: strokes and thrombosis, pneumonia and leukemia, septicemia and diphtheria. Medically speaking I learned a lot at almost ten years of age poring over Dorman's logs of dead souls.

Indeed I loved Lisette. Her face was a perfect square from the outline of her forehead to her soft double chin, and her body a squat rectangle from the tip of her shoulders to the southernmost part of her hips. She had no neck to speak of and legs so stubby they did little to alleviate the overall cubical impression one immediately derived upon first meeting her. Much like cats children often have a sixth sense when it comes to people and at one glance they can tell a probable friend from a potential foe. I had sensed from our first encounter that Raymond Langiers could be the latter. He was thirty-seven and a much sought-after bachelor, worked as senior clerk for the local notary, Maitre Pinson, played checkers with Father Rocas every Wednesday evening, went to low mass on Sundays and always wore starched shirts under the vest of his dark suits. He might have been a caricature of a small town law clerk except for one thing; he was handsome. All the young and not-so-young eligible girls of Dormans harbored secret dreams of snagging Raymond Langiers although in fairness to him he did little to encourage them. On Saturdays, market day, they would congregate outside the bookstore next to the bakery at the corner of the Place du Luxembourg, three or four of them, sometimes more, all twitters and whispers, hair piled high above their heads as was the fashion, uplifted by several centimeters of corked heels, each more anxious for Langiers to make his appearance at eleven o'clock. I did not have to search the Avenue de la Marne to know they had spotted him: one girl would touch up her hair, another would wiggle in the sheath of her skirt while a third suddenly absorbed herself in the contemplation of her painted fingernails. And Langiers invariably showed up within seconds, smiled a thin smile and dropped his expected "morning" at the lot of them before disappearing inside the bookstore. Crouched behind a vegetable stall or the weekly poster of the Empire Theater, I would utter a disgusted grunt and share my contempt with a stray dog or cat working its way through the busy square. But if Nanette, her shopping done, did not come looking for me, I would wait till Langiers exited the store. The girls waited too. Sometimes he would be out within seconds, but other times he would linger in the store for a good fifteen minutes.

He would always look preoccupied when he emerged from the bookstore, and although the pretense of preoccupation was with him a professional, and I was sure, a calculated ploy, that which shown on his face every Saturday morning as he came out of Monsieur Lucien's shop on the Place du Luxembourg always seemed genuine. He did not smile at the girls though they did at him. He would start walking blind man steps as he leafed through the magazine he had just purchased. Then he would find a certain page, stop, read intently: an obstacle in the path of every one scurrying down the Avenue de la Marne. Once I had asked Lisette about Langiers' magazine, what it was in it that so absorbed his attention. But she answered something about estate sales and auctions being advertised weekly, and how he had to keep up with such things in his line of work. I hadn't believed a word of her explanation preferring my more nefarious conjectures and I went spying on him every Saturday, fully confident that my obstinacy would pay off and ultimately reveal what it was that kept Raymond Langiers from courting the available girls of Dormans and walking about in shirt-sleeves once in a while like Bébert, and knowing how to talk to little girls like me without giving them the impression they were prize poodles: what it was in short that kept him from being and acting like the rest of us.

Indeed, on this fine Labor Day 1944, I was so full of expectations and so restless that the incident of the Boche had lost some of its urgency. And although sometimes lying in the dark immediately before sleep I would again see him as he had stood behind our house at The Gaux that night, hear again my endless screams and the struggle which had occurred between him and Bébert and Nanette, the episode no longer held my eerie perplexity. So I would think about Lisette instead, ignore the memory of the putrid well and concentrate on Mémé's strained breathing at the other end of darkness.

My task was rendered easier by the prospect of Guigui's First Communion. It was only two weeks off and the entire family was astir with planning for it. There were endless debates around the kitchen table each night, cooperation or lack of it, threats being made and promises sworn to, and discussions about the guests and the dishes, the wines and the prayers, the presents and the protocol. The main point of contention remained Bébert's flat refusal to attend the high mass at which his son was to be confirmed as "a host munching" member of Dormans Catholic community as he had irreverently put it a week earlier. The only way she would get him inside the church, he had warned Nanette, would be feet first, and even then he might well come back to life just long enough to scare the pants off of the entire congregation up to and including Father Rocas if he wore underwear under his cassock, which Bébert doubted. Bébert heathen tirade had left Mémé quasi apoplectic and had so stunned Nanette that the two whole days elapsed before she recovered enough gumption to launch a counter-offensive. But still, the matter stood unresolved: Bébert stuck to his anticlerical guns while Mémé worried her rosary beads with a litany of Ave Marias, and Nanette, for some reason which remained obscure to me, threatened to move to my old bedroom in the attic. And Guigui did not care.

I too contributed to Nanette's frustration because of my growing attachment to the condemned pig. It had been two weeks since Chalembert had made good on his part of the deal and to our surprise the pig had turned out to be plump in all the right spheres, with a pinkish gray hide that rippled over a sea of potential lard and rear hoofs with enough vigor in them to brand Nanette's shin with a couple of real shiners when we had untied it in the small yard behind Bébert's workshop on the Faubourg de Chavenay. Although Nanette opined that it was her reputation as a shrewd trader - - if not as a shrew, I thought - - that had prevented Chalembert from swindling us, I took a smug pleasure in starting from the other end of her premise and believing that Chalembert had brought us a prize pig to shut her up once and for all. At any rate, I was convinced from the look on her face when Chalembert had unloaded the animal from his old truck that Nanette had looked forward to a royal battle with the farmer. As much as she had wanted Léo the pig to be good and fat, Chalembert by denying her the opportunity of putting up a fight for it had truly put one over her. Perhaps this was why I had grown fond of Léo over the past two weeks: he had become in my eyes the symbol of Nanette's come-uppance. Besides which I had been assigned the task of tending to him during his last days upon this good earth and in trying to make them as delectable as possible, I had fallen into the trap of so enjoying my own devotion that I could no longer bear to see its object slain and quartered and devoured, in short, taken away from my tender if egotistical care. Unlike Bébert though, my struggle with Nanette was doomed from its opening salvo. Léo would die. My last desperate wish was to straddle her with guilt over Léo's demise, and to ensure that she should regret each mouthful she ingested once her nefarious scheme had been put to culinary execution. Guigui for whose glory Léo was fated to perish didn't give a darn.

But then Guigui did not give a darn about anything. He sleepwalked through the house like Saint Guigui bathed in a newfound religious fervor, contemptuous of us doomed sinners, and floated among us like a soul incarnate speaking wisdom and repentance. We did not see much of him because he had started upon his retreat and spent most of his time with the other future saints scheduled to march with him down the Church's center aisle to the high altar. Farther Rocas was his mentor, the hallowed halls of the church on the Place du Luxembourg were his home, and he had been sent upon this earth to bring about universal redemption. He had forsaken the wicked Milady and walked about with his ubiquitous catechism under his left arm, his brows knitted over the mystery of the immaculate conception and his mouth full of the Holy Ghost or the Holy Trinity: he had taken to speaking in riddles and acted through genuflections and signs of the cross. This sainthood sent Bébert into fits of demonic temper but thoroughly gratified Mémé. Nanette remained impervious to it thick as she was in planning for the pagan feast which would follow her son's first Communion while I, looking at his acned chin, cabbage-leaf ears and the tuft of brown hair blooming straight at the apex of his skull, remained convinced that the whole thing was a sham.

It was the tradition for the Germains to partake in a glass of Nanette's brandied cherries after Sunday lunch. But the Sunday before Guigui's communion they arrived at one thirty or a half hour earlier than customary. Nanette made a face and the apple pie she had just laid on the dining-room table followed a hasty retreat back to the now cold oven.

"I don't have to feed all of Dormans," she muttered, "we'll save it for tonight."

Mémé was ordered to put away our dessert plates while I went to open the front door. Although I took my time the mouth-watering aroma still wafted from the kitchen when I let them in. Aunt Louise's pointy nose positively quivered and her nostrils like the snouts of the sawmill dogs, pulsated under the sapid effluvium floating about her weasel-face.

"Mmmm! Antoinette has spoiled you child, hasn't she?" she said brushing my cheeks with her thin lips. "Do you smell that Marcel? Lisette?"

"Sure do! Only little rascals have such luck, right Tina?" he tugged at my right ear as his mustache chafed my forehead.

I liked Uncle Marcel but I did not like his Clemenceau mustache and although sometimes I would condescend to sit on his fat knees, I was grateful that the respectable circumference of his belly together with my small size prevented between us an even closer rapprochement.

"She's got the nose of a terrier your wife, Marcel!" Nanette called from the dining-room as we filed through the kitchen. "thought I would give the children a treat They ate it all, you know what a sweet tooth they have," she lied as I shot her a disapproving glance from behind Lisette.

As was the well-established custom, the Marchands got up from the table to perform the perennial kissing ritual. This family greeting every time the Marchands and the Germans got together had surprised me no end when I had first arrived in Dormans three years earlier. Except for mother whom I kissed as seldom as she would allow, my kissing was limited to special occasions such as birthdays or Christmases. I had never seen two grown men kiss each other's cheeks the way Bébert and Uncle Marcel did each time they met. And yet they did. Again I watched them from the dining-room door, amazed at this outpouring of kindred affection which for some strange reason tied a knot in my throat. Uncle Marcel opened the ritual with Mémé and his mustache was followed on her wrinkled cheeks by Aunt Louise's pinched lips and Lisette's dimpled chins. Two kisses per cheek for a total of thirty kisses to the Germains' cheeks and, mathematically oddly enough, thirty kisses also to the Marchands' cheeks there being five of us but three of them. Sometimes Uncle Marcel would get carried away and having completed his lap around the table would find himself kissing his wife or Lisette, which sent me into peals of laughter.

Marcel Germain was the son of Mémé's deceased brother Alphonse and if one were to believe her, his father's spitting image. He was therefore Mémé's nephew and Bébert's cousin but he was older than Bébert by some thirteen years, a seniority which for some reason had resulted in the entire family conferring upon his baldish head the misnomer of Uncle under which even I knew him. He was a house painter by trade and a fisherman by hobby. His Clemenceau mustache usually smelled of acetone and because of a life-time of scrubbing it, the skin of his stubby fingers was a rough as emery paper. He could be seen week-days through the streets of Dormans, his washed-out once white overalls caked with blotches of multicolored paint, the elastic of his suspenders distended to their tensile limit over his rotund paunch - - ready I often thought to catapult him into the stratosphere – and a long wooden ladder tucked horizontally under his left arm, a perpetual hazard to the friendly souls who happened to hail him too suddenly. He was a convinced socialist and thought Jean Jaurès was the greatest thing that had ever blessed France; he hated the Germans even more that the rich folks and loved his daughter more spontaneously than Aunt Louise because, as he would often let it be known, theirs had been an arranged marriage although looking back on their thirty-five years together, he had no regrets and only praise for the good woman.

I could not say I really liked Aunt Louise but I accepted her as a member of the clan and therefore some of my affection for the others inevitably flowed her way. But she left me uncomfortable. Love, like joy, tenderness and even sadness, were prisoners inside her and drifted unsuspected along the tide of her bloodstream like the silent plea for help of a shipwrecked mariner sealed inside a bottle that drifted about the oceans without ever coming to shore. She never cried, she commiserated; she did not laugh, she snorted; she did not speak often but when called upon to do so by chance or necessity, her voice had a pugnacious undertone which took me aback. Even her kisses in this kissing family, left me with the impression that they were doled out reluctantly so much so that I often felt an urge to apologize to her as if the contact between our faces had been an unfortunate collision. She was in her mid-fifties, sitting in that gray slice of life much as she sat in those granite-colored housecoats of hers, stiff and resigned, expecting little and wanting even less. I felt sorry for her but my unease every time we met stifled in me even those rare bursts of compassion which perhaps, might have made a difference.

"Well, boy: ready for the big day?" Uncle Marcel queried Guigui drawing one of the window chairs to the table and sitting himself heavily between Bébert and the Saint.

"Yes, Uncle, I think so. Father Rocas says I am one of his best students," Guigui replied looking defiantly at his father.

"Don't get too good at it, son, or you might find yourself turned into a curate, and then goodbye all the fillies. Ain't it so Mémé ?"

"You and Bébert! The devil's got your souls, I swear!"

"Maybe, but we also got something else, haven't we Bébert, and though I can't use it much anymore, sure used it a lot when I could, not like Father Rocas!" Uncle guffawed while Nanette chortled knowingly behind her cup.

"What's that, Uncle?" I piped up from my perch on Lisette's lap.

"You got big ears, child, and your Uncle has got an even bigger mouth," Aunt Louise scolded shrugging her shoulders at her husband. "That ain't fit conversation for a child."

"What isn't, Aunt Louise?" I insisted.

"Tssk, Tssk, Tina: you'll find out when you are a big girl!" Nanette shushed me rising from her chair to pour the brandied cherries.

"Will I be big enough on my birthday?"

"Not quite, child. I ain't sure even Lisette is old enough for it, look at her blush!"

And Bébert was right: Lisette turned the color of beets.

"You bullies," Nanette remonstrated at Uncle and Bébert. "Always picking on the girl. She'll show you one of these days, won't you Lisette?"

But Lisette demurred silently as she sat sipping her brandied cherries and holding on too tightly to my waist.

"By the way, Lisette, I was thinking of asking Raymond Langiers to Guigui's First Communion," Nanette said changing the conversation. "Might do him good to meet the family."

"I don't know Nanette. It may be a little forward. After all, I only see him at the Town Hall on official business. Besides, he might have other plans."

"Tssk, Tssk. He's just bashful like you. A man his age, not married: it ain't normal. We need to give him a little push, don't we, my Aunt, otherwise you'll both be dancing that silly minuet until you are too old to care. It's time to catch him before one of those trollops on the Place du Luxembourg gets her claws into him!"

"Whatever do you mean?" Lisette queried her heart skipping a beat against my scapula.

"A man is a man, girl, and I seen them; all sweet and honey-like. A wonder one hasn't caught him yet."

"I've seen them too!" I seconded. "But that's alright, Lisette, he never pays them any mind because they are just plain and ugly and silly. You are nice and very intelligent, even Mademoiselle Rouleau says so and she's my teacher!"

Lisette smiled, her dimples carving a happy hollow in the small of her upper chin.

"It's all set then. I'll ask Langiers myself, that way you won't need to feel embarrassed," Nanette declared with finality.

"Just don't tell him I'll be there too," Lisette urged her.

"Of course, I will. Anyway, he'll guess. And I'll tell him about Léo, I mean the pork roast, and the wine and the chickens. You got to get them by their stomachs, you do, and mark my word Lisette, after he has eaten my food and drunk my wine, he won't be 'Monsieur' Langiers anymore. Besides, I'm going to ask Father Rocas for dessert, make the feast sort of official like. And no use fretting about it, Bébert 'cause my mind is made up. And you'll go to the mass as well!"

Husband and wife glared at each other. Uncle chuckled behind his mustache while Guigui's eyes stayed glued to his father.

"The hell I won't Antoinette!" Bébert bellowed.

"Oh yes, you will Gilbert Marchand. I don't care about your soul but I do care about Guy and I won't let you shame him before the whole of Dormans and stay away from his first communion while all the other families go to church like God-fearing Christians and son-loving parents. Our only son! If you can't do that for him then you ain't much of a father, isn't that so Uncle?"

Nanette had made a masterly come back and her strategy which was becoming sorely apparent to Bébert left him disarmed. He now stood accused before the entire family of the most egregious crime: that of failing one of its members and bringing upon our collective heads the ominous threat of local gossip.

"I'll think about it," he muttered, pouring himself another round of brandied cherries.

"No you won't! I'll put the question to a vote right now and I am willing to abide by whatever the family decides and - - "

"Hush Nanette," Uncle Marcel cut her, "Gilbert is a reasonable man. Besides, he doesn't need to stay through the whole mass so long as he's seen entering and leaving the church no one will be the wiser if he sneaks out during the office. How about it, cousin?"

"I'll think about it," Bébert repeated. But I was pretty confident Uncle Marcel had made him see the wisdom of his compromise.

"Can't be much worse than going to the Château," Uncle digressed skillfully. "I'll tell you, these days it ain't fun working there, not that it ever was. They sure ain't as cocky as they used to be those bastards. What with Italy falling, and the walloping they just took in North Africa, not to mention the pounding the allied air force is giving them up north. They are getting so jittery that it ain't healthy and it'll be dark before dawn yet!"

"Been up there lately?" Nanette asked, ignoring Bébert who was sulking on his brandied cherries defeated but not forgiving.

"They dragged him up there last week to paint the Herr Kommandant's office," Aunt Louise cut him with a tinge of reproach as if Uncle was guilty of obeying a German diktat.

"Couldn't refuse, could I Louise? Not when they send me a whole battalion to drag you there by the tail! Don't know what happened to his office but it sure looked a mess. An explosion of some kind, the stove they told me. Warming himself on the backs of French men that swine, and in April too no less when we ain't got enough wood or coal to warm our lousy supper. But you mark my word: it won't be long now before the yanks and De Gaulle's lads have them on the run. Bastards, you just wait and see!"

Nanette sprung up from her seat.

"Not in front of the children, Uncle Marcel!"

She slammed shut the dining-room door on the kitchen, our hallway and beyond them, away from the Oberleutnant Redlich's ears next door.

"Yes, before the children, Antoinette!" Uncle Marcel insisted. "They are French like us. There ain't no shame in being patriotic and you can't keep them out of it, not when the rest of France is at war and a lot of our young men are paying with their lives for their future!"

"But they might be questioned, Uncle Marcel, and it's better for them if they can't tell them anything."

"No woman. There ain't no age to learn right from wrong: the earlier the better." Uncle huffed behind his mustache.

I sat on Lisette's knees in total awe of Uncle Marcel's righteous anger which suddenly gave me the impression of having come of age although I wasn't quite sure for what.

"We got them on the run though. One of their big supply trains was blown up at Amiens last week, and the maquis back in Troyes is creating all sorts of problems for them. Beethoven hints at a landing for next month. I got it from someone who's plugged into London if you know what I mean. And their own are deserting, lost a few last month, they did. Don't understand much German, but enough to know they were worried about defections in their ranks. The Château was all rumors about it last week!"

My mind wandered back to The Gaux, the small German convoy that Saturday and the drunk Boche that night. Bébert and Nanette, I noticed, stiffened in their chairs but kept mum.

"Come this summer we'll be rid of them!" Uncle Marcel went on totally unleashed now. "and then France will be France again. De Gaulle is not Jaurès but he's better than those bastards in Vichy! Hang them we will once this is over: they sold out France. Yes sir, we'll hang them so high when this nightmare is over that the entire country can see their yellow hides!"

"Hush, Marcel! We got a Boche next door!" Nanette pleaded.

"The hell we do, we got them all over Dormans, all over our bloody country. But not for long, not for long now!"

The storm abated and a big silence hovered over the room in which we sat huddled. I felt strangely elated. This patriotic monologue had upon me the same impact as my daily ministering of the condemned Léo. It sent me into a height of complacent exultation from which Uncle and I looked down upon the rest of the family as God upon his mortals. I left Lisette's lap to lay upon Uncle Marcel's shivering mustache a resounding kiss.

"There, enough, child: There's too much kissing in this family as it is," Aunt Louise admonished me freezing my impulse. "Your Uncle did his duty in the first war but he's got only words for ammunition now and those ain't much help," she closed with a knowing glance at the two of us.

"Shut up, Louise!" Uncle Marcel snapped. "The child has more spunk than you."

"Perhaps, but one day, Marcel Germain, that tongue of yours will hang you if you don't keep a rein on it."

"They are family, woman! Not strangers!" Uncle boomed his cheeks turning beet red. The sudden blow of his balled fist hitting the table toppled the cup in front of him and a small spoon landed in Bébert's tail first.

There followed a few moments of combative silence broken only by the rattling of Mémé's dentures as her lips spasmodically gaped and closed like that of a carp skimming the water surface. Everyone had become rapt in the contemplation of the raw white tablecloth. At the far end of the table Lisette attempted a smile, looked pleadingly at Nanette who wasn't looking at her but at her husband who wasn't looking at his wife because he was still sore. I thought the day was irremediably doomed when following the call of some higher order Guigui suddenly piped up something about an extraneous and totally irrelevant pair of long pants. Composures shifted toward him.

"What was that, son? Did you say something about pants?" Nanette queried him somewhat at a loss.

"Jean-Claude Pottin is letting me borrow his costume, the one he wore last year at his first communion and for his grandpa's funeral in January."

"Is he, now?" Nanette was landing to this new reality, fast. "And what's wrong with the ones I cut you from your father's old Sunday suit?"

"It's got short legs…"

"So?"

"I want long trousers, Ma" Guigui whispered under the now fierce glare of his mother. "It's more . . . It's less . . . After all, I'll be thirteen come next October!" he finished in a last attempt at bravura.

"You know how long Mémé has been toiling on those pants, haven't you seen her basting and sewing until her eyes can barely see any more..."

"I enjoyed doing this for Guigui, daughter," Mémé demurred. "Let him wear Pottin's pants if he wants. He's of age."

"Oh no he won't! What do you think they'll think the Pottins, us borrowing their son's clothes as if we couldn't take care of our own? Couldn't look them straight in the eyes if I were to let him do that. I won't have it, Guigui, and that's final!"

Guigui's cheeks right up to his funny ears turned the scarlet of a scalded lobster. I feared his guardian angel had taken a powder but as I was about to espouse Bébert's atheistic precepts a miracle occurred, although as it unfolded I soon suspected that it might be more in the nature of husbandly retaliation.

"Well, I am your father, son and I say you can wear Pottin's pants! Don't know what possessed your mother to cut you short ones in the first place. I ain't about to stand for a Mama's boy in my family!" Bébert proclaimed manfully. "So much for that!" he concluded with a defiant look at his wife.

"Well spoken," Uncle approved going one better than Bébert. "We men got to stick together else the womenfolk will have us hanging by our suspenders."

"Tssk!" Aunt Louise hissed while Mémé chuckled.

"Quiet, woman!" Uncle Marcel ordered his wife. "Bébert will go to mass and Guigui will wear Pottin's pants. And don't give us no sass, Antoinette, you got to know a good deal when you see it."

And so Nanette broke into a concession smirk and I laughed. Soon we were all laughing around the table, except for Aunt Louise who grumbled beside her daughter. The sun spread its fingers of light on the table and the storm within and without the dining-room drifted northward toward Reims.

* * * * * * *

CHAPTER IV

In the two weeks between May first - - Labor Day - - and Guigui's First Communion which was scheduled for the fifteenth of May, a plethora of events were to claim my attention. The rhythm of my life which until then had been a comfortable andante suddenly gained a momentum which, as the days started tumbling into my past ever faster, seemed to be building toward an allegro robusto of breath-taking and mind-boggling proportion. Although I was powerless to resist the tide during the day, I spent a good deal of my nights lying on my army cot in Mémé's bedroom trying to decipher the meaning of those events I thought more deserving of my attention. The result was often frustration. My heart was an emotional punching bag and up in my head a slew of questions were assaulting reason to no avail. The nails of my thumbs had been reduced to painful scars and I was working my cogitative way through the unfortunate nails of my fore fingers. What made this tidal wave of life about me more chaotic was the fact that it was affecting all three areas of my childish, and thus well organized, reality. The country, Dormans, and the family from which I derived my identity, started rippling in an undertow of instability.

To begin with the country seemed to be slowly awakening from its long German-induced hibernation. Despite the official and compulsory news blackout, splinters of information had started filtering into Dormans from what were even then termed "reliable sources" that events were taking place all over Europe which, although I could not interpret their meaning, were important if one went by the adults. The north was coming under repeated Allied air raids which the German propaganda machine no longer in a position to deny them had begun denouncing through ever thriller posters which bloomed overnight on the doors and walls of public buildings like ominous portents. Outside our kitchen window panzer divisions thundered their way up and down the Avenue de la Marne rushing northward and southward in an intimation of frenzied preparations which did little to alleviate my confusion. We learned through Father Rocas that the resistance had blown up two bridges spanning the Marne below Chavenay and that five hostages had been taken by the Germans in the hope that the real culprits might come forward.

In Dormans, the latent excitement which had swept the town and bred rumors of impending Allied landings back in April had turned to an uneasy silence. It was as if what had been a sustaining hope all those years had morphed into a somber realization of the price which might have to be paid before its actual fulfillment. Liberation had been a utopian dream at the back of everyone's mind while simultaneously the collective surrender to the German occupation had been so absolute that little had been real except a coerced no-man's-land in which everyone existed in an everlasting state of impermanence.

In Dormans people began to prepare in earnest for the hard times ahead. Mayor Chancel kept issuing orders behind the occupiers' backs, orders which reached our home mostly through Lisette who because of her job at the Town Hall was in the best position to convey them selectively to trustworthy town folks. Cellars designated as bomb-shelters were to be stocked with sand bags, food, water and blankets; citizens were to stand ready to seek shelter at a moment's notice; the Volunteer Firemen's Association in which Uncle Marcel and Bébert were active members was to practice weekly; at school Mademoiselle Rouleau was instructed to teach us to duck under our ink-stained desks whenever it took her fancy, which delightfully at first but tediously at last, turned out to be once a day. Soldat Mueller seldom smiled at me anymore and I had stopped visiting Lisette at her office because the Town Hall had become a major transit hub for German officers on the move who knew neither Lisette nor myself and thus might not have looked kindly on her nepotism.

At home notwithstanding the lenient influence of our resident catechumen the family suffered from and outbreak of acrimony whose symptoms first manifested themselves in Nanette who proceeded to spread the disease to the rest of us. While her son might be making a laudable attempt at saintliness, Nanette was turning into a shrew and we were made to bear the brunt of his distemper. Conversations at the dinner table were reduced to heated exchanges between husband and wife or, when Bébert refused to cooperate, to caustic monologues Nanette addressed to an invisible interlocutor who, judging from her prolixity, didn't see eye-to-eye with her either. She was at war with the Germans for being more disruptive of her life's daily grind, she blasted the allies for making their long-anticipated move at precisely the time her son was scheduled to make his First Communion, she resented Mémé for siding with her son, and as for myself, my greatest sin was to be forever "in her feet".

Even the beheading of my poor Léo - - an event upon which I had come to look forward in the hope it might dilute some of her ill-will - - turned out to be more of a bane than a boon. Indeed, the pig once metamorphosed into pork through the mere act of his sacrifice proved to be more of a challenge in death than he had been during his short life with us. As Bébert had put it there was a lot more to a dead pig than there was to a live one. Uncle Marcel suggested that, for a price, Monsieur Léon the butcher might be willing to lend a hand, but Nanette would have none of it. Instead, she and Aunt Louise took to closeting themselves in the shed behind Bébert's workshop with a panoply of saws, cleavers, cutters, saltpeter and salt, tubs of water and the dead pig as well as that volume of our encyclopedia which depicted the graph of a side of beef for surgical guidance. Each night at the dinner table she made no bones about telling us how they went about sawing Léo's. She smelled of rancid suet and dried sweat and for once I did not mind the boiled and soggy rutabagas prostrated in the hollow of my soup plate and entertained thoughts of becoming a vegetarian.

The only bright spot in this otherwise dreary fragment of my life occurred when Nanette allowed me to invite Mademoiselle Rouleau to Guigui's first communion. I had wanted to ask her ever since he had started on his retreat but Nanette's crabby disposition had frozen in its bud my attempt at such an overture. For days the question never crossed my lips: it became like a sore on the tip of my tongue which I toyed and teased to frustration. But the night of Léo's death, perhaps sensing I had nothing to lose and aware that despite her distemper Nanette was not totally impervious to my grief, I put the question to her very fast, almost in a whisper. Much to my relief she acquiesced immediately, even remarking that it was kind of me to have thought of it. Thus, the very next day, I formally invited Mademoiselle Rouleau to our forthcoming festivities and the smile she gave me when she accepted convinced me that contrary to my assumptions and despite Léo's demise, there were still many lost souls in this world one could care for from which to derive complacent rewards.

To the people of Dormans Mademoiselle Rouleau was a living, walking and breathing tragedy in their midst. Some twenty years earlier her parents, who according to the local gossip had been prosperous silk traders from Lille, had been the victims of a terrible car crash which had killed her father instantaneously but spared her pregnant mother long enough for the young woman to, prematurely and on a rain-swept roadside, deliver a seven-month old female fetus who miraculously was the sole survivor of the wreck. Thus Mademoiselle Rouleau had come about her life, orphaned before emerging from the mangled maternal womb, condemned to a wintry childhood of Dickensian gloom, in turn ward of the state or some religious institution, cared for by all but loved by none. I would often in those days as I tried to pen down her dictations or applied myself to learning those multiplication tables she gently attempted to etch upon our memories with her sing-song delivery, catch myself escaping her classroom, forgetting the chalk-stained blackboard which was her perennial backdrop. My unseeing eyes staring at a window-framed segment of the stark brownish trunk of the lone plane tree in the school's yard, I would reconstruct to its ultimate pathos Mademoiselle Rouleau's tragic beginning, retrace the painful roads of her life and almost tear up at the dizzying loneliness of her present. For she was lonely: it was in her eyes that one could detect it most. Periwinkle blue they were, forever staring at something beyond you. One might have thought her blind because of their apparent lack of focus, but after having heard her story, one knew that this seeming blindness was in fact resignation and that even though she could actually see, something in her refused to let her eyes behold more than the safe superficiality of her surroundings. It was my hope that I might one day see those periwinkle ponds of hers ripple under a sudden stir of recognition, that she might at last force herself to view her life at closer a range and perhaps discover in its immediacy that flicker of hope which otherwise would remain hopelessly buried in her miasmic perception of it unwanted infinity. Abstraction was her sanctuary. She had landed in Dormans in search of an elusive anonymity but tragedy is never anonymous and thus she lived among us pitied but no more loved than she had been before, a victim of her sad past as much as she was that of our commiseration. She had our sympathy but not our friendship and although people were considerate toward her no one in Dormans had ever thought of inviting her to a family celebration.

Besides Mademoiselle Rouleau, the guests included our neighbor, the sonorous but well-meaning Madame Tardieux, Jean-Claude Pottin so he might keep an eye on his borrowed suit, Raymond Langiers whose acceptance had sent Lisette in a fit of expectant rapture, and Father Rocas who had consented to join us for dessert after lunching with Monsignor Leduc who was coming down from his diocese in Reims for this Holy day. Apart from the "strangers" as Nanette insisted on calling our guests, the entire family was slated to participate in the festivities. Thus there were to be twelve of us for lunch that Sunday, a staggering total in those times of forced frugality but one whose individual members I trusted would show enough Epicureanism to pay Léo the compliment of a second helping.

I spent a restless night the night before Guigui's communion. In one hectic day of final preparations the family forsook its internecine combativeness, and even Nanette's ill humor disappeared swept by the tide of a resurgent esprit-de-corps whose practice was essential to the success of that day. We dressed the house with joy, brushed and ironed our holiday attires: Bébert got a haircut and Nanette a permanent wave while I got a new blue ribbon for my hair to match my new blue dress. According to Bébert, we spent the value of at least six coffins on the black market and I rushed and scurried about the Place du Luxembourg, Nanette's errand boy. And how lovingly we prepared the setting for the feast: the long table with the extension leaves spreading their wings dressed in the damask of celebration, the cheap china polished to a porcelain sheen, the disciplined rows of long stemmed glasses disguised as crystal guarding each place setting; the linen napkins so ingenuously folded standing erect before each plate like a flotilla of windblown mizzens ready to sail us through our gastronomic journey. I did not want to think about it being over yet, of having mere memories behind me instead of these sparkling patches of expectation. As always, the beautiful future of my tomorrow was, even then, a thousand times better than however memorable my past.

A shuffling of feet on the landing - - Nanette going to the bathroom - - and through the clover-leaf design of the shutters, a gray dawn, overcast and rainy, splattering and dribbling, wet against the bedroom window panes. I had slept after all, but now I was awake and just as expectant, perhaps more, than I had been the night before. Mémé still breathed her metronomic wheeze at the far end of the bedroom and above us the attic was alive and creaking: Guigui was up. This, at long last, was the dawn of our Sunday and within a few hours, our guests would be pouring into the hallway downstairs to partake of that chicory and brioche Nanette had promised them before the high mass. Later the organs would play in the Gothic church of the Place du Luxembourg, the school choir would sing and the church bells would break into their Christian song and we would parade down the Avenue de la Marne, Guigui in his long trousers and me in my blue dress. The house would be alive, Lisette in love, Mademoiselle Rouleau no longer lonely. Madame Tardieux would drown our voices and we would all savor Léo whose aroma had wafted about the house for two days.

"Mémé! Mémé!" I gushed running barefoot to her bedside, shaking her bony arm in the darkness. "What is it?" she startled. "What is it child?" opening her eyes and her toothless mouth.

"It's Sunday!" I exclaimed abandoning her bedside to romp about the room. "It's Guigui's first communion!"

"It's still night, child, hush now."

"No it isn't! Nanette is up. I heard her on the landing, and so is Guigui. It's pouring outside but I don't care, do you? You must get up, Mémé . Bet Nanette is already in the kitchen by now. Let me see your clock: five past six it is, five past six!" I sang resuming my celebratory dance around her bed. "Get up, Mémé ! I'm going downstairs. Bet Bébert is already up too, you'll be last if you don't hurry!"

I slammed the shutters back, opened the window wide open and let the dreariness of the damp spring seep in: my happiness was as determined as the tearful weather. I ran down the stairs two steps at a time, singing on top of my lungs. Behind his closed bedroom door Bébert grumbled.

It was like November all over again in the kitchen: the chill outside fogging the window panes, the lone electric bulb making the day more bleary than it was, and Nanette by the stove shivering inside the old green sweater thrown over he faded pink nightdress. But the pot of chicory was already brewing and the dining-room table perceived through the open door was still dressed for a gala.

"You're up with the chickens today, child," she remarked as I stood on tiptoes my forehead offered to her morning kiss. "You didn't wake up Mémé I hope?"

"Yes I did: You know how long she takes for her Sunday toilette. Got to be pretty like the rest of us, she has. Bet she beats Bébert to the bathroom."

"Hush, hush, child. She can't. I've got to go in there first 'cause I got a million chores to tend to yet. Go tell her I'll be up in a minute." She started cutting slices of stale bread. "Better yet. I'll go up myself and wash up first. Else I'll still be waiting for my turn come Christmas. Now you be a good girl and layout breakfast for me, child."

She was gone. Within seconds I heard her arguing with Mémé, Bébert, calling Guigui, slamming doors. I like Nanette.

I practiced my whistling while spreading home-made cherry jam on the bread, poured the chicory in our breakfast bowls. Guigui had told me you were supposed to breathe out, not in, when you were whistling but all I got doing it his way was the muffled whiz of a deflating tire. My mouth wasn't built like his, I thought, touching my pursed lips with my fingers. "Think of a chicken's rear end, Tina. You seen them often enough. Tight as a chicken's rear end: that's the way to get a good whistle!" Well, my mouth wasn't a chicken's rear end: I didn't have enough cheeks to spare, and my face muscles were too short.

"What are you doing, stupid?"

"Trying to whistle. And that's not a Christian thing to call me on the morning of your communion."

"You're right, Tina" Guigui apologized brought back to holy order as it were. "You did look funny though!"

"That's what you always say."

"That's because all girls look that way."

"Well, you boys don't look much better. Long trousers: you're going to look like an undertaker, you are!"

"I'll look fine and don't you dare giggle when you see me in church. I'll box your ears if you do!"

"I won't," I promised.

"Oh, alright. . . " he walked to the window, lifted a corner of the crochet curtain: it had stopped raining. "Gosh, I hope we get a bit of sun. Please God make it be sunny today pleaaaase!"

"It will be," I promised. How little we had thought about Guigui during these last few weeks, all of us; how little room we had left for the solemnity of his day. "It will be sunny yet, Guigui. You just wait and see. And we will take pictures: Raymond Langiers has a camera and he promised to bring it, he did." But he was just staring at me Guigui: I wasn't sure he was listening to me really. "You'd better have some breakfast, have a couple of slices with jam ready for you…"

"Can't: it's a mortal sin to eat before communion."

As I stood in my nightgown, the plate still offered to him, he did a funny thing, Guigui: he kissed me on the cheek very fast.

"Got to beat Mémé to the bathroom!" he said hurriedly. "Father Rocas wants us all there by nine for rehearsal!"

Then he was gone and I stood alone in the kitchen under the dreary light bulb munching on his forbidden breakfast. Happy, so very happy! It was going to be the shiniest, sunniest, gloriousest day of our lives.

Madame Tardieux was the first to arrive but then she did not have to come from very far as Nanette remarked. Her hat defying the weather was a garden in full bloom: poppies and marigolds, forget-me-nots and daisies grew on it impervious to their rightful season. Then came the Germains: Aunt Louise, despite the festive occasion, still dressed in sadness and resignation, Uncle Marcel as jolly as ever despite his dark blue Sunday suit, and Lisette, unfortunately lip-sticked and mascaraed but wearing a burgundy velvet dress under her old raincoat which, I thought approvingly, made her look shapelier than usual. Mademoiselle Rouleau and Jean-Claude Pottin arrived together since they had met a block up by the Co-op. She wore a black jersey dress with a demure white satin collar. On her left shoulder was pinned a gold butterfly with blue enamel wings that matched the periwinkle of her pupils. In spite of the dark dress, the raining gray outside against which her silhouette was etched, there was a strange glow about her, a certain ethereal quality that kept the smile on my lips as I returned her greeting. Behind her Jean-Claude Pottin scrubbed to a shine, beamed.

After the round of introductions, the conversation started again in the dining-room, general at first: Mademoiselle Rouleau inquiring about Guigui's whereabouts and Nanette responding that "unfortunately" he was already at church, "rehearsals, you know." Then Madame Tardieux interjected an irrelevant comment about the awesome decorum of her late husband's funeral. Bébert shrugged derisively in response and promptly drew Uncle Marcel in a tête-à-tête about the latest war rumors; Madame Tardieux again launching into an endless recital of what they had served at HER first communion: fish and fowl and lamb; "would you believe eight courses and so much wine! We finished lunch just in time for vespers and I slept through the whole service!" Nanette laughing, Aunt Louise smirking and Mémé always hiding her dentures behind her bony palm. I sat on Lisette's lap, sipped chicory from her cup while observing Mademoiselle Rouleau who, next to us, was inquiring about Raymond Langiers and, catching sight of Lisette's confusion, hastily opining that she must be overwhelmed with work at the Town Hall "the situation being what it is." I soon fell into my favorite pastime of reconstructing the precise moment of her appearance into this world. I could visualize it all except for some gynecological details still out of my reach: the rain, nothing like this morning, more like a monsoon, slashing and whipping the wrecked car. Her father soaked in blood, his eyes opened wide on death. And her poor young mother so beautiful if one were to judge by her daughter, moaning and writhing in pain and her broken arms akimbo like those of the old porcelain doll I had recently exiled to the attic.

"Tina! Teeena!"

Startled out of my self-induced pathos, I turned to Nanette.

"The door, child! Raymond Langiers probably. Just in time too: we should be leaving for the church soon."

The doorbell had just rung a second time when I opened the front door.

He seemed as startled as I was, Oberleutnant Redlich, though probably for a different reason: anticipating an adult his eyes had been aiming far above my head, and for a second neither one of us could think of something to say. At last he found my face aligned with the breast-pocket of his officer's uniform and my eyes which were lost in the middle of a dilemma: what was I to say?

"Ach, Fraulein Tina," he saluted me breaking our impasse. "Good morning."

His sea-green eyes settled on mine and although I could detect in them a polite expectation my voice remained lost somewhere inside my parched throat. But I did manage a half-smile: after all, he was very handsome, even Nanette herself conceded that much albeit reluctantly.

"A very pretty dress you are wearing, Fraulein Tina; but then it is a very special day for your family, nein? Frau Tardieux has told me all about it."

"Yes," I stammered.

"May I come in?"

As he preceded me inside the kitchen, I saw the two bottles of champagne he held in his left hand. In a flash, I suddenly dreaded what might, what could, what I hoped would not, happen when he entered the dining-room. However, this was counting without Madame Tardieux who, probably for having seen her tenant many morning in his dressing-gown, stood much less in fear of him than we did.

"Oberleutnant Redlich! What a surprise," she boomed, her voice hammering at the silence with the subtlety of a sledgehammer. "how kind of you to drop in.. and with presents too!"

She darted a glance at Nanette and Bébert attempting to draw them into a modicum of civility. And failed.

"Come in, come in, Oberleutnant," she persisted undaunted by the general discomfort. "You know the Germains, of course, and the Marchands…"

He inched inside the crowded dining-room, enough for me to sneak around him and plant myself by Lisette's chair.

"…and Mademoiselle Rouleau" she is Tina's and Guigui's teacher at school…"

Just as my attention was thus drawn to her, I saw it. It was almost imperceptible unless one knew her well, but it shone in her periwinkle eyes, in her fingers clutching the soft fabric of her dress: a jolt of recognition, a spasm of joy dilating her pupils and holding her breath captive. But as I tried to interpret the turmoil I had just perceived, her eyes receded behind their protective mist of applied indifference and her hand released the soft folds of her dress.

Nanette's voice brought me back to reality. She was saying we should be going, thanking Oberleutnant Redlich with puckered lips while nonetheless easing from his grasp the bottles of champagne. They all rose from their chairs and for a second Mademoiselle Rouleau was shoulder-to-shoulder with Oberleutnant Redlich, her chestnut hair brushing his epaulet because the kitchen was too small.

"Well, thank you again, Oberleutnant. Sorry we don't have time to offer you anything, but the priest is like your officers, he doesn't like to be kept waiting."

"I know, Frau Marchand. They are the same in my country."

"Are they now? Didn't think you had any churches in Germany - - "

Bébert elbowed his wife while the doorbell rang and Raymond Langiers stood in front of us as dark as the German was fair. Much to my frustration things were happening so fast that I had no time to delve further into Mademoiselle Rouleau's strange behavior. Dejected, I concentrated on Lisette whose face as she stood stargazing at Langiers hid not the slightest secret.

Behatted, begloved and bejeweled, half of Dormans crowded the Place du Luxembourg when we finally reached its square. There were many familiar faces come down from Chérisy and Chavenay and beyond from Epernay and even Reims, and from the Château a heavy detachment of German troops posted one each at a distance of perhaps ten feet from each other guarding the square and attempting to curb our joy with their forbidding presence. They searched our faces and randomly checked papers with the ever-present suspicion which was theirs and always made me want to be even smaller than I was. And at the dead center of the square, parked on the cobble-stones, a mastodon of a panzer, its iron trump pointed at the church stood ready to mow us down should we act less than submissive. Oddly no one seemed to pay them any mind, not Mayor Chancel and Father Rocas as they stood caucusing on the church's parvis, not the diminutive brides dressed in white tulle and muslin their veils wafting in the breeze like a flurry of dove wings, and not the boys in their long-trousers, white armbands and solemn faces.

They were in the church with us also, the Germans, but I too slowly forgot about them as we knelt in our pews. I gazed at the sun now shining blue and red and gold through the rose-window above the altar, and at the stained-glass Jesus haloed in glory looking straight at me it seemed and an insidious tide of ecstasy started to sweep over me as I tried to hold back tears. But when the church's choir broke into the Te Adoremus echoing from ogive to ogive and the communicants walked down the aisle steepled hands pressed against their breasts and I spied Guigui's profile so very close that I could almost touch him, I could no longer fight against the maelstrom of religious fervor overtaking me and burst into a fit of alarming sobs interspersed with irrepressible hiccups. My eyes squeezed to a pulp by my emotional disarray let loose a furious gush of tears. Soon my hysteria was drowning the Te Adoremus and the people of Dormans. Chérisy and Chavenay and yonder those of Epernay and even Rheims, began shifting noisily in their pews and whispering and looking for the perpetrator of this commotion which had even Father Rocas and Monsignor Leduc, though flustered, valiantly trying to ignore my outburst. Flushed with shame Nanette proceeded to slap my back while Lisette preposterously stroked my hair on my right. In the pew behind us, Uncle Marcel and Bébert started voicing their disapproval.

The sudden appearance of the black boots aborted my next sob: they were lustrous. Looking up a bit, I caught the perfectly pressed dark gray pants and up again, the Mauser gun cradled in its black leather holster. They led me out of the church like a reprobate, still sobbing and hiccupping, the German soldier leading the way, Mademoiselle Rouleau holding on to my left hand while Lisette crushed my right one, and all I could think of as I was being marched out was that Guigui would box my ears, and that, for sure, he would never understand the fervent holy transport which had been the cause of my seizure and how much he had contributed to my disgrace.

I never stood witness to Guigui swallowing Christ's body or sipping His blood. But I had other compensations as we walked back to the house. The Panzer and the soldiers were gone except for the two who stood guard by Monsieur Lucien's bookstore. The cobble-stones shone like black onyx after the morning's heavy rain, and the small houses across the square from the church were crowned by an iridescent rainbow. I can still hear the echoes of the hymns and organ streaming from the church, Lisette's and Mademoiselle Rouleau's high heels clickety-clicking against the pavement of the deserted Avenue de la Marne, still feel the breeze from the river as it funneled its way through the diagram of the narrow streets and last, the melting love of Mémé when we reached home upset lest someone had been taken ill and then kissing my forehead and offering me a tasty piece of the pork roast. I can also still smell the blended scents of jasmine because of Mademoiselle Rouleau and that of rose water because of Lisette. They laughed as they related to Mémé what had transpired at the church and even Mademoiselle Rouleau seemed to have teased mirth until it became almost genuine. Perhaps she was not as sad as I had first thought.

It was close to one when the churchgoers returned. Nothing was said about my earlier outburst although Nanette swore never to take me to church again, to which Bébert grumbled that he wished he should be so lucky because two hours of Latin mumbo jumbo and genuflecting was more than one should be made to endure to save one's soul if indeed such a thing existed. Madame Tardieux chided him quoting excerpts from Monsignor Leduc's inspirational sermon and giving a sniffle by sniffle account of the many who, although with more restraint than me, had also been moved by the "exquisite beauty of the service." And thus my outburst was mercifully forgotten.

Uncle Marcel opened the celebrations by popping open one of Oberleutnant Redlich's bottles of champagne. Guigui made them much more interesting by unwrapping the gifts bought for him by our guests: from Madame Tardieux her husband's pocket watch; from Lisette Monsieur Dumas' "Twenty Years After," from Mademoiselle Rouleau a black fountain-pen. Uncle gave him a season ticket on his fishing boat and Aunt Louise a sad gosling green wool sweater and, "from the four of us" Nanette announced radiantly as she gave him the box, a brand new pair of long trousers bought on the sly the day before from the men's store on the Avenue de la Marne. But by far the most intriguing gift Guigui received that day was a square black box of a camera presented to him by an apologetic Raymond Langiers.

"Though of German manufacture, it's one of the best on the market," he explained earnestly. "Let's face it: technologically they are way ahead of us and there's a lot France could learn from them once this war is over."

His words were followed by a dubious silence while he twirled his glass and contemplated its bubbly content.

Lisette hurried to his rescue.

"It's a beautiful camera wherever it came from." she turned to Uncle Marcel: " Father, I think you should concede to Mr. Langiers. You yourself told me not too long ago that their panzers were better than - -"

"Hush, daughter. Sure they got better equipment than we do, but who's building it for them? For all I know, might be some of our compatriots in one of their labor camps that built the factory where this thing came from!"

"You might be right at that," Langiers backtracked.

"How did you come by it?" Bébert queried at the far end of the room with a suspicious undertone which sent me on the alert. "Must have cost plenty if you found it on the black market, it must!"

"Not really," Langiers countered. "I paid a fair price for it but it's the least I could do for Mademoiselle Lisette's nephew."

"And it's a very generous gift," Madame Tardieux said with flourish, forcing the matter to a close. "Even I might take gold from the devil himself if he offered it, no offense meant Monsieur Langiers."

With that she winked reassuringly at Guigui who, I could tell, for an anxious moment had feared the camera might promptly return whence it had come from. But it was really mademoiselle Rouleau who extracted us from the impasse by offering a toast to the first communicant in which we all joined with relief. But then the roar of two motorcycle-mounted German dispatchers racing past our vibrating window over the clangor of clinked glasses drew our attention. Behind me above the sideboard the cuckoo sprung out of its wooden chalet to chirp the half-hour and from the kitchen, I heard the hiss of sizzling pork fat. It was as I reached furtively for Nanette's brimming glass of champagne that I caught sight of his hand. It was a lady's hand: long slender fingers, trimmed cuticles and nails polished to a nacreous sheen. On his little right finger was looped a signet ring of blue onyx whose gold-casing covered the whole of his third phalanx. The thought struck me that he had never worn a ring before, Raymond Langiers, not ever. Besides this one was too large for him as it kept sliding toward the sidewall of his hand while his fourth finger kept rubbing the gold band back into place. He turned abruptly to me as I reached blindly for the ring. His eyes like glazed chestnuts conveyed a warning as they bored their chill into mine.

"Beautiful, isn't it?" he whispered. "My father's. He was a big man, my father, that's why it doesn't fit. Would you like a closer look at it?" he queried slipping the ring off his finger and offering it to me on the soft, almost lineless plane of his very white palm.

I drew back: suddenly I did not want to be anywhere within reach of him. He chuckled softly as I fled to the kitchen, to Nanette and Mémé , putting as safe a distance as I could between us.

"Bet you just saw a spider back there. Shame on you, you are a hundred times bigger than it is!" She smiled waving her index finger in my face. "Be a good girl and take the pate and tomatoes to the dining-room" While I complied, she bellowed behind me: "Lunch is served. Everybody take your seats!"

There followed a mixed tremor of displaced chairs, a shuffling of feet and the dull pop of bottles of wine being uncorked. I sat between Mademoiselle Rouleau and Jean-Claude Pottin, out of the range of Langiers who sat two seats away hidden by Aunt Louise. My unease slowly ebbed and I even managed to smile at Madame Tardieux who, across the table from me, was wishing all a most hearty "Bon

Appétit!" Bébert poured the wine, Mémé forgot to say grace, Uncle talked about the upcoming fishing season while Mademoiselle Rouleau and Lisette chatted about hairdos and Jean-Claude Pottin and Guigui tied their napkins around their necks. I sat back waiting for Nanette to serve me just as the siren of the sawmill broke into a piercing shrill over our heads and the sky echoed with a sudden and ominous whirr. For a few seconds none of us reacted: we just sat there, forks in mid-air, harkening to the continuous wail, harkening to the sounds, frozen inside the innocuous reality of the prior moment and mesmerized by some incredulous fear.

"Air raid! It's an air raid! Everyone to Dr. Martin's shelter!"

Bébert shot up from his toppled chair, his eyes intense with urgency. A thunder of military vehicles rumbled past our windows while the sawmill siren still wailed in a crescendo of panic. I found myself being slapped by someone, hoisted out of my chair and dragged out by Lisette and Mademoiselle Rouleau, while Bébert shouted at Guigui and Langiers to close all the shutters, and Uncle Marcel lumbered across the avenue to their house to do the same. Nanette shoved Mémé out of the front door. Jean-Claude Pottin vanished along with Langiers who disappeared like a ghost melting into thin air. Then everything became oddly silent as we made our way across the Avenue de la Marne, an instant of pregnant stillness before the coming conflagration. Left was the deep blue sky and the budding foliage of birdless plane trees, but also the frightened faces perceived through the corners of one's eyes, and the mad, frantic rush of legs skirted and trousered and laden wheelbarrows bumping on the cobble-stones, and above all, the total confusion engulfing us and Dormans in a sweeping maelstrom. At last coming from the hollows of the hills beyond the town's main bridge which spanned the Marne behind the Town Hall, came a low persistent whirr growing closer with each second.

"It's the Americans! It's the Americans!" Lisette shouted.

"They are the only ones you can't hear until they are almost upon you!"

And as she said this, gigantic black clouds spouted on the horizon, dotting the skyline above The Gaux. Behind us Madame Tardieux doubled back and shouted something indistinct as we trouped up the steps of Dr. Martin's front door and threaded the hallway where the glass-encased Latin diplomas caught a glimmer of light from the street. I smelled the pungent odor of ether when, the trapdoor once lifted, we descended the high stone steps plunging us into the earth's bowels. Oil-lamps and candles, mattresses and blankets, empty buckets stacked in the corner and mountains of sandbags, all laid out in the musty dark underground, a shivering cold and the sepulchral silence reigning at the heart of the large but precarious safety of Dr. Martin's cellar turned shelter.

The war, the ugly war I had so far ignored, was now upon Dormans. In our flight we had lost Bébert and Nanette, but Albert the fat cat was with us, mewing its discontent, clawing at my knees, scratching and screeching. I should have known Madame Tardieux would never leave him behind.

* * * * *

CHAPTER V

We spent two days and one night in the shelter. Dr. Martin's four daughters were there as was Madame Martin and most of our guests except for Raymond Langiers and Jean-Claude Pottin whom we had lost in the debacle. Within a frantic half hour of us Nanette, proud as a peacock, made a grand descent into the cellar. Her arms weighted down by two wicker baskets while Bébert behind her, stumbled under the onus of a bulging back-pack and mumbled something about his wife having lost leave of her senses. It transpired that torn between a potential loss of life and that of her lovingly prepared feast Nanette had forced her husband to risk the former for the sake of the latter and coaxed him into helping her pack up everything from hors-d'oeuvres to dessert. Thus Léo's sacrifice proved not to have been in vain and although those in a position to do so chided Nanette, by the time we began spooning the apple tarts, the gluttonous consensus was that life was well worth the risk taken.

Alas, the anguish which we had kept at heart's bay thanks to Nanette's determination not to fall prey to it crept its way back into the adults and insidiously, like the mist of dusk rising over the marshes of the Marne, soon drew a pall over us. Uncle gave up talking first. This tacit resignation which one might have anticipated from anyone but him, brought back the reality of what was happening to Dormans, of the war being fought above our heads while we sat holed up like rats waiting for the terror to have taken its toll. Uncle's silence summoned back the anguish, and one by one, the women began to conjecture as to how their houses, their possessions accumulated along a lifetime might survive a bombardment. All they had left behind in their haste now came back to mind and the more they spoke the longer grew the list of objects, photographs, without which they just could not bear to live. Madame Tardieux expressed particular concern over the fact that she had not taken along a single photograph of her late husband. She insisted that without one she might soon forget what he had looked like, that this would be a betrayal of his dear memory, and became so distraught that Madame Martin had to force down her abysmal throat a spoonful of brandy.

"Your house will be fine, my dear. It's the Germans they aim to crush, not you." She attempted to placate the widow.

"But I have a German in my house!"

"And how would they know that the Americans? Besides they are after military targets: bridges, railroad tracks, ammunition depots. Not civilians."

But Madame Tardieux was not about to be easily extracted from the emotional depth of her despondency. She brushed aside soothing words while clinging to Albert the cat who, though stifling against her ample bosom, nonetheless massaged its two orbs with feline sensuality. Nanette suggested she might have some group pictures taken before the war in which Monsieur Tardieux was sure to figure. This hint of hope seemed to comfort the bereft widow. Somehow it did not enter their mind that should her house be destroyed, so for sure would be ours. But everyone kept mum and soon Madame Tardieux fell back into a semblance of composure which Nanette immediately seized upon to appoint herself as our quartermaster: She would oversee the organization of our camp. Sandbags were stacked up high against the wall fronting the Avenue de la Marne. Mattresses and blankets were pushed against the longest parallel walls of the cellar and since we would have to double if not triple up, the segregation of the sexes was to be enforced: women would bunk on the left side while the men would berth on the right side. I was instructed to cut out of yellowed newspapers neat and large enough rectangles to be used for their obvious purpose in our makeshift privy which was set up in the darkest end of the cellar hidden behind a charcoal blanket nailed to the dank mortise holding the uneven stones. The final touch was the heavy wooden table commandeered from the Martins' kitchen which the huffing and puffing team of Uncle Marcel and Bébert had lowered into the cellar.

At eight o'clock that evening our morose idleness was relieved by Dr. Martin's appearance. He had been called earlier in the day before the alert to Monsieur Matthieu's farm on the road to The Gaux. The old man it turned out had been feeling poorly for days and would have died for certain had it not been for his son Philippe who had finally taken it upon himself that morning notwithstanding his father's rabid contempt for all members of the medical corps, to fetch Dr. Martin.

"Found him squirming in his bed. Acute attack of peritonitis. Had to operate right there and then!"

I thought "peritonitis" was a lovely word. It rang a bell and I surmised it probably had to do with my perusal of Lisette's death registries.

"That will teach him a lesson! Was held up by the bombing though. Three hours I sat listening to Madame Matthieu's drivel until I couldn't stand it anymore!"

Madame Martin was feeding her husband a cold slice of Léo while Nanette poured him wine and all of us listened intently to the news from the outside. I had never noticed how telegraphic Dr. Martin's oratory style was but never also had I been so grateful for it. The terse bits of news rolled form his thin lips upon our silence, round and tinkling like Guigui's prize agates on the tiled floor of our kitchen.

"Met the Mayor. Says Epernay has been hit pretty hard!"

"Hush, Jacques, eat!" Madame Martin cut off her husband. "Did you have anything to eat at the Matthieu's?"

"They offered but with old Matthieu's bloody innards for an appetizer, I lost my appetite."

He did not even smile when he said that. Neither could I detect a hint of humor on the penciled hiatus of his busy mouth nor a twinkle of mirth in the brown beads of his bespectacled eyes. I discarded the fleeting image of old Matthieu's tumescent belly and waited for the next marble of news to roll out of Dr. Martin's mouth.

"Now for the bad news," he said at last after having wiped the corners of his mouth with two precise fingers which he then proceeded to lick clean.

He looked at us as we huddled around the table our faces sparsely lit by the flickering light of the candles whose flames grew longer as they grew shorter. I heard a whirr above our heads, indistinct as yet, but already nipping at the fringe of the silence.

"The sawmill has been hit, and The Gaux."

"The Gaux," Nanette sputtered her hand flying to her heart.

"And part of the Château! Saw them with my own eyes. All Hell is breaking loose up there!"

"The Gaux," Nanette repeated horrified. "Do you hear that, Bébert? Our Gaux!"

He eyed her without a word.

"Thank the Lord there are no civilians up there," Dr. Martin continued, "Might have been a carnage if - -"

But I had stopped listening to Dr. Martin: something important was happening across the table. Behind Madame Martin and two of her daughters, and beyond Louise and Madame Tardieux, shadows among growing shadows, Bébert and Nanette stood whispering, hushing their voices but betrayed by the anxious flutter of her hands as they argued.

Easing my fingers out of Lisette's grip and praying Dr. Martin would continue to hold their attention I inched my way through the maze of legs of his captive audience. I rounded the table, stopping when a silence threatened, resuming my progress when he resumed his delivery. At last I found a spot behind Mademoiselle Rouleau between her black jersey dress and the patch of darkness where, within earshot of me, Bébert and Nanette were still thick in their heated conclave. My heart hammered against my eardrums as I strained to hear them.

"It's going to swarm with Boches….the well…"

"You got to…then I will, tomorrow…"

"You won't get past the sawmill."

"We must make sure, Bébert! You know if…Mémé and Guigui and the child: all of us…"

Blast Dr. Martin: his voice had risen suddenly and was drowning their whispers snatching whole pieces of vital information from my hearing.

"What are you doing down there, Tina!" Mademoiselle Rouleau broke inquisitively above me.

In my frustration I was clutching several folds of her black jersey dress in my fist.

"Nothing," I shot back letting go of the fabric.

Too late: Nanette spun around, squinted to find my face which, since my back was turned to the candlelight, was engulfed by my own shadow. The hint of uncertainty vanished from her face when Bébert, taking advantage of the distraction, rejoined the ranks of Dr. Martin's audience. I scooted away: I did not want to be anywhere near Nanette right then. Mercifully, the good doctor leapt to my rescue with a diversion of his own which he sprung on the lot of us quite without warning.

"Herr Kommandant Blücher wants all volunteer firemen to report immediately for duty," he announced looking directly at Bébert and Uncle Marcel. "It's an order, he said. I told him I'd get the word to the two of you. Got to go back myself, some of his men got hit: not enough though!"

I heard a fat tear of melting candle dripping onto the scarred wood surface of the table. But apart from that, the silence had become so absolute that one could have heart the heartbeat of a fly.

They had all thought of the occupation in terms of its disruptive impact upon their lives. They had hated the slow erosion of what until its advent had been legitimate and thus ignored freedoms. They had resented the rape by the Nazi war machine of the once luxuriant land, a rape which had turned the French into a nation of scroungers, hagglers and profiteers; they had put up with the raw winters and lean years, with the constrictions and deprivations and executions. They had even learned to live with their fear. But until now, it had been fear of fear itself and thus one that paradoxically need not be feared.

On this at long last perceived new reality hung our present silence edged in black like a death notice awaiting the name of the next casualty, and the words we were not speaking, dared not speak right then, could be read in their eyes. In Mémé's and Guigui's as they stared at Bébert with helplessness, in Nanette's through the anger I read in them, in Lisette's as she looked at her father across the table as if for the first time she realized how dear he was to her. And yes, even in Aunt Louise's because the hatred I saw in them also held the dread that the very destruction of the enemy might also mean that of her husband whom she had loved and still loved as best as she knew how.

"Well, Gilbert, Marcel…Hate to rush you but we should be going," Dr. Martin urged breaking our silence.

Large, soft tears started rolling down Mémé's wrinkled cheeks: they washed out of her pupils the translucent happiness I had always found in them.

"Don't worry, Mother," Bébert said embracing her. "Come tomorrow I'll be right there in our kitchen ladling soup and chiding you for saying grace. You just keep praying and everything will be alright!"

She was crying openly now yet attempting a brave smile. And then we were all saying goodbyes. Madame Martin and Nanette were packing food for the men in old newspapers. Madame Tardieux was admonishing them to be sure to eat else they would not last through the long night ahead of them while Mademoiselle Rouleau was uncorking a bottle of wine opining that it was cold outside and they would need something to warm their hearts and Lisette was tying a woolen scarf around her father's neck. Aunt Louise admonished him not to be brave. Guigui was holding on to his father's hand as if he would never let go while Nanette ordered her husband to be alive come tomorrow or else! We kissed them as if it were to be for the last time and even Madame Tardieux, Mademoiselle Rouleau and Madame Martin and her four daughters joined in the effusion. I did not think of counting them but they were many our collective kisses.

At the top of the stairs, Dr. Martin was lifting the trap door when, as it to confirm our fear, a tremendous explosion rocked the very foundations of the house and sent us tumbling pell-mell down the cellar's steps. I heard screams, theirs and mine. My forehead hit a corner of the oak table while the candles blew out under the sudden gust of air rushing through the now dark cellar. Then, as I laid dazed on the cold gritty floor, I felt a hand brushing my calves, winding its way up to my bare knees: Madame Martin. Was I alright, she asked: I whispered "yes." Her fingers groped their way up the table leg; I heard her strike a match and in a second the unsteady flame of a lone candle glowed over the scene. Leaning against the table I took a census. There was no sign of Bébert and Uncle Marcel or Dr. Martin and I guessed they must have taken advantage of the confusion to make their exit. A pain throbbed above my right eye but the bump was already there: round and sore under my fingers.

"Must have hit the Town Hall," Madame Martin ventured. "Is everyone alright?"

There were murmurs of reassurance and apart from the waning stupor one could still read in their eyes they seemed to have survived this first unexpected brush with the allied bombardment.

We did not sleep much that night as we huddled around the table because the air raids continued unabated for several hours, at times hitting so close that Mémé would cross herself and knit her eyes, at other times hitting so far that we might have thought the noise was merely the rumbling of distant thunder. No one spoke except Madame Martin who had been a registered nurse before wedding her doctor husband and felt it her duty to keep us collected.

Unfortunately for Madame Martin, I was more intrigued than fearful and as the night wore on, although she seemed bent upon convincing herself that I was on the verge of an attack of childish hysteria which despite my guilt over not accommodating her, never occurred. In my innocence I still thought that the war was a game and that it being the case, none of us would die. The things which frightened me then were more tangible: Soldat Mueller, Chalembert or Langiers because of the way they acted. I was scared of true embodiments of evil because I had already felt their impact on my impressionable being and thus their discomfort was by then imprinted on my memory. But the war was merely a word with unpleasant connotations like measles, the dentist or the attic. It brought images of fleeting inconveniences such as acute cold or boiled rutabagas, ugly visions of the Easter Boche and the German army that morning in the Place du Luxembourg: not enough to catapult me as Madame Martin would have liked into those fits of anxiety the adults seemed to suffer from around me. The war's toll upon me had been minimal: Exile from Paris brought by severe malnutrition and now the bump of my forehead. I still could glean rings of happiness from the carrousel of my childish life and lived as if the German occupation was and were to be a permanent state of affairs because I had known little else.

It was late the afternoon of the second day when we received the all-clear and left the cellar. The allied planes, those which had made it through the German flak, had rejoined the safety of the British shores but the wounds they had inflicted upon the town were bleeding smoke over the scarred landscape. Madame Martin had been right: across the square from us the Town Hall stood amputated of its right wing, the one which had housed the public library and the archives, and was now a heap of smoldering rubbles. On our left little remained of Mr. Pottin's co-op except the twisted iron frame of its front display window which soared erect like some discarded stage prop hiding from our view the mass of debris which the day before had been one of Dorman's friendliest store.

The Germans had cordoned off the perimeter of the Town Hall with five panzers and three jeeps and scurried about behind their makeshift barricade, barking orders at a dozen or so Frenchmen who were busy sifting through the rubbles trying to salvage from the destruction what little history had been spared by the allied bombing. Among them I soon spotted Raymond Langiers and Uncle Marcel. Below and closer to us, curious townsfolk haggard and incredulous, still in their Sunday clothes, stood gaping at the scene much as we were ourselves standing on Madame Martin's doorsteps trying to rein in our consternation.

"Lisette! Lisette!"

The call issuing from behind the German barricade brought us back to reality.

"Lisette! Over here Lisette!"

It was Mayor Chancel, disheveled and rumpled, waving frantically in our direction from the steps of the Town Hall. Soon he was making his way between the line of panzers, attempting to reach us against the shoving and jostling tide and verbal onslaught of the crowd of townsfolk anxious to get the latest news from their elected representative. I followed the women down Madame Martin's steps and within minutes we were engulfed by the crowd which kept swelling as the Mayor reached us. Questions shot from all sides and a wall of angry citizens was inexorably coalescing about me. A strand of my hair became entangled in someone's belt buckle but my small voice was drowned in the crescendo of vociferations.

"What the hell is the matter with you folks?!" Mayor Chancel bellowed at last almost apoplectic and his fist far too close to my nose. Veins swollen with frustration bulged along his neck and forehead. "What the hell is the matter with you?" he barked again as the tumult died slowly, although a few intemperate questions still echoed through the growing silence around us.

"What do you want to know? What-is-it-you-want-to-know-that-you-can't-see-for-yourselves?" he hammered as people began receding from our nucleus and my hair minus a few strands rejoined my scalp. "Look again! You want me to tell you what happened last night? You need me to tell you we got the hell bombed out of our pants! Haven't you got eyes? Why are you here gawking? Haven't you seen enough? Hasn't the whole bloody mess sank into your thick skulls yet!"

"But Mayor," someone interjected behind me. "We got a right to know"

"What right? This is war, Monsieur Lucien. Nobody's got rights any more or haven't you learned that yet? You don't even have the right to survive: Pottin and his son Jean Claude didn't! Buried under his shop they were, look at it, look at this stinking heap of rubbles. You ask all those who didn't make it last night if they had rights. You are alive, aren't you; your bookstore is still standing up there on the Place du Luxembourg, isn't it? Well, that's all the right you got and consider yourself lucky!"

A hushed silence fell on the crowd. The news of Pottin's and Jean Claude's deaths had stunned everyone and even the contentious Monsieur Lucien was left to ponder shamefully upon his good fortune. I thought of Jean-Claude Pottin, summoned forth his features the way he had looked on Sunday as Guigui unwrapped his presents. But try as I would, I could not superimpose upon his then happy face the tracing of what death might have done to it: he kept smiling at me Jean-Claude Pottin and would forever unless my intractable memory was given a chance to erase from his face that Sunday's joy.

"I have a job to do here, we all do!" Mayor Chancel resumed after a respectful while. "And here's how you can help me. I need all the volunteers I can get, and remember, it's not the Germans you'll be helping, it's our kinfolk and this town which belongs to us no matter what THEY might think," he continued pointing toward the panzers. "You'll be doing it for the good earth of Champagne which has served you well and for the Pottins who are no longer among us and for all the others like them who might have paid with their lives trying to protect it."

The men listened gravely while a few women - - among whom I counted myself - - wiped random tears from their cheeks. Forgotten were the earlier bickering and petty selfishness, the allied bombardment and the Germans standing not too far from us: the night had delivered Dormans its first known martyrs. Poor old Monsieur Pottin among them who had lived less than a heroic life worrying about powdered milk and cabbages, shoe laces and turnips, whose only war had been the one which had pitted him against the army of rodents which kept proliferating in his store, now loomed larger in death than anyone had assumed he did while alive.

"Let's get organized," Mayor Chancel voiced authoritatively. Turning back to practical realities. "First, you are to report all deaths - - may they be few - - to Lisette Marchand here at the Town Hall. Next. Maitre Pinson is handling logistics: he is at the Café de Paris on the Place du Luxembourg. Those of you wanting to volunteer are to report to him and he'll tell you where you can be of most use. Off with you now. Once this square is cleared and we get a better overview of the damages, I'll have more to say. Matter of fact, check the bulletin board on the front door of this Town Hall come tomorrow: it'll all be there, I promise. "

Slowly the crowd began to thin around us: most of the men took the Avenue de la Marne intending to report to Maitre Pinson while the women, after one last dismayed look at their amputated Town Hall, scattered and vanished in the maze of side streets converging on the square. Aunt Louise spotting her husband behind the German barricade left us hurriedly while Madame Martin her daughters in filial tow, returned to their house mentioning something to them about having to straighten their father's consultation room which had been left in total disarray by the allied bombs.

"Have you seen Gilbert, Mayor?" Nanette inquired anxiously as we stood alone with Mayor Chancel, Mémé, Lisette and Mademoiselle Rouleau. A pang of guilt flitted through me: in the confusion I had totally forgotten about Bébert.

"He's alright, Antoinette. He's been assigned to the Château. Saw him there not more than an hour ago."

Mémé's hand left Nanette's arm. She crossed herself and mumbled something I could not hear although I was confident God had.

"I'm going up there," Nanette declared. "He'll need some food and a change of clothes." But I could almost see the thoughts churning through her crafty head. "Might push on to The Gaux after that. I understand it was hit pretty hard. Been up there yet, Mayor?"

"No. Anyway, there's nothing up that way."

"There's our house, Mayor" Nanette objected.

"So what? If you want my advice, Antoinette, you'll just stay put and not go poking your nose where there are Germans swarming about. They are in no mood to tolerate infractions - - "

"What infraction?" Nanette cut him off. "It's our property. I got a right to check on our property - - "

"Here we go again with rights!" Mayor Chancel exclaimed exasperated. "Now, I'm telling you to go home, Antoinette, and stay there! I got enough on my hands without you getting yourself arrested!"

"I won't get arrested: I will go through the fields that way they won't see me the Boches - - "

"Alright, woman: have it your way," he surrendered. "But don't send Gilbert running to me for help if you get into trouble."

"I won't get into trouble, Mayor," Nanette shot back with a tone of finality as she pushed Mémé toward our house. "Come children. Mademoiselle Rouleau, do you want to join us?"

"No, thank you Madame Marchand. I think I will stay here and make myself useful. May I, Mayor Chancel?"

She was looking toward the Town Hall as she spoke. Following her trajectory, I spotted Oberleutnant Redlich standing behind the German barricade, his back to us while talking to a mounted-courier who stood at attention next to his purring machine and whose over-sized goggles raised to his forehead made him look like a toad. As though he had sensed her presence he turned toward us Oberleutnant Redlich. He did not smile or wave, but he stopped listening to the courier as he glanced at her. After a while, the toad's lips stopped shaping words and he, too, looked at us.

"Come Tina! There is nothing more to see," Nanette voiced.

"I want to help too!" I yelped yanking my hand from hers. "I'm going to help Lisette. May I, Lisette, may I help?'

I was pleading now and looking at Redlich who had by then returned to his colloquy with the toad. My heart hammered inside my chest and blood surged to the bump of my forehead while they looked down at me startled as I was by my outburst.

"I too want to help," I tried explaining as I searched my mouth for a drop of saliva. "Just for a little while, Nanette, please!"

Above me Mayor Chancel broke into a benign smile while Lisette, with this unfortunate habit I found so prevalent in adults, patted the top of my head.

"There's a good little constituent," Mayor Chancel voiced as I smiled angelically at Nanette. "And at least she doesn't go on about her rights," he ended with a searing look at her.

"Very well, child." Lisette agreed. "I am sure I can find something for her to do, Nanette. I'll bring her back for lunch."

Upon which Guigui extracted from his mother a concession of his own to visit Madame Pottin and her remaining son, Jacques. For a moment, a slight regret cooled my triumph: I was just as eager to find out about death as I was to elucidate what was happening between Mademoiselle Rouleau and Oberleutnant Redlich. But I had made my choice. I watched Guigui turn the corner of the Faubourg de Chavenay and promised myself he would tell me all about his visit to the Pottins this evening. He might even get to see dead Monsieur

Pottin and Jean-Claude. God forbid, he might even get to see the dead, Guigui.

The German soldiers manning the opening in the makeshift barricade waved us in with the butts of their machine guns. I pressed closer to Mademoiselle Rouleau. She looked down at me, smiled. Ahead of us the Mayor was giving instructions to Lisette and on our right the line of Frenchmen was still sifting methodically through the mountain of debris.

"Fine, Mr. Mayor. I will report to you later," Lisette voiced, and to me: "Come, Tina. We have work to do my girl!"

I was about to let go of Mademoiselle Rouleau's hand when her grip tightened around my wrist: Oberleutnant Redlich's voice had broken behind us.

"Fraulein Rouleau!"

"Yes?" she queried him abruptly releasing me.

"Fraulein Rouleau," he went on as he reached us. They stood speechless for a moment, his eyes bearing into hers as if he had forgotten what he had meant to say.

Lisette called out to me again, impatiently now: "Tina? Are you coming? Good morning Oberleutnant Redlich."

"Ach Fraulein Germain," Redlich said startled. "And a good morning to you, and Fraulein Tina. I had not seen you down there," he added bending stiffly towards me, snapping his heels.

"Did you want something, Oberleutnant?" Mademoiselle Rouleau queried him with a voice that did not sound like her.

"Ach Jawohl, Fraulein Rouleau," he answered her with a tentative smile.

But she averted her eyes from his now. She was not going to stare at him in the same way she had a minute ago: I knew. So I left them and ran up the last steps to Lisette. The last thing I heard him say was something about her establishing a log of those library books which could be salvaged from the wreckage.

It was dark inside the Town Hall: the bombardment had hit unseen power lines somewhere and the long marble hall was dimly lit by a few kerosene lamps placed far apart. Eight German officers sat in the rotunda around a heavy mahogany table dragged, I recognized, from the Council Room. On its moth-eaten green felt was spread a large map of France over which they huddled impervious to the kerosene lamp which spread its jaundiced light over their conspiratorial faces. Behind them in the shadow of a pillar, Soldat Mueller stood at attention. Our footsteps resounded incredibly loud against the marble floor. The officers stopped talking and searched the patch of darkness engulfing us as we approached the table. Penetrated by the same eeriness as I was, Lisette came to such an abrupt halt that she sent my face crashing into her still velvety fanny.

"Fraulein Registrar? Is that you?"

Herr Kommandant Blücher squinted in our direction. The Château was his usual headquarters and one rarely saw him in Dormans except on ominous occasions. He was a dedicated Nazi who had fought well for his Führer and had reaped along his campaigns as many medals as he had wounds, including the one which had brought him to Dormans. Although it had been the whispered talk of the town when he had first arrived, no one had yet explained to me the nature of his wounds apart from a few unenlightening comments about their having to do with his manhood. Dormans was a far cry from Warsaw and Tobruk for a career German officer in search of glory and because of it, it was said of Herr Kommandant

Blücher that he hated all of us with as much passion as he resented the twist of battle which had relegated him to our backwater.

"Fraulein Registrar!"

There was ice in his voice as he unfolded his lanky body from the chair. Soon he towered above the table and France, skeletal and gray like a scrawny vulture because he was as bald as he was skinny. The kerosene light drew a gigantic shadow behind him and I thought he had never stood as threatening as he did just then.

"Fraulein Registrar!"

"Yes, Herr Kommandant," Lisette managed at last. She grabbed my hand. "We have come to help organize the archives…"

"Sehr gut, Fraulein Registrar, proceed!" He made to sit down again and spotted me. "Ein moment, Fraulein, who is the girl? What is she doing here?"

"It's my niece, Herr Kommandant. I thought she might give me a hand…"

"Gut! Gut! Make sure I do not ear her. I cannot tolerate kinder!"

"She will be as quiet as a mouse, Herr Kommandant."

"Richtig! Richtig!"

He dismissed us with an impatient flicker of his hand and returned to his war. As we tiptoed our way down the long corridor I felt as unimportant as the flies I had swooshed around Mémé's gaping mouth at The Gaux.

Lisette's office remained seemingly untouched. Seemingly because at first glance the wall opposite her door was as it had always been with its stained oak shelves sagging at their center under the weight of the age-worn registries, and on my left the same door still opened on the parquetry of the Council Room now missing its huge round table which Kommandant Blücher had requisitioned. The twelve high back bottle-green leather chairs now faced each other across a void as if in preparation of an occult séance. Seemingly because on my right the visitors' counter still stretched its frontier between the public side and Lisette's territory. Behind it her desk stood crowded with its usual clutter of yellowed official forms, accounting ledgers, pencil butts and ink bottles, the rack of rubber stamps and the lonely periscope of the carved ivory ink-pen presented to her by Mayor Chancel in recognition of her first ten years of service. On the right-hand side wall, Petain and Hitler still avoided looking at each other from inside their frames. Everything was as it had always been. Except, and in this exception laid the delight which presently sent me prancing about the room.

"My wall! My wall, Tina, it's gone!" Lisette cried aghast. "Sweet Jesus, what am I to do, however am I going to protect my files?"

Her hands had flown to her cheeks in a gesture of despondency and her double chin almost tripled as she hung her head down as if to ward off a potential blow. But there was nothing she could do, Lisette, to change any of it. I was delighted: not only had the allied bombs pulverized the entire right wing of the Town Hall, they had also, very neatly, carved out of Lisette's inner sanctum the entire wall which heretofore had been her backdrop, the one behind her desk.

"Oh my God!" she lamented plunking her body on the visitors' bench right under Hitler. "What will I do? I just can't work in here: it might rain, it might even snow, it has snowed before in May. And the kids: they are going to be lining up out there after school gawking at me. Drive me mad they will. Mayor Chancel never mentioned a word, did he, Tina? Never even mentioned a word about this," she moaned pointing again at the large breach yawning in front of us. I sat beside her on the bench.

"Lisette, did you notice the smell?" I whispered snaking my fingers into her hand.

"What smell?"

"The smell, Lisette! It doesn't smell of mushrooms anymore"

"No, it smells of mildewed plaster, and smoke and debris, and even worse!"

"No, Lisette, it doesn't. It smells of spring. It's chilly but I tell you it does. It smells of the river now, or like the Avenue de la Marne after rain." I inhaled deeply: "it smells like Dormans!" I finished ecstatically.

But Lisette would have none of it. She shrugged her shoulders derisively, brushed my cheek with her free hand, the one I was not holding. "What a child you are, Tina! Dormans doesn't smell, a city doesn't smell."

"Oh yes it does! Paris does, so does Dormans, and they are completely different smells, and even The Gaux doesn't smell like Dormans or Paris," I persisted, arms outstretched toward the now visible patch of sky and that corner of the street which sloped down to the bridge and the river but through which she only saw the mountain of rubble. "Look at how bright it is now, Lisette! You can see Mr. Dupont's chimney and the swallows on the electric wires, look! You must ask Mayor Chancel to build you back a glass wall, like an aquarium so you can see the street, the sky, the birds, from your office. Wouldn't that be wonderful?"

I stopped, searched for a rainbow on her face.

"I could never work that way," she said shaking her head for emphasis. "I am used to working under the electric light. I like my hole-in-the-wall. I couldn't work with daylight pouring in on me like that. Besides, the sunlight, it makes my office look even dirtier, the grime doesn't show half as much under the electric light. And the draft, have you noticed how drafty it is now. I'll catch my death in here!"

"That's because all the windows in the Council Room are wide open," I tried again at my wits' end.

I had never known Lisette to be so contrary as I stood in the center of her office drained of joy and helpless myself while increasingly angry at Mayor Chancel. After all, I knew she was not talking to me, Lisette: she was talking to him and the twelve members of the City Council, and at Herr Kommandant Blücher, or even maybe De Gaulle, Churchill or Roosevelt. But she sure wasn't talking to me. Besides, I still thought her office looked a darn sight better than it had before.

"Hullo? Anybody here?"

I spun around, faced the controversial breach. Feet spread wide apart for balance, Raymond Langiers stood atop the mountain of rubbles. He had doffed the jacket of his Sunday suit and rolled up the sleeves of his rumpled shirt almost clear up to his armpits. He looked tired and unkempt, not at all the way one was used to seeing him in the streets of Dormans. A day-old stub of beard drew charcoal smudges on his chin and his very black hair which he usually wore parted in the middle and sleeked down with a generous application of brilliantine now hung in dull strands over his ears, longer than I thought it to be. And yet despite his ragged appearance as he loosened his tie, studied the clutter on Lisette's desk and leaned against the visitors' counter, I detected in him a strange sense of purpose. He was after something, Langiers, but I did not know what.

He shrugged loose the weariness, moved away from the counter. "Guess I should get started," he said. "The men will be here soon to help clear the debris - -"

"Do you have a moment, Monsieur Langiers?" Lisette interjected. Her hand had flown to his forearm and I almost felt under my own the wooly hair her fingers brushed. But he recoiled from her touch momentarily throwing the two of us in an embarrassed silence: Whatever had been on her mind was forgotten. Instead almost pleadingly, she temporized: "You look all done in, Monsieur Langiers. You must have had a frightful night…"

"Not really, Lisette," he answered, his eyes softening. "In these times we all must chip in. Besides, I am like you: a public servant at heart!"

"I know what you mean, Monsieur Langiers," she agreed missing the undertone of mockery I had sensed in his voice. "One day, when all of this is behind us, the people of Dormans will owe you a debt of gratitude: I know all the good work you do through Maitre Pinson."

He moved away from us. "I don't expect gratitude," he countered. "Besides, there are no more ferocious prosecutors than belated patriots!"

I had no time to ponder his last remark because a sudden noise of tumbling rubbles reached us from the outside. Several men, among them Uncle Marcel, were making their way through the breach and within seconds voices were shooting from all directions. Uncle Marcel still wore his fireman's copper helmet and his face and arms were smudged with soot. I rushed to him and for once did not mind his mustache chafing my forehead. I asked him how many fires he had helped douse but he had no time to answer me because a German Korporal I had never seen before joined the group.

"The desk and all the furniture must be removed, Fraulein Registrar! The child can help you move the papers and registers to the Council Room. Schnell! You," he called to Langiers who was hovering about Lisette's desk, "You help the women with the heavy stuff! The others, start clearing the debris now, Schnell!"

So we set about the job of clearing her office: Lisette handing me piles of documents and objects which I, in turn, would hand to Langiers who would store them in neat stacks on the dusty floor of the Council Room. After a while, the German made his way outside, watched over the clearing crew as he lit a cigarette. It was tedious work but gave my mind ample time to wander off as was its habit. At a time when death loomed around me, I found myself overwhelmed by life, tugging at its sleeve to elucidate a multiplicity of mysteries. The adults around me kept assaulting my childish realm and pushing the ever open turnstile of my curiosity only to depart leaving me more confused.

"Tina! Tina!"

Lisette was handing me another stack of documents and seeing Langiers occupied, I carried them myself into the Council Room. He was crouching over the stacks already lined up and his back was turned to me. I could see the distended gray satin of his waistcoat, its two small silk flaps hanging like limp tongues over the leather of his belt; the beige soles of his new shoes as the weight of his body rested on his toes. He was utterly oblivious to my presence a few feet from him so intense was his absorption in the task which held his attention. He was thumbing through what appeared to be official documents and in a move whose stealth startled me, retrieving and folding some and promptly stuffing them inside the front of his shirt. Over and over again. After a minute at most, he stood up and I tiptoed back to Lisette's office, praying he had not caught me watching him.

I did not say anything to anyone about the Langiers incident. Not even to Guigui as we sat after dinner on the kitchen floor under the window exchanging secrets about dead men while Bébert and Nanette held another conclave out of earshot from us in the dining-room. And I did not tell Mémé either when we went to bed. But then, I did not tell them anything about Mademoiselle Rouleau and Oberleutnant Redlich either. In retrospect, it may have been that revealing Langiers' secret may have alerted me to danger. As for Miss Rouleau and Redlich, theirs was a mystery which was nobody's business but theirs, and even I was not about to babble about it, although I might be determined to discover its nature.

****

CHAPTER VI

Wednesday, the Seventh of June Nineteen Forty-Four! A day which started like none other, that events occurring on the beaches of Normandy on the other side of France twenty-four hours earlier had predetermined would remain a red letter day on the map of my life. I know the historical dice had already been thrown before we awoke, that by this remarkable Wednesday morning unbeknownst to us the shores of France were already littered with the thousands of corpses it had taken to give the world back a semblance of hope. I have read about Omaha Beach and Utah Beach and about what occurred at Ste. Mere l'Eglise and Carentan; I have visited the German bunkers which still stand between Arromanches and Cherbourg and watched the ocean from inside their concrete walls standing where their gunners had stood in the dawn hours of the Sixth of June as they beheld in one moment of sheer terror the greatest armada ever built advancing inexorably toward them.

And yet, despite what I have since learned and read, notwithstanding the inscribed graves and the statistics, the war Memoires and the biographies, for me and I suspect for all the people of Dormans who lived it, the Seventh of June Nineteen Forty-Four will forever remain etched on our memory more vividly than the previous day because it is on that day that most of us first heard about the Allied invasion.

There had been more bombardments since the first one the day of Guigui's communion, "saturation bombing" Bébert called them knowingly. At the beginning they would strike when we least expected them and the race for survival would be a confused melee with each of us scurrying from wherever we happened to be and in whatever garb to our assigned shelter in Doctor Martin's cellar. We learned to run fast in those days. Sometimes the old folk would run faster than the young perhaps because so near their natural death they were more anxious to safeguard what little life remained to them. Morning, noon or night they would hit, the bombardments, without warning except the belated siren of the sawmill which, even then, would often wail as, with their death-pregnant bellies, the allied bombers were already dotting the skyline of the near horizon.

At first, the City Council voted unanimously that the citizenry should put up as good a front as the Germans were advertising, and thus "business as usual" became the order of the day. People went about their lives as if not even the prospect of an air raid could force them into a state of petrified idleness, and although one did not know from one day to the next whether one would be alive beyond the next bombardment, Uncle Marcel still walked the streets of Dormans with his perilous ladder stuck under his arm horizontally, Mémé continued to go to the fields in the hills behind what was left of the sawmill to cut grass for our dwindling herd of rabbits. Nanette still went to the town's wash-house on the Rue de la Riviere, Lisette officiated at the Town Hall, and Guigui and I, although more reluctantly, continued to attend our respective classes. This parody of normalcy lasted two weeks. Then toward the end of May several ominous events occurred: Bébert ran short of wood for his coffins and the three economic mainstays of our small town - - the railroad yards, the sawmill and the cement factory - - got hit along with some of the low lying districts on the other side of the Town. "Business as usual" became an untenable pretense for in many instances people found themselves with neither a place to work nor a bed to sleep in. Thus the members of the City Council met again and under the aegis and with the approval of the local German Kommandatur, adopted new emergency measures among which, to Guigui's and my delight, was the early closing of all schools which were ordered to stand in recess forthwith and until further notice for the longest summer vacation of my life as of Monday, June 12.

At any rate, on the morning of June Seven Nineteen Forty-Four, I was still a little girl who had dallied in bed in the house in Dormans and was living in the only country there was, the Present and the only mansion there should be, Happiness. History, liberation, invasion, occupation, the past and the future were alien concepts to me as I stood at the top of the stairs by the door to the toilet listening to dead Pepe's clock striking the hour and deliberating whether I should make use of the privy now or wait until I really felt like it which would most certainly be in the middle of breakfast. I had almost made up my mind to follow my first option when there erupted from somewhere downstairs palls of laughter intermingled with shouts and loud voices. The rumpus froze my commendable intention and I headed down the stairs wondering what at this early hour even for Dormans could bring about such exceptional merriment. I harkened some more when I reached the bottom step and inspected the hallway. Soon another explosion of what could only be elation, this time much closer to me, burst forth again. I was peering through the lace curtain of the kitchen door when it swung open in my face and an incredible spectacle offered itself to me.

Most of them still wore their night-clothes except for Bébert who was in his blue overalls and sleeveless undershirt and obviously had taken no time to shave or comb his tousled hair. Mémé was in her long blue flannel nightgown her gray hair yellowing at the tips braided into the single plait that hung over her left shoulder. In her obvious haste she had forgotten all about her dentures so one could not tell where her naked gums began and her lips started; the gaping hole between her parted lower and upper jaws gave her an air of hilarity which made her look a few years younger. Guigui, oblivious to the June chill of the kitchen, wore only the bottom half of his pajamas and, standing by the stove still coiffed sternly in her black hairnet, Nanette's face reminded me of a portrait of Louis XI I had seen in my history book. Uncle Marcel and Aunt Louise having presumably rushed over to our house from theirs across the avenue had thrown coats over their night-clothes whereas Madame Tardieux had merely contented herself of a black woolen shawl over hers. Her head casked by an army of paper curlers was a revelation. Even Albert the cat was there purring on his mistress' lap. Only Lisette was absent.

I must have looked dumbfounded as I stared at them from the kitchen door because after exchanging knowing winks they all burst out laughing again. Each was holding a full glass of wine. I thought for sure that they just would keep on pointing fingers at me, catching their breaths only to start laughing again. After a while, they looked so silly to me that in spite of myself, I emoted Aunt Louise and smirked right back at the lot of them.

"Ha! Ha! Ha! Look at the child's face!" Uncle roared at last between two fits of laughter. He was chewing his mustache whose tips got in the way of his mirth. "Look at her!"

He pointed a chubby finger at me. The folds of his distended pajamas rippled with glee. Bébert slapped his knees and Mémé's toothless mouth became an abysmal gorge. Guigui who did needed no encouragement poked me in the ribs while Albert, outraged by the sudden quake shaking the foundation of his comfortable place on his mistress' lap, hissed and jumped off of them, landing at my feet. I thought they had all gone mad and rushed to bury my head in Nanette's nightgown.

"Stop teasing Tina," she remonstrated them. "We haven't even told her what this is all about!" I smelled the drying perspiration of sleep on her nightgown.

"Oh, oh, oh," Bébert pooh-poohed her. "We are not laughing at you, Tina, no!"

"How would she know that? You tell her Madame Tardieux!" ordered Aunt Louise.

"No, no: let me!" Guigui screeched all excited.

"You keep quiet, son," his mother admonished him. "Madame Tardieux is the one, you weren't there when he told her."

Curiosity got the better of me as I looked up from Nanette's nightgown and waited anxiously for Madame Tardieux to finish gulping some of her wine.

"Come here, Tina." She finally called to me wiping her lips with a corner of her shawl. "I've got some really big news for you!" My eyes had grown the size of plums in their sockets. "It's like this, child - - give her a drop of wine, Nanette, she won't hear that kind of news again in her lifetime - - the ALLIES HAVE LANDED, Tina, that's what! They landed in Normandy yesterday at dawn and by now they are probably half way to your mother in Paris, and it won't be long before they reach Dormans. Just like my Léon always predicted!"

"So what happens now?" I queried perplexed. The long anticipated invasion meant nothing to me. It was like the sea: I had never seen either.

"Can you believe such a question? What a happy state childhood is!" Uncle Marcel marveled. He leaned over his wife to brush my cheek. "Let me tell you what it means, Tina: it means no more Boches in Dormans or anywhere in France, no more forced labor, no more hostages being shot, no more rationing, no more curfews, no more bombardments - -"

"And no more tanks or panzers on the Place du Luxembourg." Guigui chimed in.

"And no more Herr Kommandant Blücher at the Château!" came Aunt Louise's contribution.

"And more food! Imagine, a real steak and fried potatoes. Haven't seen a decent potato in months, not since I got those from old Matthieu at Christmas: paid their weight in gold too," Nanette went one better.

"And real sugar and butter and chocolate!" Mémé chirped in her hand hiding her gaping mouth.

And they all smiled and laughed again: paradise was in sight so I toasted its promise with them and downed a quick gulp of wine from Nanette's glass.

"I'll say this much though," Bébert cut in more soberly. "Once the Boches are gone - - and I reckon it won't be too long now - - I hope that between De Gaulle and the Party, we can put this country back on its feet again, and not the way it used to be either! A popular front! That's what France will need and trust me, we'll be ready for them the next time they try something again the Krauts!"

"They ain't even gone yet, Gilbert!" Aunt Louise said tartly.

As if to validate her contention the floor began shaking under our feet. I looked out of the kitchen window with the rest of them: a long file of German panzers was roaring past headed in the direction of Paris. The beaches of Normandy suddenly seemed very far from Dormans.

"Sure they are still here," Bébert agreed half-heartedly after the convoy had passed. "Might even be here for a while yet for all we know."

"A month: that's how long I give them," Madame Tardieux opined with forced optimism. "And I'll tell you something else," she added knowingly, "Oberleutnant Redlich doesn't think it will even take that long. I could see it in his eyes when he told me about yesterday's invasion this morning."

"I still can't get over his telling you about it: and him a Boche too!" Uncle Marcel voiced shaking a dubious head.

"I've told you many times, Monsieur Germain. He is not like the rest of them," Madame Tardieux objected.

"Oh piffle!" Nanette snorted. "They are made of the same cloth all of them. Ain't not one better than the other. Mad dogs, that's what they all are."

A raw hatred streaked through her brown eyes, here and gone, fast. I had never seen in Nanette such a suggestion of cruelty, not even that night at The Gaux, because even her angers, as violent as they might seem, were always diluted by her intrinsic goodness which somehow blunted the impact of her onslaughts and promised a swift forgiveness.

"I am telling you, Antoinette, Oberleutnant Redlich is not like them," Madame Tardieux persisted not giving an inch. "You can't have a man live for two years in your house without getting to know him. He's a good man, Antoinette. Why, with my Léon gone I couldn't have managed save for that man's help: the food he brought me, the rent he paid when he didn't have to ---"

"Just buttering you up so he might spy on us!" Nanette snapped back.

"No! No! you're wrong Antoinette," went on Madame Tardieux beating her bosom for emphasis. "Besides, do you think he would have told me about the invasion if he were like the rest of them? Never mind their propaganda: it's bad news for them. They know it's the beginning of the end, and yet he told me because he knew it would make all of us happy. And you forget the champagne he brought for your son's communion!"

"You...happy, Madame Tardieux? Everyone knows you were for Petain!" Nanette scoffed with a well-aimed jab which left the widow speechless.

Our stunned silence at Nanette's mean outburst turned uncomfortable. The drip of the kitchen faucet raced with the tick-tock of the Swiss chalet on the dining room wall while I held my breath, searched their faces which were not looking at me except for Uncle Marcel. Knees spread wide apart for balance on the diminutive kitchen stool, he was shaking his head with obvious dismay.

"God forgive us!" he sighed at last. "God forgive us!" He looked at each one of us still shaking his head in that weary way. And even though his pajamas showed under the threadbare winter coat and there were sweat stains on his collar and even though perspiration greased the triple strand of wrinkles around his neck, as I stared at him I was impressed by his dignity. "God forgive us!" he said for a third time, now looking straight at Nanette who promptly looked elsewhere, at Mémé I think, "And God forgive me, 'cause I too hate

Petain and I too hate the Boches, and I too have called for retribution, you know that full well, Antoinette. And it was right then because it's the hatred that kept us going through those ungodly years. But we can't carry that hate in us forever. By the time they are out the Germans, by the time the allies are done with them, France will need all the hands it can get and that will take a lot of forgiveness! A united front, that's what it'll take to rebuild this country, not revenge. There are thousands of young men dying as we speak over there on the other side of France, Antoinette, and they ain't dying just for you: they are dying for all of us because we are all French here and one just as good as the other. So now you apologize to Ma'am Tardieux and you pour me some more wine 'cause I ain't never made such a long speech before."

Behind me Madame Tardieux was weeping silently. She leaned over Aunt Louise and patted Uncle's fat knees.

"You are a good man, Monsieur Germain, like my Léon…" she withdrew her hand, gave a look of apology to Aunt Louise. "You've got a good man, Madame Germain," she voiced through her sobs.

"Have some more wine, Madame Tardieux," came Nanette's voice: Her way of making amends without having to apologize. I smiled at her knowing it was the best she could do Nanette and even that I knew had been difficult.

At first it was thought that the Americans would be in Dormans within days, that like an equinox tide the forces of goodness having successfully triumphed over the first line of German fortifications would sweep the country transversally in a direct line from Normandy to Germany. Uncle Marcel even calculated that given the some three hundred kilometers between Caen and Dormans and allowing for an allied advance of a measly twenty kilometers a day (which was truly conservative for an army with such military supremacy), our liberators should reach Dormans within fifteen days, twenty at most if he were to make allowance for the strategic advantage of the well-entrenched Germans, "the recognized edge of the defenders over the attackers." We relied heavily on his prognostications: he had been at Verdun back in World War I, and besides, his Clemenceau mustache which we had so far taken for granted, suddenly became one more symbol of his military expertise. Bébert who had been too young for Verdun and too old for the Meuse in 1939 was at a disadvantage. Unable to contribute anything to Uncle's brilliant calculations, he took a killjoy stance and acted the Cassandra in our midst predicting a potential allied route, an all-out German counter-attack, or events of the same dismal ilk which we ignored. At first.

In Dormans itself the atmosphere had changed. Nobody spoke about the invasion openly but everyone knew about it and also knew everyone else knew about it and yet when one went to the stores or met someone on the street or went to market Saturday mornings, one spoke about everything else except that one topic. For months and years, people had whispered about a potential allied invasion, they had conjectured ad nauseam as to when and where it might take place, but those forbidden whispers of hope had been contrived like the wishes for prompt recovery one makes to a man touched with a terminal illness. Now that the invasion had begun in earnest, however, one dared not speak about it lest it should fail or, as Bébert would predict on occasion, turn into another Dunkirk.

The Germans became much more visible after what has since become known as D-Day: they were everywhere one went. They probably had been there all along, but then their presence had been part and parcel of one's life. Now they became conspicuous because the historical process was about to run its course: from victorious enemies to unwanted occupiers to now endangered losers. One no longer spoke to them unless it was essential; but then, one no longer spoke to those who were suspected of having been on too friendly terms with them. The town divided itself in three camps: the expectant pawns, the suspected collaborators and the uniformed enemies and between those three factions the chasm grew wider with each day which brought us closer to adjudication.

On the surface the town and its citizens pretty much continued to abide by the modus operandi which had been in force since the first German had goose-stepped into Dormans. The cemetery was fuller, the shelves in the stores were barer, thirty percent of the town had been destroyed and forty percent of the surviving work force was out of work, but people managed to push from one day to the next believing the misery would be short lived. Every day Bébert or Nanette would bring home to the dinner table tales of loss and tragedy but they always involved people I had never met. Thus, although the recounting of such woes satisfied my inborn curiosity, my interest remained transient. I associated such calamitous events with the sort which had beset Monsieur Hugo's Lisette: it was heartbreaking but somehow fictional. I had neither the perception nor the understanding of an adult and therefore did not have the emotional capacity to empathize with unknown individual's miseries. I lived in the present and in my own circumscribed world and so far, both remained mercifully intact.

By the first week of July, Uncle had lost some of his clout: the Americans still had not liberated Dormans. To buttress his earlier prognostications Uncle brought to us those events which tended to support his position while Bébert countered with those which gave credence to his prophecies of doom and there would inevitably ensue between the two men contentious arguments which seldom settled anything and left us women confused. Then on Tuesday, the Fourth of July, Guigui returned from confession with a bombshell which promised to settle the issue.

Contrary to the usual French catholic practice, he had not forsaken religion after his first communion and although I sometimes suspected it was more to aggravate his father than to stay on good terms with God, he still went to confession and attended mass every Sunday. In any event, on Tuesday, the Fourth of July, Guigui came home from confession cleansed of his inglorious sins and the bearer of a secret whose knowledge might involve a degree of danger but which he was ready to share with us provided we swore on the Cross to keep our mouths proverbially shut. Bébert who had little patience for his son's self-aggrandizing promptly ordered Guigui to come out with it, whatever it was.

It may have been that the uncertainty as to the allied advance and the concomitant wrangling over the issue which of late had been growing more acrimonious had so upset Guigui that he had conveyed them to Father Rocas, or it may have been that Father Rocas who viewed himself as God's agent on earth had simply wanted to pass along the word to the Marchands and the Germains that, notwithstanding these evil times, he was indeed still tuned in to God. In any case, it transpired by way of Guigui that Father Rocas kept a short-wave radio hidden within the church in one of the alms boxes. Every two or three nights so as to lessen the risk of discovery, Father Rocas would listen to the news from London and then selectively pass on the good words to trustworthy members of his flock among whom - - Guigui relayed peevishly - - Father Rocas regretted not to count Uncle Marcel or Bébert or even Nanette and Aunt Louise.

Thus the following Sunday, Nanette put on her best clothes and her funeral hat, and accompanied her son and her mother-in-law to church as she would do every Sunday after that until Dormans was liberated. Unfortunately Nanette who loved holding center stage had thus been handed the material to safeguard her starring role in the limelight of our ignorance. From that Sunday on she instituted weekly briefings which she would hold in the kitchen after high mass and before lunch, and although by then we all knew God lived in London and that His word coming through Nanette by way of the church's alms box could be relied upon for its veracity, we all soon started to regret our newfound enlightenment. Nanette's lectures were as pompous as they were dull. It had been more fun to listen to Uncle and Bébert fight every other night even if neither knew beans about the allied advance. Anyway, by then it began to look as if they would never come the Americans, so I temporarily put them aside along with the Boche, Langiers and the rest of the unanswered questions and plunged head-long into the spring. July was outside our windows and its promise was far more concrete than that of the problematic liberation.

In addition to acting as God's emissary among us, Nanette had also joined the Dormans' Women's Emergency Committee which had been organized by Mayor Chancel with a view to providing assistance to the war-made homeless and unemployed of the community. Its headquarters were located in my school. The WEC was a mixture between the Salvation Army, a soup kitchen and a refugee center, but despite the state of utter confusion in which its volunteers operated, it provided valuable services and thus was constantly overrun by the many dispossessed its purpose it was to help. At first Nanette only spent her mornings there but gradually as word got around of the valuable work the WBC was doing, its clientele doubled in size and so outstripped the volunteers that they found themselves putting in many more hours than had at first been anticipated. Although I accompanied her mornings and contributed in my small way to the general relief effort, my afternoons were gloriously free of both chores and adult supervision. I was nine years old racing toward ten, an inquisitive little girl for whom each encounter was an education, every season the source of unknown wonders, Dormans a paradise and the war an abstraction.

I visited Madame Tardieux but no longer inquired about her defunct husband because I was far more interested in Oberleutnant Redlich. I paid occasional calls to Lisette at the Town Hall but my passion for the death registries had been replaced by the more urgent matter of what it was Langiers had pilfered from her office that day. So far my convoluted questions had drawn repeated blanks from her: she no longer knew where anything was, Lisette. The place was a mess and that's all there was to it and it would take her months to straighten out the archives let alone find out whether anything was missing. Occasionally I accompanied Mémé in the fields in the hills leading to The Gaux when she went to cut grass for our rabbits but soon realized that she refused to enlighten me as to whether Nanette had made it to The Gaux after the first bombardment and she still pleaded ignorance about the Boche: "Still fretting about him, child! He's long gone. Now watch out for my billhook!" I stopped by Bébert's workshop on the Faubourg de Chavenay and plunking myself on a heap of pungent wood-shavings I watched him at his craft and queried him about the Germans at the Château or I crossed the workshop to the small garden behind it where Nanette grew a few vegetables and kept the rabbit cages. I fondled their silky fur and spoke to them about the carrots which would soon be ripe at The Gaux if Nanette's seedlings bore their promise.

However, most of all my latest delight was the Marne river and the deserted footpath which bordered the lazy waters as they meandered their way toward the Seine amid a patchwork of fields and orchards. The land was flat on the town's side of the river but across it hillocks spiked with tall marsh reeds dropped into the water. If one looked facing the direction of its flow the view was magical in the wealth of its hues which ran the gamut of diverse greens with here and there the contrasting earth brown of a tilled field, the merry yellow of the jonquils poking their heads out of the reeds or the crimson of poppies which grew wild and in clusters.

At first I took the footpath which ran along the Dormans side of the river and was hedged between the water and the railroad tracks. I followed the same itinerary three afternoons in a row taking the side street which wound around the now shattered right wing of the Town Hall, thence across the rail tracks and on to the footpath. From there I walked the short kilometer to Dormans "beach" which was little more than a clearing carved out of the overgrown vegetation but where at that particular spot the river was shallow enough to afford reasonable footing if one could not swim. Two weather-beaten wood benches and a bleached picnic table, a crumbling outhouse and a broken diving board were the sum total of the town's contribution to its recreational amenities. The third afternoon, however, I found the beach shrieking with children who, although my own age and most of them my colleagues at school, so infuriated me with their inane games and noisy antics that I promptly departed.

By the fourth afternoon, self-exiled from the once solitary beach, I decided on a bolder course: I would investigate the other side of the river, the ones where the fields ran almost flat before scaling a long ridge of hills on the far horizon. However, the main bridge which had spanned the Marne had been blown to smithereens by the allied bombs. But I knew that there was a small village buried somewhere in the hills across and deduced that there must be a means to ford the river. Soon I spotted Monsieur Jaubert, the Town Crier, sitting under his mangy straw hat, napping on his mustache at the tiller of a small row boat. His drum and batons next to him were doing likewise. He was so pleased to see a human being, Monsieur Jaubert, that in no time I had convinced him to ferry me across the river. During the passage I sympathized with his plight. The krauts would be putting a pontoon over here soon, he explained, but in the meantime Mayor Chancel had ordered him, "ordered me, Jaubert, the Town Crier, Mademoiselle Tina," to assume the functions of emergency ferryman. He let me off on the other side, promised to come back for me within an hour and ordered me to keep my ears open for the siren of the sawmill although he doubted they would be back the Allies seeing they had already inflicted all the damage they could to our town.

I made my way through the tall marsh reeds. There was just me, the milky blue sky, a few yellow butterflies and bees and a dozen skylarks flying in V formation. I walked toward the sun and Paris, inhaled the coming summer, gathered a handful of poppies while letting July impregnate me with its warmth. I might have been humming to myself or daydreaming when I spotted them. I am not sure. But I remember neither of them saw me or heard my sandals crinkling the strong reeds. I did not immediately recognize them because they stood against the sunlight in their swim suits, a triton and a mermaid born from the water on which shore they were presently standing. As stealthily as I could, I eased myself flat in the tall grass, pressed my tummy to the ground and buried my face in a patch of bluets. Peering through the curtain of tall reeds which grew dense from the river clear to the top of the mound which overhung the small cove from which their hushed voices reached me, I soon recognized them: Oberleutnant Redlich and Mademoiselle Rouleau. Their bodies glistened against the sun speckled water and her hair when she removed her bathing cap fell on her shoulders in wildly tangled chestnut curls. He stood beside her, tall, straight and slender and my heart went out to her when he wove his fingers through her damp hair. And when she raised her face to him I buried mine in the bluets afraid she might discover my presence.

"I won't have it, Franz!" she whispered to him, resuming a conversation they must have started long before I happened on them. "You'll be killed or taken prisoner. I couldn't bear it. I just couldn't! When will they reach Dormans?"

"Soon now. And then it will go very fast and this whole, wahnsinnigen …insane war will be over…" he whispered.

"It may be insane, Franz, but it is not a game. It's our lives and I shall die if they kill you!"

"You will not die, Liebling, and they will not kill me."

"How can you be so sure?"

"Because…Look at the river, Liebling. How can you think of death in the midst of such beauty. How does that French poem go: O temps! Suspends ton vol, et vous, heures propices! Suspendez votre cours: Laissez-nous, laissez-nous …How does it go, Liebling?"

"Laissez-nous savourer les rapides delices des plus beaux de nos jours! It's by Lamartine* and – "

"Ach, Lamartine, of course! A beautiful poem for a beautiful day. Do you not wish also that time could really stop, Odile?"[1]

---

[1] Oh time suspend your flight and your blessed hours:
Delay your course
Let us savor the fleeting delights
Of our most beautiful days!

"Of course I do! But it will not, Franz! And I don't care about Lamartine, I only care about you, about us."

"And I about you, liebe Odile."

The silence which fell between them at that instant prompted me to look up from my pillow of bluets. He was kissing Mademoiselle Rouleau, Oberleutnant Redlich, and I held my breath as long as they kissed, which was very short because although his arms held her in an embrace she pushed him away.

"No! No Franz! We must decide now!"

"Decide what, Odile? Who is going to win this war?"

"No Franz. We know who is going to win the war," she was pelting his chest with her small fists. "Within weeks, days perhaps, they will be here in Dormans and you act as if you did not care!"

"Perhaps I do not…"

"But you must, for us!"

He stepped away from her, turned his back on us and stared at the river.

"I am so tired, Liebling, so very tired. I was not born to be a soldier but alas I was born a German and in these days one goes with the other." He stopped speaking as if he were surprised by what he had just voiced. "You know," he started again, "when I was younger and living in Paris in 1932 and 1933, I had this plan of making my life there, finding a job with one of the German newspapers perhaps…I loved France: I loved its people, its poets and writers, I even loved its whores and its concierges," he smiled. "And its cafes: the Deux Magots, The Flore and, oh, the Brasserie Lipp: I saw Le Corbusier and Saint-Exupery there once before the war and we even shared a drink. You should have been there with me then, where were you,

Liebling? But now it will never be the same, will it? After this war, we Germans will not be welcome in your country, or in any country – "

"Stop it, Franz!" she pleaded. "I don't want to hear any more. You sound like death, farewell, never again, and all those words which mean 'NO' forever. You can run, we can run. There are places in this world where no one has been hurt by this war: South America for instance…I don't know: places. Or you could stay in Dormans, hide when thy liberate us. I would find a way to smuggle you out, hide you until then!"

"That is also what Frau Tardieux would like for me to do, Odile, and if I were a good German I would have to report you both! But I shall not, of course, because I deserted a long time ago…"

"Deserted, how? You are still wearing that horrible uniform which might kill you tomorrow!"

"Ach, the uniform! It is the only gift of Herr Adolf Hitler that I still retain. A pretty uniform, don't you think? It fits me well, nein? I think without my uniform you would not have loved me - - "

"Franz, Franz, please!"

She was at her wits end, Mademoiselle Rouleau, and near tears I could tell as I watched her through the screen of marsh reeds. Her small fists hammering away her frustration pounded the air between them with desperation. But then, quite abruptly, she drew away from him, stomped the ground with her foot and looked at him with new resolve.

"Franz, listen to me, darling," she resumed as he stopped staring at the river and bent his face toward her. "Here is what we will do. When the Americans come you will stay at Madame Tardieux's: she has offered to hide you so there will be no problem with her. Are you listening to me, Franz? I will tell her about us tonight or first thing in the morning. Later when the Americans do come, I shall move in with her. No one will think anything of it: you have left, she is a widow and still needs the rental income, so, nobody will ever guess you are still there. In six months or whenever, when things settle down, we can escape somewhere, forget about France and Germany and the war: all this horrible world that we didn't create. We will start fresh where no one will know us. Oh, I do so love you Francois, please say you will, please…"

She was begging him now as if her life depended on his answer. And suddenly I was her too, standing so very close to him that I too could feel his breath wafting on my forehead and I too wanted him to say yes.

"Ach, Liebling, Liebling! You are such a dreamer - -"

"Please tell me you will, Franz, please?'

"Do you know what they will do to you and to Frau Tardieux if I should be discovered? Do you know how much hatred you shall reap, you and her, if the French find me?"

"But they won't. It's a perfect plan and it will work, Franz, bitte, bitte!"

"You do not understand, Odile. Then I should be responsible for what happens to you. With the other deaths, the thousands of other deaths, the million other deaths, I can tell myself I was only ein Zuschauer, a man watching an accident. But then it should be different: I would be directly responsible for what the French or the Americans do to you and to Frau Tardieux -"

"But they won't, Franz, they won't even know you are still here!"

"Perhaps, but if they do find out, then they shall hurt you as much as they hurt me."

"I don't care: I would rather die with you than live without you!"

"And what of poor Frau Tardieux?"

"If they do find out, we can tell them we forced her into it, that we threatened her even, so that she had no choice and this they WILL Believe –"

His hand across her lips silenced her. Slowly his arms encircled her waist, lifted her small body. They were so beautiful as he whirled her around, the gold of summer spangling their young bodies. He kissed her neck, her shoulders as she clung to him laughing and her head tilted back. When they stopped spinning and he bent down to kiss her again and again, and when he laid her gently on the small stretch of secluded shore and they vanished from my sight behind the scarp, I felt like it was the morning of Guigui's communion all over again. I bit my lips and buried my face in the crushed bluets. Then from below I heard their whispers, their sighs, and I caught sight of their entwined legs and heard her hushed gasps and his cry as if his life breath was draining out of him. I was swept by a tidal wave of bliss. I counted to a hundred before I could be sure they would not detect my presence, and then I ran and ran. They could not hear me flee or the sound of my heart pounding inside me so frantically consumed as I was by the conflagration of their love. I just kept hoping all their dreams and mine for them would come true.

The summer exploded in my chest as I reached the row boat and poor Monsieur Jaubert never suspected what terror had made me so very breathless. I kept laughing and catching my breath and smiling at him during our journey back and for a long time after that.

* * * * *

CHAPTER VII

In the two weeks which followed my discovery of Mademoiselle Rouleau and Oberleutnant Redlich's affair, my childish world became ever more unreal. I drifted through the days and wandered about the house aimlessly like a woman who has just discovered she is at last pregnant and keeps deferring a formal announcement so as to savor the mystery of her own fecundity a little longer. Love was permanently on my mind. The lilt of its words, the glow of its sun which I had read on her face and even the sweet screams of its rite which I had overheard, kept inhabiting my memory, swelling and growing until from those minute seeds suddenly grew, like from the fabled bean, a veritable forest of delights through which my thoughts roamed at will without constrictions. Dormans had become an enchanted realm and my orphaned teacher and our German neighbor its beleaguered lovers. I devoured Andersen anew and soon convinced myself that, just as in his fairy tales, my two friends were fated to happiness sooner than later.

In this emotional state I tried applying the color of love to the people who were part of my daily life painting them with its brush, daubing its inhabitants with pastel colors which, unfortunately, turned sour on them. Mémé especially gave me a hard time: I could not imagine her young without her false teeth and her yellowing plait, and since I had never known dead old Pépé, his face when I tried to visualize their courting days remained an oval blank. With Nanette and Bébert the fantasy was more conscribed because I had heard them often recount their courting days. But then I had laughed so much at their retelling, all the things that had gone on in that little alley which led to the Faubourg de Chavenay but that they remembered as their Lovers' Lane, at the times her father had caught them petting and chased Bébert away with a Seltzer bottle because he then owned the café in which Soldat Mueller now drank his schnapps and it was the weapon of his trade, or the morning of their wedding night when his friends had put them through the traditional chamber pot ritual, tossing out of bed that I could not picture their courting days as anything but farcical. They had laughed too much about it while Oberleutnant Redlich and Mademoiselle Rouleau were more serious and thus more memorable as lovers. Yet I still went about my daily life during those two weeks trying to assign to familiar faces the glorious symptoms of the love I had witnessed that afternoon.

Bébert thought I had a touch of spring fever, Nanette opted for a touch of anemia and fed me the only remedy for which, alas, there was no shortage which was cod liver oil. Mémé came closest to my true condition when she ventured that my distraction and lack of appetite were symptomatic of my age and more of the mind than of the body. "The things that storm through their minds at her age, Nanette: you wouldn't believe!" I frequented Madame Tardieux more assiduously than in the past but her usually expressive face now seemed permanently shrouded by a veil of secrecy. Meanwhile I periodically lost my voice when per chance I happened to run into Oberleutnant Redlich or turned the crimson of guilt whenever I met Mademoiselle Rouleau.

For once the war was on my side. It was so much on the mind of the adults around me that they had little time to search the reasons for my febrility let alone waste time quizzing me as to its cause. Sometime during the afternoon of the 20th of July, 1944, we learned of the attempt on Hitler's life earlier that day and for a few happy hours in the confusion which had apparently overtaken the Nazi Kommandatur, we hoped fervently that the plotters had succeeded. The allies were still mired in the Bocage in Normandy and our side had hoped for such a God-send miracle to turn the tide. Unfortunately, the morning of the twenty-first Herr Kommandant Blücher ordered the populace to gather on the Place du Luxembourg and delivered a speech which shattered our fleeting hopes: The Führer had survived, Germany would crush the pitiful Allied invasion and the new order of National Socialism was here to stay for the good of France, for the salvation of the world and for the glory of the beloved Führer. There followed a reading of Hitler's address to the German nation the night before in which he threatened chilling retribution for the perpetrators of the outrage, topped by a rendition of the Deutschland Uber Alles intoned defiantly by the entire German garrison of Dormans. Despair it seemed then was never far away no matter how much we all might hope.

But then the following Sunday Nanette came back from church beaming: The Allies were out of the Bocage, they had taken St. Lo and they could no longer be stopped. The German defense was at last springing leaks and soon the cleansing tide of the just would unleash its hordes upon the fascist barbarians and free the whole enslaved nation. Father Rocas also relayed through Nanette London's coded warning that the French underground would soon be getting specific orders to help pave the way for the advancing Allies and that under such circumstances all civilians were advised to stay close to home so as to forestall German suspicions and concomitant reprisals. "From now until further notice, I don't want any of you roaming around Dormans unless it is absolutely necessary," Nanette ordered us. "We got to know every minute where each of us is!" I thought she was over-dramatizing as usual but remembering Herr Kommandant Blücher's virulence at the public meeting earlier that week I decided for once to play it safe and stuck close to quarters.

The month of July was drawing to a close and although its beauty still beckoned, I closed my eyes and reluctantly whittled away each of its remaining golden hours playing endless games of card or Families with Guigui and the now father-less and brother-less Jacques Pottin who had become his new bosom friend. I dreamt of love and was bored with war and not even the prospect of my upcoming tenth birthday could lure me out of the nostalgia. But then fate and reality came barging into my childish life and after their combined thrust I would never be able again to recapture the virgin happiness which had been mine until then.

There are events which took place in Dormans during the three years that I lived there which, although they must have happened because a day in one's life is made up of just such fragments, that I have now completely forgotten. There were people, I guess, many people who drifted through my life, in and out of the kitchen perhaps or encountered at market or on the country roads whose names and faces I shall never be able to remember or evoke. I sense there is also an army of small everyday joys or aggravations which I accumulated then which now stir in the dark recesses of my memory, trying to, in one last flutter, escape the guillotine of my oblivion. The incidents, the scents, the emotions, the colors and the faces, the words that I can still project on the screen of my present, toss at random on the table of the here-and-now when I empty the pockets of my memory, if strung together like so many beads, would take up no more than two months at most. Three years reduced to two months then: my past amputated arbitrarily by the surgeon of time which has hacked away that part of my life. Hard as I have tried to hang on to each retentive limb, to recall the tritest encounter and the most innocuous exchange, the tempestuous storm of the future has blown over the marching present, its mad gales sweeping aside a whole chunk of the past. And thus it is that there are probably many blessed days back in Dormans that I cannot evoke however desperately I might search my memory and most of the pages that were written then have been torn from the book of my life until what remains of the overall story is so disconnected as to make sense only to me.

And yet I remember that day and most of those which followed it as if they had happened last week. I even remember the pins-and-needles numbing my knees as I sat on the kitchen floor across from Guigui trying to pretend I really did not care that I was going to lose this game of checkers. There was an hour before supper and the sun, although it had sunk behind the roofline of the houses across the Avenue, was still somewhere above the horizon turning the sky a salmon pink behind the lace curtain of the window. Even Nanette's apron as she busied herself over the sink at the far end of the kitchen, was tainted with the pastel of the fiery dusk.

The imperative knock on the front door rifled through my discomfort. I looked up: outside the window the patch of pavement in front of the house was stirring with shadows. Within seconds came another sharp series of knocks and Nanette dropped the pan she had been scouring. It hit the stove, the oven door, rebounded twice before coming to rest on the tiled floor. Guigui and I shot up. Watching Nanette who stood transfixed for a split second before bolting to the front door. Her foot hit the pan which slid the length of the kitchen, Guigui raced after his mother and I after him.

At first I only saw young Philippe Matthieu standing inside our front door. He wasn't saying a word: he just stood there, his eyes lowered, worrying his beret between his hands, blocking our view to whatever laid beyond him until Nanette pushed him roughly out of her way with a ferocious swing of her left forearm that sent him careening against Madame Tardieux's front steps. Old Matthieu was there also, big and heavy, his rubber boots smeared with cow-dung. Madame Tardieux, her eyes dilated into saucers, watched Nanette make her way to them. Two boys from Guigui's class carrying fishing rods and buckets stood a few steps back gawking. At last I caught sight of the wheelbarrow parked by the plane tree which bordered the Avenue behind old Matthieu. It was a large wheelbarrow, yet not long enough to hold the shape which laid on it. They had put a board across its handles so the feet wouldn't scrape the ground. An old army green blanket torn in places covered the body but the left arm had slipped form under it and the hand, open and stiff, showed gray against the spokes.

"Bébert…" Nanette whispered her hand flying to her breast. She edged slowly toward the wheelbarrow as the rest of us, frozen, watched her progress. It was as if some unseen force were pulling her against her will toward the covered shape. Each of her steps was atrociously slow, painfully reluctant, and still she threw one foot forward, then the other. "Gilbert!" she wailed suddenly as she reached the wheelbarrow. The flesh shrank inside my skin and my hands flew to my ears as she howled his name over and over. At last she tore the blanket away from the shape and the scream choked inside her throat.

It was not Bébert lying like a broken doll in the wheelbarrow. It was Mémé. Her head was slumped to one side and her eyes were closed as if she were merely taking one of her usual naps. Most of the pins holding her chignon together had fallen at some point so that long loose strands of yellow-white hair hung over the backboard of the wheelbarrow. Someone had tucked her long coal gray skirt around her ankles but her shiny button boots pointed toward the sky as they rested against the board over the handles. Her other hand, the one that wasn't hanging over the side of the wheelbarrow, was clutching her breast. A small pathetic fist had tried to shore up the flow of blood which now maculated her blouse, whose stream as it had dribbled between her clenched fingers down the length of her sleeve was already coagulating in an ugly rust stain.

Nanette knelt by the wheelbarrow now. She took in hers Mémé's poor hand, the one that wasn't smeared with blood and fondled it while whispering words I could not hear. She was rubbing between her palms Mémé's hand, blowing on it like one does to warm cold fingers. On and on, as if she expected Mémé to open her eyes again and smile apologetically the way she had done so often at family gatherings. And as I stared at her, outwardly numb yet incredibly aware inside, I knew she did not know she was crying Nanette, that she did not feel those big hot drops of hurt raining down her cheeks. She just kept on kneeling there, brushing away the green stain of grass smearing Mémé's forehead, gathering to the chignon the loose strands of gray hair, smoothing the blood-stained skirt. I wanted to scream at them to do something, anything. And then she gasped on a sob, Nanette, and swallowed all her misery in one strangled choke and the tears stopped running down her cheeks. She rose slowly, looked upward at the now mauve sky darkening above the roof-tops and inhaled very deeply like a runner before a race. She held the lungful of summer air captive inside her chest for a few seconds and then let go. I had never seen her so frighteningly composed as when she turned to us again.

"Monsieur Matthieu, Philippe, would you take her inside," she directed. "Tina, you show them Mémé's room, lay her on the bed. Madame Tardieux, could you go get Louise and ask Lisette to fetch Marcel and then come to our house. Son, you come here!" Her hands framed Guigui's face, held it straight when he tried to turn it aside, hard, as if she were trying to hypnotize him out of his grief. He struggled a little but she was stronger and the determination in her eyes mesmerized him. "I know you loved Mémé, son, and I know the pain that is in your heart but you got to keep it inside. It's your poor father I am worried about because there ain't no one closer to a man than his mother. It's going to be much harder on him that it will ever be on either of us, and whatever our grief, we got to keep it bottled up 'cause your father's going to need all the strength we can give him. You understand what I am saying, don't you?" Guigui bit his lips, nodded silently. "I want you to go to the workshop, Guigui and tell your father what has happened. I can't because I got to see to Mémé: we can't let him see her like that, can we? I don't know the words you can use, but whatever comes from your heart will be right. Now, off you go, son!" She swiveled him around, pointed him toward the Faubourg de Chavenay. "You two gawkers, go on home, there ain't nothing to see here!" she said angrily to the two fisher boys before pushing me inside the house.

They wheeled Mémé inside the front hallway and I showed the Matthieus up the staircase, told them where to lay their burden of death. I turned on the light in the bedroom, closed the shutters. I threw back the fat eiderdown so they could lay her body flat on the pink blanket, and then the three of us stood at the foot of the bed watching her. You could not tell there was no life left in her: she was wounded and a little tired, and perhaps just a bit too still. But she looked to me the way she had the morning of Guigui's communion when I had awakened her as her head rested on the pillow under the crucifix. Her dress was dirty, that's all. Death didn't change a person, it just made them look like they were a paler, like their sleep was deeper because of some tremendous fatigue and that it would take more shaking to wake them up. But there was no pain on either side: not in her and not in me. Her fist was clenched but then so were mine, and I knew if I pinched her she would not feel it. There was a bruise on her neck, a dark purple blotch and her lips were too tightly drawn over her false teeth. Guigui had told me Pottin's eyes were wide open and his mouth gaping when he had seen his body but Mémé was not like that. It would have been scary if she had been like Pottin, gaping at the ceiling with her mouth and eyes. I circled the bed, walked right up to her head and peered closer at her. She looked like she always had, Mémé, and I still loved her and she did not scare me one bit. I bent toward her in a sudden impulse to feel under my lips the reassuring mellowness of her warm wrinkles, to hug her neck as I had done so many times in joy or childish despair. It was a high and big bed Mémé slept in and I had to raise myself on tiptoes, stretch over the sheets in order to reach her forehead. My lips brushed her skin and at last discovered how cold she was. That's why Nanette had tried to warm her hand between hers. Her forehead was like snow under my mouth, except it wasn't melting: it just remained cold, so very cold as I kissed her a second time. Then old Matthieu and his son took me away from her and led me out of the room and back down the stairs. As I looked at Aunt Louise coming through the front door, I finally knew that she would never be warm again, Mémé, no matter how many times I might kiss her.

Nanette and Aunt Louise quickly disappeared upstairs and I stayed in the kitchen with the Matthieus, poured them some wine as Nanette had instructed me. Then I leaned back and watched them. They sat on each end of our kitchen table, holding their glasses, afraid to drink, afraid to look at me. None of us spoke but the water faucet over the kitchen sink still dripped over the cracked porcelain sink. The pan Nanette had shooed in her haste still laid on the tiled floor under the window, its handle thrown over the encyclopedia. The checker board with its black pieces still poised for Guigui's unclaimed victory sat next to it, exactly as we had left it a thousand hours ago.

I was comforted when Uncle Marcel and Lisette arrived. I don't think I could have stood it much longer in the kitchen alone with the Matthieus. I kissed them both and they greeted Philippe and his father. Uncle was still in his work clothes and a blotch of white paint had dried on his mustache, across his cheek and I wanted to tell him but couldn't find the words.

"Where are they, child?" he asked me softly.

"Upstairs preparing Mémé,"

"Has Gilbert been told yet?"

"Guigui is with him now."

"Poor lad. Think I'll go over there, talk to Gilbert a while before I bring him back,"

We were whispering. The Matthieus, sitting on the edge of their chairs, were looking at us. They seemed more at ease now: they had done their part and that was that. They had hardly spoken a word and they had kept their heads lowered. But now we knew and the burden was no longer theirs. They respected our grief while waiting for an appropriate moment to take their leave. Lisette had left the front door open and now Madame Tardieux came back: she was wearing her house coat.

"Thought I'd come back and lend a hand. Nanette won't have time to worry about dinner, Monsieur Germain, I know. But you people should eat. Between Lisette and myself we can whip up something if the child will show us where everything is, won't you Tina?"

She patted my cheek. She was trying to whisper too, Madame Tardieux, but she was having a hard time of it and here and there a syllable would come through her usual pitch and startle me. Perhaps it was because it was getting dark in the kitchen: her silhouette etched itself, black and flat against the almost phosphorescent dusk glued to the window panes.

"I'd better close the shutters on my way out," Uncle whispered next to me as if he too had felt the same ethereal uneasiness which had just been on my mind.

There was a shuffling of feet at the table: old Matthieu half stood up.

"Time we should be going me and Philippe, Monsieur Germain. My wife will be waiting and it's quite a ways back to the farm."

"No, no, Mr. Matthieu," Uncle interrupted him hastily. "I'd be grateful if you could stay a while longer, "till I bring back Monsieur Marchand. He'll want to know how it happened."

Matthieu's shadow reintegrated the chair.

"We won't be long, Mr. Matthieu, you have my word. Lisette, pour them some more wine."

I saw his ghost framed in the window before he closed the shutters and then it was night in the kitchen and I switched on the light. We all blinked under the raw yellow bulb. From upstairs came a thud and a shuffling of feet on the bare bedroom floor. Madame Tardieux looked at the ceiling.

"A tragedy!" she voiced nodding her head in dismay. "Such a good lady she was. A real tragedy!"

After that we did not speak much. The Matthieus sipped their wine in silence and I showed Lisette where the colander was and I told Madame Tardieux the condiments and the suet were in the cupboard above the sink. I took the plates and the glasses and set them on the dining-room table and I came back for the cutlery and opened the drawer where we kept our napkins. I saw Mémé's still folded in a triangle: I took it along with ours and laid it next to her plate as though she were going to join us for dinner. I knew she wouldn't but somehow it did not enter my mind not to set up her plate: I had to do things just the way I had always done them.

A half-hour went by like five minutes and then the men came back and simultaneously I heard the door being shut upstairs and Aunt Louise came down the stairs followed by Nanette. It was hard to look at Bébert because he looked vulnerable as if he were standing naked in the middle of the kitchen and did not know it and none of us dared say a word even though his nakedness was an embarrassment. He wasn't crying now but he had cried: heavy tears probably whose sting had left red scars on his retina and puffed his eyelids. His ashen cheeks were drawn and there was a trail of wet saw-dust on the left side of his nose where he had crushed a tear with his finger. Guigui had not been as strong as Nanette had wished because he had cried too, still wept a little as he held on to his father's arm. The Matthieus had risen from their chairs and waited like the rest of us for someone to break the awkwardness.

"I'm going up to see her now," Bébert broke at last. He swallowed hard. "It won't take me a minute, Matthieu, but I have to see her first." He turned toward the door. "You stay here, son," he said shaking off Guigui's hand. "I want to be alone with her."

We all stood there listening to his heavy footsteps crushing each stair with his grief. Lisette was sobbing by the stove, the tears raining down to her double chin until Nanette handed her her handkerchief. Madame Tardieux was whispering to Aunt Louise by the porcelain sink pointing at steaming pots and pans. Philippe Matthieu had moved to his father's side and the two of them stood by the window framing the encyclopedia and toppled frying pan. We did not wait long because Bébert kept his word and returned shortly. The trail of sawdust was gone from his nose and his hair looked slightly damp: I thought he had washed his face.

He stepped right through the kitchen to the dining-room, waved for the Matthieus to follow him. Then we all sat around the dining-room table but it was no longer the runway to merriment it had been a few weeks earlier when we had dressed it for Guigui's first communion. Bébert sat at one end but no one sat across form him at the other end, not even Nanette, because that would have been Mémé's place.

"Now, Monsieur Matthieu, tell us what happened!" Bébert prompted him while staring at the empty plate in front of him.

"Well, M'sieur Marchand," old Matthieu began as if he was not sure what he had to say was all that important. "There ain't much to tell. The Boches did it, that's all about there is to it. Philippe here, he's the one that saw it all."

"Philippe?' Bébert shot looking up for the first time.

"It was like this, M'sieur Marchand. I was behind my plow working our field that's up a way behind the farm, right above the Chérisy brook. I'd seen her come up the road to The Gaux round about three just like I'd seen her many times with her basket and her bill-hook, climbing up the path slow like. I yelled to her not to stray too far up 'cause I'd seen them Boches with their dogs scouring about the countryside since noon. Guess she didn't hear me though 'cause the next time I saw her she was clear up the hill, well on her way to your place up there at The Gaux. She looked no bigger than the crows that eat up our corn. I kind of worried when I saw how far she had strayed but then I thought for sure, even if they saw her the Boches, they weren't likely to bother her seeing she was just an old lady going 'bout her business. So I went back to my plow, thinking she'd be alright - - -"

"I had warned her about going to the fields," Nanette cut in angrily, "God knows I had told her!"

"Be quiet, Nanette! Go on Philippe," Bébert snapped. His eyes had not left young Matthieu's lips since he had begun to speak.

"Guess it must've been a good hour later that it happened 'cause I had almost finished the field and the mare was puffing and slowing down and I had to whip her to get her up through the last furrows. Staring at her rump I was like I'd been all afternoon when the firing started. When I looked up the top of the hill was crawling with crows, except they weren't crows, they were them Boches, as whole lot of them come from nowhere. And they were firing those machine guns of theirs. The mare bolted and I was thrown off clear of my plow but held on tight to the bridle and gave it a couple of nasty pulls. They were still shooting behind the plow. I looked up again after a while and saw three black dots way out on my right, running, and the Boches on my left and in between the two that little speckle, lonely like and then there was another round of machine gun fire and the dot in the middle disappeared and I ducked and laid flat on the earth eating dirt. I stayed low for a long time, 'til the silence was back, still holding on to the bridle. Then I heard a jeep stop at the edge of my field and two German officers hopped off and came toward me. They looked me over suspicious like and poked my ribs with the butt of their machine guns. I told them I hadn't seen nothing, that I'd been plowing my field all afternoon and didn't know beans about them guys from the resistance. They checked my papers, looked over the plow and the mare, surveyed the field and spoke in German. After a while they headed for their jeep again but then one of the two turned to me and said there was an old woman up there, that she'd been shot and I should take care of her. I asked them if she was alive and they said "Nein." He threw his callused hands in the air, sighed and shrugged helplessly as he looked around the table. "That's about it…"

"Then the son came to fetch me and we went and got her. She was dead alright. Don't think she ever knew what hit her," old Matthieu explained as an after-thought. "No sir: she never felt a thing, I'm sure…"

"Bloody Boches!" Nanette spat between her lips. "Why didn't she listen to me, why?" she pounded the table. "Why?"

"Thank you, Matthieu," Bébert said ignoring his wife's outburst. "I am very grateful to you. Sorry we held you up so long but it was important that we know, you understand?"

"Sure M'sieur Marchand," Matthieu said getting up. "It just grieves me that it had to be Philippe and me brought her back but we couldn't leave her up there…"

They left the Matthieus, Philippe pushing the now empty wheelbarrow with the blanket tossed into it. After a few minutes Madame Tardieux, too, left. No, no, she didn't want to stay for dinner she whispered to Nanette on her way out but she would be back in the morning to help.

And thus we sat around the table in the dining-room, Bébert presiding at its head with myself sitting between Guigui and Lisette on his right. Nanette went into the kitchen, she brought back a pan of steaming leek soup, placed it at the center of the table and sat back in her chair, silently. But after a while she got up again because Bébert had not moved and started ladling the soup into our plates. The clang of the metal ladle hitting the copper of the pan was the only noise competing with the ticking of the Swiss clock behind me. Soon we were all served and waiting for Nanette, Bébert, someone to start eating so the rest of us could follow. At last Uncle Marcel, after having glanced at Nanette and imperceptibly raised his shoulders at Lisette, took his spoon and made for the soup. It had just hit the bottom of his plate when Bébert interrupted him.

"Just a minute, Marcel," he said placing his left hand on Uncle's forearm. He looked intensely at Guigui who sat to his immediate right. "You get up, son, and you say Grace loud and clear so as she can hear you." His voice choked but he held it under control. "Don't know what possessed her to always say them behind my back, poor mother. I didn't mind really, 'twas what she believed in…" He was reaching beyond death, Bébert, to the reality of yesterday which was already a memory, a frozen shrine from within which dead old Mémé from this evening hence would watch the rest of us go forward in time while we forced her backward into our past because it was the only course her death had left us with. "You go on, son speak up and say them Grace."

So Guigui rose and said Grace but not loud and clear because he was torn and his voice broke over "Jesus" and "food". We ate our soup in utter silence like we always did except it wasn't the same silence: it was something to do but you couldn't stretch the pretense and eventually we all were done with the soup. No one looked at anyone else but the things, the objects around us got our full attention and suddenly there where many I had never seen or noticed before. There was also Nanette's nervous sniffle and Uncle's heavy breathing on my left, and Lisette shuffling her feet under the table and Nanette rising again; her chair screeching against the parquet floor when she pushed it back. There were lots of things and noises to keep one pretending this was a night like any other old night. Except it wasn't and Uncle made that clear presently when he wiped his mustache and crossed his arms over his paunch preparing to speak.

"Now cousin," he began after clearing his throat. "This is war and there ain't no time for niceties. Under different circumstances I wouldn't talk to you about them nasty details tonight, but the Allies may be marching into Dormans any day now or we may be hit by another bombardment…We got to lay her to rest soon as we can, Bébert. We got to arrange a proper church funeral, have Father Rocas give her the last rites. I know you ain't much of a church goer, but like you said, 'twas what she believed in' and we got to respect that. There's the coffin to worry about and all of them formalities though I reckon Lisette can help us with them. Hate to rush you in your grief, Bébert, but in times of war there ain't no choice, not if we are going to see to it that she's put to rest next to her husband before the fireworks hit town!"

"Marcel's right, Gilbert," Aunt seconded between her thin lips. "We got to settle everything tonight 'cause we don't know what's liable to happen tomorrow or the day after."

I looked at Bébert; he sat back in his chair, stared at the unused plate I had laid for Mémé. He had not touched his soup: he had just been staring inside himself all this time while we had been stretching our alibi.

"I agree with Louise and Marcel," came Nanette's voice from the kitchen. "Bébert, we got to decide about Mémé tonight: it's what she would have advised. We'll get Father Rocas in first thing in the morning, Lisette can post a notice tomorrow and we can have the people pay their respects tomorrow night, then come Thursday we can give her a proper funeral." She was standing in the kitchen door and her eyes wandered to Mémé's plate. "God how she loved that husband of hers," she mused, "even after all her widowed years. Young too she was when he was killed but she wouldn't have anyone else though she could've. Poor Mémé … they are together now, Bébert, that's the way to look at it, her and your father up there together again…"

She was trying hard to ease his pain, Nanette, but I could tell he was only hearing what he wanted. No matter what she said, his grief spoke louder to him than she ever could.

"Don't have any good wood for her coffin…" he mumbled painfully. "…just the kind that'll rot three days after we put her into the ground. She should have better than that - -"

"And she will!" Nanette interrupted him. I think she was encouraged he had started speaking again, Bébert as she sat down. As long as she kept him talking he wouldn't have time to think about the misery. "What about my mahogany?"

"What mahogany?" Bébert asked turning a blank stare to her.

"You know very well what I am talking about, Gilbert Marchand! My mahogany, the one you've been saving for me since you did the work for the Church's sacristy a good ten years ago! Promised to make me a fine dresser, you did, one of them objets d'art like they say, except you never did seeing I'm just your wife and not a paying customer!"

She was trying to lure him into a smile but there were really too many tears pent up in his heart. So she bent across Guigui and laid her hand on his instead.

"I don't need one of them objet d'art, Bébert, wouldn't fit with what we have. I'd rather she have it," she squeezed his fingers and he looked deep into her eyes. "Where is it, Bébert?"

I thought he was going to start crying again but instead he looked at his folded napkin next to his untouched plate and started toying with it.

"I'm not sure, probably in the loft above the workshop, I don't know…"

"Yes you do, Bébert! First thing in the morning we'll get it down so as you can start…"

But another sweeping tide of misery was lapping at Bébert's shore so he got up before she had finished what she was going to say. He did not look at any of us, did not say 'goodnight' or anything as we stared at each other helplessly. But once he was out of our sight, almost out of the kitchen, we heard his voice saying he was going upstairs now. He didn't want any of us to worry because he would be alright but he didn't want any of us to come in either. I heard him close the kitchen door as I wondered where I was going to sleep, and about my nightgown. The prospect of the attic terrified me.

I slept with Nanette that night, in the big bed Bébert and she had shared since their wedding night in the room next to where Mémé laid on hers, dead. She held me tight in the dark and she talked about Mémé as if she felt it was necessary for her to explain death to me. But I had seen death and there was nothing to explain. Still, I listened to her and even asked questions. She roamed through memories like on leafs through a photo album and Mémé was in turn laughing and readjusting he dentures, her blue eyes were twinkling again and she was teasing and bashful and mischievous and contentious, and, and. She was Mémé , like I had always known her and when I fell asleep on Nanette's shoulder, she was as alive as she had been that morning after breakfast.

The following day flew by like a school day: slow while it progressed but incredibly fast in retrospect. Bébert had left for his workshop long before dawn. I found Madame Tardieux in the kitchen relieving Nanette who had gone to the church to fetch Father Rocas. Aunt Louise, she informed me, had left for the cemetery to see Morel, the grave-digger, about opening the family plot, and Guigui was at Doctor Martin's seeing about the death certificate. She served me breakfast then sat across from me at the kitchen table, sipping hot chicory from the old mustard jar. She too talked about Mémé : what a good life she had had and what a good woman she had been, and said that all things considered, if it had to happen, we should all be thankful that it happened so fast without her feeling any pain. I asked her how she could tell Mémé had not suffered in that field all by herself and reminded her how tightly her small fist had clenched her breast as she laid in the wheelbarrow. It didn't mean anything Madame Tardieux insisted: "nerves, that's all it was." Sometimes they continued to act up after a person had been dead and chickens, for instance, could keep running several meters after one had chopped off their heads. Nerves. I pushed away my plate and said I did not want to eat my slice of bread. She nodded and said she understood and that anyway I should get dressed because people would start coming soon.

Father Rocas came around ten. He wore a deep violet stole over his black cassock and carried a small black bag. He and Nanette disappeared upstairs and stayed there for a good fifteen minutes and when they returned his arm was around her shoulders. He patted my cheek on his way out. He was followed by Doctor Martin who did not wear a stole but also carried a black leather bag except his was bigger than Father Rocas'. "Terrible! Terrible!" he muttered on his way upstairs and again on his way out. He too patted my cheek as I held the front door open for him as he left.

The family joined us for a potluck lunch. Bébert who did not want any remained at the workshop working on his mother's coffin. Lisette reported that Oberleutnant Redlich had stopped by her office that morning and asked that she convey his deepest condolences to the Marchands, he had been fond of the old lady.

Nanette pinched her lips but said nothing. Aunt Louise reported on her visit to Morel: they would open the grave in the morning and they would have to move Mémé's brother to another compartment so she could be laid next to Pépé. After her, there would be only two slots left and if they all wanted to be together something should be done eventually about enlarging the plot. At any rate, the grave would be ready for Mémé at four the next afternoon. Uncle Marcel said that was fine because Monsieur Pichegrus, the undertaker, had promised to have the horse-drawn hearse in front of our house by two-thirty in time to get to the church for the three o'clock funeral mass and then take Mémé to her final resting place. I sat, ate and listened. It wasn't Mémé they were talking about. It was death, and death was just a corpse that had to be disposed of somehow but whose riddance required the cooperation of lots of people and the going through of pre-established formalities. A business, little more, and Mémé and I never had had much of a mind for business.

Later that afternoon came the people of Dormans who had known Mémé and wanted to see her one last time. There were also those who hadn't known her but owed money to Bébert and thought paying their respects would be taken on account of whatever their outstanding debt; and there were those who hadn't known her and owed no money but came because her death was what everyone in Dormans was talking about. Some I knew, most I did not. I manned the front door and watched the procession. Most wore their Sunday clothes because in Dormans one only owned one set of good clothes and thus regardless of whether the occasion be sad or happy, a funeral or a wedding, so long as the function was official, one donned one's uniform. Endlessly they filed in. Those we hardly knew did not stop in the dining-room. But those who we knew did. They included Mademoiselle Rouleau who stayed quite a while talking to the family because she knew all about grief. She wore the same black dress she had worn for Guigui's communion minus the pin because this was no time for butterflies. Love drifted through my mind then left with her when she kissed me goodbye. There was Mayor Chancel wearing his tricolor cummerbund and a face dressed for the circumstance. He said a few lofty words about sacrifices and heartbreaks and war and Frenchmen. Monsieur Lucien, the owner of the bookstore on the Place du Luxembourg came but said not a word about rights. Langiers' boss, Maitre Pinson who never looked you straight in the eyes and was well into his eighties, came dressed in a black frock-coat with a high hat led by a silver knob stick. He recollected that he had drawn up the marriage contract between Pépé and Mémé when he was a young clerk just out of law school, which didn't make him any younger. Madame Pottin, recently widowed, drew the inevitable parallel between her loss and ours. Then there was Madame Martin and her four daughters: she made the error of inquiring about Bébert and was ever so embarrassed upon being told that he was working on the coffin. There were Bébert's and Uncle Marcel's colleagues from the voluntary fire brigade who came as one, the youngest of them carrying a home-made wreath of red and white carnations with a nice blue ribbon around it inscribed with something or other, and even old grumpy Chalembert who surprisingly brought us a gift of a chicken "'cause you'll need a square meal after the funeral." Langiers, at last, who wore his mysterious ring and lingered in the kitchen whispering to Lisette for a while. People.

Well after nightfall, Bébert came back accompanied by Uncle Marcel who had gone to the workshop that afternoon to give him a hand. We were all tired from the day and ate in silence after Guigui had said grace. No one asked about the coffin until after Bébert had gone upstairs to spend her last night in the house with Mémé. Only then did Uncle Marcel say it was beautiful like they used to make before the war, with brass handles and white satin inside and they had even lacquered it and he hoped it should be dry by morning. That night I slept again with Nanette but she didn't reminisce about Mémé and her goodnight kiss was perfunctory. She rolled over to the far side of me after putting out the light: within minutes she was snoring in the pitch-black void of the bedroom. I heard Bébert pace in Mémé's room, tanks rolling past our windows. Guess I must have been dreaming when I saw the drunk Boche lying inside the casing of quilted white satin. I couldn't see his face because it was covered with potato peels which Léo the Pig was browsing with his dirty snout, but I had other ways of telling it was him.

The next morning I woke up with lead in my head and a cramp in my right arm. Nanette had pushed back the shutters and the sun pouring through the curtains drew a checker-board of shadows and light on the wall adjoining Mémé's room. I sat on the edge of the bed feet dangling, rubbing my shoulder while I watched a lonely sparrow chirping away behind the crochet curtain on the windowsill. It was a small one just out of the shell a few weeks. Soon it spread its left wing, pecked and pecked at it, then without transition it took flight in a trill of chirps. I got up, wandered to the empty landing. There were voices coming from downstairs and a gust of summer air brushed my bare calves, flew past my feet and arms. The door to Mémé's room was closed and I hesitated a second before turning the doorknob. Two days since I had looked at her, not since the Matthieus had brought her back all tired and dirty.

The door heaved a drawn out squeak when I pushed it open. I blinked: the shutters were closed but the flame of the lone candle dancing on the flowers blinded me. Slowly I made out the chrysanthemums and the gladiolas, the carnations and the lilacs and even the potted purple hyacinth sitting on the dresser next to the plaster-of-Paris Virgin Mary. My cot in the alcove was a medallion in full bloom. Flowers, such and orgy of them that it was hard to imagine Mémé could sleep in their overpowering blended scent as if the room were still the same. She was in her Sunday best, the brown velvet one with the lace collar buttoned up under her chin. Her hands were folded on her chest, peaceful like, over a mother-of-pearl rosary. She wasn't in pain or dirty any more. Her yellowing white hair was neatly combed back and there were no more wrinkles on her forehead.

"Tina? Is that you child?"

The slats of the parquet floor squeaked under Bébert's cautious steps and then fell silent again when he stood next to me.

"Saying goodbye to Mémé, are you, child?" he whispered as his arm enfolded my shoulders.

I stared up at him, surprised.

"No, just looking at her," I whispered. "She isn't going anywhere, is she, Bébert?"

He squatted next to me, his weary face now level with mine.

"No, Tina, she isn't going anywhere, not anymore." He embraced me, squeezing hard. "She's staying here, right here, in our hearts, child, and there ain't no place where she'd rather be," his voice broke in my neck. "Now off you go, Tina," he said after a while standing up. "Off you go, child."

I almost turned back when I heard him sob. But it was an isolated sob, a single lonely cry, so I continued my descent down the staircase and started thinking about breakfast.

We ate an early lunch then Bébert and Uncle brought back the coffin. It was really beautiful and you could almost see yourself in the lacquered mahogany, and the inside looked very cozy and comfortable. I wanted to go upstairs with them but Nanette said I shouldn't and asked Madame Tardieux to stay with me in the dining-room. She sat in one chair while I sat in another wondering why my heart was beating so fast inside my chest. Then I heard the hammering upstairs and I thought maybe the noise had something to do with my heart because each time the hammer fell my heart skipped a beat and it became harder to breathe. After a while Lisette came back and said it was all done and just in time too because Pichegrus was rounding the corner of the square with the horse-drawn hearse.

After that everything happened at once: People sprung from nowhere milling outside our house, the black horse-drawn canopied hearse, Bébert and Uncle Marcel talking to men from Pichegrus' staff upstairs, Guigui cold as a trout standing in the kitchen door in his long-trousers, Aunt Louise behind him holding on to her daughter's' arm. There was some shouting because the staircase was winding and narrow so that the men had a hard time easing the coffin around its bend. Pichegrus standing in his black frock-coat at the bottom of the staircase directed the maneuvers while Nanette behind her black crepe sighed and sniffled impatiently. I remember catching a glimpse of Oberleutnant Redlich drifting past the open front door, Madame Tardieux big and black in her mourning suit, the Martins and the Pottins, Langiers and Maitre Pinson, the shuffling of feet and the whispers, the lowered eyes and the nodding of heads.

At last they started to file behind the coffin as it was carried out the front door and suddenly I thought I should go get my coat and I pushed past Aunt Louise and Guigui who stood in my way, Nanette stopped me in midflight: she grabbed my elbow with an iron grip. I looked at her but could hardly see her eyes behind the black crepe: Only her mouth was not in mourning.

"You stay here, child. I've asked Mademoiselle Rouleau to stay with you. Ain't no good your coming to church "cause it will just make you cry like that other time - - -"

"But Nanette," I cut her stammering, "I have to go!"

"Better if you don't Tina. Besides," her lips attempted to smile, "I've asked Mademoiselle Rouleau to prepare supper for when we get back from the cemetery and she can't do it all by herself. She don't know where things are or how I do things round here. So I want you to show it all to her."

"But Nanette - - - "

"I have to go now, Tina. You be a good girl and lend Mademoiselle Rouleau a hand." Her dry lips touched my forehead. "Be back soon, child!"

She left, closing the front door quietly behind her. I stood there, empty, until Mademoiselle Rouleau grabbed my hand and led me back into the dining-room. There was plenty of time until they should all be back, she said as I stood behind the lace curtain watching the funeral procession glide out of my sight, and wouldn't it be nice if the two of us had a chat, or perhaps she could read me a story, or we might draw something if I would get her some paper and crayons. The street was empty now behind the window and the house was deafeningly silent around us and I was falling, falling, falling.

I tore past Mademoiselle Rouleau out of the kitchen into the hallway. I climbed the stairs two at a time and once on the landing I flung open all the doors and the water-closet and the washroom gaped at me as did Nanette's room and that of Mémé . I didn't know what I was looking for but still I had to look, find whatever it was. I tore open the door leading to the attic and flew up the steps leading to its landing and I caught a glimpse of our laundry strung up under its roof. And then I heard myself yell and call out her name over and over, and the tears, hot and heavy, drowned my eyes and cascaded down my cheeks, like an angry fist my heart pounded against my throat.

"Mémé! Mémé ! Mémé !"

I flung open Guigui's bedroom door and wrenched the window open and then I rushed to my old room and threw open its door. Then I ran back to the landing and looked upward desperately but here were no more floors to search, only the casement window open on the blue sky so I fell into a sobbing heap against the wooden railing of the staircase and a great chunk of my heart broke into a thousand pieces.

"Mémé, Mémé, oh, Mémé!" I called between hiccups. But at last I understood why she could no longer hear me. She had left the house forever, Mémé , and no matter how thoroughly I might search or how loud I might call out her name she would never again answer me.

And then Mademoiselle Rouleau came. She slid next to me on the bleached attic floor under the laundry. She pulled a handkerchief from her sleeve and told me to blow my nose hard. When I was done she took me in her arms and rocked me against her shoulder and since I kept on crying every more wretchedly, she said everything would be alright, that I was just growing up and learning about life, and that both were sometimes painful but that the human mind was a marvelous thing because after a while it only remembered the happy times and since there had been so many for Mémé and me, then very soon I would forget the tears and only remember the laughter and the smiles we had shared, the two of us. But as my sobs continued unabated to rain on her shoulder, I only knew I wanted desperately for it to be Easter at The Gaux, for Mémé to be dozing in her long chair under the chilly April sun and for the two flies to be hovering over her gaping mouth again. And if growing up meant having to accept this tremendous despair, then I did not want to be ten in a week.

Or ever!

* * * * * * *

CHAPTER VIII

Two days after they buried Mémé I began the slow climb out of my emotional prostration. I do not remember how I passed those forty-eight hours but as Nanette recounted to me later, unable to staunch my hysteria Mademoiselle Rouleau had become so distraught that she had run all the way to the church to fetch Doctor Martin. I was still in the attic crying out what was left of my heart when they had returned. The good doctor had diagnosed an acute attack of hysteria and proceed to put me under sedation thus dispatching me into a Never land of oblivion from which Nanette extirpated me at regular intervals to pour down my throat multitudinous bowls of soup that, to this day, I do not recall ingesting. I finally woke up at six o'clock on the morning the Saturday following Mémé's funeral, not so much because I had slept myself out but rather because too-long ignored physiological demands compounded by the bowls of soup Nanette had fed me propelled me out of my cot and thence sent me tumbling to the water-closet which I do remember reaching in the nick of time. I remained seated in its long tunnel after I was done, rubbing the last remnant of soporific fuzz from my eyes and dusting my mind off the cobwebs which had held my thoughts captive. At last I was able to focus on the twinkling porcelain doorknob in front of me a ways and rose shivering and dizzy from my vertiginous ascent back into reality. I crept my way back to Mémé's bedroom to discover as I stood wobbly on its doorstep, that is was no longer hers. At the far end of the dawn-bathed bedroom another head rested on her pillow, tossing and crushing its feathers to comfort: mouth agape, ears sprouting and hair bristling, Guigui slept fitfully.

Contrary to what Mademoiselle Rouleau had tried to explain to me as I sat sobbing against her shoulder, my hysterical outburst had not been a symptom of my growing up. If anything, it had been proof of my obstinate refusal to face up to the next stage of my young life by accepting the inevitability of death. Although I remember few of the conflicting thoughts which had crowded my tortured mind that Thursday, I also admitted now with a sense of shame, that they had been evidence of my self-centered nature, and that if I truly searched my heart Mémé's potential suffering had weighed little on my mind the day of her funeral. Instead, my intemperate seizure had been a reflection of a wrong which I firmly believed had been done to me by erasing her out of my life when I trusted that people I loved should be forever part of my journey for as long as I lived. I regret to say I cried that day over Mémé much as I had cried over Léo after his execution and much for the same self-absorbed reasons. My only excuse is that I was a few days short of my tenth birthday and still under the delusion that the world revolved around me and existed for my sole benefit. But I did grow up as a result of Mémé's death and to that extent Mademoiselle Rouleau was proved right. The transformation did not occur suddenly. Instead it developed more subtly over a period of several days beginning with that Saturday morning when I joined the Marchands for breakfast.

Perhaps out of the force of habit developed over too many years, they sat where they always did Guigui, Nanette and Bébert. At first

I thought nothing of it. I was shaky from too much sleep, still nauseated by Nanette's liquid diet and not too sure footed about my rediscovered vertical stance. I squeezed myself in my assigned spot between husband and wife and silently acknowledged the fuss being made over me. But after I had answered that, yes, I felt better, and indeed an egg might be a treat, there was little more any of us had to say because we were still fresh out of the grief. Thus we settled into the uneasy silence of recent mourners and my eyes studiously avoided theirs. I searched for something on which to settle my eyes and soon they alighted on the void at the end of the table and slowly I grasped what so disturbed me about Mémé's empty chair, why it had become the only thing in the room which I could not avoid acknowledging. So long as her body had laid in the house I had temporized, now I had neither a corpse nor Mémé. What had replaced both was something more disturbing than life or death: it was the total eradication of her very existence. While alive she had been a witness to my own being and now I would have to recast the actors on the stage of my life without her. Her death now endowed me with a past and since I now had a past it followed that I had gone on to the next phase of my life or "grown up" as Mademoiselle Rouleau had put it. Ten days later, events helping and my curiosity gradually reborn, I opened myself to my new life and found it contained enough novelty to deflect me from any more thoughts of Mémé.

We followed the Allied advance in Normandy but with less anticipation. When we learned on August Second that the Americans had at last reached Avranches the previous day in what was to prove a turning point of the invasion, our reaction which two weeks earlier might have bordered on rapture, was merely a tepid acknowledgement that the war might indeed soon be over. Nanette immersed herself in her work at the WEC and Bébert spent longer hours in the solitude of his workshop although I am not sure he actually worked more.

Although no one had asked them, the Germains took to joining us daily for dinner. Aunt Louise just showed up one late afternoon carrying sundry pots and pans containing their dinner. Nanette and she busied themselves in the kitchen and we all ate in the dining room, no questions asked. Notwithstanding any hope I might have harbored, this pooling of resources turned out to be a culinary letdown, their main staple consisting much like ours of the sempiternal rutabagas. If anything, Aunt Louise's were worse because through her ministering they lost all vegetal consistency and ended up in one's mouth tasting pretty much like strips of broiled papier mache. Still, we were grateful for the Germains' presence: bodies provided there be enough of them can do a lot to neutralize the void of an eternal absence.

Uncle Marcel who had developed more of an immunity to the shock of death because of his World War I service soon established himself as our resident monologuist. At the heaviest of a silence punctuated only by the rhythmical clang of forks against china, and without prompting he would embark on a discursive political monologue which at times developed into a full-fledged dialogue wherein "for the sake of objectivity" he would act out both the lines of his imaginary opponent as well as his own and carry on a surprisingly heated argument. Or, adopting a professional tone, he would deliver rambling lectures on the art of fishing which might start anywhere from the history of the design of the fishing rod, evolve to salmon spawning in Canadian waters, and invariably end up with this own multitudinous experiences with the aquatic fauna of the Marne river. Uncle interested himself and because he could become so totally rapt in his own discursive perambulations, he somehow always succeeded in drawing one of us in his loquacious discourse. Soon a general conversation would be underway without anyone of us realizing how or when we had taken that first conversational step out of grief.

Mémé's death had brought about another intriguing development: Guigui had moved into my room thereby being the first man ever to invade my privacy. This demotion from the third to the second floor had been imposed upon him by Nanette who, because of past experience, was more anxious to safeguard my peace of mind than her son's prudery. Thus Guigui had moved in with me and as I watched him living in perpetual fear of my spying the barest inch of what he considered his most promising asset, the thought developed in my mind that notwithstanding Farther Rocas' sermons, Eve might not be entirely to blame for the original sin. I tried my best to reassure Guigui by reminding him that, after all, I had seen that of the Boche and although his had truly proven repulsive because he was so fat and drunk I did not think I would get sick again if per chance I should catch an unintended glimpse of his. But Guigui would not listen to reason: he was obsessively aware of his soggy rutabaga as I had unfortunately referred to his implement once in a flare-up of exasperated female superiority. Soon the only way we could cohabitate was on the basis of my adhering to certain rules which he set and which consisted mostly of my absorbing myself in the contemplation of the flowered wall-paper whenever necessity compelled him to ambulate through the bedroom in his nightshirt. Poor old Mémé had been much more accommodating as a roommate, but then she hadn't had a rutabaga. Perhaps there was a biblical ban against a woman seeing a man's rutabaga; maybe if one did she would turn into a "pillar of salt" like Lot's wife whose story he had recently recounted to me. Still, having a man as a roommate, despite the attendant constriction upon my freedom, opened up an imaginary door to an intriguing mystery. As I laid each night on my cot before sleep my mind was better occupied trying to elucidate masculine prudishness instead of harping over Mémé lying dead under a stone slab amid the cypresses.

On August Four I turned ten but due to our mourning status, the celebrations were kept sober. The Americans still had not made it to Dormans so the glass of champagne I had looked forward to was out. Anyway, as I had discovered two weeks earlier that one didn't automatically grow up on one's birthday, but rather that one merely added another year to one's life belt and that wasn't growing up: that was aging. Nanette, by some miracle of sheer horse-trading, managed to procure some Swiss chocolate out of which, with Madame Tardieux's contribution of two whole eggs, she managed to bake a chocolate cake so memorable that ever since all chocolate cakes I have ever sampled taste like being ten all over again. You couldn't find pink birthday candles in those days so I wished on the lone flame of the fat candle we kept for blackouts thereby I hoped guaranteeing its realization. Bébert offered me as a gift Mémé's missal. In the week that followed I read its prayers from church rite to church rite by way of the portions in Latin and the italicized cues to the priest and congregation which told them what to do and when. It wasn't the most exciting text I had ever perused but I felt I owed it to Mémé to read her prayer book in its integrity.

Something else happened on my birthday which was more important than my turning ten. Madame Tardieux, on account of the two eggs she had contributed toward its creation, was invited to partake of Nanette's culinary dessert. She came after dinner, the bearer of gifts: embroidered handkerchiefs from her and a rare bag of candies from Oberleutnant Redlich. I kissed her thank-you and invited her to sit on my right. While we sat our eyes devouring the chocolate cake Nanette was carving, she made some appropriate remarks about the significance of birthdays but sent a fleeting shiver up my spine when, wagging her forefinger in front of my nose, she stressed that I was now old by a full decade. Somehow "decade" in her mouth sounded awfully close to senility. As usual the foremost topic of conversation was the Allied advance and although no one was taking bets because of past disappointment, the guarded consensus was that within a month at most Dormans stood a fair chance of being liberated. Lisette reported that Mayor Chancel was already at work on a speech for the occasion and further, that he was quite frustrated in his efforts to come up with a symbolic key to the city which he intended presenting to the first American officer to set foot in Dormans.

"He'd like it gold-plated," she added, "says he will melt his own wedding ring if he can't find gold any other way!"

"Delusions of grandeur," Aunt Louise scoffed. "That man aims to run for President one of them days!"

"Of course he doesn't," Uncle scolded his wife. "Ain't nothing wrong in trying to do the Americans right. Only thing is they won't have time to dilly-dally listening to speeches and receiving gold keys. They'll be too busy chasing the Boches once they got them on the run!"

"Hope they get every one of them," Nanette spat. "Especially those who killed Mémé"

"There have been enough killings on both sides and more of them won't bring her back," Bébert interjected nodding his head. He had spoken so little since his mother's death that we had gotten used to his silence. His eyes wandered over our startled faces: "I'll just be glad when those bastards are out of France!"

"Gilbert is right!" Uncle approved cheerfully because he was glad Bébert had started speaking again. "Let's get them out of the country and that will be good enough for me. Eh! Eh! Madame Tardieux, you're going to lose your tenant, aren't you?"

Madame Tardieux almost choked on her mouthful of chocolate cake.

"What does he say Redlich?" Uncle persisted. "Though he was never as cocky as the rest of them and he seems like a decent fellow… if there be such a thing as a decent Boche…What does he say about all this?"

Madame Tardieux fretted in her chair. Her sudden uneasiness which was so unlike her triggered a forgotten thought in my mind.

"Well, Monsieur Germain…" she stammered as though looking for words. "We don't talk much him and me these days. Guess he is waiting like the rest of us."

"You bet he is!" Uncle chortled. "But we sure ain't waiting for the same thing!"

The widow managed a strained smile while I toyed with the embroidered handkerchiefs.

At last I spoke up. "Isn't it going to be lonely for you, Madame Tardieux, in that big house with just Albert, won't you be scared?"

"The child is right," Nanette approved sensibly. "It's a big house you have Ma'am Tardieux. Ain't a question of being scared but it's a heavy burden maintaining a house that size by oneself, and the expense! On a widow's pension you are going to have hard time!"

"As a matter of fact," Madame Tardieux perked up as if she had been given the opening she had been hoping for, "I might have a new tenant to replace Oberleutnant Redlich - -"

"Who would that be?" I blurted.

"Mademoiselle Rouleau!" she beamed.

"Mademoiselle Rouleau?" Lisette echoed surprised. "She's got free lodging at the school, why would she want to pay rent?"

"It's not a question of money," Madame Tardieux explained, "as much as a question of her wanting more privacy. It was alright when the school was run as a school and she could have some peace and quiet after classes, but with the Women's Emergency Committee - - no offense intended Madame Marchand because they do a mighty service for our community - - but it has become a bit of a railroad station –"

"That's true," Nanette agreed. "The more we help the more come pouring in!"

"Precisely!" Madame Tardieux said approvingly. "She came to see me last week and we had a long chat. Poor soul, never knew her family of course, and never had much warmth in those orphanages. They gave her a trade the nuns but not much more. Anyway, I wouldn't mind having someone around the house again to cook a proper meal for and talk to over dinner. Ain't much of a life for me these days now that Monsieur Tardieux's gone."

"It's a very good idea," Nanette said looking at Aunt Louise and then back at Madame Tardieux. "You can both do each other good. Can't they Uncle?"

"Sure can! Besides, she's quite a looker that Mademoiselle Rouleau and, mark my word, the house will be swarming with young men. Might even drop in on you myself!" Uncle finished with a wink at Aunt Louise.

"Oh no, no, no! I don't think so!" Madame Tardieux retorted too vehemently, startling Uncle. "That is, maybe later she can have some young man..." she went on attempting a smile. "Don't believe she will have visitors for a while though: peace and quiet and a little bit of home life: that's what she's looking for and I think I can give her that, you understand..." she finished leaving us to complete her thought.

A four o'clock sun speckling the water of the Marne River streamed through my mind and I had visions of bluets and intertwined legs: she wasn't telling the truth, Madame Tardieux, but it was alright. I smiled at her when she looked at me, shaped a sail out of one of her handkerchiefs and steered the imaginary boat of love toward her empty plate. He wasn't going anywhere, Oberleutnant Redlich, no matter how many Americans might come marching through Dormans.

The knowledge that Mademoiselle Rouleau had begun to implement her perilous scheme contributed greatly toward my emotional recovery. I still thought of Mémé but her features when I tried to reconstruct them were already eluding me. Bébert had been right when he had told me she would henceforth live in our hearts because it was in my heart that something stirred whenever her name was mentioned. Mémé was becoming an emotion, one which would endure far longer than any blurred portraits of her I might still be able to conjure. Thus, secure in the realization that the void at the end of the table was not replicated in my heart I reintegrated the present which, thanks to Madame Tardieux's news, throbbed again with renewed excitement.

A full month to the day after Mémé's death on August 25, Paris was liberated. As had been the case with the invasion, we learned about it the following day which was a Friday. But even before Madame Tardieux soon followed by Father Rocas, rapped her effervescent knuckles against the kitchen window, we knew something big was about to break. Ever since Thursday morning Dormans had been a town sitting on the slope of a volcano: in over four years of German occupation, we had never seen as many military convoys as thundered past our windows in those twenty-four hours. Dormans overnight had become a civilian island inside a mammoth garrison and although restricted to quarters by one of Nanette's edicts, Guigui and I never enjoyed so much our arbitrary confinement. We spent Thursday afternoon our panting breaths steaming the window panes of the dining-room, our eyes riveted to the overwhelming spectacle of the German retreat. Endlessly they rolled and thundered by, heaved and rumbled, the tanks and trucks, the jeeps and motorcycles, the anti-aircraft guns and the war materiel. And the men, so many of them, on foot, riding bicycles and even horses, or being transported tame and stiff in open trucks like toy soldiers: you could have won a war with what streamed past our windows in that single afternoon. And that evening the thundering flow continued and there was no night because there was no silence and no darkness: the mightiest army in the world had chosen to bivouac outside our windows.

Thus we were not surprised Friday morning upon hearing of the long-awaited news. For all these weeks since the invasion, Paris had been a dying man's fist thrust inside the allied flank. With the obstinacy of despair and despite gradual an ineluctable encirclement, the Germans had held on to the city knowing whomever held the capital also wielded a mighty Damocles sword over the rest of the country and that no matter how dull its blade had worn or how symbolic its threat had become, the psychological impact on the French populace of knowing their capital still under the German yoke would be as crippling a weapon as might have been a sudden transfusion of fresh divisions which at that point they were incapable of mustering. Now Paris had fallen, or rather had been resurrected from its comatose torpor and the rest of the country could look forward to convalescence followed by complete recovery. We could in truth say - - and believe it for the first time - - that it would be a matter of days before "they" marched into Dormans as Bébert said at lunch that day. We were so exhilarated at the prospect that it did not dawn on us, despite the several hundred enemy soldiers camping through the town, that the physical liberation of Dormans itself might bring war, death and gunfire outside our doorstep if not in our house. Happiness is rarely realistic and in our joy that Friday we travelled the historical light-years between occupation and liberation as if the transition were to be immediate, certainly one whose evolutionary process was devoid of danger or painful transmutations. Paris was free and so were we.

However that same evening an incident was to take place which not only exposed the extravagance of our premature rejoicing but also brought within the confines of the kitchen the terrifying side of the German occupation which apart from Mémé's death we had seldom confronted in four years of living under their hegemony – and which we had completely discounted that very morning upon hearing Paris had been liberated.

As had become their custom since Mémé's death, the Germains came for dinner. But this was an unusual day and to mark the occasion Uncle Marcel, much to Aunt Louise's dismay, stepped into the kitchen brandishing a magnum of Champagne recently unearthed form its cache in their back garden. He insisted we should pop it open before dinner. He was exuberant and determined to be jolly and the women's pleas that it was the sacrosanct hour for dinner would not sway him. The rutabagas could wait but he could not, nor could the good health of De Gaulle and the Americans. "Besides we ain't drunk to Tina's birthday yet!" A churlish Aunt Louise put our supper on the slow-burner while Nanette retrieved the gala flutes out of the sideboard and Guigui and I pranced around the dining-room table at the end of which a petulant Uncle proceeded to uncork his exhumed magnum. Even Bébert seemed contaminated by our pervasive exultation and for the first time in many days, we had him chuckling again. After the champagne had been poured we sat around the table. Aunt Louise anxious to get this inane celebration out of the rutabagas' way raised her glass to her thin lips and half-thrust a gray tongue before Uncle called her to order by rattling his fork against his flute. He glared at her and for a second she sat defiantly glaring back at him. In the end, however, his eyebrows circumflexed in an intimation of outrage got the better of her. Thus we all sat back, returned our brimming flutes to the table and waited for that speech Uncle was so obviously determined to impose on us.

As Uncle speeches went this was one of his better ones and one in which I figured prominently seeing that I was from Paris, that my mother often cited, was now basking in the sunshine of freedom and that, as a result of the glorious events which had unfolded the previous day, they and I could look forward to a reunion with my mother which, Uncle added hastily noticing my consternation, would not mean a prolonged separation: they would all visit me in Paris and I, of course, should always think of Dormans as my second home. He closed with touching remarks in which Mémé was remembered and asked her to extend upon her beloved and loving relatives the blessing of the Lord whose realm she now inhabited and where we should all meet again come our respective time. We were all close to tears as Uncle himself, equally moved by his own delivery, opted not to proceed any further. We reached for our flutes and I had barely shivered under the first prickly swallow of champagne when the doorbell rang and almost instantaneously, imperative fists rapped against the kitchen window in a drumfire of urgency. Since Mémé's funeral the front door had become my responsibility so that I hopped down from my seat and proceeded towards the hallway. I spotted the outlines of several large and ghostly shadows behind the crochet curtain of the dusky kitchen when I passed it, but considering the many soldiers encamped outside our house since the previous day, I did not make anything of them. Behind me in the dining-room the conversation had resumed and I heard Uncle's thick laughter peal over some grownup joke.

I was not prepared for the fury which rushed the house as I drew open the front door. My head was still thrust forward inquisitively and my hand still clasped the doorknob when someone forcefully shoved it wide open. It slammed me into the coat rack behind the door as slightly dazed, I landed perpendicularly against the wall. Seven lustrous pair of boots marched past me, thumped their way through the kitchen and the voices, in a threatening cacophony, silenced Uncle's laughter. I caught a glimpse of a command jeep parked in front of the house but the SS standing at attention next to it didn't smile at me when our eyes met.

There were five of them in all: three SS soldiers, standing stiffly at attention at the far right of the dining-room behind Lisette. Their eyes at attention like them, stared fixedly at a point in the center of the table. Opposite them at the far left of the room, their backs to the window and facing the table where we still sat, stood an SS officer and his aide, the latter posted a few steps behind the former. The officer was not much taller than Lisette but as he stood behind Bébert's chair, so very erect that I could almost feel the same horizontal bar straining my back as must be straining his, he seemed as tall as Herr Kommandant Blücher. His face was oddly asymmetrical with an upper half that didn't match the lower half. His forehead, wide and bulging between the eyebrow line and the black brim of his officer's cap, seemed to crush the rest of his face from the eyes on down to the sharp angle of his jutting chin. His recessed eyes swept our faces while he proceed to remove meticulously his black leather gloves. As he caught sight of Uncle's bottle of champagne at the center of the table his lips twitched before tightly drawing into a thin smile. We all startled when he spoke.

"Well gentlemen," he said ostensibly looking at the three SS soldiers, "We seem to have interrupted a celebration, Nein? What do you think they are celebrating? Could it perhaps be the liberation of Paris? Tell me, what do you think?"

Hands clasped behind his back he walked around the table. His French was flawless. A hint of smile drifted on the Germans' faces as he passed each of them. I retreated a few steps inside the kitchen when he passed me to take a stand behind Bébert's chair.

"Yes, I believe that is precisely what the champagne is for. And it is as it should be."

His eyes swept the table again. The rhythmical hiss of his leather gloves slashing through the air as he flapped them against the open palm of his left hand was the only noise breaking the silence. My eyes were riveted to them and when they at last fell limp and still between his hands, I held on to my breath, every fiber of my being taut.

"Indeed it is as it should be!" he repeated. "However," he continued and in the way he let the words hang inside our continuing silence there lurked a threat. He threw back his shoulders and grew so tall that I thought only he was stopping the ceiling from crashing on our heads. "However," he said again looking first at his gloves then abruptly at Nanette: "Dormans is a long way from the capital and the Americans: is it not? And, unfortunately, Dormans is still under

German control, and so, perhaps the celebration is a little premature. Do you not agree Monsieur?" he finished bending toward Uncle.

I shot a glance at Uncle. His mustache quivered in an intimation of anger or fear, I was not sure which, but then he confronted the SS officer squarely until one could not tell whose eyes were holding whose. At last he shrugged and with forced bonhomie pointed a finger at me. I shrunk back inside the kitchen.

"That's who we are celebrating," he said calmly. "We were drinking to the health of this little girl because it is her 10th birthday!' He lied brazenly.

The SS swiveled his entire body towards me.

"When were you born?" He asked me sharply.

"She was born on July 30, ten years ago," Uncle cut me off his eyes now boring into mine. "But her Mémé was shot around about then so the child's birthday had to wait."

"What do you mean, she was shot? She died, Nein?" The SS asked rapt in contemplation of his black leather gloves.

"No I mean she was shot!"

"You are trying to confuse me, are you not, Monsieur?" the German spoke now peering at Uncle.

"No again! Her Mémé was shot and the child's birthday had to wait. Ask them!" Uncle snapped back waving his hand in our direction. "Ask them if you don't believe me!"

"That's right!" Nanette nodded across the table.

"Absolutely!" Bébert echoed her with conviction.

"And a shame it is having you lot spoil it all for her a second time!" came Aunt Louise between pinched lips.

They had all three spoken simultaneously and this sudden barrage seem to rile the SS officer. He stiffened, stepped back and took in the whole table. His eyes seemed to retreat even further into their sockets; above them, showing distinctly in the glare of the electric bulb, were the skull and eagle emblazoned on his officer's cap.

"Liars, bloody French Liars!" he screamed at all of us. "It is the Americans, it is the Allies, it is the liberation of your capital that you were celebrating! You are celebrating the defeat of the German Reich!"

A glacial shiver went up my spine and fear suddenly clamped a vise around my heart. I groped blindly for Nanette's hand which was expecting mine. She drew me to her, wound her arm around my waist. An invisible tide of anguish swept over the room as Guigui, Lisette, Uncle, Bébert, Nanette and Aunt Louise drew closer to each other.

Meanwhile the SS Officer had walked to the window under the impassive joint stares of his cohort. I too watched him around Nanette's shoulder. He put on his left hand leather glove, raised a corner of the crochet curtain with a black forefinger. Soon I couldn't hear him breathe anymore. He let go of the curtain. When he turned to us again, he smiled, the most terrifying falsely benign smile I had ever seen.

"Hemmler!" He motioned to the SS who had stood behind him. "The Report, Bitte!"

The young SS officer opened a leather satchel I had not noticed earlier. It had a brass combination lock. He rummaged briefly through its contents and pulled out a sheet of paper which he held ready for his superior.

"I am Obersturmfuhrer Steigl!" The SS officer introduced himself at last temporarily ignoring the proffered document. His voice was cold and official, the same voice which had inquired about the object of our celebration minus the sarcasm. "I have been called to Dormans from Reims to investigate a matter of importance to the German Kommandatur of your city. Hemmler!"

He took the offered document, poured over its contents. His eyebrows were drawn in a falsely deliberate frown. After a while he looked up at us again, searching our faces.

"Who is Gilbert Marchand?" he shot.

Bébert stiffened in his chair as if Steigl had whipped him.

"I am Gilbert Marchand," he said half raising himself from his chair.

"Very well, Monsieur Marchand," Steigl continued while circumventing the table, he stationed himself behind Uncle and Guigui in order to face Bébert. "Are you the owner of the property abutting the Château at a place called," he checked his papers, "at a place called 'The Gaux'?"

"I am the one who owns a house up there!" Nanette cut in. "I am the owner. It's been in my family for eighty years - - "

"And who are you, Madame?" Steigl interrupted her casting a brief glance at her.

"I am his wife, I am Antoinette Marchand."

Obersturmfuhrer Steigl smiled imperceptibly.

"Of course, of course. But if you are married to Monsieur Marchand, then it is his house too, is it not?"

"Of course it is!" Bébert agreed glaring at his wife.

"When were you there last?"

Bébert looked at Nanette. Standing so close to her as I was, I was able to read in his eyes a creeping awareness. But it flitted through them very fast, as though he wanted to silence the very thought lest it might betray him. He stared at the empty plate in front of him, fingering the stem of his flute.

"Can't rightly recall. It's been a while though," he answered in a dull voice.

Nanette's arm was crushing my waist.

"What with the bombardments we ain't been able to get up there much. It ain't safe up those hills!" she barged in.

Steigl paced the length of the table, swooped around, and walked back a few steps to Guigui who stared at his father.

"Perhaps the children can help you remember!" Steigl went on with mock concern. He gave Guigui's shoulder a gentle rap of his leather gloves. "They have a very good memory, children!"

"That son of mine can't remember what he had for dinner yesterday!" Bébert cut in.

"So, he is your son!" Steigl said satisfied with himself: he knew where he was going. "And if he is your son, then of course, he follows his parents, Nein? And he goes with them to …" he checked the report again, "he goes with them to "The Gaux" every time you visit there, does he not?"

Bébert chewed his upper lip. Lisette next to the petrified Guigui was torturing the nail of her left thumb and when the lip of the nail suddenly gave way, her hand flew to the flute in front of her toppling it. The champagne foamed on the tablecloth. She gasped, Nanette and Aunt Louise stared with dismay at the spreading stain but did not move. Steigl clenched his fingers over the sheaf of paper he had been holding and his lip drew a thin hiatus of anger.

"I am here on my Führer's order conducting an official investigation," he began, his voice hammering each word. "I shall not permit anyone, even you, to turn my questioning into a joke! Hemmler: get these women out of here, and that man, yes the fat one with the mustache! I will not permit anyone to ridicule an officer of the German Reich!"

He threw back his shoulders again and breathed, hard, as though to control his anger. Along the side of his impeccably pressed trousers his fists were clenched. The three SS soldiers moved forward as one. It was if Steigl had given them the signal they had been anticipating. In my fright I was pushing hard against Nanette who pushed me back. But when she rose from her chair, her fingers grabbed mine.

"You! You stay here!" Steigl ordered her, his index pointing to the window. "The others, raus, schnell! Hemmler!"

The three SS soldiers at the far end of the room shoved Lisette out of her chair. Her face was cast in stone but her eyes glued to Nanette were mesmerized by fear. Still she did not scream. She stumbled as the SS shoved her out of the dining-room. Then they came back for Aunt Louise. She tried to wrench herself free and in the process overturned Nanette's empty chair. It toppled between them for a second until one of them booted it clear under the table and grabbed hold of Aunt Louise's forearm again. No one spoke, not even Uncle Marcel as he struggled to get out of his seat under Hemmler's icy stare. He was plump Uncle and could not move as fast as the others. But at last he stood up. His shoulders were slumped and suddenly he looked very old. His hand brushed Bébert's left shoulder as he shuffled past his empty chair and lingered there as if he needed a prop, but it was long enough for him to give Bébert a gentle squeeze. Bébert looked up but by then Uncle was already being pushed out. I looked at Guigui, at Nanette, not knowing what was expected of me.

"The children stay here!" Steigl barked his eyes boring into mine as if they had read my unspoken question. "Shut the door, Hemmler!"

When the door to the kitchen was closed and we were left alone with him and Hemmler, Obersturmfuhrer Steigl made us all stand with our backs to the window and planted himself in front of us like Mademoiselle Rouleau sometimes did at school when we had done some mischief and she wanted to find the culprit. And I hated to be standing there like that, not knowing what to do with my hands, not knowing who to look at: it made me feel guilty for no reason.

Steigl paced up and down in front of us, slowly. My eyes followed his boots. I couldn't look any higher and I couldn't look right at Nanette or left at Guigui. If I moved for sure I would give myself away.

"Gilbert Marchand!" Steigl proceeded at last camping himself squarely in front of Bébert. His voice this time had the staccato of a machine gun. "I am going to tell you when you were last at - -" he glanced at the report again "at 'The Gaux'. You were there for Easter - - - "

My heart sank to my feet. Mémé dozing in her long chair and a butcher's stall littered with blobs of sanguineous innards flashed before me.

"- - - checked your papers, do you not remember? And they asked you if a man had been by your place, did they not?"

"And I told them…I, we, hadn't seen anyone because we had not." Bébert parried.

"You shall speak when I tell you to speak, Gilbert Marchand!" Steigl snapped. "You said you had not seen anyone that is right! But then you just told me you did not remember when it was you had been at your house at - - - " he checked the report again this time with obvious irritation, "at 'The Gaux', and that was a lie because you did remember, you could not not remember because something very important happened there at Easter, did it not?"

"Nothing - - -"

Hemmler took a step toward Bébert who fell silent.

"It happens that a German private was murdered there: a solder of the Reich, a son of our beloved Führer. Murdered!" Steigl screamed in Bébert's face. "Murdered!" he repeated. He breathed slowly. "We have not found his body yet but - - -"

"And you won't!" Bébert cut him ignoring Hemmler and Steigl's raised eyebrows. "You won't because - - - "

He was chalk white, Bébert, and his chin quivered irrepressibly. I expected Steigl to let out another glacial reminder and drew closer to Guigui. He turned and glared at me Guigui as if he were about to box my ears and I shrunk back. But Steigl kept mum this time: instead a mask of contempt covered his face.

"Gilbert Marchand," he resumed after a while: his voice soft now, just above a whisper. "You love the Americans, you hope they are going to win, do you not? You do not even mind when they bomb your town because you think it is to hurt Germans, do you not?" He fell into a short studied silence, walked to the table and back to Bébert. "Ach, the Americans!" he sighed shaking his head "But sometimes friends do things which are not very good for us. Sometimes by striking our enemies, they also strike at us, do they not, Herr Marchand?"

It was a rhetorical question which Bébert did not answer. At that point the cuckoo above the dresser sprung out of its chalet to chirp whatever half hour it was and, incredibly, we all raised our heads in unison to look at it, even the Germans. But then the cuckoo vanished again, its job done. Steigl' eyes were upon us again.

One afternoon when we were going to make herb for our rabbits, the dog of the sawmill - - the one who always barked - - had almost tried to attack Mémé and me. It had been unchained by a stack of lumber. Upon spotting us it had raised itself to a crouching position and had stayed so for a moment, snarling. Its yellow eyes a laser beam of viciousness boring into Mémé 's. She had grabbed my hand, whispered for me not to move. And as we stood frozen in mid-motion, the dog, its tail between its hind legs, its ears drawn back, still snarling, had started circling around us, wide concentric circles which grew narrower as its snarl grew more threatening. I had been petrified by terror, by the sheer agony of waiting for it to pounce on us and maul us to shreds. As I watched Steigl pace up and down in front of us, his eyes never letting go of Bébert for a moment, the same terror suddenly crept over me. I started inhaling only as much air as would not show.

Steigl stepped up to Bébert. Their faces were level, only ten inches apart at most.

"You see Gilbert Marchand, one of the American bombs hit your property. I think you have not been at your house recently because if you had, we would not have found there what we did find. Now perhaps you understand what I meant about your friends the Americans, do you not?" he asked drawing his face closer to Bébert's who abruptly pulled back. "Without their bombs the wall of the Château would not have been damaged and our dogs would not have strayed on your property." He explained matter-of-factly. "The well is filled with debris and rubbles and exploded earth but that does not matter because we shall empty it to find whatever is in it. We have also found a gun. It is a German gun, the sort our soldiers are given when they enlist into our infantry. It is rusty and unusable because it has spent many months in the earth. Unfortunately for you, Gilbert Marchand, it has a serial number engraved inside its magazine chamber and that number says it belonged to the same private that our party was looking for that Easter Sunday when you told them you had not seen anyone!" Steigl finished on a note of triumph.

Concentric circles, like the dog at the sawmill. Bébert could not talk, none of us could. I had gone beyond panic. All of me was now a sensory void. I was inside that split second of emotional numbness between fear and the actual event which will trigger it when nothing stirs, when thoughts, pulse, heartbeats, breath are all at a frightening standstill.

"Gilbert Marchand, in the face of the evidence which I have enumerated, do you still maintain that you did not see one of our soldiers that week-end?"

"I - -"Bébert started, choked, cleared his throat. "I do. We did not see anyone the entire week-end except for your lot."

"How would you explain the Luger then?" Steigl pressed him.

"Guns are found every day during war....everywhere," Bébert answered.

"Anybody could have put it there," Nanette broke in. "Might have been drunk your soldier, might have strayed on our - - "

"Shut up woman!" Steigl cut her off.

"My husband works at the Château, ask anyone at the Kommandatur!" Nanette persisted obstinately, "Our neighbor - - "

"Shut up!" Steigl ordered for the second time.

"....Oberleutnant Redlich, he knows my husband. And your Herr - - - "

"Shut UP!" Steigl hissed as his eyes perforated Nanette with cold anger to no avail.

"...our Herr Kommandant Blücher! You can ask any of them: they will tell you about my husband, they will tell you he couldn't have done what you say. He's just a carpenter: never even was in a war. He's a family - -"

Steigl slapped her violently across the mouth and she moaned in pain as her hand flew to her face. Bébert sprung forward but before he could reach Steigl, Hemmler threw himself between them. For a second we all stood frozen: them and us. And then the door flew open and the three SS burst inside the dining-room while Lisette behind them in the dark pit of the kitchen, started screaming hysterically.

"Schweigen! Silence!" Steigl screamed his eyes now two black holes like those of the skull emblazoned on his cap. "Hemmler, take care of that woman! Gilbert Marchand, I am taking you in for questioning under suspicion of murdering a soldier of the German Reich!" he recited very fast the word tumbling into each other as he tried to speak over Lisette's screams. "Raus!"

Lisette stopped screaming. Nanette caught Bébert's arm and tugged at it.

"He hasn't done anything. He hasn't even had his dinner. You killed his mother last month, you can't take him: I won't let you, I won't let you!"

She was sobbing now. And she was holding on to one of Bébert's hand while still tugging at his other sleeve so that the cuff covered both their hands and you couldn't tell where she began and where he ended.

"Schondorf! Schondorf! Get that woman out, raus!" Steigl yelled at one of the SS soldiers standing closer to him. But it was almost as if he had already walked out of the room the way he said it, as if he really did not care about any of us, as if he was not seeing anything around him but only his nice lustrous leather gloves as he threaded them almost lovingly on each of his fingers.

Lisette's scream had sent me cowering under the dining-room window and it is from there that I watched Schondorf come at Nanette. She was still tugging at Bébert's sleeve with one hand while holding on to him with the other so that the collar of his shirt bared half of his white bony shoulder. He tried to shake her off but could not: it was as if their hands were soldered together. And then, though she did not see him, Schondorf towered above her. Like a discus thrower he raised his right hand deliberately all the way over his left shoulder and let fly at Nanette with all the strength contained in his muscular body. My eyes had outgrown their sockets. The pain in my temples was excruciating.

The iron hand struck Nanette in the forehead, right above her left eye. She fell to the ground like her dress was empty of her, like there were no bones in that plump body of hers. Within seconds as she laid sprawled on the parquet floor half way under the table, a rivulet of blood started oozing out of the gash, snaking its way out of the wound over her closed eyelids, her nose, the tip of her nose, her lips and chin. Ever so slowly. I could not see anything in the room, could not hear, or feel. Nanette's blood draining out of her like the milky sap of some tree was all that mattered. Ever so slowly.

When I looked up again, my hands stifling my breath, they were gone: the SS soldiers and Schondorf and Hemmler and Steigl and his fine black leather gloves. And Bébert.

Aunt Louise, a dish cloth in one hand and a copper pan full of water in the other, knelt by Nanette.

"Antoinette!" she called softly, "Antoinette!" She bathed the wound with clear cold water and wiped the blood off of her face, and Nanette at ever so long a last, blinked her eyes open. "Antoinette! She's coming to, Marcel. Get her a drink. Guy, where do you keep the brandy?" she was propping Nanette up against the wall so that her head rested against the frame of the window. "Here, drink this, Antoinette, slowly. It's alright, everything's alright…"

Nanette sipped and I watched them all and there was a great sweeping emptiness inside of me. Uncle was saying he would go see Mayor Chancel come morning, and Lisette looking all of her spinster's years perhaps because she owed us a debt of courage was half-heartedly volunteering to speak to Herr Kommandant Blücher himself, while Guigui suggested Oberleutnant Redlich might be of more immediate assistance seeing he lived next door to us. On and on they carried on about what they might, should, would, maybe do, perhaps do tomorrow. Like a big shapeless lump of wet clay they were tossing at each other, kneading in turn, as they tried to reassure each other that something could be done, that they could get Bébert out of his straight. But none of what they suggested rang true to my ears. Tomorrow was a void and the future a black bottomless abyss in which Bébert and I were irretrievably lost and apart from each other. No matter how many times they might repeat that in the end everything would be alright, in my heart, horribly and despairingly, I believed otherwise.

* * * * * *

CHAPTER IX

In retrospect Nanette's surprising emotional collapse which, each time I evoked the events which had taken place that night in the dining-room, confounded me far more than Bébert's arrest, but it was mercifully short-lived. Hysteria was not in her nature and neither was surrender to despair no matter how justified by the hopelessness of the circumstances. She was as ashamed as I was by her own weakness and when I inquired the following morning about the gash on her forehead, she commented with an acerbity not directed at me that it had been deserved and that she hoped the scar would long show as a reminder that one never, "Never, Tina, remember that!" should allow oneself to fall prey to one's fear. "I gave him just what he wanted, Steigl," she lectured Guigui and me at breakfast. "If only I had showed more guts Bébert might still be here. Instead I went to pieces, me!" she added incredulously, "like all their craven victims: I handed them Bébert on a gold platter together with my shame!"

But as the morning progressed, it became apparent that whatever shame or guilt she felt would not stand in her way and that, if anything, like a sinner sometimes beats his breast with the sum of his earlier transgressions to attain ultimate salvation, Nanette would use both to buttress her determination to see her husband safe and free. Thus, because she was earlier and better than anyone of the Germains to view the tragedy of Bébert's arrest as something less ineluctable than an act of God, she also became the moving force behind our subsequent efforts to secure his release and indeed their instigator. I still remember her that morning standing at the center of our kitchen while Guigui, the Germains and I, her captive audience, sat around her speechless and mesmerized by the strength gushing out of her, splashing us with each word she spoke: a lightning rod against which our maudlin despair exploded in a flash of guilt at the heart of which Bébert appeared far more impotent than we had thought ourselves to be throughout a restless night of complacent prostration.

She was not pretty Nanette: never had been judging from the sepia photograph of their wedding day she kept on their bedroom dresser. She had been rectangular then, still was, from her face to her bust and her hips. There was nothing soft about her except sometimes the caress of her brown eyes when one was ailing or when Guigui brought back high marks from school. She was not demonstrative but when she kissed you it warmed not only your cheeks but your heart because her kiss was as much in her eyes as it was on her lips. She did everything absolutely and because of it, one forgave her angers because one knew her laughter whenever it came back again would be as fiercely spontaneous as the outburst which had just scalded you. Because she was all of that there emanated from her a singular energy which seldom showed better than when faced with a situation the rest of us had long accepted as desperate. And certainly, Bébert's arrest by the SS which at some point during a sleepless night she must have come to accept as a bleak reality, was the most ominous crisis she had ever faced and one in which all this strength and determination in her should yet find their greatest challenge because, just as she did everything else, so, truly did she love Bébert.

That morning as she stood in the kitchen exposing her strategy and giving us our marching orders, she managed to show us how to unearth from our hearts that nugget of hope which otherwise might have remained buried under the weight of our collective despair. She also, at a time when we had surrendered all our thoughts to the one and only reality of Bébert's arrest, showed enough unselfish pragmatism to, above desperately conniving for her husband's problematic release, remind us that Dormans was facing a potential state of siege and instruct us how best to prepare for such an eventuality.

Nanette decided that our lobbying efforts on behalf of Bébert should be directed at four individuals whose clout with the Kommandatur, even if minimal, might at least guarantee his case a fair hearing. She would approach Oberleutnant Redlich while Uncle Marcel would request from Mayor Chancel that he intercede with the German hierarchy for Bébert's release. Meanwhile, Lisette, provided circumstances at the Town Hall offered her the chance to do so, would talk to Herr Kommandant Blücher while Guigui would consult Father Rocas to determine whether the Church as an institution might make representations on our behalf. To Aunt Louise and myself fell the more inglorious task of stocking up for the turbulent days ahead.

Thus later that morning I accompanied Aunt Louise to market. Except at times of compulsory attendance to one of Herr Kommandant Blücher's virulent speeches, the Place du Luxembourg had never been as congested as it proved to be that Saturday when we reached it around eleven. One could hardly see the stalls for the bodies swarming them and the German soldiers far outnumbered the legitimate citizenry. It soon became apparent as we dove into the throbbing crowd that the news of Bébert's arrest the previous evening was the main topic of the hushed whispers which followed our progress through the stalls. In turn frightened, accusatory or concerned, stares scalded my back with their simmering curiosity, the almost culpable way in which they searched our faces for a trace of despair, a hint of anguish, only to avoid ours when we confronted them. Notwithstanding the importance of our mission I soon started wishing I had stayed home. With one hand Aunt Louise hung on to mine so tightly that the knuckles of my fingers ached, while I clasped the handles of my small shopping bag with the other. Meanwhile Aunt Louise - - with myself in reluctant tow - - proceeded to shove her way from butcher to grocer, acknowledging rare expressions of sympathy with a stiff nod of her weasel-face, haggling over exorbitant prices which seemed to prevail that day but offering a deaf ear to the whispered questions which often slowed our progress.

After about an hour of plowing our way through this human canyon we at last closed our loop around the square. Gasping for air as much as anonymity I rushed Aunt Louise through the short aisle of the dwindling bodies and heaved a vulcanian sigh of relief when at last we reached the billboard of the Empire Theater. Across the street the door to Monsieur Lucien's shop stood open to let in a constant ebb and flow of German soldiers and as I turned again toward the still crowded square behind the billboard, I confronted Hitler who glared at me from behind the penciled monocle some irreverent prankster had drawn over his left eye. I shuddered and looked at Aunt Louise.

"What's with you Tina rushing me like that?" she huffed behind the large checkered handkerchief with which she was presently wiping her summer brow. "And me loaded like a donkey!"

"I want to go home, Aunt Louise," I panted by way of apology.

"We will," her flat chest heaved under her slate-colored blouse. "Just give me a minute, child. I ain't as young as you you know! Let me have your shopping bag so as I can unburden myself a bit."

She stooped over the bulging shopping bags laying disemboweled on the pavement while I crouched next to her and we proceeded to transfer rutabagas and turnips, grey bread and shriveled beets from one to the other spreading our load more evenly. I was jingling my bag to tamp it down when a black leather shoe thrust itself between us. Aunt Louise half straightened up.

"Don't look up," a familiar whisper admonished her from above.

Still crouching between the bags and the billboard I turned my head a bit and through the corner of my eyes I spotted the neatly pressed black trousers, the shiny shoes I had seen him wear in Lisette's office after the bombardment.

"It's me, Langiers," came his voice again. "Tell Madame Marchand…"

He fell silent. Abruptly. I looked beyond his trousers: three pairs of lustrous knee high boots wandered our way. I held my breath and stared with Aunt Louise at the soil-stained rutabagas she held in her hand. The boots stopped: their toes pointing toward the billboard like Langiers' shoes were doing. He greeted them in German and they answered back to him. He had never told us he spoke German Langiers. Then they all laughed above us and his pants quivered when he repeated after them his "Heil Hitler." Within seconds the six boots fell into step, drifted past us toward the Avenue de la Marne.

"Tell Madame Marchand her husband is alright," he resumed in a whisper, the word tumbling into each other. "Steigl's holding him at the Château. It won't be long now if they don't transfer him to

Reims." His left shoe stomped out the butt of a cigarette that had just rained past my left shoulder. "It won't be long now: tell her that."

Then he wheeled his shoes around, crossed the street. We saw him enter Monsieur Lucien's shop with the German tide as we stood up.

Although we were very puzzled by its source and the cryptic manner of its delivery as we gathered that night for dinner, Langiers' message proved to be the only concrete bit of news any of us had gathered that day about Bébert. Nanette, though slightly reassured remained perplexed. Over and over she made Aunt Louise and I recount the incident, repeat word for word to her what it was Langiers had said. I kept insisting on the part where Langiers had spoken to the Germans in their own language and was much piqued to discover none of them cared. If anything it soon became apparent that my insistence upon this point irritated them especially Lisette who finally hushed me up by informing me pompously that the province of Champagne being close to that historically contested province of Alsace, one should expect its more educated citizens to take German as part of their scholastic curriculum.

"There's nothing wrong with speaking German, Tina, quite the contrary! What is wrong is to be German, and that is what Monsieur Langiers certainly is not!"

I sat back in my chair and decided love had never made anyone so blind. And what about the papers he had stolen from her office, Langiers, what about that mysterious ring and the brand new leather shoes and Guigui's German camera when the rest of us couldn't afford to buy an ounce of butter! For a righteous moment as I glared at her across the table I wished she could read the angry thoughts storming through my mind Lisette. But instead she looked at Nanette, dismissed me with a scornful quiver of her double chin.

While I sulked and vowed never again to give them the benefit of my wisdom they each went on to report on their day's activities. Nanette had failed to meet with Oberleutnant Redlich: since Friday he had been on duty almost around the clock but Madame Tardieux had promised Nanette she would speak to him the minute he came in, wouldn't leave her house until he did. Uncle reported that the Mayor was already aware of Bébert's arrest and that, although justifiably swamped because of the military situation, he had promised to do what he could to at least prevent Bébert from being transferred to SS Headquarters in Reims. Lisette hadn't seen Blücher and since the following day was Sunday, she would have to wait till Monday to approach him. Guigui said Father Rocas had been "appalled" at the news which he had not heard before seeing he had spent the night praying for the Allies. He had promised to say a rosary for Bébert and more pragmatically to attempt to visit him at the Château. Nanette inquired how Father Rocas proposed to perform such a miracle and Guigui taking an obvious pride in the ubiquitous nature of the Church, went on a limb by averring that under cover of his ecclesiastic cassock Father Rocas could get into a lot of places where the rest of us could not. He had many an alibi for doing so Father Rocas: confession, sacraments for all occasions including the last rites. Nanette shuddered.

I spent a tormented night that Saturday fleeing from one nightmare to the next. At one point Langiers, naked from the waist up, hairy arms bared, bent over an unseen Bébert spread-eagled on a rack whipping the sanguineous flesh with the gigantic fingers of an over-sized leather glove under the supervision of Steigl whose entire face had become a putrescent boil. Guigui, the Germains and

I meanwhile, each sporting bushy Clemenceau mustaches, played cards in the shadow of the torture chamber while Nanette, drowning in the folds of a heavy woolen brown robe glided up and down the length of an altar dressed in black chanting mournfully: "It won't be long now, it won't be long now!"

I woke up Sunday morning exhausted and perspiring vowing I should never go to sleep again.

Despite her concealed anguish over Bébert's fate, Nanette thought it best to go to Church with Guigui on Sunday: she might garner something form someone there, and besides, Father Rocas would give her the latest on the Allied advance. I stayed home with Aunt Louise and Lisette who had come earlier, pottering idly about the kitchen and trying to convince myself Bébert would be alright while they busied themselves preparing what seemed to me an inordinate amount of food for our dwindling contingent. Two German privates sent a shiver up our spines when they rapped on the windowpane but it turned out all they wanted was a pail of water. Half an hour later a third one rang the door-bell asking to use our water-closet but Aunt Louise told him it was clogged. I knew it wasn't but kept my mouth shut. They were still camped outside our house by the tens, and looking at them from behind the crochet curtain I wondered what peace would be like for them if it ever came.

Nanette and Guigui returned from high mass around one accompanied by Uncle Marcel who had met them on the Place du Luxembourg on his way back from the Fire House. Both Father Rocas and the Mayor had confirmed that Bébert was still being held at the Château. "A short kilometer from us and there ain't a thing I can do for him: can't even get to see him!" Nanette muttered angrily as she removed her mourning hat. Then Guigui said the word was that the Allies had taken Meaux during the night and were sweeping toward Château-Thierry; Mayor Chancel estimated that at their present pace they might well reach Dormans within the next three days. The sun was splashing my chair as we sat around the dining-room table and a whiff of warm summer air swept past my nose when Guigui leaned over his plate to say grace. A while later Uncle Marcel his mouth full of shredded carrots opined that he was torn between anticipation and apprehension. As we could all attest he had looked forward to the liberation, he said but now with Bébert held prisoner at the Château, he had second thoughts because God only knew what they might do the crazy krauts when the Allies marched into Dormans: "Might shoot the bunch of them before they retreat!". Nanette disagreed ferociously: "They wouldn't dare, besides, they'll have other fishes to fry by then!" Her vehemence did not reassure me. Lisette expressed the opinion that a lot would depend on whether the Germans decided to hold Dormans or make their stand somewhere else. Aunt Louise, pointing at the window with her angular chin, snapped that the answer to that was out there: "You mark my word, they are digging in for a long haul. A bloodbath, that's what will happen when the Allies come!" Uncle scoffed: there was nothing in Dormans worth holding. Now Epernay was something else and if his wife would grant him a certain degree of military expertise it would be his bet that that's where they would make a stand against the Allies, the Boches.

Thus went our lunch that Sunday and thus went the next two days as we prepared for war while growing ever more apprehensive of Bébert's fate. Arguments, anguish and industry: our home was a microcosm of what was happening to the town, in hundreds of houses, as Dormans readied itself for the final struggle. By Monday afternoon our bustling community was fast reaching a complete standstill: stores and shops were being boarded up, the Women's

Emergency Committee closed its doors for an indefinite period, children no longer scampered up and down the Avenue de la Marne and a stray dog crossing the Town Hall square had become an incongruity. A dwindling number of people still could be seen in the streets but their pace was hurried. Even though the August sun hung out its beckoning shingle high in the sky, they remained blind to its enticement and stopped neither for friend nor foe, gossiping or gawking. Survival had become the order of the day: living would come back later.

On the assumption that Bébert might take advantage of the battle to escape his captors, Nanette decided that rather than move to Dr. Martin's shelter at the first outbreak of hostilities, the family would remain in the house so as to be there if Bébert made it: we would use our own cellar. It was dug deep under the house and since it ran its full width from the front hallway to the far wall of the dining-room, it was large enough to accommodate the Germains and us. It had an air-vent which opened on the street through a metal grating thus letting in both air and light in addition to, by way of a wood ladder Uncle Marcel brought form their house, enabling one of us in turn to act as lookout and survey the street so as to keep the others informed of what was happening outside. We spent the Monday afternoon ferrying down food, water, wine, chamber pots, mattresses and blankets: like beavers at the onset of winter we were ready to burrow in for a long siege.

It was well after curfew that same night long after the Germains had gone home to pack necessary belongings and as we were preparing for bed that we got our first account of Bébert's situation. Oberleutnant Redlich came in person accompanied by Madame Tardieux to give us the news. He had dark smudges under his eyes and exhaustion glazed his grey pupils as he stood leaning against our closed front door. There was something worn about him and when he spoke his voice had a monotonous undertone as if he were forcing the words out of his throat one by one and it was a strain to do so. He was very sorry about what had happened to Herr Marchand, he began, and it was obvious his arrest had been a mistake. He had tried to explain that to Obersturmfuhrer Steigl but, unfortunately, even he, an officer of the Wehrmacht, had no influence on the actions of Schutzstaffel. He had seen Herr Marchand though and the latter had expressed particular concern that the family might over-worry about him. He wanted Oberleutnant Redlich to convey the word that he was alright, that there were three other Frenchmen being held in his cell and that between the four of them they were keeping each other's morale pretty high.

Nanette wanted to know if Bébert had been questioned yet and after some hesitation, Oberleutnant Redlich nodded affirmatively. Nanette shot a glance at Madame Tardieux who promptly patted her forearm and assured her everything would be fine in the end. Then Oberleutnant Redlich brushed his forehead with the back of his hand and said he should get some sleep now because tomorrow would be a hard day. Château-Thierry would fall perhaps tonight, and then they should be pulling back toward Epernay.

"Aren't you going to hold Dormans?" Nanette asked him.

"But what about Bébert? Will they take him too?" Nanette shot anxiously.

"I cannot read the minds of the SS, Frau Marchand, it is - - "

"But you can do something, Oberleutnant Redlich, you could," Nanette pleaded, suddenly taking hold of Redlich's hand. "You could, couldn't you?"

She held his eyes for an everlasting second while we stood silent holding our breath , eyes riveted to his lips. He shook his head as if confounded by the enormity of her request, but in the end after he had searched our faces for a trace of understanding which wasn't there, his eyes yielded to hers, like they had to Mademoiselle Rouleau that day on the beach.

"You will help my husband, won't you?" Nanette pressed him.

Oberleutnant Redlich sighed, looked beyond her at the far staircase down the hallway.

"I shall try, Frau Marchand…" he said at last turning toward the door. He looked back at us over his shoulder. His eyes found mine and a smile, weary, strained his lips. "I shall try…I promise I shall try…"

Then he opened the door and stepped into the uncertain darkness.

An undulated wave of shadows lapped the shores of the moonlit houses across the Avenue de la Marne and voices coming from under the plane trees whispered guttural secrets past my ears. They were still camping out there, the Germans, yet, as I inhaled one last whiff of the river breeze blowing over the rooftops, I suddenly felt that Mémé's death, Bébert' arrest, our feverish preparations for the upcoming battle that day were absurd, that it was silly for people to be busy dying and warring and fearing and crying when there was such a beautiful summer covering the world. I spotted the evening star before shutting the front door: It was perched right above Uncle Marcel's chimney.

I felt a mellowing happiness sweeping over me as I climbed the staircase ahead of Guigui and Nanette. Perhaps Mémé was not dead at all I ventured as we reached the landing, perhaps, just perhaps she was on one of them summer stars up there, like Mr. Saint Exupery's

Little Prince. Nanette kissed my forehead and patted my fanny over my nightgown. "Perhaps she is, child. Off to bed now!"

I heard her speaking to Guigui as I reached my cot in the alcove.

"He's a good man that Redlich, son, not like the rest of them anyway. Ma'am Tardieux was right about him."

I smiled. Then Guigui came in and closed the door. After a while he called out "good-night" from his end of the night and I turned toward the wall, cuddled under the blanket. I was looking forward to sleep after all.

*
* *

Château-Thierry, the main town between Paris and Dormans distant from the latter by some thirty kilometers, fell to the Allies while we slept that night and by noon Tuesday, the German troops encamped outside our windows began the hasty but laborious retreat toward Epernay. Once again Nanette confined us to quarters but as a sop we were allowed to keep the windows wide open. It was one of the hottest days of that summer. An implacable sun hung at the heart of the heat-white sky thawing the tar of pavements under the German's feet and turning the patch of street on the horizon into an intricate patchwork of iridescent puddles. Clad in our bathing suits as a means of escaping the sizzling summer Guigui and I each leaned out of one of the two ground floor windows watching the Nazi exodus. Across the street from us and all up and down the length of the Avenue de la Marne as far as I could see if I leaned over the window railing, there were other people leaning out of other windows of other houses: watching. So many faces. They showed little emotion: their lips shaped no words and smiled no joy; their eyes shed no tears. Their arms did not wave or threaten the retreating occupiers and there was no laughter of relief ringing from house to house. There was something solemn about the way the town watched the German retreat. The significance of the event had not yet sunk in, and beyond it, the freedom it portended was suddenly perceived as an awesome responsibility.

That same afternoon Mademoiselle Rouleau officially moved into Madame Tardieux's house. It was around two when the widow came to borrow our wheelbarrow to help move the young woman's books, clothes and other sundry possessions. Nanette gave her the key to Bébert's workshop, told her where to find it and within a couple of hours the two of them, the teacher pushing the loaded wheelbarrow and Madame Tardieux carrying a bulging suitcase, came back, flushed from their labors but obviously already thick in their conspiratorial friendship. They stopped outside the kitchen window and chatted with Nanette for a while. Oberleutnant Redlich hadn't gone yet, the widow explained while Mademoiselle Rouleau massaged the ache out of her hot bare arms, but it wouldn't be long now. They had thought it best for the young woman to move in before the battle started. They, too, would seek shelter in their own cellar that night and by the next day with the Allies sure to be in command of Dormans, Redlich would be gone. I stared at Mademoiselle Rouleau: her face was apple red and perspiration curled the baby hair around her forehead. Her periwinkle eyes sparkled but I knew the fever in them was only one of intense expectation. I played with the fingers of her hand and waves of love swept my heart. She inquired about Bébert and beamed when Nanette told her Redlich had promised to help. "Your husband will be back with you by tomorrow, Ma'am Marchand!" Madame Tardieux promised clasping Nanette's hand in hers, "You mark my word, no later than tomorrow!"

And then we sighted the Germains shutting up their house across the street and Nanette waved at them. Soon they were hurrying toward us. Uncle Marcel, breathless, said he had just heard from the Mayor that the Allies were within fifteen kilometers of Dormans. There was a lot of fighting below the Marne river and although it would be several hours before the Allies hit Dormans, he was of the opinion we should get ready for it now while there was still plenty of time. Madame Tardieux agreed. Uncle helped the two women get the wheelbarrow up the widow's front steps and into her hallway and then we bade them goodbye and they bade us good luck for the uncertain night ahead of us all.

Behind us people started drawing their shutters and barricading their houses as German tanks and jeeps, trucks and command cars, in a scrambling retreat began to retreat. The steps of the Town Hall became alive with officers barking orders at German privates who were busy loading boxes of documents onto waiting trucks while behind them still other soldiers fed other documents into a big bonfire. The summer day swept over Dormans and big storm clouds slate gray and pregnant with thunder, gathered over the rooftops. They had pulled back, the Germans: since morning and part of the afternoon we had watched them moving out and rolling on. But by nightfall, when the first lightning clangorously streaked over the rubbles of dead Monsieur Pottin's store, there were enough of them still lurking behind their bazookas and their submachine guns, lying in wait inside the steel bellies of their tanks, to give the Allies a fair fight. Perhaps the battle of Dormans wouldn't go down in future history books but a battle we would have: the prospect infuriated Uncle Marcel as we in turn proceeded to barricade ourselves in the house and made our ghostly descent into the cellar.

It was around three the following morning when the first outburst of gunfire jolted us out of our fretful sleep. My eyes plunged in the pitch-black void of the cellar and as I sat rubbing them, a second volley of gunfire this time followed by the blast of a shell exploding nearby shattered the silence and lit up the night. I caught a glimpse of Uncle at the foot of the ladder and my groping hand encountered Lisette's thigh on the mattress next to me. Then darkness fell over us again and I heard Uncle's heavy footsteps scaling the ladder, Aunt Louise whispering for him to get down. Angry. But he just went on hoisting his way up toward the blanket we had hung over the grating of the air-vent. Within seconds a small phosphorescent arrow of light tore a corner of the black cocoon. I sprung up. My eyes strained toward the patch of faint light but at that moment there came a sudden shuffling of running feet and Uncle let go of the corner of the blanket which covered the grating. Outside the boots hurried past the air-vent while we held our breath. It was a long time after the silence had returned that Uncle lifted the corner of the blanket again. This time I was able to make out the design of the grating. Between us and it, Uncle's profile etched itself against the phosphorescent patch: the polished brass of his fireman's helmet gleamed uncertainly. He was way above me, Uncle: his face, like a full moon, floated inside our darkness and his index, stiff against his mustache, motioned us to caution.

In the next instant all the furies of hell broke loose outside and Uncle came crashing down and swearing dragging in his fall the blanket we had nailed over the telltale grating. His helmet, rolling and tumbling, clanged its way from bottles to buckets, between mattresses and crates. The world exploded and Dormans became its epicenter. Above our heads a shower of shells hissed throughout their trajectory then exploded right and left and far and near, and the jarring roll of artillery counterpointed by rockets fired by some unseen bazooka was all around accompanied by the frantic thunder of tanks speeding past the air-vent. The house rocked and rumbled on its foundations, and I thought any minute now it would collapse and when it did not, from second to next dreaded second, I couldn't believe it had not. But soon now, with this shell. Here it comes! And the drawing of all of one's body in a knot of terror and apprehension, waiting for the pulverizing impact. My face crushed the mattress and my ears burned because I pressed my hands so very hard against them. I was sure my heart had stopped beating: but still it thumped and thumped against my temples ready to explode in my head with the next thunderous blast. I couldn't think of the others or stretch my hand toward another hand. I was petrified by terror, and thoughts, crazed, disconnected fought their way through my mind in a frightful melee of panic. I was sure we should all die any minute.

And when after what seemed to be an eternity my ears suddenly hummed with the static drone of silence, I thought I had gone deaf. I sat up, lifted the palms of my hands from each ear, then the other, slowly. I blinked and yawned, once, twice. Mechanically. To see if it worked, if I could still feel the friction of my jaws rubbing against the bones of my inner ears. It worked: I wasn't deaf! The silence I heard was real: we had survived!

The battle raged on intermittently until five. Then later, as the first bluish gray rays of the receding night sifted into the cellar, the war passed us by and drifted toward the other side of town. We could still hear echoes of artillery fire or the occasional burst of shell hitting its target, but they were occurring far away and between the battle and us a zone of spreading silence now stretched its buffer. We had not spoken since the first cataclysmic outburst a couple of hours earlier; we had not slept either. But when I sat up at last, stretched my legs on the side of the mattress and searched the dim shelter for familiar shadows, I felt no exhaustion. The silence, deeper than any I had ever known, was upon us, soothing, so loud and thick, almost liquid, that one bathed in it with all of one's body. Snug and delicate. I had never felt so small and safe except perhaps in Mémé's skirts.

Nanette was the first to break the magic. The silence bothered her she suddenly whispered to Uncle Marcel who sat on the bottom step of the cellar, and what did he think it meant? And then Lisette stirred next to me, and behind her Guigui rose from the toppled ladder against which his shadow had been prostrated. Life took over and the wonderful silence became just another silence as my ears strained toward the hushed words nibbling at it.

"I'm going to have a look," Nanette voiced, still in a whisper. "Might even see an American!"

She pushed Guigui out of her way and dragged the ladder under the air vent. A shadow moved on my left.

"Put on Marcel's helmet," Aunt Louise ordered her. "You never know what might be out there."

We all made our way toward the ladder, surrounded it, and held it while Nanette climbed its rungs.

"See anything?" Uncle queried as Nanette, her nose rubbing the metal grating swept the street with her eyes. "Any krauts out there?"

"Can't see a soul. Your house got hit: it's got a big hole where the parlor window was! But there ain't no one, no one at all out there."

She turned toward us, peered down at our raised faces.

"What do you think Uncle?"

"Reckon we'd better wait a while, Antoinette! Don't think it's safe out here yet, it's too quiet…Better wait for the Americans…"

"But there ain't no Boches, Marcel! There ain't no Boches and no French and no Americans. Here, have a look!"

She clambered down from the ladder, anxious suddenly. We made way for Uncle and then closed ranks around the ladder again while he plodded his way up toward the air-vent. The blue was turning gray around us and I could clearly see Aunt Louise's face on my right and Lisette's on my left: pale gray, they were, the color of paper ashes, and flat like they were drawn over the dark background of oozing mortar joints of the cellar walls. And between the rungs of the ladder Guigui looked just as flat: his cabbage leaf ears were in line with the tip of his nose. I touched my face. Maybe I was flat too.

"The bastards!!" Uncle exploded above me. I looked up: his face was full of shapes, and mad. "They sure hit our house Louise. It's got a hole as big as an elephant's ass up front, window's gone - - "

"Dear Lord," Aunt Louise gasped next to me while Guigui, from his pigeon hole between the ladder's rungs shivered under an irrepressible attack of the giggles. "Is it big enough for someone to sneak in, Marcel?"

"Sure is! I tell you: an elephant's ass, that's how big it is!"

"They'll be stealing us blind!" Aunt Louise hissed.

"We got nothing worth stealing, woman!" Uncle snapped shrugging his sagging shoulders. "But the damage, that's what worries me, and where am I going to find bricks. Besides it won't be safe sleeping there until - - "

He stopped abruptly. I had heard the noise too, like a trap door being slammed shut behind us somewhere. Uncle Marcel held his breath and his lower jaw quivered under his mustache. And then that first noise was followed at short intervals by a shuffling of feet coming from somewhere above us, a heavy door squeaking open and then being shut with a dull thud. We all harkened to the silence which followed. Guigui was frozen in his giggles and Lisette's thick eyebrows were arched like gothic porches over her drooping eyes. Within seconds we heard footsteps outside and two bare calves suddenly extended their poles on the other side of the metal grating. My hand flew to my mouth.

"It's Nanette! It's Nanette!" I shrieked a premonition streaking through my head.

Aunt Louise shot a glance at me, surveyed the cellar and then we all looked up.

"Sure looks like her feet," Uncle voiced hesitantly. Then his hands clasped the top of the ladder as he looked some more. "It's her alright! The woman is mad: Antoinette!"

We all started to whisper anxiously and Guigui called out his mother's name as he attempted to find some space next to Uncle on the ladder. The calves disappeared and soon her face replaced them behind the metal grating. Big. She looked like one of our rabbits in its cage. She was lying on the pavement, Nanette, and she was nose to nose with Uncle Marcel.

"Keep quiet! Want to give me away!" she breathed angrily. She was panting like she was afraid.

"You get back down her this instant, Antoinette!" Uncle ordered her just as angry as she was.

"No I won't, I ain't coming back till I find Bébert!" she hissed back. Her eyes were darting glances right and left. "I'm going after him - -"

"You are mad, woman! It's probably crawling with krauts out there!"

"I'm going to find my husband I tell you!"

And then she got up and for a second there was a big gray blank behind the grating.

"Antoinette! Antoinette!" Uncle screamed thinking she had already gone. The ladder shook with his anger. But then Nanette gave a great whack to the grating with her shoe and Uncle pulled back sharply.

"I tell you Louise, the woman has gone mad! Guigui, your mother has gone mad!" Uncle exploded taking us as witnesses.

"I'm going after Bébert, now!" came Nanette's panting whisper once more but we couldn't see her any more. "Took a carving knife, just in case! But there ain't no one around to stop me Uncle!" Wherever it came from, her breath was heavy. "You see to the children, I'll be back!"

She was already out of ear-shot. Gone.

Uncle Marcel turned his back to the air-vent, clonked the whole of his defeated body on the top rung of the ladder. No one spoke; we just surveyed each other's faces impotently.

"At least she's got my helmet," Uncle said at last above us.

We all stared at him. He pulled a rumpled handkerchief from his pant pocket and started wiping his glistening forehead. On and on, as if he were tracking a thought and had forgotten about his hand and the handkerchief. And then there was rumble in his tummy: a faint sound gurgling its way up from his paunch to his throat. He drew the handkerchief away from his face, looked down at us, seriatim like, and his body started rippling, really rippling, like he were sitting on one of the conveyor belts of the sawmill.

"By God she's got guts that Antoinette!" he exploded at last. "She may be mad your mother, son, but she's got guts!" He was laughing now: his whole body was one big roaring laughter. "Her and her carving knife and my brass helmet: and escaped lunatic!" he was choking he was laughing so hard. "She's mad but she's got guts, though, ain't she?"

And soon we were all laughing and catching our breath and panting and laughing again like Uncle Marcel. My ribs started aching and my jaws felt sore. I knew there was something crazy about our outburst and I wasn't sure it was right for us to be laughing when Nanette was out there: lonely. But I couldn't stop. It was like a collective hysterical fit that had to run its course, that only the tears and the spasmodic hiccups when they finally came would stop.

*
* *

CHAPTER X

We left the cellar much later after Uncle Marcel, shuffling restlessly under the onslaught of a natural urge, adamantly refused to use one of the chamber pots we had brought down with us the day before in prevision of a longer siege. Like almost all the others Uncle and she had ever acrimoniously debated, Aunt Louise lost that argument: Uncle who saw no reason to lower his trousers in front of us, and even if he did (which he wasn't about to do!) to hold himself back because of the dribbling noise. With an exasperated huff and an angry puff, vowing to brave death itself for his bladder's cause he stormed out of the cellar and from thence hurried to the water closet on the second floor. He was followed in short order and in that order by Lisette, Guigui and myself, but not by Aunt Louise who remained steadfastly ensconced in the bowels of the house long after we had transacted our business and moved to the shuttered kitchen.

Slowly then, while Aunt Louise mortified attempted to save face in the cellar, the four of us opted for a return to normalcy as the only means of palliating our concern about Nanette's foolhardy mission. Trapped inside the house as we were, afraid to open the door or to speak above a whisper, cast out of a war that had exploded so terrifyingly above our craven bodies mere hours earlier, the unsettled present took on a surrealistic quality. We sat at the kitchen table, harkening to the cuckoo-clock chirp each creeping half-hour in the dining-room. Through the clover leaf design of the shutters we watched the dawn bloom into morning. Like sun baked soil, her two day old makeup had long cracked on Lisette's face and Uncle's beard was growing grizzled gray. Everything was real, even the familiar knifescars on the surface of the wooden table under my fingers. And yet, I had a growing suspicion that beyond the walls inside which we sat as perennially intact as the familiar objects, the noises and the colors, the shapes and scents that surrounded us, everything else was strange and unreal. Our house had become the castle of the Sleeping Beauty and a hundred year old forest encircled us stretching its impenetrable density between us and the rest of the world.

It was shortly before nine when the sounds returned. At first numbed as we were by the silence we ignored them. Uncle shrugged and pointed toward the cellar with his chin: Aunt Louise tired of her self-imposed stoicism, probably. We sighed and drifted back into our individual meditations. But within seconds as the cuckoo struck nine the sounds broke out again, or rather the sound: like someone's nails scratching the shutters in a stealthy entreaty. Uncle stiffened in Mémé's chair. We all looked at him, searched the light oozing from the clover leaf patch above his head. An then there came a faint rap, one lone, three short, one long again in a definite pattern, as if whoever was outside on the Avenue meant to signal to us they were friends.

Uncle rose from his chair. His hand stiff and fingers spread wide apart bade us to remain seated. His eyes appeared to be under the hypnotic spell of the kitchen door-knob. He tip-toed toward it. Stopped. His eyes glided toward the window opened on the drawn shutters. I held my breath and clenched my fist against my right knee. He was heavy, Uncle, yet we did not hear him as he took three more steps and at last reached the kitchen door. The lock squeaked when he turned the porcelain knob. Then the signal came again: one long, three short, one long. This time whoever it made no attempt at muffling its sounds. I swung around on my chair. My mouth gaped as I watched Uncle make his way into the hallway. One more step and he was out of sight.

"Marcel! Uncle Marcel!" a voice called from behind the closed shutters. "Open the door!" An impatient hush, slightly anguished. "Forgot my key, Marcel. Louise, can you hear me?"

Then simultaneously the trap-door of the cellar flew up in the hallway and Uncle opened the front door. Daylight flooded it and the top half of Aunt Louise popped out of the cellar like a Jack-out-of-the-box.

"Marcel, it's Nanette!" she yelled

And he:

"I know it's her, I got eyes!"

And Aunt Louise still:

"Just saw her face through the grating!"

And then we were all crowding the hallway and pushing and shoving behind Uncle to get a look at Nanette. We were laughing because we had been scared and suddenly she was back and the war was almost over and she was kissing us in turn and sniffling between laughter. Almost crying. Uncle patted her back and nodded his head. Aunt Louise now all out of the cellar berated her for her imprudence and Lisette told her mother to be quiet because Nanette was back and that was all that mattered. Our words collided with each other: the din of our joy shattered our collective anguish.

I was tugging frantically at Nanette's waist, trying to get her attention when I saw him. The smile froze on my lips and something rasped against my throat.

I don't know why I was so surprised because Nanette had said she wouldn't come back without him. Perhaps after fearing for both of them so much the mere sight of her had thrown by the wayside our anxiety. He wore his slippers still, and the same blue overalls he had worn when they had arrested him. But his belt was gone: one of Nanette's safety pins held the trousers around his waist. The upper right front side of his overalls was torn. There was a piece of it missing between the waist and the brown bud of his left breast and his skin, white, gaped from it like an indecent wound. His face was like those of the vagrants who scour the summer country roads: unkempt and hunted by a hell within, intimate yet inexplicable. His nose, like Mémé's the last time I had laid eyes on her was pinched and slender like the body of a butterfly and on each side of it, two violet wings spread their wary planes under his hollowed eyes. The stubble of his beard, older and dirtier than Uncle's, devoured the bottom half of his face and his upper lip was drawn tightly over his lower lip as if he were biting it in an attempt at holding something back. But down the length of the two violet wings of exhaustion, two symmetrical tears were raining. Only Bébert could cry like that. So silently.

I had not noticed they had stopped talking. But now, as Uncle moved toward Bébert I heard the silence: it was so thick that it pushed against my mouth and I felt like breathing deep and long but could not because it was so hard to move. Behind me Lisette started weeping. Uncle Marcel who was shorter and fatter than his cousin drew his short arms and clasped Bébert in a bear hug. Above Uncle's right shoulder, Bébert's eyes were still crying.

"I'm glad to see you, cousin!" Uncle choked at last drawing away from Bébert. "Louise, Lisette, you get him something to eat while I get the wine! Bet you ain't eaten in a while, have you, Gilbert?" he said turning again toward Bébert. "Well you come in and sit yourself down. And don't you talk till we get something into you." He sat Bébert in his chair, took a few steps back, looked at him. "You do look a fright! Still, we'd be glad to see you even if you looked like the plague itself, wouldn't we, wouldn't we?" Uncle choked looking at the rest of us and started to laugh. Already.

He looked as if he were visiting, Bébert, even though he sat in his own chair in his very own kitchen. He did not speak and hardly stirred and his eyes, dried now, kept sweeping the room as if he had never been in it before. When Uncle handed him a glass of wine, he bent his head and whispered a word of thanks. The shutters were still drawn and we had locked the front door again, but we were all together now and whatever happened outside no longer mattered. I sat on Uncle Marcel's lap my eyes guzzling Bébert's face, hypnotized by disbelief as much as love.

Aunt Louise and Lisette had breakfast ready for Bébert in no time: three of the six eggs we had bought at exorbitant black market price that Saturday went into his omelet. But incredibly, it took all of our pleas before he could bring himself to poke his fork into it.

"His stomach's shrunk!" Uncle explained while we watched Bébert reluctantly force each mouthful down his throat. "Better feed your man good, Nanette, like you did Léo the pig, right, Tina?"

"Right Uncle," I agreed though I really felt like crying.

There followed a second silence as we continued to watch Bébert struggle through his omelet; and then Uncle slipped his hands under my armpits and put me down. "Getting too heavy for my paunch, child, go see Lisette." He whispered while I proceeded to do so, his voice broke again behind me, his elbows planted firmly on the table he stared at Bébert.

"It's all well and good to have you back, Gilbert, but I want to tell you: your wife gave us no end of a fright taking off like she did with them krauts still out there –"

"They weren't there," Nanette cut him darting a concerned look at her husband. "They weren't there at all, at least not until I got to the Château."

"—and them shells and gunfire hitting all over town!"

"There was no shelling where I was," Nanette cut him off again, "and anyway I got him back, didn't I? That's all I wanted: to get him back!" she finished shaking her head obstinately.

"Nanette's right," Lisette opined conciliatory, "It doesn't matter now, father, they are both here and –"

"Sure they are," Uncle kept on, "But what about us? Three hours we sat up here, so scared we couldn't talk, worried sick out of our skulls something would happen - -"

"I'm sorry…" Nanette apologized awed by Uncle's irate tirade.

"As well you should be, you crazy woman!" He was still glaring at her, Uncle, but his disapproval had weakened. He took a generous swig of wine, wiped his mustache with the callous edge of his hand. "Well? What are you waiting for, ain't it about time you told us what happened out there?"

"That's all you're interested in, ain't it Uncle?" She was teasing now Nanette and poking her husband's elbow. Bébert attempted a smile and winked feebly at me like he used to before Mémé's death.

"Sure it is!" Uncle shot back. "Well???"

Nanette searched each of our faces to make sure she had our attention. "Well…" she echoed Uncle, satisfied that she did. "Twas like this…"

I climbed on Lisette's knees, wound my arm around her neck. A fat and round beam of sunlight pouring through the clover leaf design of the drawn shutters bathed Guigui and his father. Between Nanette and Lisette and I, Aunt Louise sat upright on her stool, bony arms crossed across her flat bosom. An unseen bird outside answered the cuckoo when it chirped the half of the ninth hour as Nanette proceeded to recount her story.

"Twas still pretty dark when I left," she began. "All them houses were shut and there wasn't a soul in sight and for a while, I tell you, I was scared out of my wits being out in them cat-and-dog streets by myself. 'Twere like all of Dormans was dead and buried along with Mémé and somehow I was the only one alive. And the silence! You wouldn't believe the –"

"We heard it too," Uncle cut her.

"YOU heard it?! Out there 'twas worse, heathen almost, that's what it was!" she drank some wine, wiped her lips with the back of her hand, and then resumed: "Anyway, after a while I got used to it, even was sort of grateful for it. There weren't any krauts at the Town Hall: doors wide open but none of them around. I held on tight to my paring knife with one hand and with the other kept pushing back Marcel's helmet - - you got a big head, Uncle! - - 'cause it kept sliding down over my eyes - - "

"By the way, where is my helmet?" Uncle interrupted her. Aunt Louise hissed impatiently next to Lisette and me. "T'ain't mine you know, belongs to the city!"

"I lost it, that's what! The racket it made when it hit the cobbled stones in front of Rigaux's warehouse! So I left it there 'cause it was more trouble than help. After that I made good time till I got to the Empire Theater. I tell you, though, I thought my heart would stop: it beat so fast it hurt. Still, I knew I had to get as close to The Château as I could before daylight moved in on me completely and it sure was moving fast: by the time I got to the Theater the sun was already rising. And still no one and not a sound around me. I got scared again, but not like that first time. There weren't a living thing but me in that street, not a stray bitch or a bird and the air was kind of dead. Even though I was running and pretty fast at that, I had the weirdest feeling I wasn't moving at all. Really scary it was! Anyway, I was moving 'cause soon I got to the cemetery. I looked in through the open gates at all them tombs and just prayed and prayed for Mémé to help me. I was so scared I was actually talking to her in my crazy mind and telling her all about Steigl and how she had to help me get her son back…Then, as I got to the end of the cemetery, a red robin shot up from nowhere on the road ahead of me, swooped around and down and skimmed the ground a couple of times. I'd stopped running by then and was just standing there, gaping at the bird as if I'd never seen its likes before. And I swear, that bird was looking straight at me, and suddenly I wasn't afraid anymore - -"

"'Bet 'twas Mémé that sent it!" Guigui blurted enthralled.

"Of course not!" Uncle demurred. "Just one of them red robins that nest in the cypresses. Bet you were glad to see a living thing though, Nanette?'

"Sure was! I tell you, after I'd seen it I wasn't scared anymore!"

"And then? What happened then?" I intervened because she seemed on the verge of distraction, Nanette.

"Well…I started running again through them back streets and finally made it too the corner of the Avenue du Château. I'd just about reached the end of Oak Street and was about to make my turn into the Avenue when someone grabbed me so hard from behind I was near swept off my feet. My mouth felt like for screaming but before I had time to catch my breath, he slapped his hand across it, kept it there so tight I could hardly breathe!"

"A Boche? Uncle shot his mouth gaping.

I had slid down from Lisette's knees and was holding onto the table's edge, tight.

"Was it a Boche, mother?" Guigui asked anxiously.

"Well, was it?" came Aunt Louise, impatient.

"Let me tell it my way, will you?" Nanette snapped with a frown.

She picked up her glass from the table, took a fiendishly deliberate sip, then another sip, while we seethed with curiosity around her.

"Well?!" Uncle ordered her at last.

"It wasn't a Boche…" Nanette started again, setting her glass back on the table ever so slowly and looking at Lisette in an odd way. "'Twasn't a Boche at all…Anyway, there I was, wanting to scream and break lose and scared but he was still holding on tight to me and pulling me back against one of them doors. It was right about then that I heard a rumbling of engines coming from somewhere on my right toward The Château. The door of the house back of us flew open and they dragged me in and locked the door again. And when we were inside, this one man let go of me and I made as if to scream - - "

"Who was he?!" Uncle exploded unable to contain himself any longer.

"'Twas Langiers, Lisette, that's who it was!" Nanette beamed at her. "it sure was him, Lisette," while Lisette blushed and squeezed my waist. "He wasn't in them fancy clothes, just overalls and a military helmet and he had a machine gun slung over his shoulder. I was so stunned seeing him there in that get up that I couldn't speak! There were five other men in there with him: four I didn't know but the fifth was the apprentice mechanic of the garage on the road to Epernay. They were armed to the teeth. Then the rumble of the engines grew louder: we could hear them coming towards us. Langiers barked something and the others scattered through the house as he yelled at me what the hell was I doing out there and I told him I was going after Bébert and he said I was out of my mind 'cause some SS were still inside The Château and what the hell did I think war was any way. God he was angry!"

"He had a right to be, you crazy woman!"

"Let her go on Marcel," Aunt Louise ordered her husband.

"The noise of the cars was growing outside," Nanette continued, "'Twas real close by then. Langiers pushed me inside the parlor of that house and said for me to lie on the floor 'cause there was going to be some fireworks in a minute. He said they had been waiting for the SS to pull back most of the night, that all the krauts had left except the SS bastards 'cause they always were the last to go, and it had been a long night but they were going to get it now 'cause Oak Street was crawling with Americans and maquisarts and I was going to see something I wouldn't soon forget. There was as small table pushed against the wall under the window ledge and he set up his machine gun on it real fast like and pointed it at the street, just in time too 'cause within the next few seconds the first car loaded with SS turned into Oak Street.. After that everything went crazy! There was a lot of shooting back and forth and grenades exploding all around, one of them even hitting dead center one of the SS jeeps and turning it into an inferno, black Citroens speeded past the window and Langiers yelled like a mad man behind his machine gun! Then after a while, the others came rushing downstairs and them and Langiers went running outside with their guns and their grenades and when I looked up again, the window was in slivers and there were no more cars speeding past it. The gunfire was moving down the street, real fast like. I tell you, the whole thing was over in seconds and I was by my lonesome in that house, not quite sure what had happened!"

"An ambush, that's what happened, a bloody ambush!" Uncle burst out slapping his fat knee with glee. "Hope they got every last one of those bastards!"

"Did they Mother?" Guigui queried.

"That Langiers," Aunt Louise cut him. "Always as prim as a sissy and then pulling a stunt like that."

"Like what?" I snapped because I still did not trust Langiers.

"Like this!" Lisette answered pinching my ear. "Like what Nanette just told us. A brave man - - "

"He still talks German!" I objected.

"Hush Tina," Uncle ordered pinching my other ear. "You just don't like him, that's all."

"They'd left the door open," Nanette resumed. "so I sneaked into the hallway, took a look outside. There was a Citroen burning and a couple of dead krauts lying next to it way down the street on my left. I saw the rumps of three American soldiers rounding the corner heading toward the cemetery. After they had gone I just took off like a hare. I ran down the Avenue, till I got to the main gate of The Château. Wide open it was. The park looked deserted. I could hear gunfire behind me, far, and I thought Langiers and the Americans were fighting it out with what was left of the SS. I thought for sure there weren't any krauts left in The Château but I wasn't taking no chances. Someone had set fire to the outbuildings and there was black smoke snaking up from them rubbles, but down the gravel path, ahead of me some ways, the Château seemed intact. Windows wide open except for those on third floor that were all boarded up. I crossed the gate and started edging my way from tree to tree, the grass so thick I couldn't hear my footsteps. First time I'd been back there since before the occupation and I tell you, Louise, I'd forgotten how pretty it was in that park: green and quiet and thick and scented. Rich, real rich, even after them Boches had been in there all those years!"

"It sure used to be pretty there," Aunt Louise mused startling me. "Still remember when the Count's family gave it to the town, years ago…They would open it Bastille Day. We'd just been wed, Marcel and me, and we'd take food and wine, Marcel his fishing gear and me my sewing and we'd spend the whole day by the big pond that's up a ways behind the Château going toward The Gaux: cows grazing, hawthorn in the air and morning-glories - - "

"What's with you woman?" Uncle broke in staring at his wife with as much disbelief as I was. "Talking like a bride you are!"

Aunt Louise caught herself, pinched her thin lips and averted the onslaught of our eyes.

"I got memories too," she snorted chin thrust forward. "And I can remember them old days." She looked up from her crossed arms, squinted her eyes at Uncle like her old usual self was straining to get back behind them. "Ain't I got a right to remember them pretty days, ain't I?"

Uncle's eyes retreated toward the bottle of wine sitting at the center of the table. He mumbled a few inaudible words and his brows quivered over his mustache which was doing likewise.

"Look at your parents, Lisette!" Nanette teased, "Lovebirds they must have been in those days."

Lisette's chins rippled with mirth. Her hand searched her father's.

"Let go of me, daughter!" Uncle scolded her. "this ain't no time for your female drivel. You finish your story Nanette else we'll be liberated long before you're done. Go on, woman, go on!"

Nanette chortled and presently resumed her account.

"I had no idea where they might have put him, Bébert, but I was hoping he would be there somewhere. I thought I'd start with the main building so, like I said, I made my way to the Château and soon got to the main staircase. Still couldn't hear a human sound but there were plenty of birds chirping away behind me by then, happy as could be. It was dark inside the marble hall and for a while I couldn't see much 'cause my eyes were still blind from the outside sun. I took off my shoes because the wooden soles were making a racket every time they'd hit the marble floor. I had just about passed the big staircase that's on the right when I heard a door slamming upstairs and voices, funny voices. I made a line for the staircase and hid under it: lots of room under there and even a stone bench like they got in the church. I was too scared to sit, I just squeezed under the ramp, strained my ears. Four of them were coming: I could see their hands sliding down the stone ramp, and then one of them started talking and the others answered him. They talked like they had oatmeal in their mouths and I knew immediately they were Americans, you know how they talk. I mean, even without seeing them I knew they weren't Boches 'cause they didn't sound like they were scratching throats all the time.

I poked my head out a bit and, sure enough, they were Americans, just like you've seen them in the movies: Errol Flynn, Clark Gable, Laurel and Hardy, they all look like that to me! I shot like a bullet out from under the staircase, ran up the stairs and grabbed the first one. Laughing I was, like I was possessed, and hugging that poor man till he was crying out for mercy...By then the others were pulling me away 'cause I still held on to that carving knife and they were sure I was crazy enough to use it: must have been! Anyway, soon they had me sitting on one of the steps, trying to explain what I was doing there. I don't talk American as you know, but one of them spoke a little French, enough so as I could make him understand about Bébert. When it got through to him what I was after he looked at the others like he had just had a brainstorm or something and talked to them in American and they all broke into grins and slapped my back and started talking all at once and pointing upstairs. Then the one that spoke French said for me to follow him 'cause they had found four Frenchmen locked up in the basement chapel and Bébert was sure to be one of them. They had moved them upstairs again..."

She was breathless, Nanette, and her eyes sparkled with retrospective excitement but so close to the denouement, Uncle was not about to countenance an intermission.

"Well, go on!" he prodded her urgently.

"I got to breathe, don't I?" she remonstrated him her hand clasping her runaway heart.

"You can breathe later!"

"Well, when they told me that I flew up the stairs, calling out Bébert's name and slamming doors open on the landing till I got to the right one and I saw several men standing and sitting around desks in that office, and Bébert way behind them sitting by his lonesome near the window. I shoved the others out of my way, climbed over a desk and grabbed him. I hugged and kissed him, right in front of these people, didn't I, Bébert, didn't I?"

We all turned our heads toward Bébert. He sat in his chair, still dirty, as erect as a king under his ancestral crown, and as profoundly asleep as an old curate over his prayer book.

"Poor cousin," Uncle smiled nodding his head gently. "Bet he hasn't slept since they took him away!"

"That's also what I thought when I saw him," Nanette whispered as her hand brushed Bébert's unshaven face.

He didn't even stir under her caress. He was lost in the labyrinth of his exhaustion and it would be a while before we got him back.

"Did he tell you what they did to him?" Uncle inquired of Nanette in a whisper.

"Wouldn't talk about it…I asked him several times, but the never gave me an answer."

"Probably too close to him yet, poor Bébert!" Lisette offered.

"He did say one thing though - - "Nanette voiced as if she had just remembered an important detail. "Redlich apparently kept his word: That man really did help like he said he would.

"How?" Guigui queried.

"From what Bébert was able to tell me, ever since they took him away the SS, him and the others had been locked up in a room on the third floor - - apparently that's where Steigl did his dirty work! Anyway, remember when that first round of shell fire hit us last night? Well, it hit them too! Bébert said when it broke there were lots of shouts and a confusion outside their cell and for a while they thought the SS were coming for them. 'Twas pitch black in the Château according to Bébert and him and the other three kept waiting for Steigl to come in and finish them off before decamping. Instead what happened is that Redlich - - and Bébert says that man really stuck his neck out because Steigl could have shot him for it - - Redlich at some point in the confusion smuggled them out of their cell. He couldn't set them loose 'cause that would have been too dangerous, so he took them down to the basement and hid them in the Chapel. Redlich told them no one ever went down there and that he hoped between the fighting and them having to pull back, Steigl and his men wouldn't waste any time looking for them once they found out they were gone. And it worked, it really worked because that's where the Americans found them this morning gave them some rations and instructed them to get back upstairs until the resistance showed up and gave them the All Clear and - - "

"And Redlich?" Lisette interrupted anxiously. "What about Redlich?"

"Gone with the others I guess," Nanette opined. "A shame too! I would have liked to thank that man, even if he is a Boche. I really would have liked to - - "

She stopped abruptly. I too had heard the whirring echoes of distant vehicles: we all had. We fell silent around the table except for Bébert whose breath as he slept rhythmically whistled its way out of his parted lips. We sat harkening to the growing roar coming ever closer to us. And then within seconds the thunder broke outside and behind the closed shutters, the Avenue exploded into a storm of shouts and we were all standing and rushing pell-mell toward the front door because we knew by then that the clamor outside could only be that of freedom.

They were at a standstill down the next crossroad to our left the Americans: five tanks, six jeeps and one open truck over-spilling with GIs. A small detachment considering the military might with which the Germans had overwhelmed us during four years of occupation. There was no way they could have made it to the Town Hall. People had stormed their convoy and were besieging their men like a swarm of ants assaulting a jar of honey. Except it wasn't like that. No.

It was more as if Dormans had been a giant slumbering beast all those years and suddenly the beast was coming alive and shaking loose its lethargy in a volcanic spasm of surging life, and the people streaming out of the side streets toward the Americans were the new blood rushing through the beast's arteries, and the hundred shutters being slammed back against the facades of the houses were a hundred eyelids raised to behold a new day and the thunderous clamor born from a thousand throats was the jubilant cry the beast let out as it rose from its deep slumber and stood against the sky of victory.

"Good Lord! Good God!" Uncle exploded jolting me out of my trance. "It's them, it's them alright! It's really over, the war is really over!!"

Incredulity and many emotions like joy and confusion made him talk in duplicate, Uncle.

"Look at them! Look at them, Louise! Aren't they beautiful, aren't they the most beautiful sight you ever saw!"

He was nodding his head and slapping his thighs and he was rocking back and forth and clasping his chest as if he were nursing the elation throbbing inside of him. And then Nanette burst out laughing next to me while Lisette broke into tears and I hung on to my breath, my heart and Aunt Louise's bony fingers, unable to do either because the conflicting emotions were wedged inside my throat like two people stuck in a narrow door.

"There's Jacques Pottin!" Guigui screamed excitedly behind me as he spotted his friend amid the coagulating throng. "Jacques! Jacques!" he yelled.

He sprung between Aunt Louise and I and tore toward the crowd and in the next instant we were all running after him except for Bébert whom we had left to his restorative slumber inside the shuttered kitchen and Aunt Louise because even at that incredible moment she was as much a prisoner of her inhibition as she had ever been. I caught a glimpse of her over my right shoulder: she was walking, just walking, with only the slightest hint of haste but her thin lips were split open over her yellowed teeth in what was as near to a smile as she would ever come. Then Nanette grabbed ahold of my hand and I forgot Aunt Louise. She yelled to Lisette over my head that she didn't want to lose me. My heart was exploding, my feet had left the ground. Ahead of us Guigui and Jacques Pottin crashed into the crowd and within seconds we were doing likewise and I was suddenly straddling Uncle's shoulders.

They were about twenty heads ahead of me, the Americans, dazed and flustered, dirty and overwhelmed by our adulation. Wine and champagne dribbled down their chins and lipstick flowers bloomed at exuberant random on their chins, cheeks and even their lips. Many of the girls that used to wait for Langiers Saturday mornings on the Place du Luxembourg were there hugging and kissing them to suffocation. There were hands outstretched, so many hands, and flowers flying and people screaming and echoes of accordions playing American tunes. A gale of laughter, a wind of hysteria. A cold dribble down my bare knee. Nanette laughing, wiping the bubbly champagne off my sandaled foot, dabbing her wine-soaked finger behind her ears for luck. As my small hands crushed Uncle's forehead, I thought for sure we had all the luck we would ever need and that peace was a far greater thrill than love had been that lonely afternoon by the Marne river. At any rate, I was hiccupping again, and quite wrenchingly as a big burly Yankee soldier hoisted me from Uncle's shoulders, bussed my cheeks and laid a fat juicy orange in my hands: the first orange I had ever seen let alone tasted.

Like one intractable knot of coagulated humanity, it took some time for the Americans and us to travel the three blocks which separated their convoy from the Town Hall Square. I do not know where all the people had come from which crowded it. There were hundreds, perhaps a thousand faces, all straining in the same direction as each one tried to catch a glimpse of the liberators. So many faces! Like an endless field of big sunflowers, fluttering, wavering, streaming to the limits of my horizon. All the men and women of Dormans were there, and the children also from the newest born to the oldest acned adolescent, with only wonder in their eyes. Then as the throng rounded the corner of the Town Hall, the deafening noise which had accompanied our slow progress gave way to a whispering tide that started at the American heart of the crowd and slowly rippled its course toward us. Uncle's mustache tickled my bare calves as he craned his head toward Nanette and his warm breath streamed down my knees when he spoke.

"What's happening?" he asked anyone who would answer.

"Pichegrus says some big wheel is coming!" Nanette voiced uncertainly as she too tried to read the faces around her.

"Who is coming?" came an imperative voice behind me: Monsieur Lucien ever worried about his rights. "Do you know who it is, Monsieur Germain?"

"Ain't got the faintest idea," Uncle poured down my right leg again.

And then everyone started questioning and searching each other's faces and there were names mentioned with question marks tagged after them: De Gaulle? Leclerc? Maybe even Eisenhower?

"They ain't got no cause to come to Dormans," Aunt Louise sassed peremptorily. "We ain't important enough!"

"Tut! Tut! They got to come through Dormans to get to Germany," Uncle retorted sharply under me.

Several voices shot up in support of Uncles position including that of the indomitable Monsieur Lucien who not only thought he had rights but also viewed himself as the belly-button of Dormans and thus by extension, thought Dormans was the belly-button of the world. He and Aunt Louise glared at each other. But as we all held our breaths in anticipation of an acrimonious skirmish the familiar voice of Mayor Chancel blaring out of the bull-horn somewhere brought the crowd gathering on the square to startled attention.

The American convoy with the command jeep leading the way, had come to a halt along the curved front steps of the Town Hall. The sun, now high above the fields across the river, the fields where I had first come upon love, was ascending to its noon zenith, setting ablaze the glistening slates of the sloped roof of the Town Hall as it slowly arose from behind the building. Across the crowd from me, Dr. Martin's window panes were of pure gold, blinding, and a little to the left of it, the many slivers and splinters of broken glass strewn throughout the rubles of Monsieur Pottin's store scintillated like iridescent gems. Since Mayor Chancel's jolting bull-horn blast the crowd had fallen into a whispering hush but it would not be long before they grew restless again. Even Uncle under me was beginning to shuffle and strain. The soldiers had alit from their vehicles. Machine guns sporting carnations slung over their shoulders and helmets dangling over their rumps, they milled about their vehicles while their commander, two of his aides and Mayor Chancel, held council on the steps of the Town Hall. After and interminable while, the Mayor detached himself from the official group and waving his bull-horn high above the crowd, he made his way to the command jeep and hopped upon its hood with surprising agility. I had barely time to whisper to Uncle and the others to be quiet before Chancel, standing erect, taurine and rubicund upon his commandeered stage brought the bull-horn to his lips. Within seconds a sweeping tide of silence washed over the crowd and even Monsieur Lucien behind me, unseen but ever vocal, grudgingly came to attention.

"My fellow citizens!" Mayor Chancel began, testing the bull-horn for effect, "My dear fellow citizens!" he surveyed the crowd, inflated his basso's chest. "The day has come to pass! This day which we all have been praying for and fighting for, this day which even the darkest hour of our national agony we never once kept hoping would come, this marvelous day I am grateful, honored and proud to say, has indeed come to pass - - - " he stopped again, turned dramatically toward Town Hall. His arm offered us the Americans: "They are here at last!" He exploded. "They are here and ---"

A thunder of applause drowned his voice as the crowd roared its approbation and cheered the Americans. The outburst was deafening but thoroughly exhilarating. Even Uncle at his patriotic loftiest had not sent through my spine this shiver of national pride which, had he not been holding on tightly to my legs, would have, I was sure, sent me soaring from my launching pad upon his shoulders. I screeched with delight and banged his head with gusto and laughed at Lisette red as a newborn below me whose voice although she tried, could not begin to match my shrieking pitch. It was a gale of collective madness and swept over the crowd and reason was gone and nothing, not the full incandescent orb of the August sun poised in full glory over the slate roof of the Town hall, not the American commander as he attempted to still the uproar with an impotent wave of his braided officer's cap, could bring the crowd under control. After four years of submission to tyrannical orders extracted at the price of fear, of national silence because of national shame, freedom was back and no one was ready to let go of it again any time soon.

At last, after a good five minutes of sustained acclamations and exhausted by its boisterous hysteria the crowd lapsed into a heaving spell. Mayor Chancel who had been taken aback by the passion he had unleashed hastily brought the bull-horn back to his lips while the American officers closed rank on the steps of the Town Hall.

"Please! Please!" the Mayor pleaded through his bull-horn, wagging a scolding forefinger at a cluster of die-hard vociferators in front of Dr. Marin's house. "We can do better than that, can't we? I know and they know" he said pointing to the Americans, "what this day means to us but behaving like a mob isn't going to make it better than it already is! We may be free but we have a lot of work to do and I am counting on every one of you to ---"

"The Mayor's right," Uncle whispered under me. "Behaving like ---"

"Schhh!" Aunt Louise admonished him while Nanette giggled silently to Uncle's right.

"Restraint and industry: that's what I expect from each and every one of you." Mayor Chancel went on blaring. "And this applies to me too. That's why I shall dispense with a speech at this time even though I shan't soon have your willing ears like I have them now!" A few laughs shot through the crowd. "But much as I hate to pass the opportunity, there's important work to be done." He nodded toward the American commander who blinked his eyes gratefully. "There are two things I have to say and then you can all go home and start this town working again. First, we understand there may still be some Germans hiding around our parts. Now, I know a lot of us think we have a score to settle with the krauts and even I myself might like to get my hands on one of them bastards! But this is a law-abiding town and prisoners of war must be treated within the framework of the Geneva Convention. I know the Germans never did play by those rules and more often than not they wiped their asses with the Geneva Convention, but we are better than them and that's why, if we do find one of those sons-of-a-bitches hiding in our town, we will immediately, and I stress immediately, turn him or them over to the Americans or to the local authorities. This is an order and I expect everyone to abide by it! Let the authorities deal with them. They will get what's coming to them, don't worry and - - -"

"Don't worry! Don't worry! Monsieur Lucien spat behind me. "Just let me find one of them bastards, just let me!" he whispered threateningly as I turned toward him startled. His beady eyes behind the steel-framed lenses of his spectacles were an aspic of hatred. A cold shiver ran down the back of my neck as I watched his lips spit vengeance and a thought, indistinct really yet frightening, streaked through my subconscious.

The crowd exploding into another round of cheers prevented me from tracking the reason behind my apprehension.

"------General George S. Patton!" Mayor Chancel was blaring as the cheers shot up again. "He will be arriving in Dormans at about five this afternoon and we got to give him a rousing welcome! He's the commander of these men, the Commander in Chief of the U.S.

Third Army, the brain behind the liberation of Dormans and the man to whom, besides our friends here, we owe our freedom!"

"See, Louise," Uncle scolded her under me. "I told you they had to pass through Dormans to get to Germany!"

"Patton! Patton!" Aunt scoffed shrugging her angular shoulders. "Who's Patton anyway?"

"Yes, who is Patton?' I echoed her.

Uncle squeezed my knees and craning his neck attempted to find my face. "He is a great General, girl! Don't listen to your Aunt, she's just bitching."

"Schhh!" Nanette, this time, glaring at the three of us.

I shrunk my head inside my shoulders and came to attention. Mayor Chancel was still exerting himself behind his bull-horn.

"They tell me the General ain't one for ceremonies but he's going to get one whether he likes it or not!" he declared with finality to the approval of the crowd. "I want to meet with the town's officials in the school at 13:00 so we can lay out plans for a proper tribute. As for the rest of you, I will see you at four-thirty sharp on this square so we'll all be ready and in place for him when he arrives. Now, get on home! The war is a far cry from being over for these lads and we have to let them rest a bit so they can go on to Epernay tonight winning more battles."

With a dismissing sweep of his hand, Mayor Chancel packed his bull-horn under his left arm, hopped down from the jeep and made his way to the Town Hall steps. Within seconds he and the Americans, followed in short order by Lisette who, unseen, had left our side, and the town crier, Monsieur Jaubert, disappeared inside the building to begin the slow and laborious task of salvaging out the shambles left by four years of German occupation whatever structural scraps might serve as a basis for returning Dormans to its pre-war condition.

Almost reluctantly but not without anticipation the crowd proceeded to disband: five o'clock and Patton would be here and then the celebrations would resume and the joy would be unleashed again upon our town. As we slowly made our way home, Uncle predicted that people would be dancing on the Place du Luxembourg that night while Nanette already schemed to have me deliver the traditional hero's bouquet to General Patton and took no time in convincing herself that Lisette could arrange the honor. Guigui and Jacques Pottin dreamt of catching a German deserter and, notwithstanding the Mayor's admonition, daringly proposed to dispose of him in various but equally gruesome ways. Aunt Louise worried about lunch and the shell hole in her house while I, listening to the desultory drone of their conversation began to suspect the sandman had paid me an early visit. I tightened my grip around Uncle's neck and let the whole irresistible weight of my head fall upon his. It smelled of coarse tobacco and something else, perhaps that thin, moist film of summer sweat which coated our skins as they rubbed against each other. Bébert was no longer in the kitchen when we reached home: he had gone to bed. Butter yellow scraps of his omelet had fried on the flowered edge of his plate.

Thus, amid the flowers and the echoes of accordions, the kisses and the spilled champagne, the confusion and Mayor Chancel's bull-horn admonitions, we surrendered our town to the Americans together with our gratitude and celebrated the return of yet another peace to the streets of Dormans. I thought little of Oberleutnant Redlich that morning and did not realize until much later that day that neither Mademoiselle Rouleau nor Madame Tardieux had been among the celebrants gathered on the Town Hall Square. My attention was all taken by the events erupting about me. I had never known there could be among adults such a universality of emotions, a unanimity of hopes, a consensus of love. The town was one in its exuberant madness and even if my ears caught vague echoes of a recriminating strain that must have played in the background of our joy even then, I thrived with the majority inside the happiness, convinced that together with the fear, the Germans and the war, it had crushed the hatred and would be our sole emotional substance for a long time to come.

*
* *

CHAPTER XI

It had been a thoroughly confounding day I thought as, preened and beribboned, clutching to my throbbing breast a bouquet of red carnations, I towered over the crowd assembled on the Town Hall Square. Behind me Mayor Chancel sashed by his tricolor cummerbund argued over a point of protocol with Father Rocas whose wide-sleeved and lace-trimmed surplice fluttered about him like wind-blown sails whenever he threw up his hands, which was often. Below us the school children under the stern eye of the town's academe opened up a parterre which began at a respectful distance from the steps of the Town Hall and fanned out into the far side streets on the other side of the square. The children were followed by the twelve members of the City council among whom Bébert stood, still disturbingly remote and thin in his Sunday suit. Behind them came Dorman's six-man brass band followed by the local chapter of the World War I Veterans' Association consisting of thirteen much decorated sexagenarians proudly bearing the moth-eaten standard of their defunct regiments. Uncle Marcel somewhat restless could be seen among them. The loss of his brass helmet accounted for his exclusion from the more colorful ranks of the Voluntary Firemen's Association whose members were lined up behind the Veterans.

After the firemen the assemblage became eclectic Maitre Pinson under his black top-hat wobbled between Dr. Martin and the undertaker, Monsieur Pichegrus, in a line that also included some of Dorman's tradesmen and functionaries such as Monsieur Jaubert and his ubiquitous drum. At last, in a chaotic grouping, came the backbone of the citizenry: the housewives and the old folks, the young men Aunt Louise was often berating, the farmers from the nearby villages including Monsieur Matthieu and his son Philippe an even Dorman's only street sweeper.

I knew I should have been proud for the privilege of being among the handful of officials about to greet General Patton that I should have been happy too in spite of Guigui who from behind Langiers' camera was set to record this historical event and Nanette who kept signaling for me to straighten up my blue socks. Yet I couldn't bring myself to overcome the creeping foreboding which had overtaken me earlier that afternoon.

I had recovered from my weary spell when, soon after lunch, Jacques Pottin had burst into the kitchen to lure Guigui in a grand tour through liberated Dormans. They hadn't wanted me along but Nanette, quick to notice my discomfiture, had told them it would either be Guigui and me or neither one of us. So I had tagged along with them. Like carnival it had been, merry, noisy: a thousand Christmas mornings rolled into one mad emotional feast that left one breathless yet craving for more. There had been the Americans jamming the Place du Luxembourg among their tanks, their jeeps and killing machines as they waited to be billeted for the night. They were not at all like those other soldiers we had known for four years so we had promptly befriended a group of them. They had given us candy and chewing-gum - - a discovery - -, showed us the inside of their tanks, we had talked in sign language and laughed a lot. There had also been the people whose faces had worn the bitter frown of defeat for many years but who that hot August afternoon had gone around offering the soldiers a place under their roof, a piece of their heart, who had begged for a chance to give because the Americans had given them so much that day. How many emotions I had reaped during our foray through liberated Dormans, the flags and the vows of eternal friendship, the tears that were laughing and the laughter that meant one was on the verge of tears, the school choir practicing anthems out of tune and Monsieur Jaubert drumming our ears with a deluge of public announcements. Yet, despite our collective joy, Bébert could not be coaxed to join us because even as he watched the madness from the kitchen window, his mind was full of Steigl and the Easter Boche and whatever it was they had done to him at the Château.

Even as I stood waiting for Patton my shins overtaken by pins and needles because it was so long since I had arrived, I knew I had no reason to feel anything but the exhilaration I had felt earlier when heart ready to burst I had left the boys behind me to run to the Town Hall and tell Lisette about my joy. How fast I had run down the Avenue de la Marne, and how crushed I had been when she had not been there the first of the many people crowding the rotunda. I had dashed upstairs to the Mayor's office, raced through the Wedding Hall; I had even gone up to the third floor where there were more offices that I had never been in before because under the Germans the third floor had been off limits to all, even Lisette and the Mayor. But she had not been anywhere among the people bustling inside the Town Hall as I had searched for her with growing desperation.

I don't know what had made me think of the basement: perhaps it was my growing frustration. Lisette had told me about it on my first visit to the Town Hall two weeks after I had arrived in Dormans.

Like the third floor it was off limits to French civilians ever since the Germans had turned it into emergency living quarters. There was a large dormitory under there Lisette had explained her foot tapping the marble floor of the rotunda, big enough for twenty-four of them. They had even lugged the piano down from the Wedding Hall: she had heard them often enough banging on its keys! That afternoon, in my thwarted search for her, I had remembered her telling me about the basement and I stumbled down the forbidden staircase, guessing at the stone steps because they were so dimly lit. A long narrow corridor had unfurled at the bottom of the staircase at the end of which a single door had gaped open. Light had splashed from it, raw white like the August sun was pouring through the earth. I had soon identified Lisette's voice out of the several echoing from the far room and immediately a tide of relief washed aside my incipient discomfiture and I had bolted for the door at the end of the corridor my hands brushing the walls as if to push them faster behind me. I had run, run! Then about halfway down the corridor my foot had tripped over something lying on the floor: I could still hear the startled cry I had let out when in the next instant my eyes had found his body brushing against my shoe.

He had always made me uneasy, Soldat Mueller: even his greeting whenever I used to pass him on my way to school had sent icy shivers up the back of my neck. Now he was dead, I had thought, dead like Mémé and Monsieur Pottin; but unlike Mémé, he even looked dead. Yet incredibly I had felt no horror as I had stood watching him more stunned than frightened. I still wanted to run to Lisette, my heart was still been brimming with excitement. But something kept holding me back, something having to do with his eyes, the glassy way they had of following me at whatever awkward the angle without really seeing me at all. So I had pulled a handkerchief out of the pocket of my blue pinafore, a big one that had belonged to Pépé and now belonged to me because Nanette had given it to me after Mémé had died. It was yellow with age, big enough for a man, and it had covered all of Soldat Mueller's face, his mangled throat and even part of his hair which haloed his head on the cement floor.

No he had not scared me, Soldat Mueller: he was only a tiny part of what had happened that afternoon to make joy such a remote memory. If it hadn't been for what had happened next and then later at our house, then on the emotional map of my day his corpse could have remained a mere inconvenience and I could have gone on being happy just as I had been leaving him under Pepe's handkerchief to resume my flight toward the elusive Lisette. But there are days in a child's life when events make staying happy about as futile as trying to swim a river upstream, when no matter how hard one may try, the current of life is so overwhelming that it soon turns one's determination into helplessness and a ten-year old girl's happiness into a heartful of nothing. The scene which had confronted me upon reaching the doorsill of the Town Hall basement room coming as it did on the heels of my encounter with dead Soldat Mueller was about as happiness-shattering an event as I could not have anticipated.

It was an extremely long and dreary room which had opened to my left after my eyes had adjusted to the raw light, much like those endless metro corridors at major transfer points I remembered from Paris. Every surface of it was of reinforced concrete, from the drab walls to the hard stone flooring under my sandals, the arched ceiling that spanned its full depth. In an arrangement similar to that of a hospital ward, twenty-four iron bedsteads with neither mattress nor bedding opened up a central aisle that stretched the length of the room. Above my head a single file of naked electric bulbs of high wattage dangled from their respective wires at different heights because of the knots the Germans had tied into them to reduce the offending glare. At the far end of the room, sitting at an army-green metal table upon which there was only the inkwell in which she kept dipping her pen and an open register over which she was bent, Lisette was at work.

They were stretched between her and me, the dead, one each to eight of the iron bedsteads on my right. The nearest two were covered with bloodied sheets from the waist up because like blotting paper the linen had soaked up what was left of their faces; their unlaced boots poking up from the metal slats were of German make. Beyond them the next three wore civilian clothes; their faces, waxy white, were turned upward. One still clutched his gored belly with distorted fingers as though he had died trying to claw the pain away while another, right arm flung across his chest and fingers clenched, had been caught by death trying to find his missing left arm. The last three were too far from me to make them out but it was easy to tell the last one had no legs because the metal slats showing where they should have been broke the perspective drawn by the seven that preceded him.

In addition to Lisette and the corpses, there had been three American soldiers in the basement room: the tinkling of dog tags, of keys and change, the rustle of materials brushing against their hands as they searched the pockets of the dead and beyond them the uneven scratching of Lisette's pen against the page of the register as she wrote down the names they intermittently called out to her, were the only whispers of life disturbing the otherwise sepulchral silence. There was also the odor, a strange blend of mildewed mushrooms and dank leather, of singed skin and clotting blood, and even for some unexplainable reason of winter apples growing to wrinkles in a country attic: even Mémé hadn't smelled like that.

I had stood a long time hypnotized by horror against the jamb of the basement door. Then Uncle's voice had whipped me out of the stupor. I had not heard him and the other brass-helmeted fireman as they had staggered down the endless corridor their hands full of the last body.

"Lisette! What in God's holy name is that child doing here?" Uncle had thundered behind me.

"Didn't even know she was here father!" Lisette had parried after a quick glance in my direction. "You go on home, Tina. This is no place for you," she had lectured me already resuming her writing as I had stared at her uncomprehendingly.

One of the American soldiers had walked up to me: he had started easing me out of the room, down the corridor, whispering words of comfort and reassurance I did not understand. But beyond his voice I had strained to overhear Uncle's

"Who left Mueller out there?" he had asked.

"Where?" has come Lisette's voice

"In the corridor for God's sake!"

"Didn't even know he was one of them…"

A brief silence had followed behind the American and me, then:

"Ouff," Uncle had heaved. "There are fifteen at the school, mostly French I am afraid, twenty-four in the church and that's nine here with Mueller…Reckon there can't too many more out there but we got to make sure… what a hell of a job!"

"Mmm," Lisette had sympathized too rapt in her task to offer more.

"I tell you, they better bury them soon in this heat, 'cause…"

At that juncture someone had slammed the door shut behind us, Uncle probably, and peering over my shoulder at the dark pit behind me, I had vainly tried to find Soldat Mueller and waited for the American to fumble his way back to the far door.

Then I had climbed out of the basement, crossed the rotunda: soldiers had crisscrossed my path, yelled and laughed, shouted and obeyed orders. But I wasn't seeing anything, I was adding up in my head Uncle's dead: fifteen and twenty-four and nine, that came to forty seven or was it forty nine, but either way, there were too many for me to feel anything. Tragedy in bulk didn't make one cry, it was just numbing. I had remembered the morning and thought it would be nice if people could go about having their peace without the killing, if they could get together and decide to hold a peace like they decided to hold a picnic at the first of spring, for no good reason, because before the dead, peace had been fun: the best fun I had ever had.

There had been lots of thoughts running through my mind as I walked home from Town Hall that afternoon: bits of memories half-perceived melting into immediate oblivion when I tried to cull them, flitting emotions trying to prick at the rising numbness, but nothing whole enough to thread into one rational meaning all that I had seen since the previous day. Yet, even so, I could have lived with the confusion like I had done before, like I had done with the Easter Boche: I could have put the Town Hall dead on the back-burner of my curiosity until something happened to give them a meaning within my emotional reach. I had learned to forget a lot since Mémé's death and thus when I got home I was all set to try as hard as I could to forget about Soldat Mueller and the other dead. Once again, however, the tide of life that day was running at cross-current with my efforts to swim against it and thus it is much sooner than I had anticipated that the unsettling scene in the Town Hall came to have a meaning.

It came most unexpectedly when, stepping into our kitchen, I found Madame Tardieux and her day-old lodger paying the family a visit. It came in the periwinkle lightning that struck me when the teachers' eyes collided with mine over the widow's head and an as yet inchoate flash of perception streaked through my jumbled mind. Instinctively I sensed that in it laid part of the answer to the day's confusing onslaught. However, as usual, Nanette would not let me be. Absently, I answered her questions as to my afternoon meanderings holding as much back as I could, but then I found myself objecting with startling vehemence when she suggested I should get dressed for the ceremonies. There was still time, plenty of time, I insisted. Time to make myself small in the corner of the room and like Bébert put a smile on my face, a smile that was just a disguise enabling the mind to wander while giving the others the impression one was really attentive to each word being spoken. Time soon, to unseen and forgotten, scrutinized Mademoiselle Rouleau's flushed profile and wait until something she said, a move she made, brought the blurred outline of her nose into focus again and ignited that spark of recognition I had perceived a moment earlier.

And out of the light the present unrest had been born: if he had not laughed when Nanette had recounted once again how she had smothered the frightened American that morning at the Château; if, when she had not thrown back her head, laughing, those auburn curls had not rained out of her chignon as they had that day when she removed her bathing cap, then it should have been harder to make the connection. But she had made it so easy: the pride on her face when Nanette had told her about Redlich and how much the family owed to the German. So painfully easy. And suddenly there had been like a cloudburst in my mind followed by an outpour of images: the dead of the Town Hall, the hatred in Monsieur Lucien's eyes that morning, Redlich the day of Guigui's first communion. "A very pretty dress you are wearing, Fraulein Tina...a happy day, no?", Mayor Chancel's admonitions about German deserters, Guigui dreaming of gouging a kraut's eyes, Soldat Mueller's gored throat, Redlich again standing in the sunlight, glistening gold in his bathing trunk...A dizzying avalanche of recognition! All the pieces of the emotional puzzle had fallen into place that afternoon in the kitchen. And I had been scared, scared as I had never been before, not even that time when Steigl had come to take Bébert away. I had resented Mademoiselle Rouleau because I had sensed the reason behind her happiness and because like paper dolls Uncle's forty-seven or forty-nine dead had suddenly all had Redlich's face. Even now, echoing through my reborn anguish like some distant death knell I could hear the German's voice: "A beautiful day, no? A beautiful day, Fraulein Tina!" And I hated love as much as peace, longed to believe Redlich had gone while deep down hopelessly dreading the worst for him and the teacher.

The din of the church bells breaking over the square together with the sudden roll of an approaching motorcade abruptly jolted me out of my fretful state. The square became alive with people scrambling toward their assigned places while I began to scrounge for reality amid the muddled thoughts occupying my mind. On my left Mayor Chancel inflated his thorax, preened the red fringe of his cummerbund and Father Rocas hastily took in sail while I clutched the stems of the carnations and attempted desperately to grasp the reed of reality. An undercurrent of expectation rippled through the crowd and then, when the school children began to stomp the cobbled stones with their excitement, as suddenly as it had returned while we had waited for Patton, the fear and the anguish in me receded toward an emotional limbo out of reach of the joyful present. Within the next confused seconds as the last echo of church bells met a muffled death in some remote alley, a roar of urgency rounded the corner of the Town Hall and four jeeps came to a screeching halt between the throbbing mass and us. The brass band fearful lest they should miss their cue from the Mayor in the surf of excitement awash over the square, hurriedly broke into a jarring rendition of the American national anthem. At last, the dead of the Town Hall sank into my temporary oblivion.

Mayor Chancel buoyed by the long-awaited historical event remained impervious to the musical massacre while next to him Father Rocas, hands joined piously over his surplice, stood rapt and deaf in holy contemplation. The American officials unfairly caught by the zeal of the amateur band froze in their aborted attempt to alight from the jeeps saluted the Star Spangled Banner to gallop its cacophonous way out of the trombones and clarinets. At last, much to the collective relief, still at the same spirited tempo but this time more justifiably the band broke into the Marseillaise. I eased my grip around the flower stems and proceeded to search for the much heralded General Patton among the faces of the officers crowding the footsteps of the Town Hall.

He was older than Bébert, perhaps even older than Uncle Marcel and thus there was no reason for his eyes to linger on mine when they collided in the haphazard way eyes sometimes have of doing in crowd. Anyway, he was not seeing anyone right then. His eyes were like those funny one-way mirrors behind which the powerful often hide and there was nothing any of us could do to draw his attention. Below us, far away, the crowd had emotionally intoned the second verse of the French national anthem but I was not hearing any of its words: his face was all that mattered. I knew little of uniforms, stripes and decorations and yet I knew the carnations were his. It was his frown that told me he was a general and something else besides the frown: a nose which stabbed his face, thick white eyebrows jutting over the dark beads of the gleaming pupils, two wrinkles bitterly digging their furrows on each side of his nose and hair cropped to near baldness. But beyond the striking features and the frown he had a chin, strong, thrust forward in something akin to perpetual defiance. Perhaps that told me who he was for his was the face that had surely liberated Dormans.

I was still under the spell when the last martial bar of the Marseillaise came to an end and the crowd exploded into a roar of approbation. I watched him acknowledge the popular tribute with a perfunctory military salute then whip on his heels and start up the steps of the Town Hall. I could tell he was anxious to return to his war but this was counting without Mayor Chancel. Patton took the Mayor's offered hand as he had taken the acclamations: without a smile. He had been welcomed so often since D-Day, been thanked by so many small towns like ours that official tributes had come to mean little to him: they were the inevitable snags along the path to conquest that threw one off one's primary course and meant Germany was just that much farther. All this and more shown on his face as he listened sternly to Mayor Chancel's welcome, trying to control his impatience.

After it became apparent that Chancel carried away by his own delivery might proceed forever with his opening remarks, the General motioned to his aide and whispered a few words to him. Mayor Chancel watching the exchange alighted abruptly from his oratorical self-exaltation and fell into a confused silence while I began to suspect Patton was not the great man Uncle had led me to believe that morning. The crowd behind us had fallen into an expectant silence.

At last the aide turned toward Chancel. The General was now hiding behind the one-way mirror of his sunglasses and his frown had grown sterner.

"General Patton appreciates your welcome, Mr. Mayor," the aide began in surprisingly flawless French. "But he requests that the ceremonies be kept to a minimum: we have to proceed to Reims in the morning to set up headquarters for General Eisenhower and prior to that General Patton has to brief his staff to ---"

"Oh certainly, I understand," the Mayor hurried awed by the name of Eisenhower. "Have your people liberated Epernay then?"

"Not yet Mr. Mayor," the aide replied patiently. "But the coming night should change that. Now if we may- - "

"You won't mind if I tell them, do you? Mayor Chanel cut him again pointing to the crowd.

The American smiled, threw a helpless glance at his commander while Chancel interrupted him for the third time. He proceeded to shout the news of the upcoming liberation of Reims, the capital of Champagne, to the citizenry which immediately broke into another round of dilatory acclamations. My ears were afire with embarrassment. Patton glared at his aide and made a move to bypass Chancel only to be stopped by Father Rocas who, on behalf of the church, was as anxious to reap his moment of glory as the Mayor was to do so on behalf of the state. And suddenly I lost interest: more than ever peace was a disaster. I wanted it to be like it had always been with time to sort out one's thoughts and take one's emotions one at a time. I longed for it to be last week before Bébert's arrest and Uncle's dead, before Monsieur Lucien's threat and my fear about Oberleutnant Redlich's fate which was again creeping up in me as I looked at Nanette smiling at me so proudly and beyond her at the windows of Madame Tardieux's house.

"Tina! Tina!"

I jumped at Lisette's call: she had sprung up before me, was already grabbing hold of my free hand.

"The flowers, Tina!" she whispered her chin pointing at the official group. "Remember to curtsy now!"

I walked with her as if the whole thing were a dream. It had grown dark all of a sudden and except for Father Rocas' surplice which appeared almost phosphorescent in the crepuscular light, everything had become shadows and blurred contours, flat like a horizon yet infinite beyond the cluster of silhouettes etched against it.

He did not bend toward me when I curtsied, he didn't even acknowledge my name when the Mayor introduced me to him, and I feared if I raised my face to him the frown would still be there. At last he drew his hand out because it was what was expected of him and I handed him the flowers because it was what was expected of me but our hearts were not in it: his was full of war and impatience while mine was worn to numbness. I didn't even mind when he promptly handed the carnations to his aide: like this morning's joy they were wilted and no amount of hope would bring either back to life I turned my back on him without curtsying, searched for Lisette amid the shadows which had closed in around us. Then I felt her fingers around my wrist: I made a small fist and snuggled my whole hand inside hers. It was warm inside Lisette's hand and even though I was still tired and miserable, I did not feel as lonely as before.

Meanwhile, at some point during the ceremony Patton's men had apparently inched their way to the area fronting the entrance of the Town Hall because when the lights suddenly came on inside the building, flooding the square through the open doors, the windows, we found ourselves surrounded by them. I couldn't see the crowd anymore because of all of the people standing between it and Lisette and me but as I blinked under the sudden glare, I heard it: a man's voice rising far to my left, a tide of whispers there, a clear laughter shooting from my right somewhere in the night and closer by a lonely full note blowing out of an unseen trombone - - the opening echoes of a ball. Uncle Marcel had been right: there would be dancing on the Place du Luxembourg tonight. I was just comfy-tired now, and I didn't mind so much Patton, the dead and Oberleutnant Redlich. Lisette's velvety hip was soft and full under my cheek and soon I knew she would take me home, right after Mayor Chancel who was moving ever so slowly finished presenting that nice beribboned gift to the General . . . funny how naked the fourth finger of the Mayor's left hand looked: his skin was all dressed in suntan except for that one narrow strip close to his knuckle. I surrendered to an irrepressible yawn.

". . . in appreciation of what you and your country have done for my town and my country, General Patton," Mayor Chancel was saying, slowly because the aide was translating each sentence for the General, "As a small token of our gratitude I hereby present you with the key to our good city of Dormans. Actually it doesn't open any doors save the door to my cellar 'cause it was the only key big enough to look like it might open a town..." Chancel stopped, waited vainly for that hint of a smile which had appeared on the aide's lips to transfer itself onto the General's, "but I give you my word that from this day forward this key will open our hearts and our homes to you and stand as a symbol of our eternal gratitude."

I was quite close to the two men suddenly and my eyes didn't smart so much as they watched the General's hand struggle with the ribbon. I gasped with wonder when the lid fell back under his fingers. It was a good twenty centimeters long with a body as thick as my middle finger, an old-fashioned key with a finely chiseled head, and it glittered like gold as it rested on the padding of white satin. Not even the key to the Church's tabernacle was as pretty: it was the beautifullest key I had ever seen. Patton took it between his fingers, weighed it in the palm of his left hand. The frown was creasing his brow deeper than ever when he motioned to his aide. I was quite awake now.

"Mr. Mayor," the aide said at last turning toward Chancel who looked expectantly at him. "Is this a gold key?"

"Of course it is!" Mayor Chancel boasted. "It's the least we could do for the General!"

"I...the General understands," the aid voiced softly, ever so slightly embarrassed as he shot a glance at his commander. "But you see, it is against our military rules to accept such a precious gift and - - -"

"Well it's not all gold," Chancel came back hurriedly baffled by the turn of events. "Actually it is only gold plated but - - - "

"It's much more than that!" someone suddenly interjected, the voice throbbing with indignation.

It was Lisette. She had let go of my hand and stood confronting the three men, glaring in turn at Patton and at his aide.

"It's much more than that!" she huffed again as the men stared at her in astonishment. Her eyes bored their fury into those of the aide. "It may not be all of gold...anyway we don't have any gold left in

Dormans 'cause the Boches took it and we had to sell what was left to make it through the last four years, even our gold teeth, but it's - - - "

"Hush Lisette," Mayor Chancel attempted to intervene while Patton stung by Lisette's attack for the first time seemed to emerge from behind his one-way mirror. The aide was translating furiously, trying to keep pace with Lisette's indignation.

"It's much more than that!" she went on brushing aside the Mayor's objections. "It's priceless, that's what it is! It's our hearts in this key, General Patton, and it's the Mayor's wedding ring and the wedding ring of his wife. They both gave up their wedding rings so the key to our city could be gold-plated and look as precious to you as Dormans is to us!"

My eyes were agog with admiration: she was making up for the night Steigl had arrested Bébert, Lisette, and for the past four years of submission. It was as if the General's indifference coming on the heels of what we had all suffered during the occupation had ignited in her a latent courage and, for a while at least, it blazed even out of her control.

Too soon she ran out of words and as the Mayor taking advantage of the uneasy silence proceed to frown at her meaningfully, she began to realize all of sudden whom she had been berating for the last few minutes.

"You just got to accept the Mayor's key, General Patton," she finished after a blushing while. "You just must!"

This time she was looking for my hand and as I grabbed it, squeezed it tight between mine, the unexpected happened.

"I do..." General Patton started. The frown was still on his forehead but that was probably because he had been born with it, and his lips still weren't smiling but when he looked at Mayor Chancel and at

Lisette and when he looked at me and then at the crowd, it was like the sun breaking out in the middle of the night, like for the first time since he had arrived, he was actually seeing all of us.

"I do accept it," he said again loud and clear this time as he addressed the crowd. "It is a fine city and I hope one day I can return to it. Meanwhile, I shall send your gift to Washington so that together with the other gifts we have received, it may be preserved in a special repository as a symbol of the friendship which binds our two nations. Thank you all!"

I couldn't see much because my eyes were sort of blurry but as the hiccups suddenly interrupted my patriotic sobs, I thought perhaps peace was not all that bad. I knew the dead were still dead in the Town Hall basement and that it was sad, but perhaps for the living life could still be good: like after Mémé had died, you just had to forget a lot. And when we rejoined the rest of the family under the starlit August sky and Nanette hugged me, I thought I had been silly to fear for Oberleutnant Redlich. Today's were the war's dead but now peace had come to our town for good and it was Uncle Marcel who the day after the invasion had explained to me that peace meant that no one got shot anymore. I looked fondly at Madame Tardieux's closed shutters before stepping inside our house: she had been right Mademoiselle Rouleau, everything would be alright after all.

I don't remember much of what happened after we got home because within seconds after we were all inside, Uncle Marcel had the unfortunate idea of suggesting a drink might be in order. I took no more than a tiny gulp out of Nanette's glass but it was enough to summon the sandman: he threw a beachful of sand in my eyes and I went blind with sleep. Bébert carried me upstairs like a bran-stuffed doll while Uncle guffawed from the kitchen that I could sleep my way through ten bombardments tonight and Guigui from the foot of the staircase jeered that I would miss the dancing as if he were really thrilled at the prospect. Bébert closed Mémé's bedroom door behind the two of us and he laid me on my cot in the alcove and said I shouldn't worry about undressing because Nanette would see to it later.

He sat on my cot in the small of my waist and his fingers lingered on my forehead, brushed back my hair. I still couldn't open my eyelids because they were so heavy but I drew my arms up, wound them around his neck and told him how much I loved him and how glad I was he was back. He said "Hush now!' Later, when I asked him about Steigl and the Château, he covered my lips with his fingers like he didn't want me to go into that. Then he unwound my left arm from around his neck and held my hand between his and it wasn't more than ten seconds after that that I fell asleep.

*

* *

"Wake up Tina! Wake up!"

Someone was whispering above me. I could feel a hand pawing at the blanket, trying to grab my shoulder through it, my wrist.

"What time is it?" I whispered.

"A little after three."

"Why aren't you asleep? Why did you wake me up?"

He sat on the cot next to me, pointed at the closed shutters at the far end of the bedroom. It was still pitch dark but my eyes had grown accustomed to the night and on my left I could make out the outline of Mémé's bed, the chest of drawers alongside the right hand wall, the two mahogany chairs on each side of it with Guigui's and my clothes thrown over then like dust-covers.

"There are people outside, several of them," Guigui whispered, his face real close to mine.

"Who?" I breathed.

"One of them sounds like it might be Madame Tardieux: you know how she can't keep her voice down."

He stopped talking, listening intently to the silence pouring in from the Avenue through the clover leaf carving the shutters.

"What are they doing?" I asked.

"I don't know!" he snapped as if he thought my question was dumb. "They sound like they are arguing about something. There's a man with them. I can't hear what they are saying 'cause they are kind of whispering!"

I listened. "I can't hear anything," I said after a while.

"That's 'cause they stopped! But you mark my word, they are still out there: I've been listening to Madame Tardieux's door and they ain't shut it yet."

"It may just a drunk from the dance that rang her door bell," I ventured, "for a prank! With all those celebrations I bet half of Dormans is intoxicated."

"A drunk wouldn't whisper," Guigui shot back quite sagaciously, "And anyway - - "

The bells of the Church on the Place du Luxembourg interrupted him: it was three-thirty. After the silence had returned he stood from the bed: the oak slats squeaked under his weight. He threw his right foot forward but at that point the voices broke out again outside and in the next room Nanette called out Bébert's name. I jumped from my cot, froze behind Guigui.

"See! I was right! There's something funny going on out there!" he whispered fast turning toward me. "Maybe we should have a look," he said looking at me through the corner of his eye like he wanted to convince me we should.

"Mind they don't see you." I cautioned him.

He started toward the window which was wide open on the closed shutters. He was being cautious, traveling the same length of slat to avoid stepping on the squeaky joints: I hung on to my breath. He passed the chest of drawers. There were just a few steps between him and the window, a space devoid of furniture, without an anchor if he should trip.

"No! No!" a voice suddenly yelled outside.

Guigui froze. My heart skipped a beat. Then again came the cry: "No! No!"

It was hard to tell whether it was a man's voice or that of a woman. It was more like a disembodied choke: half startled, half terrified. In the next second, the beam of the flashlight lit up our bedroom, swept the ceiling wildly before coming to a rest on the sleeve of my nightshirt, and from the landing behind us, there came a shuffling of feet, a frantic spate of whispers. Guigui meanwhile had made it to the open window: his fingers were already on the shutter's latch when I tiptoed my way up to him. A shoe tumbling down the staircase behind us jolted us but then Bébert swore and we relaxed some. The latch fell back with a click: nothing stirred outside. Guigui eased the shutters out about thirty centimeters, peered down. Then slowly he pushed them open further out. Farther and farther, until I understood he wasn't aware of so widely opening the shutters, that whatever he was seeing in the street below had made him plum forget he was exposing us. I let go of his waist, weaved my way under his right arm. I pushed him hard but he didn't pinch me purple or poke my ribs like he always did when I got in his way. He just stood there like he were made of stone and he couldn't feel anything.

In the next bewildering instant my chin crashed into the razor thin edge of the window ledge and I saw them.

It was Mémé and I cornered by the mad dog in the sawmill yard all those months earlier, the four of us lined up against the dining-room window the previous Thursday before Steigl arrested Bébert. They had been caught by danger in the same way, unexpectedly, so that even at that instant when the threat was a mere arm's length away from behind that unseen hand aiming the flashlight at their faces, their expression was not yet one of fear but of incredulity, of a horror barely perceived. This was especially true of the two women. Mademoiselle Rouleau still faced Redlich, her hand still gripped his shoulder the way it had a moment before when she had tried to keep him from leaving: only her face was turned toward the flashlight like she had been called quite suddenly. Madame Tardieux on the other side of the German was moon-eyed under her paper-curls. It was she who had let out one of those blood-curling "No's" because even though no sound came out of them now, her lips continued to shape the vowel in a silent and desperate plea.

Redlich between them wore the same startled expression but that was all it was. Even later the fear which gradually swept over the women's features never once shown on his face. He was till handsome, Oberleutnant Redlich, even though he wore one of dead Monsieur Tardieux's old suits and it ill-fitted him because the station-master had been skinnier and shorter than him, but his lips were still ripe for a poem or a smile, and his eyes, even after the startled expression faded to be replaced by one of fateful resignation, were still as deep and gray as they had always been. He looked at the five shadows hidden behind the flashlight in the same remote way he had looked at the Marne river that day when I had come upon them, like nothing mattered anymore, like everything had been written in the Book of Fate and you had to fall into the words and do what they said. I don't think it took me more than five seconds to take the whole scene in, every single detail of it. I wasn't frightened yet: I just went through one of those moments of absolute lucidity before a major emotional upheaval in which one's perception is magnified tenfold by the subconscious realization of the event about to occur.

It was pitch black on the Avenue: one of those moonless nights that the eye probes vainly forever encountering the same infinite black void, a void which lurks either as deep or as shallow as one's instinctive fear will allow but which in reality is absolute. It was a night when one has to button one's eyelids to find a star and I found none that night. Thus I did not see who the five men were hiding behind the flashlight one of them was using as much as a shield to mask his identity and that of his companions as a weapon with which to threaten our three neighbors. Neither did I recognize their voices because when they finally spoke again, it was in hoarse whispers, raucous sounds which revealed little except the hatred spewing from their lips as they taunted the now terrified women.

"Ain't that cozy: the Boche and his whore going for a midnight stroll!" came the voice behind the hand which held the flashlight.

And:

"Reckon we should give them an escort: it ain't safe these days for a good German to be by hisself in the streets of Dormans and he is a good German, ain't you mein little Führer?"

A mock clicking of heels rose from the black void behind the flashlight.

"Heil Hitler!"

"Heil!"

"Heil!"

My fingers were encrusted into the stone of the window ledge and fear, like a paralysis, was rising toward my heart. Except for my knees which weighed a ton I had stopped felling my legs under me. The women stood petrified under the glare of the flashlight but Redlich between them looked like someone who has been confronted by the ominous event he has been anticipating and accepts it as ineluctable.

"Hey bitch! He don't look too good your friend! What became of his uniform, his shiny boots?" rose another threatening whisper from the darkness. "You could do better, couldn't she boys?"

"Sure could!"

"Sure could!"

"Ain't you heard, girl, we got Americans in town now," the leader of the pack taunted again. "Don't know about their screwing but they sure look better than your man here, no offense meant mein Führer!"

Another clicking of heels and another mocking chorus of "Heil Hitler!" rose from the night. The numbness had reached my chest. I couldn't take my eyes off the blinding orb of the flashlight because that was where the threat was coming from…I wanted to touch Guigui, wondered what was keeping Bébert and Nanette from bursting out of our house. I wanted to yell maybe or at least to be able to breathe or move but found it impossible to do any of these things. If my eyes for one moment, even for a split second, let go of the flashlight, then everything would explode.

"Maybe we can do something about his clothes," the hoarse whisper came again from behind the flashlight. Mademoiselle Rouleau's hand grasped that of Redlich which had been hanging limply by the seam of dead Monsieur Tardieux's trousers. In her eyes when she slowly turned to look at him, the fear had turned to panic. "Or maybe we should do something about his pretty face…yeah… reckon that's the better idea: we'll make him look like a Frenchman just out of them Gestapo beauty clinics! Then he can pass for one of ours and the bitch won't have any trouble keeping him in Dormans!"

The man took a step forward. As if on cue the other four, still careful not to step inside the light, spread out in a half circle around the German and the two women. It was worse than Steigl, worse than the sawmill dog. My heart thumped and thumped. There was no way they could escape the human threat closing in on them. I knew there was no way they could run back inside the house because the five men were far too close to them by then and in two seconds flat they would be up the steps forcing that door open. They were all poised now on either side of the light as each braced himself for the final fray. I was looking so intensely at Redlich that my eyes kept rolling toward my nose and I had to draw them back from its blade to erase the intermittent blur. I don't think he knew he was clutching my neck so tight, Guigui.

But I forgot the pain when I heard the head man wheeze behind the flashlight. He wasn't whispering anymore. There was just his heavy breathing, the halting breaths of the others as they started to converge on Redlich and the women. Like some hellish monster the night had come alive: soon it would devour us all. It had already swallowed up Redlich's legs and those of the women.

The flashlight was no more than a meter away from Redlich's face when the German reacted. For a few timeless seconds he had been caught by the hypnotic spell of the imminent danger but now something was shaking him out his numbness: a noise, a memory, perhaps the pain that had irradiated his forehead when the glare of the flashlight boring into his eyes had become too acute. His face hardened. It was like he were drawing forth all of his will power, like he were fighting the hypnosis as much as the danger, and himself as much as the five shadows hiding behind the glare of light. He took a deep breath, held it captive as though he were telling his heart: "Here, here, stop it now," and he jerked his hand free from Mademoiselle Rouleau's so violently that she caught her bruised wrist in her other hand and started rubbing it.

When he spoke at last his voice was unrecognizable, it was that of Herr Kommandant Blücher telling Lisette he couldn't tolerate children the day after the first bombardment, it was Steigl telling Bébert he was lying, it was a German voice and nothing else.

"You let the women go!"

The five Frenchmen came to a halt. None of them said a word. Even the wheezing and panting had stopped. Redlich took a step forward: the flashlight followed him.

"I order you to let them go!" Redlich repeated speaking directly to the flashlight. There was no plea in his voice, no begging: he wasn't giving them the slightest edge. "You get back into the house, Fraulein Rouleau, and you too Frau Tardieux: this is between these men and me. Schnell!"

But neither one of them moved. Guigui's fingers were welded to the skin of my neck.

"Odile, go back into the house!" Redlich commanded weighing each word carefully as if he were desperately trying to get through to her.

And still the women stood, eyes dilated by fear. Nothing happened for a second: there was just Redlich cast in the raw beam of the flashlight, the two women behind him now. And then the wheezing started to rise again from the black void, more threatening this time.

"We ain't after the women, Boche!" the hoarse whisper come from the darkness. "Later maybe …Right now we got a score to settle with you and your kinsmen. You are the first one so we'll make a special job of it, won't we, boys?"

"Yeah!"

"Your own fucking mother won't know you when we get through with you pretty boy!"

"A real fancy job!"

There was no fear in Redlich's eyes when the others finally moved in on him. I remember he raised his face towards the black void up there in that ultimate second, like he were searching, searching. But he must have known there was no moon and no stars and no hope, that the sky and the earth that night had become part of the same evil about to crush him.

The upper part of my body was out of the window by then. I didn't feel Guigui's fingers in my neck any more. Watching and breathing had become synonymous: survival depended on both.

I stopped breathing then as the flashlight went dark. I heard it tumble, roll down the pavement as my eyes went blind with night. I heard the thuds, the clashing of bodies. I heard Mademoiselle Rouleau's goose-pumping scream and Madame Tardieux begging and yelling.

"Drunkards! Let him be! Let him be!"

And then:

"Get out of my way you old hag!"

And another voice still.

"Get the whore off my back!"

Guigui had caught my hand: he was crushing it.

"Can you see anything?" he blew in my ear.

I couldn't answer him. All I could do was strain my ears, my eyes until the pain inside my forehead became intolerable. Somehow I had climbed the window ledge. Mute with dread and pain and choking with frustration because I still couldn't see anything, I listened to the fierce struggle outside, hoped against each moan, each punch and thud, that somehow Redlich would be spared.

Our front door flew open below the bedroom window and as the light from the hallway poured into the street, engulfed a plane tree, I heard someone yell and saw two shadows bursting from our house.

"What's going on here? What are you men doing?"

It was Bébert. Nanette behind him started screaming too.

"Is that you Madame Tardieux? Mademoiselle Rouleau? Are you there? Answer me?"

But no one answered her except the dull echoes of the frantic struggle which had moved beyond Madame Tardieux's house as it had grown more fierce. Bébert shot a glance at Nanette. Then he started to walk toward the pitch black void from whence the scuffling sounds were coming. He was about to step outside the pool of light streaming from our house when Madame Tardieux screamed.

"What have you got here," her voice shrill with terror, gored my eardrum. "What are you holding in your hand? What…Don't! Please, no!"

I heard three shots and inside my head there was like an explosion of pain.

Guigui grabbed hold of my arm, wrenched my fingers loose from the railing, pulled me back inside of the bedroom. I fell against him. For a second everything reeled, swirled and spun in front of my eyes: the plane tree, Uncle's house across the street, the window ledge, and I hung on to Guigui's hand as if the harder I crushed his fingers, the quicker everything would fall back into place.

Then there came a mad scrambling of bodies disengaging themselves from each other, a rush of running footsteps. I poked my head between the ledge and the railing just in time to see the five shadows fleeing, dispersing, being swallowed up by the night. Then as suddenly as all those windows lighting up the night along the Avenue, as jarringly as the two jeeps screeching to a halt in front of our house, the scream exploded. It was a scream such as I had never heard before, a scream which drowned Nanette's words, Madame Tardieux's nervous sobs, the American's voices, the shouts and the calls, a scream that tore the night with its demented grief.

He was dead by the time the Americans reached the scene, dead like Soldat Mueller that afternoon, dead like the others in the basement of the Town Hall. I didn't need to see him close to know: I just knew. That's why Mademoiselle Rouleau had screamed, still screamed in that crazy way of hers as Nanette vainly attempted to comfort her. It was freezing cold suddenly and inside me everything had gone dead like in him. And yet I wanted to see it all, as if seeing could turn back the clock, bring him back to life and love.

I couldn't take my eyes off that patch of pavement where he laid in a stream of blood surrounded by all these men staring at him. I heard a voice say "he was just a Boche", as if it made his murder more acceptable. Someone else said he had gotten what he deserved: "What was he doing here anyway? After all the others had already pulled back? A yellow Boche that's even worse than a plain Boche! Women, you know …He probably begged them to hide him and those crazy do-gooders went along with him!" But I knew it was a lie, that he was not what they said. I knew he had loved and kissed her, that he had probably saved Bébert's life, that he hadn't been a German like Blücher or Steigl. I knew he had felt guilty and sad when his people had killed Mémé: Lisette had said so. And besides, he had looked at me and smiled the night before when Nanette had begged him to help Bébert.

I watched it all through the tears. It was very wet and unreal. Madame Tardieux had stopped sobbing: she was holding a glass of something Aunt Louise suddenly popped out of nowhere had just handed her. She was explaining to the American officer in charge standing in front of her how Redlich had had a change of heart, how he had wanted to rejoin his own lines: "That's where he was heading when those five thugs came upon us: he said he had one chance in a thousand to make it, but he had to try. It was she who kept arguing otherwise he would have been long gone by the time they cornered us!" She went on telling the same story, over and over, as if somehow in the retelling all that happened after the moment they had been out there, the two of them trying to hold on to Redlich could be undone, forgotten, erased.

Uncle and Bébert had joined the curious gathered around Redlich's corpse: they were talking in whispers like men do sometimes when something they don't approve of but cannot openly denounce has happened. The tears kept streaming down my cheeks but Guigui's hand was across my mouth, stifling the hiccups. It wasn't tears like for Mémé, it was different tears. It was just a tiny chunk of my heart breaking this time because, after all, he hadn't been my room-mate Oberleutnant Redlich. He was just someone I had grown fond of because of that day by the Marne River, because of her, then because of what he had done for Bébert. But there had been all those "becauses" between him and me and thus his death could never have the same impact upon me as that of Mémé.

After Madame Tardieux had told the Americans she absolutely couldn't recognize them, that they were not "from these parts," that all she remembered was the flashlight in her eyes, the gun in that man's hand, after the people in preoccupied dribbles started to leave the scene, the Americans tried to take Redlich away but Mademoiselle Rouleau, who had stopped screaming by then, wouldn't let go of his head. Her arms were cradling it and her face covered his. She was kneeling beside him like she had gown roots into the pavement and wouldn't, couldn't be uprooted from the patch of earth where he had fallen. It took Aunt Louise, the widow, Lisette and Nanette to tear her away from his corpse. She was in a state of emotional collapse by then and the four women had to carry her inside the widow's house.

Everyone had left by the time the Americans loaded his body on the back of one of the jeeps, covered it with a canvas for the short ride to the Town Hall. There was only Guigui and me at the bedroom window, and Uncle and Bébert standing by the curb under the plane tree. They had stopped whispering: they just stood there shoulder to shoulder, watching the rear lights of the jeeps recede into the night. After a while they walked back toward the house, Uncle leading the way, and then Bébert closed the front door behind him and it was pitch black again outside, and real quiet.

We stayed at the window a long time Guigui and I. We didn't talk, didn't touch, we didn't even look at each other. But I felt real close to him, like that day when we had met in the kitchen the morning of his first communion. He was alright, Guigui.

A sudden pool of light splashing the pavement through the windows of Madame Tardieux's parlor startled me: she would be telling them about Mademoiselle Rouleau and Redlich I thought. They'd probably take him down to the Town Hall basement, put him on the metal bed frame beside the one that had no legs. I wondered what they did to a Boche after he was dead: did they bury him in the nearest cemetery? Did they burn him and put his ashes in a black urn so they could save it for his relatives in Germany after the war was really over? What did they do with all the dead Boches? Then without transition I started thinking about Mademoiselle Rouleau and the more I thought about her the more ashamed I began to feel. I remembered how she had held me against her shoulder in the attic the day of Mémé's funeral, about the days I had spent in her classroom fantasizing about the death of her parents in that car crash, and I felt guilty because I had enjoyed my fantasies. I thought of her by the riverside that shimmering afternoon, and about her tonight piercing the night with her grief.

And then an idea struck me and I left Guigui at the window and ran to my alcove. I turned dead Pepe's footlocker upside down trying to find it in the dark. After I had found it I slid inside my sheets, cuddled it tight against my chest. I had never prayed before, but that dawn, crushing Mémé's missal in my arms, I think I came close to it. At any rate, I told her what had happened that night and asked her to please ask God to do something nice for Mademoiselle Rouleau, something real nice and good. I didn't say it right out because I wasn't sure He would take it but I sort of hinted that He hadn't been paying much attention to her because from the day of her birth everything had gone wrong for her. I also told Mémé she should explain to Him that I believed it was all probably and oversight on His part because I knew how busy He was, but that this was an emergency and to please do something real soon.

I don't remember what else I told Mémé. I just remember I started crying again crushing her missal and talking to her. I must have still been talking to her when I fell asleep.

For some unexplained reason, I went on to dream of General Patton.

*
* *

CHAPTER XII

We didn't talk much about that night over the two days which followed Oberleutnant Redlich's murder. Only once, the morning after it happened, did Bébert speak of the German. We had finished a late breakfast during which hardly a word had been exchanged when, nursing a last glass of chicory he told us what Redlich had done for them that list night at the Château. He was never, that morning or in the weeks which followed, to tell us anything about what he had suffered at the hands of Steigl and his men during the four days the SS had detained him. If he told anyone it was probably Nanette but I think he did not even tell her, that no sooner had he walked out of the Château a free man that dawn, he had promptly entombed the story of the degradation he had suffered through his short-lived captivity in that dark recess of the soul where human beings keep their guilt and secret shame. At any rate that morning, as the seven of us crowded around the kitchen table listening to our thoughts and basking like shipwrecks in the sun pouring through the open window, Bébert told us how Redlich had saved their four lives. Contrary to what we had assumed, they had not been the only prisoners the SS were holding. There had been twelve in all scattered throughout the third floor cells of the Château, all of them men, many of them young, members of the local underground the Boches had been holding on suspicion of sabotage. Peering through the key-hole of his cell whenever he could, he had seen eight of them as they were being taken for questioning or dragged back to their own cells after each session with the SS interrogators: he would never forget their faces.

He didn't know what time the shelling had started that last night because it was dark inside their cell and anyway, the SS had taken their watches along with their belts, wallets and other possessions. He did remember that as they were attempting to surmount a first bout of panic, someone in the cell next to theirs had started to curse the Boches, to welcome each new blast and cry out for more, always more. And soon, as the thunder of war had pressed closer to the Château, to them, they too had started to feel the same demented exhilaration. They had hugged in the darkness and forgotten their fear. They had told each other the Germans were done for this time, that out of the ruins Dormans would surely emerge a free town! Bébert said it was like they had all four gone crazy the way they had whooped and hollered at each new explosion, like they were children watching a display of fireworks rather than grown me likely to be blown up any second.

They were still hollering and banging the walls of their cell, there was even one singing The Marseillaise Bébert related, when suddenly there had come a tremendous blast from outside and simultaneously the SS had rushed the corridor, many SS, booting and hastening their way past their door. Then as the building had begun to rock under the increasing allied shelling, as the exhilaration of the moment earlier began to recede in them under the more concrete threat stalking past their door, the night had suddenly exploded into German shouts. Huddled in the dark they had heard the far doors at the end of the corridor being slammed open, they had heard shouts of hatred coming from the French, and they had heard the staccato of several machine guns mowing down the hatred. And when their door too had suddenly burst open in the dark, they had believed death was at hand, that like the others down the hall their turn had come;

Yet, Bébert explained, it was not the executioners lurking for them in the darkness and it was not death waiting for them inside the sudden night which covered the Château because the allied bombs had at last hit the power lines. It was a voice that Bébert said he did not recognize at first when it called out his name in an urgent whisper and ordered him and the three others out of the cell: quick! Instinct being more compelling than reason they had heeded the whispered admonition. Within seconds, while behind them the cries of hatred quickly thinned down to a frightening silence under the unabated fire of the SS guns, they had filed silently behind the faceless voice, down the service staircase, their hearts pounding as much because of what they were leaving behind as in fear of whatever unknown laid ahead of them. After they had gone down and down for what Bébert remembered as an eternity, the voice had ordered them to a halt. It had pushed open a door which sounded like it had not been used in centuries because it squealed on its rusty hinges and creaked and squeaked when forced away from the door-jamb. Then the voice had whispered for them to file inside.

"He called my name again," Bébert said staring blindly at the center of the table like he was trying to remember every detail of what had taken place next. "I still didn't know who he was but then he struck a match. The flame danced between our faces and for the first time I knew who he was. I was so surprised I couldn't talk. He spoke real fast, like he was in a hurry to go. He said he would lock the door behind him and for us not to move. He said he thought we had a good chance of making it and that he was sorry it was all he could do for us. Then he blew out the match because it had started to burn his fingers…I was raking my mind 'cause I wanted to thank him - - I knew what Steigl was liable to do to him if he found out about his helping us - - but I couldn't find the words. I heard him move toward the door, slow-like, like there was something else on his mind. He didn't whisper the next time he spoke normally, like what was happening outside and on the third floor, like what he had done, suddenly didn't matter. And he said - - you know how stuck up he always sounded - - anyway, he said something like: "Herr Marchand! I shall never see you again but in bidding you farewell I have a personal request to make of you," and he said, "I ask you to remember that not all Germans are born evil, that one should not condemn a whole nation for the sins of however many there be. I ask you to remember that in trying to help you tonight I am as much a German as SS Obersturmfuhrer Steigl."

We were all silent around the table. Even Uncle usually so loquacious was out of words.

"I don't' think I understood what he meant then," Bébert continued after a while staring at his glass of chicory, "I was still trying to thank him when he closed the door," He brought the rim of the glass to his lips: none of us was looking at him by then, or even at each other. "Darndest thing is that I couldn't find them words…I just couldn't…Guess the last four years stuck in my throat…"

I heard him slurp some chicory as I continued to stare at the handle of my knife. He sighed, laid the glass in front of him on the table. He unfolded then refolded his napkin, laid it back to the right of his glass.

"I saw the other eight in the school morgue this afternoon..." I only sensed he was looking at each of us because I still couldn't look up. "Like Redlich said, not all Boches are bad..."

That's the only time we spoke of Redlich after he was killed except for another time two days later when something we couldn't have foreseen that morning occurred, something violent and ugly which, dead as he was, brought the Germans and all of the other Boches that had ever occupied Dormans back into our lives for the final chapter of a war we thought had ended with the arrival of the Americans.

But after breakfast that morning, Aunt Louise decreed that the first order of business was the repair work to be done on their house. Guigui and I were assigned the task of scrounging enough usable bricks out of the war's rubbles to fill the shell-hole in their front wall. I am not sure what Guigui offered him in return, perhaps a ride in Uncle's fishing boat, but whatever his price, Jacques Pottin agreed to give us a hand when we ran into him on the way back from fetching the wheel-barrow from Bébert's workshop on the Faubourg de Chavenay. It had never looked like such a big hole until we tried to fill it: all told, perhaps on the account of all the other scavengers, it took the three of us the best part of four hours and twenty-two trips before Uncle was satisfied he had enough bricks. Guess he had been right: it was really as big as an elephant's ass, more like ten elephants' asses! Anyway, that's how Guigui, Jacques Pottin and I spent that first morning after Redlich's death.

Considering we had longed for it for what was then incredibly half of my life, we came to accept the advent of peace remarkably fast and forty-eight hours after the liberation of their city the people of Dormans began to gather the scattered strands of their interrupted lives and resume normal activities. There was joy in the air and although people were still circumspect in what they would discuss when they met on the street or at the market, one could sense the fear which had made a virtue of mistrust for the over four years of the German occupation was beginning to wane. It was not quite peace we had yet because the war was still part of our existence, but it was an emotional freedom which no one had exercised for so long that when it became ours again if affected us more deeply than might have the regained prosperity which in the longer term would be a byproduct of peace. There was still food rationing and shortages of every imaginable commodity and a third of the town had been left in shambles by the war, but endowed with this new freedom the citizens rolled up their sleeves and began to look forward to the rebuilding task. Two days after Redlich's death and Patton's visit the Women's Emergency Committee reopened its doors at my school and Nanette resumed her volunteer work. Bébert, meanwhile, after having succeeded in overcoming what Mayor Chancel had referred to as a "totally understandable reluctance," returned to the Château to work for its new Allied occupants. Uncle Marcel, ladder tucked perilously under his left arm again, resumed the practice of his painter's trade while Guigui worked with other volunteers at repairing the railroad yards and Lisette chirped and twittered inside the Town Hall. Even Aunt Louise seemed anxious to do her share and much to my dismay took to cooking lunch for the American officers billeted at the Town Hall but somehow they survived her culinary ministrations. We still observed the twin rites of rutabagas for dinner and curfew for evening socials and we remained alert to the sawmill siren should it howl a potential air-raid, but suddenly the rutabagas tasted like French fries, curfew as a joyful time and the sawmill siren remained silent. No it wasn't quite peace we had yet because peace would not come until the following spring, but the fear and suspicion were almost gone and by the third morning after

Redlich's death as I knocked on Madame Tardieux's front door, I had every reason to believe the worst was behind us and that between the widow's gentle care, Mémé's spiritual intercession with God and my own determination to love her back into joy, even Mademoiselle Rouleau could eventually be made to surmount her grief.

Once again however events were to prove me wrong for something happened that first Saturday after the German's death which not only exposed before my bewildered eyes the depth of the wounds inflicted on my compatriots by the occupation but also, though it was just another in a series of incidents that had begun with Mémé's death, the cumulative impact of which sent me reeling out of childhood and into a premature and unwanted adolescence. Never again would I be able to retrace my steps to the child I had been that Spring for what took place that Saturday tore such a big hole in the chrysalis of my innocence that I was forced to catch a glimpse of life as it laid beyond the fairy tales, of life as a staggering symbiosis of ugliness and beauty, as a monstrous paradox of evil and goodness.

But I knew none of this that Saturday morning as I accompanied Nanette to the communal wash-house on the Rue de La Rivière. August had drifted toward September without transition the previous day: the mid-morning sun, as free and warm as it had been then was beginning its ascent in the cloudless sky and rising out of the morning haze, far, the hills of Champagne still etched their soft green outline against the heat-white horizon. It was market day and normally Nanette and I would have been heading for the Place du Luxembourg but, as she had explained at breakfast in an understatement, this had been a week like none other and consequently laundry had been the last thing on her mind. Now, however, with the problem of spare underwear and especially clean sheets on account of the Germains having moved into our attic's bedrooms, the situation had become so dire that it could countenance no further delays. Aunt Louise was entrusted with performing whatever miracle she could at market with our shopping list while Nanette, pushing the laden wheel-barrow with myself riding high on its pile of laundry, a large pail containing two blocks of Marseille soap and a stack of scrubbing brushes for armrests, proceeded to the wash-house. We took the side street which ran along the damaged wing of the Town Hall and sloped toward the river, to make a left turn into the Rue de la Riviére. The narrow street delineated by two identical rows of identical drab gray houses was deserted as we rolled down its cobble stones and soon Nanette pulled up inside the wash-house.

It was a long rectangular building topped by a flat roof of concrete supported by four square stone pillars at each of its four corners. The front of the building was completely open to let in the flow of washerwomen, wheel-barrows or an occasional stray dog or cat in search of shelter, while the other three sides were closed by low walls which stopped midway between the floor and the roof letting in the bitter cold winds of February in winter or the gentle May breeze in spring. There were four waist-high deep rectangular vats under the concrete roof: two were for washing and the other two were for rinsing. On a good wash-day it could accommodate four housewives but this being market day Nanette and I had a run of the place. She proceeded to fill one of the vats and wash our dirty laundry while I filled one of the rinsing ones with water. The sun pouring through the open façade played shimmering games with the water and lit up the concrete ceiling with wide arcs of reflected sunlight. When you spoke inside the wash-house it was like there were several of you all jabbering at the same time: your voice, captive inside the concrete box, rebounded and ricocheted in an echo that took forever to die.

Nanette didn't like to talk once she started washing our laundry. Sleeves rolled up high over her muscular forearms, primed with mean and rough brushes, a laundering wooden beetle and a large handkerchief girding her forehead like a warrior's helmet, she assaulted dirt with a vengeance, scrubbing, thrashing and flogging underwear and sheets, napkins and socks as if they were her own private enemies. I never bothered her once she had begun her weekly struggle until the war over dirt nearly over and the dripping laundry piled high and heavy into a pail ready to be transferred to the rinsing vat she would wipe her sweat-greased brow and beckon me back with a smile and half-pooped half victorious grunt that signified the worst was over.

Thus that Saturday morning following our established ritual I idled time away while Nanette fought her perennial battle with dirt. I took a couple of spins around the wash-house with the empty wheel-barrow in tow, chased a butterfly as far as the edge of the rail-tracks and wished on a ladybug sunning itself amid the weeds growing behind the concrete structure. The morning was slow and lazy with only a hint of a breeze wafting through the air and tatters of clouds adrift on the dun-bleached sky. It was a morning for letting the flow of life heavy with yesterday's emotional flotsam roll by.

An hour later Nanette, the worst of her chore over, summoned me back. We loaded the pail heavy with the dripping laundry onto the wheel-barrow and she holding one handle and me the other, we rolled it to the side of the rinsing vat. Once there she hoisted the pail onto the concrete ledge and with a single deft move eased its contents into the clear cold water. Then, with her wooden beetle on one side of the vat and me straining on tiptoes and armed with a long wooden stick on the other, like two witches concocting an evil brew, we sloshed and swirled the laundry till the water turned a murky color of whey. At last came the moment I enjoyed best out of wash-days when arms bared to the shoulders we would both plunge them deep into the cold water to fish out the soaking laundry.

She had barely wrung her first sheet to a sausage that morning and I was wading for my third pair of underpants when our water games were abruptly interrupted. The shout was indistinct yet: it might have been calling out for anybody and the clangorous roll of wooden-soled footsteps pounding the cobble-stones might have been hastening toward any one of those drab gray houses which made up the street. Yet, perhaps because the past four years had honed our instinct to a razor-thin edge of self-preservation, Nanette and I froze and looked at each other across the vat and then it wasn't more than a few seconds later that we found ourselves outside the wash-house searching the street for the embodiment of the danger we had just perceived.

She was tearing down the street, Madame Tardieux. She started waving frantically in our direction when she spotted us, calling out Nanette name with her stentorian voice and trying, from too far away, to shout something we couldn't make out. I was straining my ears when Nanette took off like a shot. I bolted after her and within seconds we reached Madame Tardieux halfway up the street. She crashed into Nanette's wet arms. For a while we couldn't get anything out of her: she sobbed and sobbed and clawed at her bosom. Her eyes were dilated by some unknown calamity and although she had taken the curl-papers out of it she hadn't combed her hair so that the empty gray coils dangled and quivered on her head like the bursting entrails out of some disemboweled mattress. At last Nanette pushed her aside, shoved her forcefully on a nearby stone marker and instructed her to breathe: deep and slow, there! Again! But after she had breathed thus a couple of times, she burst into another round of tears, Madame Tardieux: gigantic tears to match her built and stentorian voice, a flood that even Nanette had a hard time bringing under control. At last, after a few minutes of coaxing her Nanette had her calmed down enough so that between the tears and the sobbing the widow managed to hear Nanette's questions.

"What is it, Ma'am Tardieux, what on earth has happened?"

But now Madame Tardieux's nose was in tears too. However between her powerful sniffles and a corner of Nanette's working blouse, the situation soon became more manageable.

"What is it?" Nanette prodded her again.

"It's Odile! It's Mademoiselle Rouleau…oh my God, Antoinette!" and again she erupted into another round of volcanic sobs.

"What about Mademoiselle Rouleau?" Nanette pressed her. "Hush! Hush! You got to tell me Ma'am Tardieux, else I can't help you! What about Mademoiselle Rouleau?"

"They've taken her away! They've taken her away, that's what! Forced her out of the house, and she barely dressed too!" Slowly despair was turning into something else in the widow: a hint of rebellion streaked through her glaucous blue eyes as they drew a trajectory between the cloud tattered sky and the slate of the roof tops. Then they hit upon Nanette who at that particular moment was drawing her body between the houses and the helplessness like an impregnable tower of determination. Her eyes never let go after that and she began to talk so we could understand her. "They weren't satisfied with Redlich, they had to come after her as well! And she ain't well, she ain't well at all!"

"Who are 'they'?" Nanette asked interrupting Madame Tardieux's rambling outpour, "Who are they, Ma'am Tardieux?"

"It's that Monsieur Lucien behind it all! He's got to show he's better than the lot of us! He's the - - "

"Now Ma'am Tardieux," Nanette came back with a whiff of exasperation. "It ain't no use your ranting on like that 'cause I don't know what you are talking about!"

At last the widow relented.

"I'm truly sorry, Antoinette! It's just…it's just…" Madame Tardieux blurted out, brushing a remnant of a tear with the inner edge of her hand. She was still looking at Nanette but now the helplessness was back in her eyes. She heaved a defeated sigh. "I don't rightly know who they are, Antoinette…The two mechanics from the garage on the road to Chavenay: I saw them! And old Matthieu - - can you believe it, old Matthieu! But there were maybe thirty of them, women too, just vicious, vicious…"

"What did they do?" Nanette broke in trying to put the widow back on the track again. "What did they want?"

"Banged on my door, they did, and before I knew what was happening they poured into my house, asking for her: for Odile! She was back in the kitchen 'cause we had been having a late breakfast. They just stomped through the parlor and the dining-room and then, of course, they found her…It was like an invasion. Madame Pottin was there too, guess on account of her dead husband and son…"

"And then? What did they do then?"

"Well by then I started shouting and asking them what was going on, what they wanted in my house, but they paid me no mind, no mind at all, and me in my own house too!"

"I know, I know, Ma'am Tardieux! But what happened next?"

"I got to the kitchen: had to shove my way to get in. Just mobbed it was, mobbed! Odile was sitting at the table, eyes glazed, like she has been doing since he was killed. She isn't right in her head, you know, not since that night. Hasn't spoken a word since. It's like she doesn't' even know she is alive. I got to feed and help her dress, and tell her when to eat and when to go to bed…It frightens me. Dr. Martin says its' shock and she'll get over it with the rest and care and the laudanum he is giving her, but it grieves me to see her. It ain't up to me to say whether she was right or wrong: all I know is that he was a decent man. He was kind to her. He wasn't like the rest of them Boches - - "

"We all know that, Ma'am Tardieux, we know! But what happened then?"

"I couldn't stop them. Vicious they were, plain vicious! A sick girl like that! Said she was nothing but a German whore who needed to be taught a lesson. But she wasn't: she didn't love him for food or money, she didn't go from one to the other. It was just him she went with 'cause she loved him and there ain't a thing one can do when one loves someone like she did Redlich.'"

"Where did they take her, Ma'am Tardieux?" Nanette cut her off again.

"Place du Luxembourg, and on market day too! I heard one of them say they aimed to make a show of it so's the whole town could see…" She rose from the stone marker. She didn't look so big now, Madame Tardieux.

And suddenly I bolted up the Rue de la Riviére. I heard Nanette yell for me to come back but kept on running. I had to get to the Place du Luxembourg even if there wasn't a thing I could do! I had to be there: she had to see me there, even if she was a little crazy in her mind like Madame Tardieux had said.

I tore up the Rue de la Riviére and into the Rue du Marché that was still the same street but changed name on the other side of the pontoon bridge. It was all uphill but it was shorter than retracing my steps to the Avenue de la Marne by way of the Town Hall. My sandals, wet from the wash-house, slid on the cobble stones but each time I picked myself up and kept on running and it wasn't more than ten minutes later that I got to the alley that cut across the Rue du Marché into the Place du Luxembourg. I threaded it and soon, out of breath and heart throbbing with hope and panic, I reached the corner of Monsieur Lucien's store.

It was the first market day after the Liberation of Dormans and in addition to the town's citizens, the people from Chavenay and Chérisy and other nearby villages had come to town to see peace and the Americans. It was like the foyer of the Empire Theatre at intermission: packed calve to calve and shoulder to shoulder, so thick there was no street left and no patch of pavement or storefronts to be seen as I strained on tiptoes trying to locate a breach in the impenetrable human barrier. But I knew I had to get through, find her no matter how insurmountable the obstacles. Nanette's sudden call behind me threatening potential reprisals gave me the push I needed: home would surely be my next destination if I let her catch up with me. I took a runner's breath, made two small fists with my hands and buttoning up my eyelids plunged blindly into the first row of legs. Despite a storm of protests for a while I made steady progress punching my way through: at least I had lost myself and escaped the more immediate threat of quarantine. The problem was that unable to see anything beyond the thick growth of fannies through which I was plodding my way I couldn't tell whether I was getting closer to the center of the square or actually turning in drunken circles. The noon sky was no help: anyway I wasn't good at reading stars. After a while I stopped, craned my neck in search of an identifiable rooftop, a familiar face to whom I could claim to be lost and get a free steer to where I aimed to go. If only I could fine Aunt Louise! She would surely bawl me out but at least she wouldn't send me home by myself for I was in too deep now, and under her mantle I might have a better chance of getting to Mademoiselle Rouleau if they had brought her there like Madame Tardieux had claimed.

I was talking to myself by then and I had resumed my subjective progress through the human forest. It was as I continued to push and shove my way through that, ever so gradually, it dawned on me the legs weren't talking any more, that the hips weren't thick in gossip as they had been earlier, and that the faces, when I looked up a bit, were all straining in the same general direction, a little to the left of where I had so far been blindly heading. Something was going on that had the market crowd church-quiet all of a sudden. They weren't even grumbling anymore as I punched my way between them: they just glared, and... The pain was fulgurant! My hand flew to my forehead and a thousand candles lit up the September sky. After a reeling while I stood up and discovered the sharp edge of the trestle-table with which I had just collided in line with my nose surmounted by a wobbling pyramid of dirt-caked potatoes. I dug my handkerchief from the pocket of my pinafore, spit on it and pressed it against the swelling bump. The pain was not as concentrated now: it had spread to the back of my head but strangely in the spreading it had lost some of its blinding hurt. The candles were gone, vanished, and beyond the potatoes suddenly I saw the clearing.

They had drawn the vendors' stalls into a circle at the dead center of the square. People pressed behind the improvised barrier but were kept at bay by a handful of men among whom were the two mechanics of the garage on the road to Chavenay whom Madame Tardieux had recognized as being in the group which invaded her home earlier. They still wore their grease-stained overalls and one of them still held a wrench in his hand as if their participation in what was about to happen was something they had joined in on the spur-of-the-moment. Inside the circle, slightly right off center toward the Church, a heavy trestle-table, a big one, had been erected. Three wooden produce crates, one turned upside down and the other two piled on top of the other next to it like a rudimentary flight of steps led to the makeshift podium on which a single wooden chair stood as a lonely prop. No none else was inside the clearing besides the handful of men policing it.

I was straining toward the cluster of adults pressing behind me, trying to catch a phrase, a word which might tell me what we were waiting for when rising from way behind the poster of the Empire Theater to my left, there came a faint drone. I dove under the trestle-table, made my way to the inner edge of the clearing and crouched against one of the legs of the make-shift podium keeping out of sight of the ubiquitous mechanics. The drone meanwhile had grown to a rumble. A tide of expectation rippled through the square and soon behind me people began to search each other's faces, to question and to press ever closer to the makeshift arena. And then the shouts came, shrill, shooting above the crowd like the calls of the blue jays that has so startled me that afternoon at The Gaux, and out of their rising number, the clamor was suddenly born. And as I pressed my hands to my ears, trying to shut out its threat the crowd surged toward the poster of the Empire Theater only to be repelled by a contrary force under whose impact it suddenly receded and, like the Red Sea before the children of Israel, opened up a narrow aisle through which they could pass.

Monsieur Lucien led the group. He was no longer the mousy bookstore owner hiding an anemic frame behind and oversized cash register and a bilious vindictiveness behind an ever glib claim to arguable rights. Looking at him that morning from my hiding place under the trestle-table, I remembered something Langiers had said that morning at the Town Hall after the bombardments about the implacability of belated patriots and thought for the first time I understood what he had meant. Madame Pottin was there too bent on making someone account for her widowhood, and old Matthieu in his bib-trousers and the cow-dung caking his rubber boots, who had been so good when Mémé had died but had lost half of his acreage to the war and most of his crops to the German Commissariat. There was also Monsieur Pichegrus, the undertaker, dressed for mourning like always, who had buried so many Frenchmen that bitterness had come to replace on his face the professional air of compassion, and for some obscure reason Monsieur Léon, the butcher, wrapped in his blood soiled apron as if he meant to show the town that the blood splotching its white linen were his own rather than that of the too many steers he had sold to the occupiers at shamefully discounted prices. I didn't know who the others were, but I counted a good twenty of them as they poured into the clearing helter-skelter pushing before them the women.

They were a pathetic trio, with little or no affinity except the nature of the crime for which Monsieur Lucien and his cohorts had brought them together on the square that morning. There was Big Renée, the waitress of the café across the railroad station. She was fat and vulgar and always accosted me on the streets of Dormans when our paths would accidentally cross with a naughty twinkle, some esoteric remark or other about Paris, and an inane laughter she spewed in my face as if the two of us were privy to some secret joke. She was in her early forties, always outrageously made up with lipstick that perennially hemorrhaged down her chin, flabby cheeks rouged to a dramatic blush and eyes charcoaled to keep the tears at bay. To all the upright housewives of Dormans she was a disgrace but

I had once heard Bébert and Uncle Marcel talk of her with jocular exuberance and because she had told me so, I knew that Guigui and Jacques Pottin spent a good deal of their time while helping clear the railroad yards ogling her through the dirt-stained windows of the café. There was also Yvonne. She was originally from some farm up in Chérisy but had hired out her services to the Château after her parents had died and her brothers had split up the farm. She was in her late twenties, nondescript, with flesh that hung on her bones like an empty dress on a coat-hanger, all drawn in and yet surprisingly cheerful. She seldom talked but she giggled a lot. I had met her a couple of times when I had gone to fetch Bébert from work at the Château. Bébert was very protective of her, said she wasn't quite right in the mind and that even though she didn't answer my questions, I shouldn't stop asking them of her or mind her giggling.

Thus there was Big Renée and simple Yvonne lined up on the makeshift stage and between the two of them so out of place that my heart ached, more beautiful than I had ever seen her, there was Mademoiselle Rouleau. She still wore her peignoir. Blue it was, washed out, held around her small waist by a man's necktie someone must have tied around it at some point. There was no more periwinkle in her, not in her dress and not in her eyes as she stared above, lost in the infinity of her grief, as if her soul had left her body the minute he had died. Perhaps in a way grief was her salvation because it made everything happening to her so unimportant but I had no such escape and because I pitied her so much that morning the shame which was meant for her instead became mine.

They started with Big Renée. But she was twice as big as Monsieur Lucien and in a pugilistic mood so that after a while he motioned to the two mechanics to come and lend him a hand. They clambered onto the trestle-table and it tilted a bit but then several men from the group that had brought the women rushed to hold it down. They were laughing and some in the crowd laughed back. After some sparring the two mechanics finally got hold of Big Renée and they shoved her on the chair, locked her arms tight behind its backrest so that she couldn't move without her face twitching. But they couldn't do much about her tongue and she was sure using it. She had bounced so many drunkards in her time that she could be as foul-mouthed as the best cusser in town. I didn't know half of the words spewing out of her lipstick-smeared mouth but she didn't seem anywhere near running out of them as she took on the mob and returned insult for insult. Soon the whole crowd was involved in a crescendo of invectives: it was like the more she gave them, the more they relished taunting her. Monsieur Lucien positively beamed as he surveyed the square from his post behind Big Renée's chair. He had gotten hold of a pair of hair clippers and held it high in his right hand like a maestro his baton. When the crescendo of vituperations at last reached such a cacophonous pitch that even he winced under its ear-rending assault, he raised his hands wide above his head, threw his anemic chest out as far as it pathetically could go and motioned the crowd to silence. But Big Renée couldn't see him since he was behind her. She looked around half quizzically as the deluge of invectives petered out about her but still kept dishing hers out. On and on, but only half-heartedly by then, until suddenly the cold kiss of the metal clippers fell on her startled neck. Her mouth dropped in mid curse and she shivered as the hair clippers plowed their first deep furrow into her black mane: a neat linear furrow that started at the small of her neck and ended at the very fringe of her forehead between her two bulging eyes.

 The crowd broke out into a round of cheers while I looked with a sudden apprehension at Mademoiselle Rouleau's copper halo ablaze about her wan face in the noon sun. Then a woman's voice behind me said the whole thing was cruel and unchristian, even if they had slept with a few Boches: that the authorities were bound to deal with the likes of them once things go sorted out. I turned hopefully toward the voice, discovered it was Madame Martin a few bodies away. But then some man said they deserved it, that anyway no one was doing them no harm except in their pride, and that the young ones of Dormans needed to be taught what public wrath one could incur by shaming France like they had done. So I crouched back under the trestle-table and forgot all about trying to reach Madame Martin.

Something new was happening inside me, something I had never felt before. I didn't feel like tears or hiccups. I wasn't scared either. It was different: uncomfortable. Even though I knew a lot of the faces cheering Monsieur Lucien as he proceeded about his avenging task, if suddenly someone had asked me whether I knew any of them I was sure I should have pretended that I had never laid eyes on them, that they weren't my friends, that they weren't even from Dormans maybe. I crouched under the table. I didn't look at Big Renée anymore. I looked at feet and table legs and stared at a turnip that had dropped out of some farmer's crate and laid sort of lonely and quiet in the center of the clearing. I just didn't want to look at faces, not even at Mademoiselle Rouleau's though it kept popping up in front of me, especially when I looked at the turnip. I wanted to hide under the table till it all went away: the jeering, the cheering and the stomping of feet. I could feel the goose-pimples on my arms but it wasn't goose-pimples like for Guigui's First communion. It was icky goose-pimples like when I had to stand up in the tin tub after Nanette had given me my weekly cold bath in the kitchen and she had forgotten the clean towel and I was made to stand there, shivering, till she went and fetched it. It was lonely and miserable and I wanted desperately to find someone I knew: even Aunt Louise would do if she happened to be the first familiar face I saw.

As it turned out, she was. My heart leaped to my throat when I spotted her dour face in the second row across the clearing from me. I bounded from under the trestle-table. No one noticed me: they were too busy gawking at what was happening on my right. I was still a ways from her when she turned her head as if in some mysterious way she had heard me call out to her even though I had not. She sprang forward, elbowed her way out of the crowd and grabbing my outstretched hand, yanked me to her side. She looked real upset and pinched my hand so tight between her bony knuckles that all my fingers were piled one on top of the other inside her grip.

"What in God's name are you doing here child?" she upbraided me as she pushed me back inside the crowd still holding on so tight to my hand that my fingertips shown beet red at the exit end of her grip. "Where is Antoinette?"

"I don't' know," I stammered. I knew she was mad because she had said 'Antoinette'. She was right behind me..." I lied giving her only the safest half of the truth.

"Well a fine thing! Ain't a sight for a child to behold! And the Mayor busy kowtowing to the Americans at the Château while this is going on. Even Father Rocas - - don't look up! - - even Father Rocas! All this happening in front of God's church and old Maitre Pinson has to pick this time to kick the bucket - - "

"Maitre Pinson's dead?" I blurted out.

"Dead or just about from what I heard. That's why Father Rocas ain't here when he should be. God's business is here more than with that old crow - - don't look up I tell you!" she shoved me behind her, grabbed hold of both my hands and held them tight to her waist.

"Keep your head in my fanny, child, it's a darn better sight than these shameful goings on! Look at them - -" but she didn't really mean for me to look at them so I kept my head in her skirt. "- - after blood they are ...You mark my word: after blood!" The roller coaster of her scorn was way up the decibel ladder. "No better than them Nazis! That's what they would have done too! That's what they had done to France!"

This time she had done it.

"Boches lover!" several voices shot around us. "Boches lover!"

I buried my face deeper in her skirt. I knew she wasn't going to be that easily deterred: even Uncle Marcel couldn't scoff her off when she was really angry Aunt Louise. It was worse than watching Big Renée, worse than under the trestle-table.

But as I waited fearfully for Aunt Louise to return the accusations something stirred outside my self-induced blindness. In the next instant someone grabbed hold of my collar, yanked me out of Aunt Louise's skirts and I found myself face-to-face with Nanette. Madame Tardieux was behind her sobbing at regular intervals as she looked beyond me at Monsieur Lucien's makeshift stage.

"You devil you!" Nanette sputtered. She was so mad she couldn't find the words to be mad with. She held onto the collar of my pinafore, shook me like a cherry tree. "Never do that again! Never!"

Her angry breath streamed down my lips with a mist of her saliva. She had only looked that way once, that time the day after D-Day when she had accused Madame Tardieux of having supported Marèchal Pétain. The same icy lightning which had streaked through her pupils then was sending a bitter chill up my spine. She wagged a thick forefinger a hair's breadth from my nose: it was all wrinkled from the wash. Her chin quivered. But after a sputtering while all she could add was another "Never do that again!" because no other words would come through her white anger.

My heart was pumping. I snuck in an avid swallow of life, then hit upon her eyes still boring into mine and stopped breathing. We stared into each other's eyes. Slowly I read in hers the extent of the anguish I had caused her and she read the fear and confusion in mine, and after a while, without either one of us having spoken a word, the conflict ended: her anger melted, my sin was forgiven. She took my hand between hers, slapped it half-scoldingly. But as I opened my lips for an apology the crowd broke into ominous cheers and all the hostility we had forgotten in those intense seconds of mutual surrender became reality again. Big Renée was done.

You could not help look up, however disturbed or frightened the sight of what you saw made you. There was a crowd all about, screaming, jeering and cheering, people pushing and shoving and straining in a sweeping maelstrom to get a sight of her. There was Monsieur Lucien, big suddenly, big with the hatred that can sometimes make giants out of small men, and there was Madame Tardieux now sobbing uncontrollably behind me and Aunt Louise and Nanette trying to make their scorn heard over the noise and the confusion and me suddenly right in front of everybody, nose to waist with Big Renée after they pushed her down the improvised steps, forced her to run the shameful gauntlet through the angry crowd as the ultimate price of her sins. She was still cussing them but it was through the tears now and it only made them laugh. The charcoal in which her eyes had been enshrined, mixed with her tears, dribbled ink black down her cheeks, a sullied sullying stream rushing to the bloody wound of her mouth and above it all that incongruous shaved head. Glossy it was, with skin so chafed by the hair clippers that it shown an obscene pink like the bare rump of a baboon I had once seen at the Paris zoo. I couldn't take my eyes off that head. After a while it was like Big Renée was no longer under it, like that absolutely bald head had become a hideous thing of its own that floated disembodied amid a sea of snarling faces. Even after I had lost sight of her, Big Renée's head kept bobbing up and down in front of my eyes, up and down, up and down to the cadence of the crowd's angry chant: "Ger-man-slut-Ger-man-slut-Ger-man-slut…"

But they had stopped their singing now. They had stopped singing and they had stopped jeering and a big silence covered the square. It caught me so by surprise that for a second my thoughts rang so loud inside my head I was sure everyone should hear them. Even Madame Tardieux had stopped sobbing behind me and Aunt Louise and Nanette were no longer venting their scorn at the crowd.

There were just the two of them on the podium now: Yvonne who was no longer giggling and seemed to have burrowed even deeper inside the bony womb of her shoulders, and Monsieur Lucien who had doffed his jacket and rolled up his shirt sleeves way above his gnarled elbows because he had never shaved a woman's head before and discovered it was hard work. And there was Mademoiselle Rouleau, standing in front of the chair that Big Renée had just left rising out of the carpet of the waitress' shorn black locks. There was a radiance about her at that instant that took away one's breath. Perhaps it was the way the noon sun caught her in its shimmering light or the aura of grief about her that gave her such a remote quality and made her so beautiful despite her disgrace that for a second the crowd stood in awe of her, cheated out of its due reward. But the magic, like all magic, was short-lived. Monsieur Lucien soon touched her shoulders and like the swooping petal of some dying rose, she dropped into the chair. As she did so the whispers started to nibble at the silence all around me, and then the whispers themselves became voices and the voices soon where on their way to becoming another clamor.

"I can't let them do that to her, Antoinette, I can't, I won't" Madame Tardieux voiced suddenly behind Nanette and Aunt Louise. "I must do something - - "

It was if she were struggling to wake herself out of some trance the way she spoke, Madame Tardieux, in a monotonous tone of voice as if she were afraid that to utter them in any other but a deliberate way would shatter the meaning of the words she was grasping to motivate herself to action. Her washed-out blue eyes had a febrile fixity as they stared above my head at the podium and when she attempted to make her way between Aunt Louise and Nanette who stood in her path, her outstretched arms poked blindly at the obstacles like those of a sleep-walker. For a transfixed second I thought she could even walk through me. But then Nanette grabbed her left elbow and Aunt Louise her upper right arm and they held on to her.

"There ain't a thing you can do, Ma'am Tardieux," Nanette admonished her frantically in a whisper. "Not a thing. They got to have their pound of flesh!" Her hand had forced the widow's face toward hers: she held on to the woman's eyes like a snake-charmer staring a cobra into hypnosis. "You just go on that podium, you just try to help her and it'll be ten times worse 'cause you will be giving them exactly what they're thirsting for, like Big Renée did! Are you listening, Ma'am Tardieux?"

"Nanette's right," Aunt Louise agreed in a whisper. "She ain't hurting, God bless her. She don't even know what's happening to her, it'll be over soon, and her hair it will grow back."

Madame Tardieux looked at Nanette, then at Aunt Louise. Slowly their words were beginning to reach her. She breathed noisily under her uncombed gray mane, looked even at me.

"See, they ain't even shouting like they did for Big Renée," Nanette came back. "She ain't fighting them and they don't enjoy it when you don't fight them! They'll get through with her in no time, you mark my word, then we'll take her home and - - "

Madame Tardieux broke into muffled sobs. Nanette drew her arm around the widow's neck, brought her head to rest in the small of her shoulder. She brushed back the tangled curls.

"There, there! Have a good cry, Ma'am Tardieux. They didn't know Redlich like we did and they sure don't know Mademoiselle Rouleau like we do, do they? Four years they've had to live with nothing but hate, it's got to come out some way. Hush now, hush…"

But suddenly I had no room for Nanette's apologies. I didn't care if it was four years they had had to live with hate like she said. All I knew was it wasn't a Boche up there on the podium, it wasn't Blücher or Steigl. It was my teacher, it was Mademoiselle Rouleau! I bolted for the podium: Nanette didn't attempt to stop me. Anyway I was so mad by then I could have wrenched my way through ten like her. One of the mechanics thinking I wanted a closer look even helped me onto the makeshift stage. "Here, you got a front row seat now, girl!" he laughed as he let go of my waist, relishing his generosity. I ignored him.

I sat there on the edge of the trestle-table, feet dangling in the void, so close to her that I could smell the rose water like I had smelled it the morning of Guigui's first communion. They weren't taunting her like they had Big Renée, and they had stopped jeering. Some were looking, others had begun to talk among themselves like the whole thing bored them: just because she wasn't cussing and fighting back! I stretched my arm toward her ankle. My hand could only circle half of it because my fingers weren't long enough to go around but I hung on to it like Nanette had held on to Bébert's wrist that night when Steigl had come to arrest him, and I prayed she should feel my pulse throbbing against her cool skin, that she might feel that the patch of warmth radiating up her leg to her heart and know it came from me. Her hands laid in her lap, limp, with fingers half closed over her offered pain; a few stray auburn locks had rained into their hollow. She did not stir when I reached towards them nor when my fingers brushed against her palms. The locks were warm from lying in the sun, soft and light as silk. Monsieur Lucien gave me a frown behind his steel framed spectacles when he caught me stuffing them in the pocket of my pinafore but I glared right back at him.

She was almost done now. My eyes swept the crowd and, as the tide of public contempt began to rise again around us and as inside the pocket of my pinafore my hand suddenly shaped a fist around Mademoiselle Rouleau's hair, something started to swell in me, a feeling I had never known before, alien and ugly, halfway between anger and rebellion yet more overpowering than both. It froze everything in its emotional path: the fear and the earlier anguish, the shame and even the love I had felt for her a moment before. All of a sudden I found myself wishing upon their sneering faces all the horror and misery I had ever experienced or simply heard of before and I mined and scraped the darkest of my childish memories to come up with an evil which might match what I then felt was theirs. In a dizzying flash I hoped they should be mauled to putrescent shreds by the sawmill dog, wished Steigl should suddenly rise from the bowels of the square with his elite squad and mow them down in an infernal volley of machine gun fire. I visualized them as mangled corpses heaped high and many in the Town Hall basement and in short begged God to unleash His holy wrath upon them all. The cursed thoughts, the next ever more cruel than the last, streamed through my mind in a searing scorching torrent whose impetus was as irresistible as it was irrational. I had never been possessed of such evil nor had my imagination ever served such a tyrant master as the thirst for revenge that overpowered me at that instant. For the first time in my life, I found myself hating: blindly, indiscriminately, passionately.

The church bells struck one as the last of Mademoiselle Rouleau's hair fell victim to Monsieur Lucien's avenging hair-clippers. Her eyes were the first sight I hit upon struggling out of my inner turmoil: they appeared larger and deeper now that the auburn curls no longer foamed about the thin oval of her face, and perhaps because of some secret memory she had suddenly remembered, the periwinkle was back in them. She didn't look at all as I had feared she might, like Big Renée perhaps, or some other equally monstrous incongruity. The sun had dabbed pink on her cheeks and between the pink and the periwinkle and the delicate china white of her skin, her face looked like that of a porcelain doll: pretty, real pretty. Even Madame Tardieux was taken aback when she reached the podium and at last dared to look up at her young tenant. I could tell easy because she had stopped crying and her glaucous eyes widened in mid-tears, like something wonderful has just happened to her. I was still sitting on the edge of the trestle-table and she squeezed my knee, emitted a sound halfway between a choke and an aborted laughter. Then Nanette behind her winked at me meaningfully so I got up on the podium, took Mademoiselle Rouleau's hand in mine. It was as cold as one of the granite tombstones of the cemetery but I had no trouble at all making her stand up from the chair, and she followed me down the makeshift steps as if she were the little girl and I the teacher. I didn't look at Monsieur Lucien but I guessed he made some sort of derisive gesture behind our backs because there was a rustle of snickers in the crowd. But they weren't screaming and stomping as they had for Big Renée and they didn't stop Nanette when she took the large checkered handkerchief from around her forehead and covered Mademoiselle Rouleau's bald head with it. Most of them knew Bébert had nearly died at the hands of SS Obersturmfuhrer Steigl and his men and that gave us no small clout - - at least they not dare accuse us of being "Boche lovers".

Nanette put her arm around Mademoiselle Rouleau's shoulders as if it were an invincible shield and we started to make our way out of the crowd. Aunt Louise and I led while Nanette, the teacher and the widow followed behind us. We walked slowly to show them we weren't scared. They opened up in front of us like they had earlier when Monsieur Lucien and his cohorts had brought in the women, but they were silent as we filed past them. I looked at every single face: I didn't want any of them to die anymore, that was over, but I was determined to stare each of them down, no matter who they were, to show them how grievously wrong they had been to do what they had just done to Mademoiselle Rouleau. I felt like I stood ten feet tall suddenly and they were ants I could crush under the tip of my sandal if I were in a mood for it. I don't think I have ever walked as proud as I did that morning of my life nor that I ever shall again.

We had barely reached the poster of the Empire Theatre when a small detachment of American MPs, no doubt called upon by some anonymous Christian soul to restore public sanity, screeched to a halt in front of Monsieur Lucien's closed bookstore. They cascaded out of the three jeeps, spotted what to them must have looked like our threatened group and surrounded us. Nanette immediately proceeded to explain to them that we were in no danger, that ---she bared

Mademoiselle Rouleau's scarred head as she said it - - the shameful deed was done and if they really wanted to salvage some virtue out of this sinful day, there was one more victim in need of assistance: simple Yvonne whose drab mane Monsieur Lucien was no doubt about to assault. Two of the Americans stayed behind to see us safely home while the others, in a riot control formation, went on to plow their way through the reluctant crowd. It was amid the ensuing confusion that a fourth jeep abruptly crashed to a halt at our feet and that, to my everlasting discomfiture, Raymond Langiers, making a startling and grandiose reappearance, sprung out of the driver's seat like a jack-out-of-the-box. Bébert and Uncle who had apparently hitched a ride with him from the Allied Headquarters at the Château where they had been working that morning, stumbled out to the contraption after him. There followed much gesticulations and more explanations as Nanette soon joined in by Aunt Louise attempted to apprise the men of what had taken place. Langiers looked at Mademoiselle Rouleau as if he didn't remember sitting across from her at our gala table the day of Guigui's first communion! For a while he kept staring at her bald head in the most embarrassing way and I am sure he couldn't make heads or tails out of what Nanette and Aunt Louise were trying to tell him about her and Oberleutnant Redlich because you really can't explain a love like theirs in one minute of gushing explanation. He still wore his black notary trousers but they were topped by a military jacket with several gold stripes emblazoned on the shoulders and one of the American soldiers kept calling him "Lieutenant." Whether I liked it or not, it was suddenly painfully apparent to me that Raymond Langiers commanded much respect and even Nanette promptly shut up when Langiers at last wearily motioned her to silence.

He had always been tall but he seemed to grow even taller when, standing by the disgraced Mademoiselle Rouleau, he slowly tucked his thumbs inside his leather belt, threw back his shoulders and swept each of the faces that made up the circle of gawkers for whose benefit we had been unwittingly performing. Then without transition except perhaps the fact that the words had been building up inside him for a very long time, he proceeded to lash out at them. He told them hadn't risked his goddam life for three years so they could attack helpless women even if they were German whores; that he hadn't lost men - - too many good men - - so they could do THAT! And he also told them they had been sitting pretty most of them all those years, the craven lot of them, while he and his men risked their balls and more so the likes of them might one day see France rid of the Boches! And what had they ever done to help the too many slaughtered in the ungrateful task, he yelled, when had they ever bothered to thank the unsung heroes whose ultimate sacrifice allowed them to stand as free men this Saturday morning! He told them all of this and more because he was real mad. I didn't understand everything he said because in his anger he was using a lot of Big Renée words but he lashed out at them like I would have wanted to do for sure had I been bigger, so even though I liked him no better than before, Langiers, in a grudging sort of way I was kind of proud to have him on our side. He had fooled me, perhaps more easily than he had the others because I had been such a willing dupe in his game. And it was all because of Lisette: she had been so frustratingly infatuated with him that I had wanted nothing better than to think the worst of him. With what eagerness I had gathered the damning evidence! His weekly trips to Monsieur Lucien's store for that mysterious magazine, the ill-fitting ring around his little finger - - a secret identification mark perhaps - - the documents he had pilfered from the

Town Hall that morning after the bombardments, his unlikely games of checkers with Father Rocas every Wednesday night, his flawless German. How much I had relished my suspicions. But it had all been a ploy, and all along while I suspected him of collaborating with the Germans he had in reality been taking his orders from London rather than Berlin and serving a worthier if more desperate cause. That's why they had made him a Lieutenant, that's why his words brought shame to their eyes when there had been only contempt and viciousness in them as they had watched Mademoiselle Rouleau's ordeal. Maybe he was alright, Langiers. I had to grant him at least that much. But I was glad, darn glad, Lisette wasn't with us to see him in his moment of glory and I sure wouldn't be the one to tell her about it. She was already silly with love for him and I didn't want her blinded by it as well else how would she see me, how on earth would she still even know I was there.

We rode home in one of the American jeeps while Langiers, Bébert and Uncle followed us in the other. It was the first time I had ridden in a motor car since coming to Dormans and despite the anguish and anger of the morning, I enjoyed the treat, especially knowing how sick with envy my telling them about it would later make Guigui and Jacques Pottin. Anyway, it was the nicest part of this horrendous day. As always when something unpleasant happened we closed ranks around the family fires and Mademoiselle Rouleau, Madame Tardieux and the three Germains all joined us for a late lunch. The teacher sat to Bébert's right. He was very solicitous of her throughout the meal and acted as if he didn't notice her bald head. I think being good to Mademoiselle Rouleau made him feel like he was finally able to say Thank You to the dead Oberleutnant Redlich. At any rate during the soup, he said what she needed, what we all needed, was a holiday and before I knew if, it was decided that come the next morning which was Sunday, we would close our respective houses, pool resources, lug my cot and Uncle Marcel's army cot, load bicycles and mattresses on our two wheel-barrows and trek up to The Gaux for a healing stay and a bit of needed peace. She still didn't speak, Mademoiselle Rouleau, but form the way she looked at Bébert as he winked at her affectionately, I got the feeling Doctor Martin's laudanum was at last working. We didn't talk about what had taken place on the Place du Luxembourg that morning so that at least for a while Lisette was kept in the dark about Langiers feat. After lunch Nanette and Guigui went back to the wash-house to pick up the laundry we had left there while Uncle and Bébert returned to the Château to finish their work so as to be able to leave for The Gaux with a clear conscience come the next morning. Aunt Louise and Madame Tardieux sat at the kitchen table tailoring and sewing two fancy turbans to hide Mademoiselle Rouleau's bald head while I, as she had done for me the day of Mémé's funeral, sat up with her in the dining-room, trying my best to interest her in the drawings I hadn't drawn then, chattering one-sidedly so my noise would stop her from thinking, and pretending as she had done then that in spite of the grief and the shame the future held some hope and even the present could be as soothing and loving, if one were determined enough, as the tick-tock on the dining-room wall clock that counted the slow hours of that afternoon.

I had the hardest time falling asleep that evening. I didn't cry and I didn't go searching for Mémé's Missal and I didn't hide under the blankets. I laid the back of my head flat against the pillow and stared smack into the night of the alcove. There was no more fear in me but also no more fancy hopes. I thought about dead Mémé and Redlich, and about Big Renée and the ugly crowd that morning, and I thought also of that last night in our basement the night before the liberation of Dormans, and of the corpses in the Town Hall, of Nanette and Bébert and Uncle and Aunt Louise, Langiers and Lisette: all the things that had happened to us. But strangely none of the images, the events or the faces that fleeted through my mind in this disconnected way memories have of doing in the thick of a lonely night stayed long enough with me to evoke an emotional response. It was like I was empty inside and all dried out, like I had become an old walnut which when cracked open is found to contain only the blackest, most shriveled up remnant of the fruit it once sheltered. That's how my heart felt inside me that night as I waited for sleep. It was sort of frightening being only a shell.

*
* *

CHAPTER XIII

Apart from Lisette who since the arrival of the Americans had developed a surprising sense of duty and left for Dormans Tuesday afternoon to resume her functions at the Town Hall Wednesday morning, the rest of us remained at The Gaux through Friday. We left Dormans late Sunday morning around eleven as the church bells were calling the faithful to high mass. So much had happened since that Easter week-end that the matter of the Boche had slipped my bloated memory. That morning though it was once more brought to the forefront of my mind when, stepping into the kitchen, I found Aunt Louise tending to Guigui's and my breakfast. Bébert and Nanette had gone on ahead to open the house before the rest of us got there, she explained. I spoke little during breakfast or later during our trek up the hills of Champagne but I suddenly remembered a lot. I remembered my fright that April night when the German private had startled us, weaving and stumbling in his drunken stupor behind the weed-grown tangle behind the house. And I also recalled Nanette's determination despite Mayor Chancel's admonition to go to The Gaux the morning after the bombardment, the things Steigl had accused Bébert of, Bébert and Nanette whispering feverishly in a dark recess of Dr. Martin's bomb shelter. All my earlier suspicions were rekindled with such urgency that I had only the merest thought for Mémé as we walked past the field where a German bullet had felled her. My thoughts were on reaching The Gaux as fast as I could to throw light upon what had motivated the two of them to leave a good five hours ahead of us: what mysterious errand laid behind their alacrity. I seethed each time Uncle Marcel ordered a halt along the way to allow Mademoiselle Rouleau and the widow to rest and pushed relentlessly up each hill hoping they might replicate my brisk pace. But Uncle who was by his own admission out of practice and besides had to push his laden wheel-barrow up the stony path would not be rushed. As for Aunt Louise she chose that morning to display a rare appreciation for beauty. She kept slowing us down by turning back to take in the view of the Marne Valley unfolding ever more picturesque at our feet as we rose up each hill urging Madame Tardieux to do likewise and remaining deaf to Lisette's suggestions that the view was even better from up at The Gaux. It was the first time she had been out of Dormans in years, she snapped, and she aimed to make the most of the outing. Meanwhile, harnessed though he was with the over-spilling rucksack and in an infuriatingly transparent ploy, Guigui pretended to search for inexistent worms in the August-dry brook hugging the path, hoping Uncle Marcel would keep his word and suggest a fishing trip on his crummy boat. Mademoiselle Rouleau, wrapped in a combination of grief and laudanum, strolled through a world of her own more impervious than ever to her surroundings. After a while, exasperated by their snail's pace and Aunt Louise having raised only the most tepid objection, I took off ahead on my own, rushing up the next sunny hill as fast as my curiosity about what had really happened to the Easter Boche propelled me.

 I ran the remaining kilometer to The Gaux, stopping only once briefly to catch my breath as my heart threatened to explode in my throat. I was aching from the strain when at last I sighted the familiar wrought-iron fence with its wicket gate ajar on the garden up a ways to my left. My calves were sore from the climb and my knees, though I fell to walking as soon as I knew I was almost there, were shaking uncontrollably as if they might give way any moment. Like a caged bird between my temples, my pulse hammered against the thin layer of skin holding it captive. I remembered Nanette's cure-all remedy and proceeded to breathe, deeply. I inhaled and took one step, exhaled and took another step, again and again, in carefully measured sequence that soon brought me to the fence in front of which I came to an abrupt halt stunned by the spectacle that laid beyond it.

In spite of my skepticism, Nanette's predictions had been borne out. Her April seedlings had grown beyond even her own expectations and those neat and invisible rows of string beans, tomatoes and corn seeds she had so lovingly planted, were all obliterated by the density of the vegetation which had sprung from them. I could only see the roof of our house way in the rear of the garden above the inextricable denseness and height of the lush vegetation. It was not until I reached the gate and stared down the center path which laid beyond it that I caught my first glimpse of the roof. Bébert and Nanette were nowhere in sight as I proceeded down the alley. The early September sky hung high over the abandoned garden and little disturbed the industrious swallows, jays and titmice as they bustled about in search of their noon feed. Halfway down the alley I found a less obtrusive wilderness, that of the carrots, cabbages and potatoes which grew just as dense but hugged close to the earth.

The door of the house was open and on each side of it the weather beaten shutters had been pushed back. Even the windows were wide opened. One of the bicycles with the cart still strung to the underpinning of its saddle rested against the right-hand wall, unloaded but hastily so because parts of its contents laid strewn all about it. I poked my head inside, ascertained though I did not need to, that neither Nanette nor Bébert were inside and after the merest hesitation made for the right corner of the house. I was about level with the cistern when I heard them. Their voices, like distant voices do in the green void of a summer day, shot upward clear and yet indistinct but still I detected in their strain something akin to exhausted relief. Anyway, it sounded as if Nanette was doing all the talking while Bébert assented to whatever she was saying. After a while I resumed my progress down the narrow side of the house. It was not my intention to surprise them since I suspected that having left Dormans at day break they had had ample time to attend to the mysterious errand that had spurred them on so early. Yet, I walked with due stealth toward the rear of the house, holding my breath, treading the underfoot padding of leaves and grass ever so cautiously while monitoring the noise of my own heartbeats. Something lurked in that enshadowed tract of forgotten nature overgrown with brambles, nettles, mulberry bushes and littered with discarded scythes, shovels, hoes, rusting watering cans and broken bottles. A sense of fear I had experienced once overtook me again for an instant.

They did not see me at first as I came upon them and stood knee-high in the wilderness that grew behind the house. They had their backs to me and for a while the three of us stood there perfectly still, impervious to each other's presence, watching the secret oasis that had laid hidden all those years behind the forbidding wall the Germans had erected to cast us out of their stolen realm like so many pariahs. But now that wall was gone, shelled down by the bombs of peace. It was as if its skies had never known war, as if none of the horror, the fear, the death and misery they had inflicted on the country for over four years, the hateful toll they had extracted from man and land, had ever touched the Château and its grounds. Rolling meadows streamed endlessly before our eyes sprinkled with poppies and morning glories and there was hawthorn in the air…just like Aunt Louise had said…and cows grazing, two of them, brown and white and peace-fat, lazy and water-lilies asleep with summer on the still waters of the pond below. Butterflies aflutter and robins atwitter and flowers, wild, swooning blue, red and white in the green spread of nature. Watching what had laid beyond the demolished wall at that instant was like catching a glimpse of peace, understanding at last why Mémé and Redlich had died, why the dead of the Town Hall basement had had to be, accepting Mademoiselle Rouleau's shame and the terror of that last night before the liberation, and yes, even suddenly learning the wisdom of casting out of one's childish mind one's awful suspicion about the fate of the Easter Boche: the ultimate wisdom of choosing ignorance over knowledge.

She did not scold or question me Nanette when turning away from the grounds of the Château she spotted me. She just looked up and smiled and called to Bébert to look who was there! I offered my forehead to their morning kiss and then Nanette put her arm around my shoulders and asked wasn't the park beautiful, wasn't it just as poor Aunt Louise remembered it from her courting days. Then Bébert vowed never to rebuild the wall. There hadn't been one between The Gaux and the Château, not ever, not until the Germans had come to Dormans anyway, and there wouldn't be one if he could help it now that they were gone because the wall and they had been part and parcel of the same evil. At last I asked what happened to the well and just as I knew she would, Nanette answered that its water, what little there had been of it, was tainted and stank so she and Bébert finished the job begun by the allied bombs and filled it up.

Killed two birds with one stone that way: found a place for them rubbles from the wall and done away with an eyesore. And didn't it look better, she asked.

In my heart I knew now Nanette had been right that day when she had tried to convince me I had been fretting about him long enough. And besides, perhaps it was just as she had told me, him back in Germany with his folks, getting drunk all over again and scaring other little girls. They hadn't caught the men who had killed Redlich, probably never would; those that had shamed Mademoiselle Rouleau would go unpunished and no one had found out yet what had become of Rigaux the collaborator so the unsolved fate of the one Easter Boche wouldn't make that much difference.

A convalescing man hardly wants to dwell on the causes of the long-term disease which has brought him to the edge of recovery after months of misery and thus it was with us that week at The Gaux. We spoke not of the recent past and little of the future but we lived each day as if it were a blessing. Madame Tardieux and Aunt Louise kept house and cooked our meager meals while Nanette, Guigui and I weeded the wilderness out of her vegetable garden and held big bond fires each afternoon at four in a ceremony which by the second day turned into a collective ritual with all of us gathered around the entangled heap of misbegotten nature waiting for it to be sacrificed to the gods of fire. Bébert and Uncle hunted for game in the meadows and fields of Champagne while Lisette dreamt of Langiers now more than ever and Mademoiselle Rouleau, just as Mémé had that spring, spent her afternoons napping under the September sun in the long chair we had set up for her by the cistern. We laughed around the dinner table, sang in garden, whispered under the starlit skies. We argued little and loved and teased a lot. Madame Tardieux had brought with her in an old picnic wicker basket Albert the cat: he was more obnoxious than ever and Uncle daily threatened to serve him to the widow as a stew come each next day. We retired early, the men sleeping in one room while us women crowded the other on mattresses, cots, chairs, pillows and sleeping bags because there were more of us than there were of them, and washing mornings was a problem because of the waiting line. But it was all fun and it was all love and we did what we wanted when we wanted to do it because there were no more curfews and no Germans and no fear and no more restrictions. It was heaven and I could not understand why Lisette chose to return to Dormans that Tuesday afternoon. I wanted nothing more than to be able to stay at The Gaux with them forever, to roam the rediscovered meadows of the Château or the hills of Champagne, to sit loved and loving among them, a little nothing of a thing living for each day, almost, but not quite, as I had that spring because I had learned now the precious reason for my happiness.

We left The Gaux Friday afternoon after Nanette and Aunt Louise, concerned over the depletion of their respective pantry, insisted they had to make market come Saturday morning. I watched them close the house and then we all stood outside the garden gate while the women made sure we had packed in and strapped to the wheel-barrows and the cart everything we had brought up with us supplemented now by a cornucopia of fruits and vegetables. Uncle and his wheel-barrow then took off first with Aunt Louise again in ludicrously raptured tow. They were promptly overtaken by Guigui whom Nanette had incautiously put in charge of one of the bicycles. After bellowing to him to slow down she too started on the long trek down accompanied by Madame Tardieux who kept reassuring a mewing Albert through the wicker of the picnic basket that his incarceration would be short lived. I stood with Mademoiselle Rouleau in the dirt path waiting for Bébert to give the garden gate the last turn of the key. I was in no hurry to go. Her hand was in mine and it was very quiet all around us now that the others had gone. The late summer sky hung still and infinite over us and below, far away, the sun-speckled waters of the Marne river dozed amid a miniature patchwork of already fall-hued fields. At last Bébert joined us pushing his wheel-barrow and catching sight of the valley made some remark about the beauty of France. I couldn't speak right then but as I squeezed his callous hand something marvelous happened: I felt Mademoiselle Rouleau's hand against my arm and as I looked up at her, a periwinkle stream bathed my face. Her lips moved as though she wanted to say something and then she looked at Bébert, inhaled deep and long, half closed her eyelids and whispered "Thank You". It wasn't much but it was the first time she had spoken since Redlich's murder. At any rate, it sure made Bébert happy and as for me, it made it easier to leave The Gaux and even necessary that I do so. There was an old Missal I wanted to hold and someone to whom I owed urgent thanks of my own: Mémé who had finally answered my prayer, a little late perhaps, but who was I to question her timing.

She got better and better Mademoiselle Rouleau in the two weeks which followed our stay at The Gaux. A piece of her heart was gone but one can live with half of a heart because it isn't so much how much one has left that matters but that one have at least some of it left, even a tiny piece will do. Her hair, when she took off her turban, had begun to grow back: it wasn't much more than a stubble but it was a copper as it had been before and much more lovely than Uncle's Sunday morning beard. I spent long hours with her, drawing and reading when it rained or taking long walks when it did not. She would always head for the river back across the pontoon of the Marne river but I never told her I knew the reason why she did nor why she could remain for an hour or more sitting in the hidden cove: it was her secret, not mine.

The month of September was drawing to a gilded end. It throbbed with promises long deferred but now suddenly realized, with all manners of hopes, all of which had become possible: a new life laid ahead of us and as I prepared for the new school term, I could look forward to the future with no small degree of anticipation. Now that it had become reality the people of Dormans began to hail what they viewed as a return to blessed normalcy. Paradoxically I found myself viewing peace as the aberration because I had known little else but the German occupation and thus could not grasp that peace might actually be a permanent condition, alas one with implications far beyond that of its festive reality. I seldom thought of Paris and though I sometimes thought of my mother, so much had happened to me over the last few years since I had left her, that that phase of my life which had preceded my coming to Dormans had taken on a remote and strangely unreal quality. It was a life which was something of the past and thus it never entered my mind, if indeed I even thought of it, that those last days of September 1944 might bring about its imminent resumption as a concomitant to peace. I just went about each day doing what I had learned to do since joining the Marchands. I accompanied Nanette to the washhouse on laundry days, called on Madame Tardieux and her defunct but ubiquitous husband. I helped Mademoiselle Rouleau toward the recovery of oblivion and fought with Guigui a lot. I sat on a cushion of wood-shavings in Bébert's workshop listening to his stories and submitted to Aunt Louise's grudging kisses with rediscovered unease.

I had also resumed my visits to Lisette at the Town Hall. Her infatuation with Langiers, now that together with dead Monsieur Pottin and his son Jean Claude had joined the ranks of Dormans' confirmed heroes, had grown desperate. With Mademoiselle Rouleau on the way to a distant but certain recovery, Lisette soon became my pet worry and by the last of September, knowing that within a few days the constrictions of school would prevent my doing so, I visited her practically every day. It was on one of those visits to Lisette, by a very overcast and wed Wednesday afternoon as I sat atop a corner of her cluttered desk trying to convince her once more that heroes make for terrible husbands that my life in Dormans came to an abrupt end.

She did not speak right way after she had flung the door of Lisette's office open, Aunt Louise. There was just this raw gust of air whipping Lisette and me out of our chatter as we turned toward the door, and Aunt Louise standing with her knuckled hand still on the doorknob, looking at me as if I were staring back at her almost from an already fading photograph and she was poring over it with great intensity of concentration to bring back to life the memory of me. I had looked at pictures of Mémé the same way shortly after her death and catching on Aunt Louise's face the same intimate anguish which had shot through me then suddenly made my heart sound tocsin, and I don't know why, because she still had not spoken a word, I felt we were on the verge of some inexorable calamity.

Her face was ashen and her mousy hair was drawn back to a pinch over her unseen ears and folded into a stingy bun at the nape of her neck. The rest of her was swathed in one of those sad granite-colored and overlong frocks she favored. I watched her make her way to the counter which stood between us with the same helplessness I had watched Nanette move toward the wheel-barrow that day the Matthieus had brought back Mémé's body. I wanted to scream as I had then, but also, as I had then, could not. She looked at me again as she reached the counter and stood behind it, her hand never touching it. And then Lisette rose from her chair behind the desk and Aunt Louise shivered like she were shaking off a nightmare and her small steely eyes left my face.

"You look like a ghost, mother!" Lisette spoke at last. "Has something happened?"

Aunt Louise did not answer the question directly. Instead she motioned me down from Lisette's desk with a sharp nod of her chin and her brooding eyes braced themselves toward reality as she looked at her daughter from behind her glasses.

"Mayor Chancel is sending Jaubert to take over from you Lisette. Said it would be alright for you to take the rest of the afternoon. We got to get back to Nanette's right away 'cause there ain't much time."

"There isn't much time for what, Mother?" Lisette pressed her behind me.

"You'll find out when we get back to the house. Get your coat and the child's. Do you have anything of yours here, Tina? Exercise books, pencils? Better take them with you if you do. Nothing? Let's go then!"

She buttoned up the front of my coat. Her face was very close to mine as she struggled with the top button but she wasn't looking at me anymore. Lisette said she better lock the door until Jaubert came. I heard her rummage through the top drawer of her desk, close it. Then the latch of the counter gate clicked when it fell shut behind her. Aunt Louise held my right hand tight in hers while we waited for Lisette to lock her office and then the three of us walked the long marble hall toward the rainy afternoon. The American MP guarding the front gate came to mock attention as we walked through the portals and sort of winked at me like he did whenever I came to visit Lisette. But there was no smile left in me so I just stared at his gun-belt and fought back something swelling in my throat. I kept wanting to swallow though my mouth was bone dry and crushed Lisette's right hand in my left as we walked down the Town Hall steps. I was staring at the tip of my shoes because I knew if I looked at Dr. Martin's house or at the rubbles of Monsieur Pottin's store, I might burst into tears.

They were all sitting in the kitchen when we entered it, except for Nanette. Uncle and Bébert were sitting at each end of the table in their work clothes like they had been called from work unexpectedly while Guigui and Jacques Pottin stood by the sink in the dark recess of the kitchen and Madame Tardieux leaned against the dining-room door. They were not talking and they were not looking at each other and somehow I knew they had been there a while. When Aunt Louise pushed me inside the kitchen they all looked up from their silent thoughts and stared at me like I had become very important and it frightened me. And then Madame Tardieux turned toward the dining-room as if she did not want me to see her face, and Bébert turned on his stool and as I had done so many times since coming to Dormans, I went and leaned between his knees and wound my arm around his neck. He brushed back a strand of hair from my forehead but as I searched his face, his eyes glided down the front of my red coat and Uncle across the table from us quickly lowered his over his mustache.

It was winter dark in the kitchen and for a while the only noise disturbing their awful silence was a hail of angry rain pattering furiously against the window panes. Soon there came a series of thumping noises from upstairs and within seconds Nanette's voice calling for Aunt Louise boomed from the second floor landing and Aunt Louise left the kitchen hurriedly, as if she were real glad to go. Lisette who had been behind her mother all this time stepped inside the doorway and raised her eyebrows toward her father quizzically but he frowned back at her as if he wanted her to keep quiet. It was at this moment, as my eyes were watching their furtive exchange with growing alarm, in the sweeping motion they made from one to the other, that at last I caught sight of him.

He stood in the shadow in the corner of the window wall. I could not see his face clearly except for the glimmer of his teeth as he smiled tentatively at me, but his silhouette was vaguely familiar. He was tall and thin, dressed in the midnight blue of a French Air Force captain. His braided officer's cap laid flat on the seat of the empty chair against whose backrest his left hand rested and as I left Bébert's knees and took an instinctive step toward him, his right hand fumbled with his upper left breast pocket, fingered its gold button as if he were searching for a pack of cigarettes, but then fell back along the seam of his trousers as if he did not think smoking would be appropriate right then. I was still looking at him as if there was no one but the two of us in the kitchen though I knew the silence had changed, that they were expecting the next move: his or mine. And then he moved, quite unexpectedly, as if he had decided suddenly to take charge of this impossible situation. He leaned forward a little and his teeth were abruptly bared by and overly broad smile.

"Remember me, Tina?" he voiced at last crouching against the empty chair, his arms opened for a hug.

I stopped dead in my track. Tina was a memory, it was many memories, all of which had absolutely nothing to do with Dormans. Tina was Paris. It was my mother, it was her friends, the concierge of our apartment building, and Mr. Michoux from upstairs and Madame Dupré from downstairs when I met them in the elevator or in the lobby. Tina was a thousand lives ago.

"Pierre Delvaux…except now it's Capitaine Delvaux but you can still call me Pierre because we go back a long time you and I, don't we Tina?"

And instantly I had a flash of him laughing at me across a holiday table a few Christmases back. It all came back to me now, tumbling. I could still hear mother commenting after each of his frequent visits: "A rake and a dare-devil, but a thoroughly brave man! Always the same thing: "A rake…a thoroughly brave man." And I had liked him, I had liked him a lot, Uncle Pierre.

"Don't you have one of those big Tina kisses for me?" he insisted at the end of the kitchen.

And I ran toward him because for a flash of a second a vignette of the past had suddenly become present again. He crushed me against his officer's jacket as if he were relieved and kissed my forehead and my cheeks. "This one is form your mother, and this one is from me!" he kept saying between each kiss. But then after he had kissed me and we had laughed uncertainly, he held my waist at arm's length. He was still crouching by the chair and his face was level with mine but I felt trapped, as if he were about to take an unfair advantage of me.

"She's waiting for you, Tina! I know it's very hard for you to leave Dormans on such short notice, but the war isn't over and nothing is normal yet: there was no way to let you know. You understand, don't you?"

But I didn't!

"It's impossible to telephone and the mail doesn't work half of the time," he went on apologizing. "I happened to have some business at Allied Headquarters in Reims and she asked me to bring you back on my return trip to Paris. She is waiting for you, Tina, she has been waiting a long time for her little girl!"

Now I understood why they were all gathered in the kitchen and the reason for their awful silence, and I knew why Nanette had called so angrily after Aunt Louise and about the thumping noises. They had nailed Mémé that way inside her coffin: he was taking me away just like Pichegrus had taken Mémé away! Thump! Thump! And I didn't want to go because I wasn't ready: Mademoiselle Rouleau would be expecting to see me tomorrow, and Lisette still loved Langiers too much, and Monsieur Pottin's store hadn't been rebuilt, and, and, I had to start school next week!

I broke away from him and ran to Bébert and tugged at his right knee but he just caught me in his arms and buried my face in his neck and kept whispering in my hair, "hush, hush, Tina, hush, girl!" while Madame Tardieux disappeared inside the dining-room stifling a sob.

"Breaking our hearts, you are, and hers!" Uncle Marcel burst out angrily at the other end of the kitchen table. "I know these are difficult times and I know it ain't your fault Capitaine Delvaux, but just the same, there was no call for this and a few more days wouldn't have made that much difference!"

"I - - "

But here was nothing he could say, Delvaux. So he just sighed. I heard him between sobs and I learned then that one can be drowning in one's overwhelming sorrow but still hear life trampling the shores of the present. I had heard every word Uncle Marcel had spoken and I could hear Guigui and Jacques Pottin shuffling uneasily by the sink and I knew Lisette, too, had started to cry. I had been wrong about her for no matter how besotted she was of Langiers, she still loved me as much as before. The realization made me cry even more in the fold of Bébert's neck. I heard Madame Tardieux blow her nose, I also heard the tick-tock of the dining-room clock and the spasmodic drip of the kitchen faucet as I choked on my tears and prayed Nanette and Aunt Louise would never come downstairs again.

"She's all packed, Capitaine Delvaux! She's got one more trunk than we she came to us 'cause we loved her and treated her like our own. You can tell that to her mother! That one there was my father-in-law's and she'll have to send it back because my husband is partial to it."

Two heavy plonks on the tiled floor of the hallway underlined Nanette's barely suppressed anger. Delvaux kept silent.

"Come child! Let me have her, Bébert. I want to talk to her for a minute…"

She took my hand from behind Bébert's neck. He pushed me gently away from him because I was holding so very tight to his knee. Then Nanette put her arm around my shoulders and buried my face in her apron.

"I won't be a minute, Capitaine Delvaux!"

We walked together out of the kitchen and down the front hallway. Once we had reached the staircase she sat on one of the bottom steps, took both my hands in hers and forced me to look at her. I was still crying and her face was all blurred like she were looking at me from the other side of the rain-pattered kitchen window.

"Now Tina I am going to talk to you like you were my own, like you were Guigui also because you are a big girl now! We have gone through a lot these past few years and although in my heart I wish it had been different, there ain't nothing us simple folks can do to prevent a war. So you've shared our lot: the grief, the joy and whatever else came our way and that makes you part of us. Nothing can ever change that. But now the war is over. You've grown big and strong like your mother asked me to raise you when she sent you to us, and it's only fair she should want you back 'cause I'm sure she's missed you as much as we're going to miss you here!" I had started sobbing irrepressibly again and she stopped talking to wipe my tears with a corner of her apron. "Anyway, I don't need to tell you all that. But I want you to remember that if ever you feel like life ain't treating you right, not now of course, but later or maybe when you grow up, or if you ever need help, I want you to remember that we'll always be ready to have you back 'cause this is your home as much as the one you are now going back to. Will you promise me to remember that, will you Tina?"

I nodded my head and she kissed my forehead as she had done every morning since I had come to Dormans and rose from the step on which she had been sitting.

"Now we better go 'cause Delvaux and you have a train to catch! Just as well 'cause you shouldn't be crying when you get to Paris. Your mother wouldn't like that, would she? With the train ride you got a couple of hours to cry yourself good and dry. Besides, you'll be back to Dormans in no time: there's Christmas coming up and Easter, and then of course your summer vacation next year. You'll be back here before you know it!"

I knew she was right as we walked back to the kitchen, that I would be back for sure, but I also knew deep inside me that it would never be the same between us whenever I returned to Dormans because I would no longer be part of their lives. And that's why it hurt so much and why I couldn't stop crying even though I was resigned now to the fact that peace had come for good and that I was going back to Paris.

They all came to the railway station with us and though I was still crying, I could not help remembering the way they had walked behind Mémé's coffin the day of her funeral as I had watched Pichegrus and the horse-drawn hearse move past the dining-room window. It took us forever to reach the station. Delvaux had taken the lead and walked alone ahead of us as if he didn't want to intrude on our last moments together. But there was nothing to intrude upon because I had already left them and they had already put me on that wretched train: there was nothing more to be said. I held on to Guigui's hand and stared at Bébert who pushed the wheel-barrow with my two trunks in it. Behind us Nanette kept a whispered conversation with Aunt Louise, Madame Tardieux and Lisette while Uncle walked silently by Bébert's side. I did not look at the Town Hall or at Dr. Martin's house, and I did not look at the Place du Luxembourg or at Monsieur Lucien's store as we made our way past each familiar landmark. I kept staring at Bébert's feet, just staring, as if I were afraid to look at anything else.

The train was on time like all trains. Delvaux boarded it as soon as it came to a steaming halt at quay, and then Uncle and Bébert hoisted my trunks toward him and he disappeared with one, came back for the other, while the rest of us stood in the rain waiting for the misery to come to an end. Then there was a sharp ear-rending whistle and they all rushed toward me and kissed my cheeks my forehead but I could not tell who was kissing me or whose cheeks I was kissing because there was this blinding feeling of panic exploding inside me, making my heart, thump and thud and my thoughts hurt inside my head. Then the train started to move slowly, ever so slowly, and I tried and tried to catch a last glimpse of them through the rain and tears and the panic, but could not.

I saw the wash-house as the train sped out of Dormans, the beach and the cove across the river from it, and then for a long while there was nothing but a dark endless tunnel. It was very cold in the corridor. Drops of rain swooshing through the lowered window whipped my forehead, streamed down my face and inside the collar of my red coat. After a while Delvaux suggested I might be more comfortable inside a compartment but I told him I preferred the corridor. It was too bright inside the compartment and full of soldiers and I did not want to look at anyone right then or have anyone look at me. I just wanted to be cold and wet with rain and lonely. And dead, really dead, like Mémé so that I might stop thinking about them getting ready for supper, about Mademoiselle Rouleau to whom I had not said "goodbye" waiting for me tomorrow, and about Lisette and Langiers, Bébert and Uncle Marcel, and especially about Nenette, about them going on without me, drifting, drifting. Drifting always farther away, hopelessly farther away from me.

*

* *

EPILOGUE

It will soon be over she thinks as the four men lower the coffin into the open ground: human pulleys straining under the weight of Marcel Germain. Antoinette has told her that he had become abnormally obese in the past couple of years: a glandular imbalance of some kind which had gone undetected most of his life and finally smothered his heart to death four days earlier. The wind does not help their task: a wind foreboding rain and thunder, lashing at the top of the cypresses and rushing through the patchwork of granite tombstones in erratic squalls. Louise Germain stands across the grave from her shrouded in her widow's weeds, more inscrutable than ever under the black muslin covering her face. She keeps her grief sealed inside that skeletal shell of hers like she has everything else, always, and the tears, if any, will be shed in the cold womb of her widow's bed in those blue hours of dawn when loneliness turns to fear. Lisette at her side makes up for her mother's stoicism. She has not stopped crying since they have embraced the previous afternoon. One would think there could be no more tears left in her, that by now she would have drained herself of all that sorrow. But no, she is still sobbing as the young priest stands over her father's open grave, commanding his soul to the mercy of God and the memory of them all. Louise Germain does not heed her daughter's tears, nor does she seem to notice the white handkerchief which disappears intermittently under the black veil. She stands alone, with memories of him perhaps, remorse for past misunderstandings and longing for that bittersweet strife which bound them together. It is a time of intimate accounting that transcends death in which the sum of their two lives together takes on a meaning she has too late recognized.

They will only have each other now, Aunt Louise and Lisette. Theirs will be a silent and dreary life because at close to a ramrod eighty, Louise Germain has become more taciturn than ever. Marcel Germain always did much of the talking and most of the laughing in their house and now that he is gone Lisette will probably rely more heavily on Guy's three sons to brighten her spinster's lot which much stretch ahead of her as bleak as a rainy Monday morning. Thank God she still has her work cut out for her at the Town Hall: she has logged close to forty years in the town's service and hopes to make it fifty. The best Registrar a town ever had Antoinette says. She can name them all: the ones who have died and of what, the young ones who have become men and women and are now marrying and raising another crop of children. She gathers those arid vital statistics to her barren womb and turns them into tales of human lives which delight Guy's boys and might delight Xavier one day. She will invite Lisette to Paris: she would love Alain and especially the baby. Antoinette says she dotes on Langiers' twelve-year old daughter though it isn't hers as she might have hoped at one time.

She is not bitter about his marrying Odile Rouleau. If anything, she was one of the few to approve of their wedding years ago when many in Dormans were ready to condemn Langiers for even thinking of marrying the teacher. Reputations in small towns are often made on appearances and for a long time after the war, Odile

Rouleau was still tainted by her association with Redlich. Things are different now: willy-nilly, De Gaulle had forced Frenchmen into accepting a Franco-German rapprochement as a necessary step to his grander design for a United Europe, which does not mean that the old wounds are completely healed, but at least no one in a position of leadership is exacerbating them. Now that Chancellor Adenauer has come to Paris on official visits, there is little the people of Dormans can do but to absolve Odile Langiers. And they seem to have. She looks like a contented matron in her early forties, and though she has become somewhat portly, her eyes are still the same periwinkle blue whenever she talks of her husband, her son or her daughter. Her hair which she wears drawn back in a respectable chignon, is still bright copper and shows not a strain of gray hair. She is proud of what she has done with Madame Tardieux's house since they inherited it form the widow and has shown Tina through it earlier that morning with an almost childish pride. She says her husband's practice has quadrupled from what it used to be when old Maitre Pinson was alive. The town's phenomenal growth has been a blessing to them. Three industrial parks have attracted new blood: a super-market where Monsieur Pottin's store used to stand, three cinemas, several laundromats have replaced the communal wash-house and banks from Paris are opening new branches: her husband will have to hire another a clerk to handle the new accounts, she beams.

Business has been good for Guy as well now that Gilbert Marchand has finally retired and his son has taken over the old workshop on the Faubourg de Chavenay. He has done wonders with it: expanded it by building additional work space where the rabbit cages and Antoinette's garden patch used to be, brought in the latest machinery from Germany and counts a staff of three full-time hands and one apprentice. Gilbert who frowns on mechanization complains that carpentry is a lost art but he and Antoinette live more comfortably in retirement than they ever did when Gilbert was working. Guy is good to them. His wife Martine complains about his long working hours but she also shows with pride their station wagon, their color television and the sparkling kitchen equipped with the latest gadgetry including a dishwasher and a laundry washer-dryer unit. They are also remodeling the old family house at The Gaux, adding three rooms to the back where the well used to be and a second floor with enough bedrooms and bathrooms to accommodate the entire family when they go up there for the month of August. They will have to think of buying land for a new summer home pretty soon. Antoinette had told her because with the town expanding the way it is, one of these days even the Gaux is bound to become another one of Dormans suburbs.

They have finally wedged Marcel Germain's coffin inside its compartment between Gilbert's mother and his grand-father. It has started to rain but at least the wind has died down. "Ashes to ashes" the young priest chants letting a handful of earth rain inside the open grave. Lisette has stopped sobbing and Martine and Guy are attempting to keep their three restless boys in line. Louise Germain has not moved but Antoinette Marchand has: she stands at the widow's side, ready to console and support as she has, always.

She wanted to get back to Paris and Alain tonight but has promised Antoinette to stay for the family dinner which will follow the funeral. Anyway she has already missed the day's last train to Paris. Just as well: she will catch the morning express, a fast two hour ride because it only makes one stop at Château-Thierry. She can call Alain tonight from Guy's house and make a date to meet him for lunch tomorrow. She will go to the hospital straight from the Gare de l'Est and they will have a quiet lunch at the Court of the Mandarins:

he loves Chinese food. What has he done these past two days without her? Has he missed her as much as she has missed him and Xavier? They have a lot to catch up on: how his speech was received at Congress, about her mother - -he will probably complain - - about Xavier's latest baby drivel which he insists he can interpret. And of course, she has a lot to tell him, awful lot - -

"Tina! Tina!"

- - she has to tell him at last all about Dormans and the funeral of Marcel Germain and above all to explain to him her fear of trains - - why

"Tina!"

She looks up. Antoinette's lips are still shaping the angry whisper and her eyes are stern: they bring back memories of long forgotten scoldings.

"It's your turn, child!"

She takes the offered spade from the funeral attendant. The handful of earth sticks to her black leather gloves: the rain probably. She lets it fall through her fingers over the open grave.

"Rest in peace, Uncle Marcel, rest in peace dear, dear Uncle Marcel!" she prays silently. "And you too Mémé."

THE END

ACKNOWLEDGMENTS

Being quasi illiterate in computer science, I wrote TINA'S WAR on my old IBM Selectric typewriter. When it came to getting the manuscript ready for publication in this computer age, I had the huge luck of having the support, expertise and especially the patience of three loyal friends whose contribution to this project proved to be invaluable. So with much gratitude: Thank You Savio D'Souza for guiding my first and second purchase of computers and programming them for me. Also, Thank You for transferring the manuscript to eBook format and hard cover print book. Thank You Sean Costello, my computer engineer friend, for taking on the inglorious task of retyping the entire manuscript into its computerized version and for her faith in TINA'S story, and Thank You Bruce Steinke, once my colleague at the now defunct NEW REPUBLIC, for designing his marvelous cover of TINA'S WAR. You are all three truly the best!

mN
NW